# THE EDGE OF IT ALL

## JESSICA GRAYSON

Purple Fall
Publishing

Published in the United States by Purple Fall Publishing. Purple Fall Publishing and the Purple Fall Publishing Logos are trademarks and/or registered trademarks of Purple Fall Publishing LLC.- purplefallpublishing.com

Publisher's Cataloging-in-Publication Data

Names: Grayson, Jessica, author.

Title: The edge of it all / Jessica Grayson.

Series: Mosauran

Description: First Edition | Pleasanton, TX: Purple Fall Publishing, 2020.

Identifiers:

ISBN: 978-1-64253-011-7 (paperback) |

ISBN: 978-1-64253-019-0 (Ebook) |

ISBN 978-1-64253-029-2 (Audiobook) |

Subjects: LCSH Vampires--Fiction. | Dragons--Fiction. | Shapeshifting--Fiction. | Human-alien encounters--Fiction. | Science fiction. | Romance. | Love stories. | Paranormal romance stories. | BISAC FICTION / Romance / Science Fiction | FICTION / Science Fiction / Space Opera

Classification: LCC PS3607 .R3978 E34 2020 | DDC 813.6--dc23

Edits by Tera Cuskaden

Cover Design by Maria Spada

PRINTED IN THE UNITED STATES OF AMERICA

## Dedication

*To my parents and my sister: Love never dies. I carry your love and your memory with me always.*
*To my husband: You aren't just my husband, you're my best friend and I love you more than words can say.*
*To my sister: I love you to the moon and back.*
*To my Neelix (my muse): Who's the bestest cat? Is it you? Yes, I think it is. :-)*

# CHAPTER 1

LIANA

Ascream of pure terror startles me awake, and my eyes snap open to pitch-black nothingness. My pulse pounds in my ears as I listen for any other sounds, but there is only silence. Maybe this is a stasis sleep nightmare. I've had them before, but this feels much more lucid.

Taking a deep breath, I exhale slowly through pursed lips, attempting to calm myself. I just need to wake up. Using the tried and true method of pinching my arm, I'm shocked when it doesn't work.

Blinking several times—as if that will somehow help me see in the dark—I'm desperate for light. I reach out to tap the stasis sleep pod controls, but my hand hits cold, hard metal—some kind of grating where the smooth glass panel should be. Confused, I trace my fingers along the strange pattern.

This isn't my sleep pod.

I reach across to activate my wrist communicator and alert the flight doctor that I'm awake, but it's gone.

Instinctively, I tap my hand to my right upper chest for the backup comm in my breast pocket. But instead of my flight suit, a thin, lightweight material covers my body. Fear skitters up my spine when I realize it's some sort of paper-thin gown that stops mid-thigh, and it's the only thing I have on.

*What the hell is going on?*

A piercing scream shatters the silence, and I still. Long tendrils of dread begin to unfurl and wrap around my spine.

Closing my eyes, I draw in a shaking breath. Please let this just be a bad dream. Only now does my brain register the rancid smell that permeates the air, and I wrinkle my nose as a wave of nausea rolls through me.

A woman's voice cries out. Her words are a frantic stream of language I don't understand. A deafening roar cuts them off, and a rhythmic thumping begins. Muffled whimpers echo in the distance.

Goosebumps prickle my flesh as the understanding of what those sounds mean trickles into my awareness.

*Oh, God. Where am I?*

The woman releases another frightened cry that's answered by an inhuman bestial sound--even more terrifying than the one before. My heart stops and then begins hammering. I have to get out of here.

Desperate to escape, I twist my body and sweep my fingers out to feel for some kind of opening. Cold metal bars lined with patterned grating surround me on all sides. I freeze as the terrible realization hits me.

*Oh, God, I'm in a cage.*

It's too small to stand or sit up. I've never been claustrophobic, but my chest tightens as my anxiety grows with each passing moment.

*Where is the rest of my crew?*

Panic twists deep inside me, but I push it down. Squeezing my eyes shut, I try to focus on the last thing I remember before waking up in this nightmare.


We were on our way back to Terra from Mars Colony, preparing to go into stasis. Amanda was trying to coax Barkli into her sleep pod. The normally fearless Golden Retriever let out a small, distressed whimper and ran behind my legs. She'd been through stasis before on our outbound trip to the red planet, and she wasn't eager to get back into one of those chambers.

I didn't blame her. Between the occasional terrifying nightmares and the jarring discomfort when you're woken back up by the computer, stasis is definitely not for the fainthearted. I reached down to comfort her, running my hands gently over her soft, thick fur.

"It's okay, Barkli." I kissed her forehead and was rewarded with a quick lick on my nose. Trembling slightly, her expressive, dark-brown eyes searched mine, and her tail gave a small, hesitant wag as she cast an anxious glance over her shoulder at Amanda.

Amanda's saddened gaze drifted between Barkli and me. An expression I'm almost certain was mirrored on my own face as well. We knew this would be hard on our dog, but we didn't feel like we had another choice. We had to bring her with us.

Although she technically belongs to Amanda, we share an apartment back on Terra, and Barkli is kind of like our shared child. After the last trip we made to Mars, we both agreed we didn't want to leave Barkli behind again. She'd been so distraught by our absence that she refused to eat or drink hardly anything. She had lost a lot of weight by the time we'd returned. Even my little niece, Elizabeth, whom Barkli loved, was barely able to convince her to eat.

Reluctantly, I held out her sedative laced treat, and she took it from my hand, swallowing it whole. The complete trust in her eyes broke my heart. I hated having to drug her.

It didn't take long to work. She laid down, her eyelids drifting open and closed as she struggled to stay awake. Gently, I held her and stroked her fur as the sedative took effect. "When we get back to Terra, we'll go to that park you love, and you can chase all the pigeons you want, okay, girl?"

She's such a smart dog. Recognizing the words she knew and loved so well, she began to wag her tail slowly, giving a final thump against the floor before she closed her eyes and fell asleep.

We carefully placed her into the smaller pod. Amanda's teary gaze met mine. "You think she'll forgive us when she wakes up?"

Looking down at Barkli's small form, I ran my hand once more across her soft, golden fur before sealing her pod and whispering softly, "I hope so."

Amanda and I shared a commiserating hug before she stepped into her pod, next to Barkli's. She gave me a small grin. "Just think, Liana, we'll actually be home in time for Christmas."

I nodded and watched as she closed her eyes and settled into stasis sleep. Amanda—our ship's doctor—is like a sister to me. She reminds me so much of my actual sister, Angela, who I can hardly wait to see when we get home.

Resting my hand lightly against the glass, I took one final look at my friend. "Sleep well," I whispered. "I'll see you on the other side."

I walked along the row of pods. As ship's commander, it's my job to check that each of my seven crew members enters stasis and that everything is functioning normally before I go to sleep as well.

When I reached Jeff's pod, it was empty. I gasped in surprise as a large pair of hands covered my eyes, pulling me back against his solid chest. "You didn't think I'd go to sleep without trying for a kiss, did you?" His breath was warm in my ear, and I could hear the smile in his voice without even seeing his face.

With a slight smirk, I turned in his arms, shaking my head in mock frustration. "You're supposed to already be in your pod, you know."

He grinned as he leaned down and pressed a soft kiss on my lips. His blue eyes stared deep into mine with a look somewhere between possessive and teasing. "Now, I can go to sleep and dream of you," he whispered. His hand slid down my back to the curve of my hip, his thumb lightly tracing along the waistband of my pants. "We're the only two awake now, you know?"

I tensed. Placing my palm to his chest, I gently pushed him away, putting just enough space between us that he couldn't try to change my mind with another kiss. "I'm not ready yet."

His face fell, and despite his reassuring grin, the mild impatience behind his eyes was obvious. "I respect that. We'll just wait until you are."

We'd been flirting. Heavily. For two months. I'm trying to be really careful. Jeff and I met during flight training. And in those past two years, I've seen him go through several women. And, despite my better judgment, he somehow got under my skin with his subtle charm, good looks, and disarming smile.

But *because* I know his history with women, I'm not quite ready to make the leap to being his girlfriend yet, which is something I suspect he's not used to. If we did date, and we ever slept together...for him, I could end up being just another conquest, but for me...he'd be my first. And that's not something I want to do before I'm sure that he's *the one*. Especially after I witnessed all the heartbreak my sister went through with her ex-husband.

Trying but failing to hide the rejected look on his face, Jeff gave me a final, reluctant hug before he stepped into his pod and sealed it behind him, closing his eyes as he entered stasis.

After confirming our course destination, I took a deep breath to steady my nerves and pushed the sequence to activate my pod, sealing me inside. I've always hated going into stasis. But I love flying, and it was part of the job.

A bright light flickers on and floods my vision, ripping me away from my memories. Temporarily blinded, I raise my hand to shield my eyes, blinking several times to adjust my focus. Loud footsteps approach my cage, followed by a harsh clicking noise with a strange and frantic cadence. A large shadow falls overhead, and my jaw drops as I look up to find huge compound eyes staring down at me.

Fear wars with disbelief as I study the odd creature before me. What I'm seeing can't be real. It looks almost like an insect, but it's the size of a Terran.

Light reflects off the chitinous, deep maroon shell that covers its entire body like armor, reminding me of a gigantic, humanoid ant. Standing upright on two legs, it lifts two of its four arms to the cage bars. A thumb and three fingers tipped with sharp claws on each hand fumble with the latch a moment before it opens.

It tilts its strange ovoid head, and the two antennae on top move

5

back and forth as it studies me. Frozen in place, my own terrified green eyes reflect from the multiple lenses of its own. Two large mandible-like pincers where a mouth should be click several times, and an involuntary shudder of revulsion ripples through me.

It reaches inside, and I scramble away, slamming my back against the metal bars in my retreat. Determined, it lunges forward and clamps down on my shoulder with an iron grip. A feral cry of panic rips from my throat as sharp claws slice through my skin like knives to drag me from the cage.

Primal instincts surge through me, and I kick out wildly. With a loud crack, my foot makes contact with something solid.

It screeches in pain, the sound blasting my ears like a high-pitched siren as it loses its grip. My reprieve lasts only a moment before a loud thump against the metal floor is quickly followed by a low, buzzing hum. The hairs rise on the back of my neck, and paralyzing fear snakes through me at the ominous sound.

Without warning, something rams against my ribcage. The air explodes from my lungs in a silent scream as the burning fire of electric shock rips through me. My back arches, my body contorting in a series of twisting spasms as I writhe in agonizing pain.

Just when I think I can't take anymore, it stops, and I collapse. Shaking uncontrollably, I gasp, panting heavily to catch my breath as I roll onto my side and clutch my chest.

Something sharp scrapes against my scalp as it twists in my long, auburn hair, forcibly gripping the strands. Panic floods my system as it jerks on my head and drags me from the cage and onto the cold, metal floor. The menacing low hum of the shock stick fills the air, and I scramble toward the doorway, desperate to escape my captor. It shocks me again, and I collapse.

My eyelids flutter open and closed as I fight to remain conscious. It drags me by my hair down a long, dark hallway, past row upon row of cages. My every muscle is limp, unable to move. It's difficult to concentrate through the fog-like haze that's wrapped around my brain. Desperately, I try to focus as strange creatures swim at the edge of my vision, staring at me with terror-filled eyes.

Despite the stark metal walls, floors, and ceiling, the air is thick with filth, sweat, and blood. The alien beings back away from the bars as we pass, cowering as my captor clicks out a harsh cadence in warning.

Devastation washes through me. No help is coming. No one is going to rescue me; I have to save myself.

An image of my family flashes through my mind. My parents, my sister, my niece...I have to get back to them. But everything hurts, and the peaceful void beckons me to take refuge from the pain. My head lolls back, and I fall away into oblivion.

*"Aunt Liana, wake up," a small voice calls out.*

*My eyes snap open to find my niece standing over me, her long red hair— so like my sister's—pulled back from her face into a cute little ponytail.*

*I inhale sharply but relax as soon as I realize there's no danger here. "Elizabeth, what are you doing here, my angel?"*

*She grins, her piercing blue eyes sparkling with excitement. "It's Christmas. Hurry, so we can open presents."*

*I sit up. "Christmas?" Relief floods my system. Thank God, it was all just a nightmare. Smiling widely, I reach out and wrap my arms around Elizabeth in a giant bear hug.*

Sharp pain snaps me out of my dream and back into awareness as I'm hit with the shock stick again. When I open my eyes, blinding white light assaults my vision; I quickly squeeze them shut.

Without warning, my body lifts from the floor. Terrified, my limbs flail wildly as I do a slow spin into an upright position, my feet hovering just above the ground. No sooner do I stop when my arms and legs are roughly gripped by an invisible force and spread apart, rendering me completely helpless.

Ice-cold fear floods my veins as I scan my surroundings. Sterile, reflective, gray metal panels line the floor, walls, and ceiling. A long table to my right, laid out with several sharp instruments, only amplifies the panic building inside me. I struggle against the invisible bonds that hold me in place and gasp as a vise-like grip tightens painfully in response around my wrists and ankles, instantly immobilizing me.

A harsh click draws my attention to two insectoid creatures

standing off to the side. They circle me as their unnerving compound eyes rake over my barely clothed form.

The closest one reaches out to lift a tendril of my long auburn hair, looking back at its companion and clicking its mandibles together in its strange and disturbing speech.

The other steps forward and swipes a cloth roughly across the bridge of my nose. It pulls back to study the material, cocking its head to the side in a puzzled look. The fabric is as coarse as sandpaper, and my skin burns like fire from the contact. When it leans in as if to try again, I yell at the creature to stop.

It points at my face and then back at the cloth, sharing what looks like a confused glance with its companion.

Realization hits me. It's trying to wipe the freckles from my olive-toned complexion. "They're just freckles!" I shout. "Permanent spots on my skin!"

The insectoid's head jerks back. Dropping the cloth on the table, it steps closer.

Did it understand me? "Do you know what I'm saying?"

It nods.

Hope fills me. "Let me down. Please, let me down. I promise to answer all your questions if you just—"

It presses a button, and my mouth slams shut, an invisible force holding it closed so I can't speak.

Raising four claw-tipped, lethal hands to my face, it tilts its head to the side as if studying my reaction.

My chest rises and falls rapidly as I take in shallow, panicked breaths. I have a strong feeling that no amount of crying or screaming will win me any sympathy from these alien creatures. They've already indicated that they understand me.

They understand, and they do not care.

Something small and metallic glints beneath the light, drawing my attention to the closest one's claws. Without warning, it reaches behind my ear. A sharp sting pierces my skin. Warmth blooms out from the spot; heat builds into a fire that burns throughout my skull.

The insectoid leans in. "Can you understand me now?"

I open my mouth to respond, but the pain steals my breath. Somehow I manage to nod before my eyes roll up in the back of my head, and I fall away into nothingness.

～

A subtle hissing noise startles me awake. Something cold and wet slicks up my neck to my jaw. My eyes snap open, and I go completely still—paralyzed with fear. Two enormous black orbs stare back at me, mere centimeters from mine. With a face like a cobra and covered in dark crimson scales, the creature's lips pull back in a snarl, baring two large fangs as a red, forked tongue retracts into its mouth. With two arms, two legs, and a long, tapered tail, its entire body is all thick, corded muscle beneath shiny interlocking scales. What little clothing it wears only covers the lower half of its body, and as my gaze travels down its sinuous form, it's easy to see that this alien is male.

It leans in, studying me intently. An involuntary shudder ripples through my body. After at least three weeks of this hell, you'd think I wouldn't be fazed by anything at this point. But this creature is more terrifying than any of my darkest nightmares.

Long black claws tip its three fingers, just like the insectoid aliens —my Zovian masters. Its eyes are large, obsidian orbs with a yellow vertical slit pupil. A second nearly transparent membrane sweeps across them as it blinks to regard me.

"Her scent is intoxicating," it says in a low and sinister hiss. "She tastes delicious. I will take her now."

With the Zovians, it's shock sticks...that's how they take their pleasure. As I study the snake-like alien, a shiver of panic skitters up my spine. There's something lustful in his expression as his eyes rake over my form.

He reaches out to touch my face. The scaled pads of his fingers are rough like sandpaper, snagging my skin as they trace across my cheek.

Disgusted, I jerk my head back.

He takes my jaw in a bruising grip, forcing me to meet his furious gaze as he bares his fangs in a threatening hiss.

I grit my teeth and return his glare with defiance. I *will not* be a compliant slave.

Surprise registers briefly behind his eyes before they narrow, and he turns a dark gaze to my Zovian master. "This V'loryn shows emotion. She has already been broken. You would dare to sell me damaged merchandise?"

This is the third prospective buyer to mistake me for a V'loryn, but I don't correct his wrongful assumption. V'loryns bring more money on the slave market. Because of this, they are less likely to be sold to the gladiator rings—given as a prize to the champions to be force-mated.

My Zovian master shifts his antennae forward and bows deeply. "I would never sell bad merchandise to you, Sszar." His mandibles click in a frantic cadence. "This V'loryn is small. We believe she is not yet fully matured. She is unbonded...untouched. I offer her to you along with the Aerilon female for the low price of 60,000 credits."

Sszar tips his head to the side, as if considering before he finally nods in agreement.

A heavy metal collar clamps around my neck from behind, and a terror-filled scream draws my attention to the side as another woman is dragged into the room.

Taller than me, with snow-white hair, her skin is a pale shade of violet, and her eyes are a striking golden color. This must be the Aerilon. As Sszar collars her, two large sparkly fairy-like wings shoot out from her back, and I stifle a gasp when I realize that they're broken and deformed.

Sszar looks to the Zovian in disbelief. "You did not pinion her?"

"Aerilons bring more money with wings," he answers. "But I can assure you, her venom sacs have been removed, as well as her claws. She won't put up much of a fight to anyone now."

Appearing pleased by his answer, Sszar nods again before tugging on our chains and dragging us toward the door.

The Aerilon's eyes go wide as she stares at our new master—the snake alien—and then looks back at the Zovian. "Not an Anguis!" she cries out. "Please, you cannot sell us to an Anguis!"

Turning with inhuman speed, Sszar jerks on her chain, pulling her close to his face as he bares his fangs in a twisted snarl. "You think *I* am the worst thing you have to fear? You have not yet met your true master." He narrows his eyes. "Once you find out who I've purchased you for, you will wish *I* was your owner and not him. But until I deliver you to him, you will earn me many credits. Do you understand?"

Eyes wide with terror, tears stream down her cheeks, and I know she's so scared she cannot speak. If she's smart—and I suspect she is—she knows exactly how he expects us to earn credits for him.

Fury burns in his gaze as he glares at her, his long tail curling at his feet like a cobra readying to strike as he waits impatiently for her answer.

Something inside me snaps, and I step in front of her, wanting to protect and shield her from him. I meet his eyes evenly. "She understands."

The narrow slits that form his nostrils flare as he regards me, his tongue flicking out so that the tip skates across my cheek.

Fear and disgust twist deep inside me, but I clench my jaw and tilt my chin up in defiance. I *will not* be afraid.

His thin lips curl up in a tight smirk. "My Lord Talel has a penchant for the difficult ones. He will enjoy breaking you." With that, he turns, jerking the chain attached to our collars.

The Aerilon stumbles forward, and I catch her just in time to keep her from falling, barely avoiding hitting the floor myself in the process as he drags us to his ship.

When we reach the airlock the door hisses open, flooding the entire compartment with the putrid smell of death and decay. My stomach twists and I swallow hard against the bile rising in my throat as he pulls us forward, dragging us past four other Anguis. Long, forked tongues flick out from their mouths as they scent the air, no doubt tasting our fear as they do so.

A dark, musky odor radiates from their bodies, so thick that with each inhalation, I feel as though I'm drowning in it. It reminds me so much of the stench of Terran snakes that I have to force myself not to recoil instinctively as we pass them. I don't want to appear afraid. From my experience with the Zovians, I've learned that most masters are thrilled by the fear they inflict on their captives, and I don't want to become anyone's favorite slave on this vessel.

Sszar presses his scaled palm to a panel, and the doors whoosh open to reveal a cargo hold full of cages—all of them crowded and occupied except for one. Cowering in their cells, some of the species I recognize from my time on the Zovian ship, but many I've never seen before. I take a deep breath and close my eyes briefly, praying that I'll somehow wake up from this nightmare. That I'll open my eyes and be home again.

The painful jerk on my collar brings me back to the present as Sszar drags us to the empty cage. Roughly grabbing my arm, he throws me inside. Pain shoots through my left shoulder as I slam against the metal bars at the back. Hard sandpaper fingers scrape against my already-raw flesh as he unsnaps my chain before pushing the Aerilon in after me. Shutting the door behind us, he secures the lock and then steps back, hissing angrily at the other slaves.

His forked tongue snakes out, tasting the air before he moves to the cage beside ours and jerks the door open. The alien woman inside cries out as he wraps his hand around her ankle. Gripping the bars tightly, she fights against his hold.

A bloodcurdling scream rips from her throat as he extends long black fangs, dripping with thick, yellow venom, and sinks them deep into the back of her thigh. Her body instantly goes limp, and I watch in horror as he drags her across the floor.

As she slides past, her eyes meet mine, and a tear slips down her cheek. I clamp a hand over my mouth to stifle a gasp as I realize she's conscious but paralyzed as he pulls her through the door and seals it behind them.

Still in shock, I turn to my cellmate, the Aerilon. Trembling, she cowers in the corner. Tears spill down her cheeks as she hugs her legs tightly to her chest.

Gently, I place a hand on her shoulder. "He's gone," I whisper, unable to give her any more comforting words than that because I don't know when he's coming back or what he's going to do. I only know that for right now, nothing is going to happen to us *until* he comes back.

She shakes her head, staring at the now closed doors with a far-away look on her face as she whispers. "No one survives an Anguis force-mating."

I shake my head in disbelief. "But if he kills her, he would gain nothing. Why would he do that?"

She lifts her gaze to mine. "Didn't you smell his scent?"

"They all smelled terrible. What was I supposed to notice about their—"

"Their musk is stronger during their mating cycle. If there are no Anguis females available, they will take any female to satisfy their need. They choose from the slaves that will bring them fewer credits." Her eyes scan the cargo hold, and her voice drops to a low whisper. "So that means you and I should be safe. For now."

Cold fills me. I press my hands into my lap to still their shaking. I can't break down. Not now. I need to concentrate on surviving, finding a way to escape. I have to find my crew and get back to my family.

Taking a deep breath, I push down my fear and extend my hand to her. "My name is Liana. What's yours?"

She stares at my outstretched hand a moment before finally lifting hers.

I carefully grasp it in mine and give it a gentle shake. A warm buzzing sensation travels across my palm, but before I can ask about it, she answers. "I am Tr'lani. Thank you for protecting me on the Zovian ship."

"You're welcome." I do my best to give her a small smile. "We have to stick together. Maybe we can figure out a way to break free."

Her expression is full of despair as she looks at me. "We will be fortunate if we survive."

"There's always hope," I offer.

She shakes her head. "Anguis slaves do not live long."

Her gaze drifts over the room, and I do the same, noticing all the terror-filled eyes that watch us. I suck in a sharp breath when I realize several of the cages have inhabitants that are already dead and rotting.

Pulling my knees to my chest, I take several deep and calming breaths to focus and push down my fears. If I'm going to survive, I have to stay strong. I place a hand on Tr'lani's forearm and meet her gaze evenly. "We will get through this, Tr'lani. We'll find a way, somehow."

She lowers her eyes from mine. "I hope you are right, Liana."

# CHAPTER 2

SORAN

My nostrils flare as the airlock door opens and the scent of putrid air wafts in from Vylax station. It burns my lungs with each inhalation. My silver-gray scales darken to match my already dark-gray wings folded tightly against my back. My dark claws extend, and the muscles ripple beneath my scales as I struggle to suppress the urge to shift into my draken form. Much larger than my current form, I know I'd probably damage much of the station if I were to change right now. Although it is difficult, I force myself to calm.

Releasing a quick puff of air from his nostrils as he wrinkles his nose in disgust, my brother Rowan turns to me. His silver reflective eyes, so like my own, stare at me intently. "I forget how wretched these outer stations can be. I am sorry we had to stop here, but it was the closest place to refuel."

I wish *I* could forget. I spent three cycles on stations like this while I was a slave. The stench is as familiar to me as my home on Mosaura. If Rowan hadn't rescued me, I'd probably still be in the fighting pits...or dead by now. I was nineteen cycles old when he finally found me ten cycles ago. He refused to believe I was dead, even though our enemies claimed I'd been killed along with my father. I owe him my life.

"I understand," I reply as we walk down the platform. "But the sooner we leave this place and reach V'lora, the better."

Rowan smirks. "I never thought *you* would be in such a rush to see the V'loryns."

He is right. I detest the V'loryns. But now that the civil war is over, my mother, the Empress, needs to formalize a new trade agreement with them. Our people need their L'sair crystals to power our ships. There is still much dissension among the Great Houses of Mosaura, and my mother's fleet must be prepared if any should challenge her right to rule.

The strong smell of fear permeates the air, and bile burns its way up my throat. I remember this scent well. Every station and port that allows the sale of slaves reeks of it. Clenching my jaw, I look to my brother. "The V'loryns may be a deceitful, duplicitous people, but on one thing, our two races can agree: We both detest slavery. If we can convince them to engage in shared patrols of the neutral zone between our two territories, it will make it harder for slavers to practice their despicable trade."

"I agree. As much as I dislike the V'loryns, at least they enforce anti-slavery laws in their region of space as we do in ours."

When we reach the bottom of the ramp, a dockworker rushes to meet us. "Refuel?" he asks, bowing his head in a submissive manner.

"Yes," Rowan replies. "Work quickly and contact us as soon as the glider is ready."

Regarding us warily, he bows again and then practically runs to the ship to begin the refueling process. Our race—the Mosaurans—is feared throughout every sector of space. We are known as fierce warriors. It is times like these that I am glad of our reputation. I don't want to spend any more time than necessary on this wretched station.

Rowan claps a hand on my shoulder. "It will be at least a few hours until the ship is ready. Let us go find a meal." He grins. "And perhaps I can win a few hands of kartu."

I smirk. "I have a better idea. Why don't you watch *me* play kartu? We'll lose far fewer credits that way."

He narrows his eyes. "The only reason I lost so much at the last station was because that corsair must have been hiding extra zari up his sleeves. I'm certain of it."

I arch a brow at him. "Is that the story you're going with, for when I tell Caryn about our trip?"

"Yes," he replies indignantly, "because it is truth."

A smile tugs at my mouth. "*Sure*, it is. You forget that even when we were children, you were unable to hide your expressions during a game of kartu. Caryn and I could tell just by one look on your face if you'd drawn a winning hand or not."

"The two of you always used to team up against me. Why was that? Is it because *I* was the youngest?"

I laugh. "Don't start *this* again. I've told you many times before: you're my favorite brother, and Caryn is my favorite sister. Therefore, you are both equal in my eyes."

"That does not mean anything," he huffs. "We are your *only* siblings."

I spread my hands wide. "Then...what is the problem?"

He purses his lips. "I wish our parents had decided to have more children. Then, maybe I'd have had someone on *my* side for a change when we were growing up."

Teasingly, I elbow his ribs, and he shoves me away, slamming me against the side wall.

I make a dramatic show of rubbing at my shoulder as if I've been grievously injured.

His eyes flash with concern but then narrow with anger when I try but fail to suppress a grin.

He smacks my shoulder. "You, maltak. I thought you were really hurt."

I chuckle as he glares at me accusingly for a moment before a smile tilts his lips, and he shakes his head in mock frustration.

As we make our way through the station, our laughter dies and our moods become more somber as we take in the filthy, decaying state of the interior. Rusted metal panels line the dozens of shops along the promenade. Bright flashing signs promise customers all kinds of illegal indulgences, and I fight a wave of nausea as we pass a pleasure house.

A female slave I was offered as a reward for winning in the arena ended up in one of these places. I thought I was being honorable for refusing her. Mosaurans mate for life, but most other species do not know this about us. I believed my refusal would grant her at least one night of peace. Instead, I found out she was sold to a pleasure house the next day.

To be rejected by a gladiator meant she was already considered too damaged to be a prize anymore. I did not know this until it was too late. After I discovered what happened to her, I never refused another female again.

Although I never mated any of them, they still feared me because of my race. Afraid that I would kill them just for sport. Rumors of savagery and violence run rampant about us among the other species. Despite my attempts to reassure the females that I meant them no harm, many cried themselves to sleep on the nights they spent with me in my cell.

When they were returned to their masters, I would lie and say that their "services" had pleased me. After that, they were then given as a prize to another gladiator, the horrific cycle continuing until they were either broken or dead.

Only a few other fighters did the same as I. One of them was Grex. A Lacerta. I did not realize they were an honorable people until I met him. He never mated any of the females given to him as a prize. I can only hope he somehow escaped the fighting pits as well. I've searched for any word of my friend, but in the arena, we are all nameless; gladiators are only known by their race and their stats. All slaves are considered expendable and unworthy of being named.

Walking past the open doorway, a Hawkan male pulls a collared slave behind him, and my blood boils with rage. Instantly, my claws extend, and my scales darken. Rowan grabs my forearm and shakes his head. "We cannot. The station is too small to shift into your draken form."

My nostrils flare with barely contained anger, but I nod in acknowledgment. He is right. Changing into draken form in such an enclosed space would likely injure innocent bystanders and possibly tear a hole in the outer hull of the station.

Rowan's eyes meet mine evenly. "When the V'loryns and the Aerilon agree to enforcing the laws in these unpatrolled regions, we will be able to free the slaves that are held here."

As much as I dislike them, the V'loryns and Aerilon are necessary. I can only hope they will accept our proposal. Surely, they realize it would benefit all of us. It is rare for slavers to dare take any from our three races because the punishment inflicted by our laws for such crimes is death. But, still...many risk it for the high price our species fetch in the illegal markets.

Something rams into the back of my leg, triggering my warrior's training. In one swift movement, I retract the knife from my belt and spin to face my attacker.

A wide-eyed Lacerta child stares up at me in horror before cowering to the floor. "I'm—I'm sorry." The light-green scales of her cheeks darken slightly as she curls her tail protectively in front of her. "Please, don't kill me."

Her words break me. Sheathing my dagger, I drop to one knee. Gently placing two fingers under her trembling chin, I tip her little face up to mine. Tears roll down her cheeks as she stares at me warily. "I am a warrior of Mosaura. We do not hurt children. I would never harm you, little one. I swear to the Creator."

She sniffs, wiping a tattered sleeve across her nose as she gives me a watery smile.

"Now, what is your name, and where were you going in such a hurry?"

"I'm Rella. A male stole our box of leetka fruit. Mother says we don't have enough credits to leave this station unless we can sell it. So, I was trying to get it back."

Turning my head, I scan the room, remembering the cloaked

person that rushed past us only moments before the child ran into me. I look back at her. "Where is your mother?"

A panicked cry rips my attention away from Rella to find a Lacerta female rushing toward us with fear in her dark-yellow eyes. Her cheeks and neck are bright orange with alarm, standing out in sharp contrast to the rest of her light-green scales.

I stand to face her. When she reaches us, she drops to her knees, bowing her head and trembling before us. "Please, great warriors of Mosaura, spare my daughter. She was just trying to get our fruit back from the male that stole it."

Rowan and I exchange an incredulous look before I turn my attention back to the mother. "We would *never* hurt a child."

"It is not our way to harm an innocent," Rowan adds.

Her head snaps up. "Then...you are not angered?"

I sigh heavily. I hate that this female and her child believe we would harm them. Sometimes our fierce reputation is a blessing, but right now, it feels more like a curse. "Give me your forearm."

She gives me a wary look as she raises a quivering arm up to me. I tap my wrist comm and then touch it to hers. After a moment, it beeps, indicating the transaction is complete. "There. I've transferred enough credits to your account to buy you both passage off this station and back to your home world."

Her jaw drops.

"Take your child far from this place. It is not safe here."

Tears fill her eyes. "Thank you, Mosauran warrior. Thank you," she sobs, gathering her daughter in her arms and leaving quickly. Rella gives us a small smile over her mother's shoulder as they disappear into the crowd.

We make our way to a nearby eating establishment, and the host greets us with a nervous grin. Bowing his head, I notice the slight tremor of his hand as he motions to the nearest table. He's afraid of us, and I am glad. Perhaps that means we will be undisturbed during our meal. I detest the idea of being solicited while we're here.

Movement catches my attention, and my gaze shifts to the far wall. Two females are chained together and being dragged behind their

Anguis master to be paraded in front of the patrons—an invitation for anyone to make an offer for them.

My jaw drops when I realize they are Aerilon and V'loryn; my blood begins to boil. Their owner is foolish indeed to have them. It is an automatic death sentence if either of their people ever found out he kept them as slaves.

The Aerilon trembles, fluttering her wings at her side, and I inhale sharply when I see that although she has not been pinioned, they are broken. Badly. I'm shocked to see the V'loryn wrap her arms around her, whispering in her ear as if trying to soothe her. V'loryns, as a general rule of their nature as touch telepaths, dislike touching others. It appears this one is not that way. Their race is known for their lack of emotions, yet she openly displays kindness as she tries to comfort the Aerilon female. I did not know V'loryns were even capable of empathy.

There is something strange about her appearance, and as she looks down at the Aerilon, I realize that while her eyes are green, they do not glow like they are supposed to. All V'loryns have glowing green eyes. As she turns in the light, I notice her brown hair has a slight reddish tint—a shade I have never seen among her people.

But that is not all that's strange about her appearance. The top of her ear is a curved shell instead of the usual pointed tip. And she lacks the three slight cranial ridges that should be on her forehead. She is so small for her race. Anger churns in my gut. What have they done to her?

An A'kai approaches the Anguis, eyeing the two females, and my muscles tense when I realize who he is. Distantly related to the V'loryns, all A'kai have varying green shades of skin, stark-white hair, glowing green eyes, cranial ridges, and pointed ears. But only Talel, brother of the First Prime of A'kaina, has a long, jagged scar that spans the entire length of the left side of his face.

Subconsciously, I reach up and run my fingers over my own deep scar that runs from just above my right brow and down to the sharp ridge of my cheek. I almost lost my eye when we fought each other. But his scar is worse than mine because it is a mark of dishonor.

He challenged me to a fight in the arena, paying my master handsomely to make sure I would lose. Although a gladiator, I still had my honor. A Mosauran warrior never gives up. I fought him, and I beat him, slicing his face with his own silic-tipped blade. No medical repair unit (MRU) can heal wounds laced with this acid. He was so enraged he had his men hold me down as he scarred my face in return.

My betrothed turned her back on me because of this disfigurement. Although our relationship was based on mutual respect and friendship instead of love, it was an honor to have been chosen by such a strong female. The pain of her rejection took many moons to heal.

The Anguis motions for the females to step forward and display themselves to Talel. The Aerilon remains frozen in fear as the V'loryn tries to comfort her. Their Anguis master jabs his shock stick into the Aerilon's back to urge her forward, and she collapses to the floor.

I stare in shock as the V'loryn lunges at him, kicking out and making contact with his monstrous face, causing him to stumble backward. Taking advantage of his imbalance, she rushes behind him, wrapping the thick slave chain around his neck and pulling with all her might to strangle him.

She is as fierce as she is brave. A communal gasp comes from the crowded restaurant as all eyes are locked on her.

The Anguis reaches back and pulls at the chain, pitching her forward as he hisses in anger. When she charges him again, he jabs her with the shock stick. I watch in horror as a silent scream forms on her face before she drops to the floor, writhing in pain beside her friend.

The Aerilon gathers the V'loryn in her arms, tears streaming down her face. Quickly regaining her footing, the V'loryn steps in front of her friend to shield her as the Anguis stalks forward. Fire burns in her eyes as she glares up at him.

A tight smirk plays on Talel's lips as he watches. Known for his immense cruelty, he will break them of their fighting spirit. Of this, I am certain. And I do not want that for either of them.

I turn to my brother and drop my voice to a low whisper. "We must help them."

His wide eyes meet mine. "Do you not recognize who is purchasing them?" he hisses under his breath, staring daggers at Talel. "We wouldn't make it out of this sector before A'kai Centurions descended upon us, shredding us and our glider to pieces. We would be fortunate to even make it off this station alive." He shakes his head. "We must contact their people first. If they have a ship nearby, they will come for them."

I start to protest, but he raises a hand between us to silence me. "And—more importantly—*they* will bring reinforcements. We do not know how many A'kai he travels with. He is the First Prime's brother. I'm certain he must have an entire contingent of soldiers somewhere nearby. We will both surely fall in battle if we attack him now, Soran."

Clenching my jaw in frustration, I look back at the females. He is right, but we cannot wait. "There is no time to contact their people. Do what you will, but I cannot leave them with him a moment longer." Dark memories flash through my mind, and I give Rowan a grave look. "You *know* what he does to his slaves."

Rowan grits his teeth, but I recognize the look in his eyes. My brother agrees with me. "I cannot bear the thought of leaving them in his hands either. We will have to free them diplomatically. We will be killed if we openly challenge him here."

There should be nothing diplomatic about this. Talel knows slavery is illegal. We should kill him where he stands. But my brother is right. If we charge him, we'll likely end up dead, and that certainly won't help the females. Balling my hands into fists, I reluctantly nod in agreement.

His eyes drift down to my hands before he lifts his gaze back to mine and gives me a pointed look. "We do this *my* way. We cannot rush into this without careful preparation. Understood?"

"Fine," I grumble.

The V'loryn female's fierce cry draws my attention back to her as she attacks Talel. Lightning quick, he wraps one hand around her throat, lifting her into the air as if she weighs nothing.

Clawing at his hand around her neck, her legs kick wildly before she goes still.

Worried that she's unconscious, I start toward her, but Rowan's hand clamps down on my shoulder, stopping me. "R'ugol," he whispers in shock.

I clench my jaw as unbridled rage floods my veins. R'ugol—a forced mind link—is the most heinous of crimes. The equivalent of force-mating, except it involves the mind instead of the body. He will die for this. I swear it to the Creator. And I don't care if he's the First Prime's brother. I will not wait for her people to render their justice; I will kill him myself.

A silent tear slides down her cheek as she stares at him in wide-eyed fear. After a moment, he slings her over his shoulder. She dangles limply over his back as he drags the crying Aerilon by her chain behind them.

Fire licks at the back of my throat as anger courses through me. It takes all my control not to shift into draken form and burn him to ash. We trail him through the station, making sure to stay back just far enough that he does not notice us following.

# CHAPTER 3

LIANA

His hand tightens around my throat in a vise-like grip, constricting the air from my lungs. I wrestle against his hold as the edges of my vision begin to go dark.

Blood rushes through my ears, drowning out all other sounds as pressure grows in the back of my mind like a giant wave building behind a dam. Without warning, the barrier crumbles, and I instantly feel him inside me. I want to scream as the full force of his consciousness invades and expands in my mind, but my body won't respond. A heavy fog envelops me, and I'm drowning in darkness as the crushing weight of his consciousness bears down upon my own. Searing pain rips through me as the sharp blade of his thoughts cut through mine, forcing them into submission as he asserts his will.

Panic fills me and I struggle to break free only to feel the unyielding brutality of his command over my body. The razor-sharp lash of his thoughts whips at my mind, and I collapse before it.

He is A'kai. A race spoken of in scared and hushed whispers among other slaves. As I stare at the cruel lines of his face, his glowing green eyes turning into obsidian orbs, I understand now why his people are so feared.

A tear slips down my cheek as his dark desires flood my mind, whispering all the things he will do, the ways he will break me and make me his. With overwhelming panic, my consciousness cries out to the void a moment before it's silenced and forced to retreat.

Throwing me over his shoulder, he releases the hold on my mind, and a small whimper escapes my lips as the suffocating pressure lifts away from my consciousness. I'm too weak to move or do anything more than breathe, and I've never felt more helpless.

Despair washes through me. Is this how I will die?

Vaguely aware of Tr'lani's cries of terror behind me, I want to call out to her. To try to comfort her somehow, but I cannot push words past my lips. I want to scream and rage against what he's done. But he grips my thigh, forcing open another telepathic connection. His mind holds mine in an iron vise, and I can do nothing but hang limply over his shoulder, praying for a miracle that I doubt will ever come.

After what feels like an eternity, we reach a ship. Two pairs of boots the same as his step aside as we enter. When the airlock seals behind us, we're plunged into darkness.

The interior is dimly lit as if to simulate night. Muted glowing green light reflects off the dark metal panels of the walls and floor, but it's so weak I cannot make out any details. We travel down a long hallway and through another set of doors.

When he throws me down onto something soft, my heart stops when I realize it's a bed. He forces Tr'lani into a cage nearby. Her head slams against the bars, and she goes limp. He turns back to me, crossing the room so quickly I gasp. How am I supposed to escape a monster who can move so fast?

I close my eyes and concentrate on trying to force my limbs to move, but it's no use. He sits on the edge of the bed and pulls me into his lap, straddling his hips to face him. He wraps an arm around my waist while he gathers my hair in his other hand and roughly jerks my head back. Tilting my chin up, he forces me to stare directly into his eyes as a cruel grin crosses his green-tinged face.

The heavy press of his mind enters mine; invading tendrils snake and wrap through my consciousness. Something sharp twists deep inside my skull, the pain excruciating as he tears through my thoughts, asserting his dominance and forcing me again into submission.

The hard length of him presses insistently against my center, and a tear slips down my cheek. I'm a virgin, and the moment this enters my thoughts, his consciousness wraps thickly around it. A perverse feeling of satisfaction spears my mind, and I realize it's his. He derives sick pleasure from knowing he will be my first...and my last. An angry sob rises in my throat, but he chokes it from my lungs.

"*I will not be gentle,*" his mind whispers to mine.

An involuntary tremor moves through me at his words before he forces me to still.

Bright light flashes in the corner of my vision. He turns toward it, releasing his hold on my mind as he focuses on a large screen against the wall. Strange symbols scroll across the display and he groans. He pulls me off his lap and throws a blanket over my body.

His glowing green eyes burn with anger as a low and menacing growl rumbles deep in his chest. "Remain silent and still or I will kill your friend first and make you watch."

Too weak to do anything else I somehow manage to nod, and he covers my head. His vise-like grip clamps around my forearm, tightening until the bones feel like they'll snap beneath the pressure. Despite the pain, I stay quiet, remembering his threat about Tr'lani.

"Greetings, my beloved. Is it done?" he asks. "Is that why you've contacted me?"

A woman's voice fills the room. "No. I simply wished to talk to you. It has been too long." She pauses. "Unfortunately, Marek still lives."

"He should already be dead." A hint of irritation seeps into his tone. "What is taking so long?"

"He is off-world, working on a translation program for a new species we made contact with."

"How are *we* supposed to move forward if you are not bonded to him?"

"Do not worry. It will be done soon. After that, I will make sure he and Kalvar meet an untimely end."

"Excellent," he replies. "The sooner, the better. Our bonding will unite our two races, and together, we will form an Empire to rival even that of the Mosaurans."

"Yes, my cherished one."

A male voice calls out faintly, "Princess, a transmission from the Embassy in Seattle is coming through for you."

"I must go," she says. "It is probably Menov calling with an update."

My heart stops. The voice said "Seattle." She has to be talking about Terra.

A low purr rumbles deep in his chest. "I ache for you, my beloved."

"And I for you," she replies in a seductive hiss.

"Perhaps we can arrange to meet off-world again for a few days, like we did on Romlin 3?"

"That would be most agreeable," she purrs. "Until then."

"Until then," he replies.

When he finally turns his attention back to me, he rips the blanket away. "Until I can be with my beloved again, *you* will have to do." His glowing green eyes turn into raven black orbs as they rake over my form. "I believe you will make a delicious pleasure slave." His lips turn up in a sinister grin and I watch in horror as his canines extend into long, sharp fangs.

Vampire! The word flashes through my mind. Fear gives strength to my weakened limbs, and I scramble back. I cry out as he lunges forward, pinning me roughly beneath him. He invades my consciousness, forcing me to still.

Panic steals my breath as he leans down to scent me, grazing his teeth along the curve of my neck and shoulder. Goosebumps prickle my flesh as something warm and wet drags across my skin, directly over my pulsing artery.

His dark desire floods my thoughts and I choke on a scream as he sinks his teeth deep into my neck. The heavy scent of iron fills the air. The sick pull against my skin is agonizing torture as he drinks of my blood. His hands clamp down on my arms in a bruising grip and I'm unable to move as his consciousness holds mine prisoner.

My pulse pounds in my ears as I begin to grow weaker, my life slowly fading as he drains me. Perverse delight dances across the landscape of his dark and twisted mind. He reaches one hand between us, roughly pushing my threadbare dress up to my waist and then fumbling with his pants. Pulling at the fastenings to free himself, he forces my thighs apart to settle between them.

Darkness closes in at the edges of my vision. Rage wars with devastation as my body begins to fail, and I struggle to keep my eyes open. I can't believe I'm going to die this way.

Paralyzed under the crushing weight of Talel's invading consciousness, tears of despair and anger roll down my cheeks. I think of my parents and how sad they'll be never knowing what happened to their daughter. I think of my sister and my little niece, Elizabeth. I wish I could see them one last time. All the things I've ever done and all the things I'll never do run through my head, and a broken sob escapes me.

"Let her go!" Tr'lani's panicked voice calls out.

He rips his teeth from my neck and growls over his shoulder, "Silence! It will be your turn next!"

Blood covers his mouth and drips from his chin. He looks every bit the terrifying monster of ancient Terran lore.

Desperate to escape I test the movements of my body, flexing and extending my hands at my side. Determination fills me as I muster all that is left of my strength. I have to fight. If I don't, he'll rape me and kill me. And then do the same to Tr'lani.

He wipes his hand across his bloody mouth. Staring down at the crimson liquid, he frowns. "Your blood. It is red." He narrows his eyes. "What are you?"

My gaze flicks to his belt. Taking advantage of his confusion, I grab his blaster, pulling it free.

Lightning fast, he rips it from my grip and backhands my cheek with the hard butt of the weapon. Pain shoots through my jaw as the taste of iron fills my mouth.

His nostrils flare as he wraps one hand tightly around my neck. "Look at me," he commands. "I *will not* tolerate disobedience."

Channeling my fear into rage I meet his gaze evenly and grit through my teeth. "Then you should kill me now, because I *will not* obey."

His eyes widen in shock, as if he cannot believe what I've just said. He throws his head back, and an evil, guttural laugh erupts from his throat. "I enjoy a challenge. I think I will keep you for a while."

Anger twists deep inside me. I am strong, and I vow that I will kill him and save Tr'lani. Even if it is the last thing I do.

The door chimes, drawing his attention away. "Enter!" he calls out.

Booted footsteps enter the room. "Lord Talel, you have visitors."

"Who is it?"

"Prince Soran and Prince Rowan of Mosaura."

"What do they want?"

"I do not know, my lord, but they have requested to speak with you."

He huffs out an irritated breath. "Show the princes to the reception room. I will receive them there."

"Yes, my lord."

I inhale sharply, wincing as his hand clamps tighter around my forearm. "You will sit beside me like a good pet and accompany me to meet with the princes."

Fire burns through my veins as I glare up at him.

His glowing green eyes meet mine in challenge. "Behave, or I will make you watch as I kill your friend. And I can promise, it will not be a quick death."

Clenching my jaw, I force myself to nod.

He jerks me to my feet, and my legs are so weak I worry I'm going to collapse, but I somehow manage to remain upright.

He tips his head to the side to regard me. "I usually share my slaves with my men. But *you*, I will keep for myself. Your blood is the finest I've ever tasted. What species are you?"

Fear spikes through me but I do my best to hide it. "I'm Martian." The lie is close enough to the truth that if he invades my mind again, it should hold up against his assault.

I was the first baby conceived on Mars Colony. My dad was a pilot back when the shuttles to Mars were done without stasis sleep. With the old Z80 ships, it used to take three months each way. My mom was a botanist, traveling to work in the hydroponics bays on the new settlement. That's how they met.

Shortly after my older sister, Angela, was born on Terra, my parents decided to return to Mars. Other babies had already been born on the red, barren planet, but I was the first one conceived there. Dad always teased that I was a Martian, and it stuck with me ever since.

Talel gives me a suspicious look. I answered him too quickly. I should have feigned hesitance.

"A Martian." He repeats the word to himself as he clips the chain to my collar. "My people will be very interested in yours." He jerks me forward. "Follow me and do exactly as I say."

As we pass Tr'lani's cage, our eyes lock briefly. I put my hand to my chest in the gesture she taught me was one of deep affection for her race. Although it's only been a few weeks since we were sold to the Anguis, she's become like a sister to me.

I want so much to reassure her that we will find a way out of this, but I can't. All I know is that I will do everything I can to make sure that she, at least, survives. I can only hope that she understands as I whisper the word, "In'ari."

It is the sacred Aerilon word for family, but it means so much more than this. It's a promise to honor the ties that bind you—to never forget or leave anyone behind.

"In'ari," she repeats solemnly. A sad, low trilling hum emits from her throat, following me out into the hallway before the doors close behind us.

We walk down a long corridor. My eyes are now adjusted to the muted green lighting. It casts just enough illumination that I'm able to visualize more of the ship's interior. Sparsely decorated, this vessel appears to be strictly utilitarian. Dark metal panels line the floors, walls and ceiling. It's strange that there don't appear to be any signs or visible markers, making me wonder how they discern one hallway or door from the next.

We pass several other A'kai. All of them tall, green-skinned, elf-like beings with white hair and three slight cranial ridges on their foreheads. One goes straight up their forehead from between their brows, and the other two start at the same point but go out like a V to their temples.

They watch me curiously as we pass. Their nostrils flare as they scent the air, probably to smell my fear or my blood...or maybe both. All I know is that these guys are monsters, and if I don't figure out a way for us to escape, we're dead.

I pay close attention to my surroundings, making a mental note of our path. It's difficult because it is so much darker on this ship than it was on the station. I wonder if it's because the A'kai are trying to simulate some kind of nighttime, or if it's that they prefer a darkened environment.

We stop in front of a large door, and Talel turns to face me. "You are my property, and you will keep your head down and your gaze trained on the floor. Do you understand?"

I cannot afford to make him mad. He's already threatened to kill Tr'lani, and I have to do whatever I can to protect her. So I will obey. For now. "Yes."

"'Yes' what?" he growls.

His eyes turn into obsidian orbs and a feral snarl twists his lips as his fangs extend into sharpened points. He is every bit a vampire from the ancient Terran myths. My childhood nightmare made manifest before me.

Lowering my gaze to the floor, I push down my fear. "Yes, Master."

With a soft whoosh of air, the door slides open, and we enter a brightly lit room. In stark contrast to the rest of the ship, I can only assume the extra lighting is for his guests. I blink several times as my eyes adjust. From my limited field of vision, I notice two plush dark-gray sofas hovering above the ground, separated by what looks like a floating coffee table between them. It's so similar to something you'd find on Terra, except our furniture doesn't levitate.

He drags me behind him, pulling on my chain to direct me where he wants. Clamping a heavy hand on my shoulder, he forces me to kneel at his feet as he sits in the chair beside me. Not wanting to incur his wrath, I keep my eyes down and notice two large sets of boots directly across from us. These guys must be huge. The leggings of their uniform are a dark, metallic, tightly woven material, molded to what little I can see of their form from this angle--almost like a second skin.

Talel speaks first. "What brings you two here today?" he asks in a surprisingly friendly voice.

"Slavery is illegal, Talel," one of the men says. His voice is deep and smooth like velvet, and I find myself wondering what he looks like because I think he might be a good guy. Especially if this is his conversation opener.

I flinch involuntarily when Talel's hand touches the top of my head to pet my hair. "So it is, Prince Soran," he replies. "But we are in the neutral zone, and the laws are a bit vague here, so you'll have to forgive me if I indulge in a few guilty pleasures."

A low and menacing growl rumbles from Soran's chest. "Give us the females."

A spike of panic goes through me. Maybe he's not a good guy like I thought. But my fear quickly disappears when he speaks again.

"I vow if you give them to us, we will return them to their home worlds and not mention your name, for you know it is death if their people find out you kept them as slaves."

Cautious hope fills me as I wait for Talel's answer to Soran's bargain. I squeeze my eyes shut, praying to whoever may be listening that he accepts their terms and lets us go.

A sharp jerk of my collar makes my eyes snap open. "What are you doing?" Talel hisses.

Full of nervous anticipation, I don't have time to think of a lie as I keep my gaze down and stumble over my words. "I'm—I'm praying."

He scoffs. "Prayers will not avail you." He leans forward to address

Soran. "I will not give up my pets. I haven't finished playing with them. Perhaps you can have the scraps when I'm done."

Soran growls and shoots up from his chair so quickly I cannot stop myself from looking up.

The moment my eyes meet his, the growl dies in his throat as he stares at me in shock. His mouth drifts open, and so does mine.

Large, silver, reflective eyes stare down at me, and they look so familiar, my breath hitches. He's covered in smooth, grayish-silver scales that shimmer softly beneath the light with accented highlights of red across the sharp ridges of his cheeks and brows. A small, bony ridge starts at the top of his forehead and spreads out across his skull in a V, disappearing into short-cropped, obsidian hair. A long and deep scar starts just above his right brow, stretching down to his cheek.

My heart stops. This is the same man I've seen many times in my dreams. The sharp angles and aristocratic features of his cheekbones, brow, and nose are exactly as I remember. I've drawn his face so many times, I would recognize it anywhere.

He's just as I've imagined. He is fierce and beautiful all at once, and as he stares down at me, he whispers the word "Ashaya" so low that I wonder if he actually said it or if I just read it from his lips. Although I do not understand what this word means, I know it is not spoken harshly or in anger. There's a kindness reflected behind his silver eyes, and despite all I've been through, my instincts tell me I can trust him. After all, he is bargaining for our freedom.

The man beside him draws his attention as he wraps a hand around his forearm. With a thumb and four fingers tipped with lethal black claws, it's obvious these guys could be dangerous, but I'm not afraid.

"Brother," he says, looking to Soran, "you must calm yourself and sit down."

Soran's eyes dart back to mine a moment before he narrows his gaze at my master. "What do you want for the females? Name your price, and we'll pay it."

A wicked grin spreads across Talel's face. "I never thought *you'd* be so interested in something outside of your own species."

Soran bristles, his nostrils flaring in anger.

Talel sits back down with a feigned air of casualness. "Let us have tea and discuss our terms."

The muscles tic on the side of Soran's jaw as he takes a seat next to his brother.

Talel hits a glowing panel on the table between them, and a man enters the room, setting a large tray with what I assume is a strange square teapot and three small cups.

When Talel reaches out to pour the steaming liquid, I notice the slight trick of his hand as he tips his ring. A single drop of what I suspect to be poison dollops into the two cups he pours for Soran and his brother.

"I don't want tea," Soran snaps. "Just tell me your terms. How much for the females?"

"Tea is a part of every A'kai negotiation," Talel replies smoothly. "It is part of our custom, and we will honor it."

Anxiety twists deep inside me as Soran and his brother reach forward to each take a cup. This is it. I can't stand by and watch them be poisoned. Drawing in a deep breath, I steel my courage. If this is how I die, so be it.

The world shifts into slow motion as I jump up from the floor and swipe the cup from Soran's grasp, throwing it back at Talel.

He only has a moment to look surprised before the liquid splashes across his face. Crying out like a wounded animal, his skin sizzles and burns from the caustic poison. Chaos erupts as Soran and his brother rush forward to attack.

Talel jerks my chain, sending me flying backward. Pain explodes across my back and skull as I slam against the wall and slide down to the floor in a crumpled heap.

Darkness swims at the edges of my vision. I blink several times, trying to focus and stay awake. The violent sounds of struggle followed by the muted blasts of an energy weapon drift across the room. Booted footsteps rush toward me, and I curl onto my side just as Soran falls to his knees. His face is a mask of concern as his gaze rakes over my form. Everything hurts. It takes every ounce of my strength to move, but I somehow manage to reach out to him with a trembling hand, staring deep into his silver eyes.

"Please," I whisper. "Save my friend."

~

**Soran**

Striking sea-green eyes stare up into mine as the V'loryn female asks me for help.

*Ashaya.*

The word ripples through me, suffusing body and soul as awareness spreads like liquid fire through my veins. My soul recognizes I am irrevocably hers; she is now as much a part of me as the heart that beats solidly within my chest. I am bound to her by celestial fate.

Fierce protectiveness rushes through me as I stare down at her small form. "I swear to the Creator, we will help you and your friend to escape."

Her gaze holds mine, and I recognize the cautious hope behind her eyes. Hope is a dangerous thing when you're a slave—more precious than L'omhara. And I vow I will not shatter hers.

"You have to find my friend," she says, pushing up on one arm as she struggles to rise. "We cannot leave her with these monsters."

She collapses to the floor with a sharp cry. Tears sliding down her cheeks as she grits her teeth in pain. Her hand drifts down to her left leg, swollen and bleeding. She slams her fist against the floor in frustration before lifting a tortured gaze to mine. "I can't walk; I'll only slow you down. Just leave me and go help my friend."

I'm shocked by her strength. I've seen males on the battlefield with injuries nowhere near as severe as hers who cried out like wild kravens. Yet this female just grits her teeth against the pain and implores me to leave her behind to save her friend? She may be small, but she has the heart of a warrior.

I carefully scoop her up into my arms, and she buries her head in my chest, muffling a loud cry of agony as I stand.

She looks up at me, her green eyes brimming with tears that she struggles to blink back. "I'll just slow you down. Please save my friend."

As her determined gaze holds mine, my chest tightens. She is much lighter than I imagined. V'loryns are built much like my people, and the slight weight of her body is concerning. I don't know what horrors she's been through that altered her appearance and her make-up so drastically, but I admire her unbroken strength of will. "I will not leave you behind."

Carefully tucking her against my chest, I rush back to Rowan. Talel's crumpled body lies on the floor, quivering as he draws in a ragged breath. I shot him with my blaster set to kill, ensuring his wound is fatal and he will die this day. Although I could shoot him again and end him quickly, I do not. He deserves nothing less than a long and painful death.

Rowan's eyes are wide as he looks across at me. "We have to go before someone comes. We cannot fight an entire regiment of A'kai by ourselves."

"We cannot leave without the Aerilon."

Panicked, he paces back and forth as if trying to come up with a plan. He runs his hand roughly through his hair and then leans down to ask my Ashaya. "Where is your friend? We have to hurry."

"Left down the hallway," she replies weakly. "Third door on the right."

We move to the door and press the panel to open it. Rowan cautiously peeks his head out to scan the passage. "It's empty," he whispers, not bothering to look back as he motions for me to follow.

Sweat beads on my forehead as we move as quietly as possible down the corridor. The sound of raucous laughter echoes from some-where nearby. I don't know how many A'kai are on this ship, but certainly more than my brother and I could ever hope to defeat on our own. The Creator is with us as we make our way unnoticed to the room that holds the Aerilon.

As soon as we enter, an A'kai soldier spins to face us, his fangs dripping with the Aerilon's blood as she fights against his hold.

Rowan rushes forward to attack, but a burst of light flies past him, hitting the A'kai square in the chest. The life fades from his eyes as he drops to the floor in a crumpled heap.

My brother stares in shock at the V'loryn in my arms, still holding my blaster out in front of her. She must have pulled it from my belt without my notice.

Her eyes are wide and burning with anger as she glares down at his body. "You will never touch *anyone* again."

Lifting her gaze to mine, she holds the non-lethal end of the blaster out to me.

I shake my head. "Keep it. You may need to use it again before we reach our glider."

Weakened from blood loss, the Aerilon's gaze is unfocused as she struggles to stand. Rowan moves to help her but she recoils from his touch as if it were fire. "Don't touch me, Mosauran!"

I understand her reaction to my brother. There has always been a deep level of mistrust between our two species. But we must push that aside for now so we can escape. I open my mouth to speak, but my Ashaya beats me to it.

"They're here to help us, Tr'lani. These are the good guys."

She stumbles forward but Rowan catches her before she falls, lifting her into his arms. "Allow me to carry you," he says softly.

The Aerilon looks up at him through slightly narrowed eyes. "I can walk."

A small smile twists his lips, no doubt he admires her determination. "As you said, I am Mosauran. Your weight is slight; it is no burden to carry you. We need to be able to run if we are going to escape. I beg you not to be stubborn about this."

Reluctantly, she nods, and we start for the door. It feels like forever before we finally find the exit. A guard puts his hand out to stop us.

"Where are you going with these two?" he asks in a booming voice.

I step forward, lifting my chin to stare down at him. "We bought them from Talel."

He eyes us warily. "Where *is* my Lord Talel?"

Before I can think up a lie, the V'loryn blasts him, and he collapses at my feet.

Irrationally, given the amount of danger we're still in, I'm practically beaming with pride at her ferocity and deadly accuracy with a weapon. She may be V'loryn, but she most certainly has the heart of a warrior.

Shouting voices echo behind us. Blood pumps through my veins like liquid fire as we race down the platform across the docking bay. Our glider is just up ahead, and I see the dockworker we spoke with earlier. A mixture of terror and surprise mars his features as we run toward him, and words leave his mouth in a panicked rush. "Your— your ship is ready, my lords."

"Good," Rowan says. He pauses long enough to tap his wristband at the male's while somehow managing to keep the Aerilon balanced in his arms.

From the wide eyed look on the worker's face, my brother obviously gave him more than enough credits to cover our fuel.

We race up the ramp to the airlock. As soon as it closes behind us, we seal the doors and head straight for the bridge.

I gaze down at my Ashaya. All the color is drained from her face, and her eyelids flutter open and closed as she fights to stay conscious.

Panic fills me. "Are you—" I start to ask if she's all right, but she cuts me off.

She grips my collar with a strength I did not think her capable of in her current state. "I'm fine! Let's go!"

She struggles to stay awake as I place her in the seat beside me on the bridge. When I tighten the harness across her chest, a small cry of pain escapes her, and her eyes snap open to meet mine.

"Forgive me," I whisper.

Breathing heavily, she clenches her jaw and nods before her head falls back against the seat. Her hands grip the chair rails so tightly her knuckles turn white, and I know she must be suffering greatly. Wanting to comfort her somehow, I offer what little words of reassurance I can. "We will contact your people as soon as we are free of the station."

She doesn't answer.

Rowan's voice calls out behind me. "Soran, we have to go! Now!"

With one last look at my Ashaya, I turn and slam into my chair, haphazardly buckling the harness around me as my fingers fly across the controls to spin up the FTL (faster than light) engines.

A harsh A'kai face appears in the viewscreen. Rage fills me when I realize it's Talel. How is he alive? My blaster was set to kill; I'm certain of it. I glare at him. "You should be dead."

"That one." He points to my Ashaya. "Her blood. It healed my wound faster than anything I've ever partaken before." He drags his tongue across his lips as if still savoring her taste. "And I've had the blood of many creatures. Give her back to me at once, or else I will order the entire A'kai fleet to hunt you down."

Fierce protectiveness rushes through me. A low and menacing growl rumbles deep in my chest as I level a dark gaze at the display, baring my fangs in aggression. "You *will not* touch her ever again. And when her people find out what you've done, *you* will be the one who's hunted like an animal. You will die for what you've done to her."

He leans forward, narrowing his eyes. "I might be worried *if* she were V'loryn. But I've been in her mind, and I've tasted her blood. I do not know exactly *what* she is, but I know, for a fact, that she *isn't* V'loryn."

Despite my shock at his statement, I glance down at the control panel. The engines are ready, and my eyes snap up to meet Talel's evenly so he can see the truth of my words. "I give you my vow as a prince and warrior of the Mosauran Empire. If you come after her, I will end you."

Before he can answer, I slam my fist down on the panel activating the engines, and the stars begin to blur as we enter FTL travel. Once the autopilot is set, Rowan activates the glider's cloaking mechanism before turning to me. The intense worry in his expression is surely mirrored in mine.

We are far from the borders of our Empire. And because of this, we cannot send a direct signal requesting aide to our people. Any transmissions sent from this distance, are unlikely to ever even reach Mosaura.

I turn back to the females. Worried golden eyes meet mine before darting to her companion. "Liana needs medical attention."

My heart seizes when I notice my Ashaya's limp form slumped forward in her seat.

I rush to the chair and unbuckle the harness, lifting her into my arms. Her head lolls back and I tuck her to my chest as I race to the door and down the hallway to medical.

Her hair falls back from her face and my eyes drift once more to the curved shell of her ear. As the scanner moves over her form, I notice a strange pattern of spots only a shade darker than her light brown skin. I should have known she was not V'loryn. But what is she?

"She's Terran," the Aerilon says, answering my unspoken question. "I've never heard of their race before. She is the first one I have ever seen."

"Terran." The word feels strange on my tongue. "Where is her home world?"

She shakes her head softly. "I do not know and...I do not think she does either. Her species has not yet left their planetary system, much less made any contact with other races."

The scanner zips over Liana's small form as we watch the display readout anxiously. Although she lacks many of their features, I can understand how she could be mistaken for a V'loryn female.

The Aerilon looks to me. "It will take a few moments. I am Tr'lani of the High Clan of Al'ani." Her voice quavers slightly. "I...I was a Healer back on Aerilon."

The despair is easy to read in her eyes as she speaks of her former life—her profession. Her use of the past tense suggests she must have been a slave for a very long time.

I understand this. After having been a slave for so many cycles, it took me a long time to realize that I was still a warrior and a Prince of Mosaura. Placing my closed fist to my chest, I bow slightly. "I am

Prince Soran of House Mosaura and this"—I motion to my brother —"is Prince Rowan." He inclines his head in greeting before bowing as well.

"Thank you for saving us." Her gaze shifts to Rowan. "I am sorry for my reaction when you found me. Our two races have fought for many cycles over the neutral zone, and we've been enemies for so long. I—"

Rowan interrupts her. "There is no need to apologize. I would probably have reacted the same if our roles were reversed." He cocks his head to the side. "You are of one of the High Clans on Aerilon. How were you taken?"

Tr'lani looks down a moment before she lifts her gaze to his. "Zovians invaded the colony I was on. Those they didn't kill, they sold into slavery. The neutral zone between our two Empires is supposed to be protected. If your people and mine could stop fighting with each other, perhaps the slavers would not be able to operate so close to the edge of our shared borders."

This has always been my concern. I know all too well that traffickers take advantage of the petty bickering between Empires to operate undisturbed in the neutral zones. Rowan opens his mouth to speak, but the scanner beeps that it's finished with its readings.

Anxiously, I step back, allowing Tr'lani better access to Liana and the med scanner. Her eyes widen slightly as she looks at the display. "The closest match to her anatomy is that of a V'loryn but...there are still so many differences. She is weak from blood loss and has several minor fractures and a broken leg, but I believe she is stable." Taking Liana's smaller hand in hers, she stares down at her friend. A low trilling hum begins in the back of her throat as she whispers,"In'ari."

Rowan and I exchanged a stunned glance, surprised that she uses this term for one outside of her race. That word is sacred among the Aerilon—a sign of deep and great affection reserved only for clan and family members.

Tenderly, she brushes the hair back from Liana's face. "She is like a sister to me. We have been through much. She has protected me ever since we met. I would be dead now, if not for her. I have never known anyone so brave or so—" She swallows thickly before continuing, her eyes brimming with tears, "So kind."

Rowan inhales sharply and my jaw goes slack as my gaze follows his to the 3D scanner display of Liana's injuries. A thick pattern of jagged, deep-red scars mar the full length of her back—a branding from one of her owners. I cannot imagine the level of pain she must have endured when she received these.

Reaching back, I brush my fingers over a long scar across my shoulder and clench my jaw in anger. Zovian marks can never be healed. They cut their slaves with Hawkan steel and pour silic acid into the wounds to ensure they are permanent. No MRU can heal these—a physical reminder of unspeakable acts of torture and time spent as a slave. She must have been very fierce indeed to have been given so many markings. Only defiant slaves are cut this brutally and deeply.

As Tr'lani studies the scans, I allow my gaze to travel over Liana. Much like the V'loryns and Aerilon, she has skin instead of scales. It is light brown with pinkish undertones and covered with several small, dotted specks of a darker shade of brown that seem to be a bit more pronounced across the bridge of her nose and cheeks. This strange spotted pigment variation of her outer dermal layer must be specific to her species; I have never seen a V'loryn or Aerilon with spots.

Tr'lani is silent for so long, it worries me. "Will she be all right?" I ask, mentally bracing myself for her reply.

She nods. "The MRU is already working to heal her. She's similar enough to a V'loryn that it should be able to repair the damage she has suffered."

Relief floods my system at her words, and my protective instincts surge as I stare down at Liana's still form through the glass casing. Something inside me recognizes that she is mine, and I both love and hate this knowledge in equal measure.

The fated mate bond is a gift from the Creator of all things—the highest blessing that can ever be bestowed upon a warrior. And yet, I cannot help but feel that it is also a curse. This bond could mean the end of everything I've ever known. After all I survived to return to my family, I cannot bear the thought of losing them again.

Rowan clamps a firm hand on my shoulder and meets my eyes evenly. "We must speak."

I glance back to Liana, reluctant to leave her side.

As if sensing my hesitation, Tr'lani looks to me, "I will stay here to monitor her."

Satisfied that my Ashaya is under the care of a Healer, I follow Rowan out into the hallway.

His brow furrows deeply. "Something is wrong with you, brother. What is it?"

I look down at the floor as I search for the words to tell him—to explain that which I do not even understand myself. Softly shaking my head, I lift my gaze to his. "Liana is my Ashaya."

Stunned, his mouth drifts open in disbelief. "Are you certain?"

"Yes."

The gravity of my answer hangs heavy in the silence between us. The red-orange scales of his cheek grow pale as he stumbles over his words. "But, she's—she is not Mosauran. How could she be your Ashaya?"

I meet his gaze evenly. "I do not know, and I cannot change what is."

# CHAPTER 4

SORAN

R owan begins pacing. He often does this when he's under
stress. The fact that he's doing so now means he understands all too well the implications of what I've just
told him.

His eyes flash with worry. "It is forbidden to take a mate outside of
our race. You would be Outcast. You are a Prince of Mosaura. You
cannot bind yourself to her."

"I cannot deny this calling. I already feel her here, brother." I
thump my fist to my chest, directly over my heart. "You do not
understand."

"You're right," he snaps. "I *don't* understand. How can you throw
away your life for this strange female? A species we've never heard of
before? You don't even know her."

Shaking my head, I meet his eyes evenly, hoping he will understand. "My soul is tied to hers. It is not something I can just ignore or
pretend that it does not exist."

He gives me an incredulous look. "Do you even love her?"

Do I? I drop my gaze to the floor as I contemplate my answer. I feel protective and possessive of her in a way that I've never felt with anyone else. And yet, I know almost nothing about her aside from the fact that she is as brave as one of my people despite her fragile form. I look back up at Rowan. "How could I? I do not know her."

"Then, that decides it." He gives me a firm nod. "You cannot give up everything for a complete stranger."

Despite my misgiving, my soul rebels at his words, and I lash out. "She is *not* a stranger. She is my Ashaya."

Roughly running a hand through his hair, he gives me a pained look. "I...I do not want to lose you again."

His despair echoes my own, and I place my hand on his shoulder. "I do not want to lose you either. Perhaps there is another way. If I can convince Mother to accept her, maybe she can convince the Council to change the laws and—"

He cuts me off abruptly, slashing his hand through the air in a gesture of frustration. "There is no other way. You know the laws as well as I. You will be Outcast, and I will never see you again." He gestures animatedly to the door and begins pacing again. "She may not even want you as her mate. Have you even considered that?"

My thoughts drift to the scar on my face and the look in Maina's eyes when she first saw it. All those cycles in slavery, I held onto the hope of not only finding my family, but of returning to her. We grew up together. Although we were not in love, I was honored that she had already decided upon me. She called me her Chosen One...vowed that she'd take no mate but me when we finally came of age. But when I returned, she cast me aside, telling me she could not bear to look upon my disfigurement because it reminded her that I'd been a slave. As if it were something I could ever forget, even if I had no visible scar.

I meet Rowan's gaze evenly. "Perhaps you are right. She may not desire me as hers."

He looks at me but says nothing. His pitying expression speaks volumes. He remembers the day Maina turned from me. She turned her back and chose him instead. And although Rowan refused her, something inside me broke that day, and I swore that I would never take a mate. If Maina found me lacking, why wouldn't another?

With a heavy sigh, I turn back to the med bay doors.

Rowan calls out behind me. "Where are you going?"

"She has been through much. I will sit with her until she wakes. Even if she does not want me, I wish to help her...to help them both in any way I can."

When I enter the room, Tr'lani looks to me. "She should be awake in a few hours."

I nod, taking the seat next to the MRU. My eyes drift to Tr'lani's broken wings. "I will sit with Liana if you wish to use the other unit on yourself."

She studies me a moment before reaching her hand out in the Aerilon gesture of greeting. The instant her skin touches mine, warmth flows from her hand, and a strange buzzing sensation travels over my palm.

I've heard of this but have never experienced it before now. This is how the Aerilon read someone—judging if their intentions are good or bad. It's not exactly touch telepathy, like the V'loryns and A'kai possess, but it is close.

When she finally releases my hand, she gives me a solemn look. "I have taken your measure. You are an honorable male, willing to protect us with your life if necessary. I thank you for your protection. I did not expect to find such kindness from a Mosauran."

I give her a subtle nod, waiting and wondering if she sensed anything else. If she knows what Liana is to me.

She continues. "The A'kai did not intend to let us live."

My eyes drift to my Ashaya. I wish I had killed Talel all those cycles ago in the arena. If I had, he and his men would have never hurt her or Tr'lani.

After a few hours, Liana begins to stir. A soft moan escapes her lips as her eyelids flutter and open. Striking sea-green eyes meet mine, something close to recognition flickering briefly behind them. I'm both surprised and grateful that she does not look upon me with fear as most other races do when face to face with a Mosauran warrior. "Where am I? What happened?"

I open my mouth to answer, but Tr'lani speaks first. "We're safe. You had many injuries, and you lost consciousness. I treated you and—"

Her eyes dart nervously around the room. "You're sure we're safe?"

My heart clenches at the slight quaver of her voice. I remember the cautious hope in my soul when I woke to find Rowan standing over me—the day he rescued me from slavery—wondering if I was finally and truly free. I meet her gaze evenly, so she can see the truth of my words. "I am Prince Soran of House Mosaura, and this"—I gesture to my brother—"is my brother, Prince Rowan. You are both safe. We are going to find your people and return you to your home."

Rowan's eyes meet mine, and I recognize the hope that flickers briefly across his expression at my vow to return my Ashaya to her people.

"Thank you for rescuing us."

Lost in her striking eyes, unbidden words fill my mind that I dare not speak aloud. "*I would gladly dedicate my life to ensuring you are protected.*"

She recoils as if struck, fear marring her beautiful features. "Are you—are you in my mind?"

So shocked that she heard me, it takes me a moment to respond. "Forgive me. I did not mean to project my thoughts to you."

A small tremor moves through her form, but she quickly hides her unease. "You don't have to apologize. It was just...surprising. My species is not telepathic, but I realize that many are," she says, clenching her jaw as she blinks back the tears gathering in the corners of her eyes.

Guilt fills me. This is part of the fated bond. I hate that our connection allows her to hear my thoughts. That it reminds her of the R'ugol—Talel's unspeakable violation of her mind. Her fear quickly disappears behind a stoic mask, and in this way, she reminds me of the V'loryns. They are experts at concealing their emotions.

Aerilon, V'loryns, and A'kai exhibit varying degrees of telepathy, but I do not know the extent of their abilities. As for my people, we can only communicate in this way with our Ashaya. I do not tell her this, though, because from what she just explained, I understand it is not the way of her people. Remembering the panic in her eyes, I wish it were not the way of mine either.

Rowan steps forward, a deep frown creasing his brow. "You heard my brother in your mind?"

Liana nods.

His expression changes to open concern. "But that is—"

He stops speaking abruptly as I cut him off with a firm look. I know what he means to say, and he's right. We are two different species. It should be impossible. But it is not...and this is proof that she is, in truth, my Ashaya.

~

**Liana**

I sit further up in the bed and instinctively band my arm across my rib cage and stomach, bracing for the inevitable pain. To my surprise, I feel nothing, and a wide smile spreads across my face. "Nothing hurts."

Tr'lani grins. "I put you in the MRU, and it healed most of your wounds. You might have some pain later, but not as much as you had before."

Swinging my legs over the side of the bed, I tentatively stand and realize that nothing hurts...at all. I haven't felt like this since... Tr'lani rests her hand lightly on my shoulder. I swallow hard against the lump forming in my throat as her eyes meet mine. My voice is thick with emotion when I finally manage to speak. "Thank you. I haven't had a single day without pain since...before I was taken."

Soran steps forward. "Tr'lani said you do not know where your home world is. Would you like to study our star charts to see if anything is familiar?"

His words jog my memory, and my eyes snap up to meet his. "Talel's beloved." The words escape my lips in a panicked rush.

Soran gives me a puzzled look.

I continue. "I heard Talel speaking to a woman. He called her his 'beloved.' She mentioned the name of a city on my home world. Her people have made contact with mine."

He and his brother give me a shocked look before Soran steps forward. "Are you certain?"

"Yes."

"I remember him speaking to a female," Tr'lani adds. "From the way she talked to him...they must be mates. But she was not A'kai."

"How do you know? Did you see her?"

Tr'lani shakes her head. "No. But she is a Princess. Talel spoke of their bonding uniting their two races to forge an Empire that would rival that of your people."

Soran and Rowan listen intently as Tr'lani and I relay everything we heard.

When we're finished explaining, Soran's brow furrows deeply. "She did not say anything that could help us figure out who she was? What species?"

"No. And—because Talel doesn't know what *I* am, he didn't realize she was speaking of my planet...my people." Panic coils tight in my chest. "I have to find my home world before it's too late."

Rowan gives me a pitying look. "I've already set a course for Mosaura. It is the safest place for us to go now. I am sorry, I wish we could help you, but we cannot just wander aimlessly in search of your planet. It will take us four weeks to reach home as it is, and at least two before we are able to communicate with our home world to request assistance from our Empire."

I stare at him in shock. "Why will it take so long?"

"In order for the glider to remain cloaked, the engines must sacrifice efficiency and speed. And I believe it wise that we remain cloaked for the entire journey. On the bridge, I overheard several transmissions. Talel has already placed a bounty on all our heads."

Despite my frustration, I know he's right. We can't just blindly search for Terra without some idea of where to look. The A'kai are hunting us.

# CHAPTER 5

LIANA

A deep voice calls my name, startling me awake. My eyes snap open. My heart hammers in my chest as I spin in the direction of the sound to find Soran staring at me with an apologetic look. "Forgive me. I did not mean to scare you."

A long exhalation of relief escapes me. I place my hand atop the MRU casing directly over Tr'lani's still sleeping form, reminding myself that we are free and we are safe. At least for now. The gentle hum of the machine fills the room, echoing off the reflective metal walls as the unit works to repair her damaged wings.

I inhale deeply, relishing the fresh, strong scent of disinfectant that seems to permeate the entire ship. From what little I've seen of the glider so far, everything is meticulously clean and polished to a brilliant sheen. A sharp contrast to the places we were held when we were slaves.

I lift my gaze to Soran. "It's okay. I'm just used to—" I stop short, about to say, "shock sticks and beatings," but instead say, "I was just surprised. That's all."

Reflective silver eyes stare down at me intently. "Are you hungry?"

It is so strange to be face to face with the man that's haunted my dreams for so many years. And I only realize I haven't answered him when he cocks his head slightly to the side in confusion. So, I quickly reply. "Yes, but I can wait."

He frowns.

I glance down at Tr'lani. She looks so much like a fairy princess from the ancient Terran legends. Asleep like this, she reminds me of another childhood story—the one of sleeping beauty. After everything we've been through together, I am very protective of her. "It doesn't feel right to leave her like this, Soran. What if she wakes up while I'm gone? What if she needs me?"

He leans forward and taps the control panel attached to the MRU. The display flashes brightly with a series of symbols. He studies it a moment. "She should awaken within the hour."

Curious, I stare perplexed at the strange hieroglyphs that move across the screen. "Is that how you tell time?"

He nods.

I huff lightly in frustration. I have so much to learn. I can't even do something as simple as tell time here. I've always been fiercely inde-pendent; I hate having to rely on others to help me do things. But, in the same breath, I realize I should just be grateful that we're alive and finally free.

"I could bring the food to you," he offers.

While I am hungry, the truth is that my stomach is all tied up in knots. And it probably will stay like that until Tr'lani wakes up. I really don't think I can hold anything down until I know she's okay.

He continues. "Tr'lani said you lost a lot of blood and that you needed to eat so your body can replenish itself."

My hand instinctively goes to my neck, feeling for the two small puncture wounds from Talel's bite. The echoes of remembered pain whisper across my newly healed flesh. I look up at Soran. He watches me with a pitying expression and opens his mouth as if to speak, but I interrupt him. "I'll eat later. Please explain this clock to me." I gesture to the glowing symbols on the panel. "I need to learn how it works."

He dips his chin in a subtle nod before taking the chair next to mine. As he goes through the various characters and what each of them means, a thought occurs to me, and I turn to face him. "Is this clock specific to just your people? Or do the other races tell time this way as well?"

He studies me with a piercing gaze. "You are a survivor." The words leave his lips in a hushed whisper as if speaking more to himself than to me.

I tilt my chin up slightly. An image of my father flashes through my mind. He taught Angela and me a mantra when we were growing up. It carried me through difficult times, and it is the singular thought that kept me alive during my captivity, the reason that I survived. I meet Soran's eyes evenly. "I am a Garza, and I come from a line of strong women. We are not easily broken."

A hint of something akin to admiration flashes behind his silver eyes as they stare deep into mine. "Never broken," he says solemnly. "Those are the words of my House. The words of House Mosaura. Your people...House Garza must be the same as my own—brave and strong of will."

Allowing my gaze to drift over his features, I realize he is doing the same as we regard one another. He's much taller than any Terran male and covered in thick, corded muscle, visible even beneath the obsidian, metallic armor that seems molded to his body like a second skin. From his height, broad shoulders, and the lethal grace of his muscular form, I would know he's a warrior even if I'd never heard anything about his people before.

Despite his alien features, he's ruggedly handsome. His scales shimmer with an almost iridescent glow under the ship's lights—smooth gray-silver stretched over hardened steel. And I wonder if they're soft like Terran skin.

The deep scar on his left brow travels down to the top of his cheek, and I'm amazed he didn't lose his eye to this injury. It doesn't detract from his appearance though. There's a warmth, a softness behind his silver eyes as they gaze back at me. His cheeks have a slightly red-orange hue to them that seems to grow darker as I continue to stare, and I wonder if that's his way of blushing under my scrutinizing gaze.

I'm struck by how eerily accurate my dreams of him were. He is just as I always drew him: a combination of fierce and beautiful. And although his people are warriors—feared throughout the quadrant--I've never once felt afraid in his presence. Not even the first time his eyes met mine on Talel's ship.

He opens his mouth to speak, but quickly snaps it shut again when the MRU panel chimes loudly. The casing snaps apart, a quick hiss of air escapes, and Tr'lani's eyelids flutter and open.

I smile down at her as the top of the unit slides away and she sits up. "How do you feel?"

She swings her legs over the edge of the bed and stands, spreading her sparkly fairy wings out behind her.

My heart clenches at the pain in her expression as they flutter softly on either side...beautiful, but still broken.

Her eyes brighten with tears. "It didn't work."

I rush forward and wrap my arms around her, wishing I could take away her sadness. Her voice quavers softly. "I'll never fly again, Liana."

Running my hand soothingly over her long, snow-white hair, I offer the only comfort that I can. I speak of hope. "Maybe someone on your home world can repair them. Don't give up yet."

"Maybe," she whispers.

Rowan walks in, his expression troubled as his gaze darts briefly to Tr'lani's still-broken wings. He steps forward. "Tr'lani," his voice is soft as he speaks. "I have calibrated the transmission panel. If you would like, we can try to send out a coded message for your family whenever you are ready."

Wiping her hands across her cheeks to brush away her tears, she gives him a warm smile. "I'd like to try it now."

He inclines his head. "Of course."

She gives me a crushing hug and then leaves with Rowan for the bridge.

After they're gone, I turn to Soran. "What about one of your Healers? Do you think they might be able to do anything for her?"

He gives me a hesitant look before he responds. "We will ask a Mosauran Healer to assess her, but our people do not know much about Aerilon anatomy. Our two races have been at odds with one another for many cycles."

I think I understand what he's reluctant to say, and now Tr'lani's sharp words at Rowan when they first rescued us make sense. "So...Mosaurans and Aerilon are...friendly enemies to one another?"

He tips his head to the side. "Something like that."

Despite his cryptic answer, I ask the question that's been burning in the back of my mind. "Why did you help us?"

The look he gives me is intense, and as his eyes stare deep into mine, something flashes briefly behind them, but it's gone too quickly for me to know what it was. "Slavery is illegal."

"Yes, but why us?" I press. "There must have been dozens of slaves on that station. And yet, you risked your life for us. Why?"

"I saw you when Talel first took you from the Anguis. You fought them both bravely to protect your friend." He leans forward. "Something about you called to me, and I...I could not leave you to your fate."

His gaze holds mine, and I don't quite know what to make of his words. He stares intently at me—as if he's waiting for something, but I don't know what. After a moment, I break the silence between us. "What about the other slaves?"

He shakes his head. "We cannot risk freeing anyone else."

Frustration burns through me. "We have to. It's not right, Soran. All those people... My crew could even be among them. I—"

He cuts me off abruptly. "I agree with you. Trust me. I do. That is why I am trying to convince the races whose sectors border ours to consider shared patrols of the neutral zones between us. I want to stop the slavers as much as you do."

"Have you seen any others like me? Any other Terrans?"

He gives me a pitying look. "No. I thought you were V'loryn. If I had seen any of your kind, I probably would have mistaken them as such."

Despair settles deep in my chest, and I sink back in my chair.

He leans forward. "I give you my vow as a warrior of Mosaura. I will help you find your people, Liana. I swear it to the Creator."

Even if Tr'lani hadn't "taken his measure," as her people call it, I'd still trust him. The expression on his face is sincere as he gives me his solemn vow. He and his brother risked their lives to free us. And I've dreamed of him all my life. I have to believe that my dreams meant something, even if I don't completely understand it all now.

He continues. "You should eat now that your friend is awake."

I nod. "I'm a pilot back on my home world. I'd like to get my bearings, take a quick tour of the ship before we eat, if that's all right with you."

With a subtle dip of his chin, he stands and motions for me to follow him out into the hallway. Just like the med area, every surface from floor to ceiling is shiny, polished and meticulously clean. Unlike the A'kai's vessel, everything is brightly lit.

As Soran shows me around, he mentions more than once how small the glider is, explaining that it is built to hold no more than four to six people. But it's actually bigger than any of the ships I've ever piloted back and forth between Mars and Terra—and those were able to fit a standard crew of eight.

This vessel is beautifully designed. Smooth, elegant lines and gleaming, seamless metal panels line the floor, walls, and ceiling. There are no sharp corners or hard angles here. Everything is curved or softly rounded in some way. Perhaps that's for safety. He explained that the glider is built for speed, stealth, and maneuverability. So, I guess it makes sense that you wouldn't want anything sharp for people to run into in case of a sudden course adjustment.

It doesn't take long to reach what I'm assuming is the crew mess. We sit at the only table in the center of the room, surrounded by four chairs. There are several compartments along the far wall, and he opens one of them, pulling out two liquid pouches.

He takes the chair opposite me and opens a liquid packet, handing it to me to eat, or drink...or whatever this is in here.

I sniff it first, and it doesn't really smell like anything, so I take a small sip. As soon as it hits my tongue, my stomach twists in a violent knot. I rush to the nearby sink, coughing and sputtering as I gag on the vile liquid and spit it back up.

Soran rushes up behind me and quickly hands me another packet.

"What's this?" I barely choke out, trying not to throw up again.

"Water."

I take in a big mouthful and swish it around before spitting the last of the foul sludge into the drain and cleansing my palate. After that's done, I eagerly drink the rest of it as I try to wash away the sewage taste still lingering on my tongue.

When I'm finished drinking, I gesture at the first packet. "What the hell was that?"

"Liquid proteins."

I give him an incredulous look. "Not to sound ungrateful, but were you *trying* to poison me?"

At first, his eyes go wide as if he thinks I'm serious, but when a slow grin spreads across my face, he laughs. A great rumbling belly laugh that's contagious. And that's when I notice his fangs.

His teeth are long and sharp, like something you'd see on a Terran wolf. A long time ago, this probably would have given me pause. But after everything I've seen and been through over the past few months, they're actually not that scary in comparison.

After a moment, he pulls out what looks like a foil-lined bar. Of what? I don't know, and he hands it to me. "Try this." With a slight quirk of his brow, he flashes a devastating smile—sharp fangs and all. "I can assure you it is not poison."

Slowly unwrapping the bar, I study it carefully. I've decided to be a bit more cautious about alien food. It looks like a generic protein bar, similar to something you'd find on Terra, but I'm not sure. "What is it?"

"A nutrient bar."

After a mini internal pep talk, I lift it to my mouth to bite a small piece off, but it's really hard on my teeth. Since I'm practically starving, I'm not so easily deterred, and I begin gnawing on it. From the expression on Soran's face, I must look like some kind of ravenous animal.

He stares at me in horror.

"What?" I ask, mildly annoyed at the look he's giving me.

"Are you"—he hesitates a moment before finally asking—"fully matured?"

My jaw drops, but I quickly snap it shut again. "What kind of question is that?"

"Well," he begins, and I can tell from the tone of his voice he's being cautious with his words, "you are very small, your claws are short and blunted, your fangs are pitifully tiny, and they do not appear to be sharp."

A quick puff of air escapes my lips in a surprised laugh. "Pitifully tiny fangs? Really?"

He nods in earnest, and I realize he's serious.

A sobering thought hits me, and my heart sinks. My gaze drops to my hands. "I am a stranger in a strange land," I whisper more to myself than to him.

His reflective eyes search mine, so familiar and yet so foreign. "I have upset you," he says softly.

I open my mouth to deny it, but the words won't come. In truth, I know he meant no harm, but his questions have upset me...more than they probably should. Folding my arms on the table before me, I blink back the tears that threaten to come. "Ever since I woke up in this nightmare, I haven't seen another Terran. None of the masters or any of the other slaves even knew what I was. They always just called me 'the V'loryn.' Every time someone mistook me for them, it was like a blade through my heart because it reinforced the fact that my planet must be really far from"—I look out the window at the stars blurring past the viewscreen—"wherever this is."

I swallow hard against the lump forming in my throat before I take a deep breath and push down my sadness. "And just for the record, I *am* considered fully mature for my species. Are you"—my gaze travels up and down his form—"fully mature?"

To be honest, I wouldn't even have thought to ask him this question, given his overly masculine appearance. But there's a lot about this part of the universe I don't understand, and I shouldn't take anything for granted.

Looking down at himself as if my question were ridiculous, his eyes snap back up to meet mine, and he puffs out his chest as if to emphasize his massive form. His mildly insulted expression tells me he obviously didn't expect me to ask this either. "Yes, of course, I am."

I stop just short of rolling my eyes when I realize I've probably wounded his pride. Frowning, I turn my attention back to my nutrient bar. I'm going to have to figure out how to eat this thing.

"May I?" he asks, reaching for my food.

I nod and hand it to him.

He takes it from me and breaks it into several smaller pieces.

Carefully lifting one to my nose, I sniff first before taking a small bite. I chew slowly, and the dry chunks coat my tongue. It tastes kind of like cranberry and apple mixed together with sawdust. I smile. Not bad...not bad at all. Definitely much better than the liquid nutrient packet.

His piercing gaze studies me. "You...like it?" he asks a bit cautiously.

I grin and take another bite. "Best thing I've tasted in a long time." And I mean it.

He smiles widely in return, and it makes him appear almost Terran. And for the first time, in a long time, the tension eases in my neck and shoulders. Tr'lani's okay. I'm okay. It almost seems too good to be real. Part of me worries I'm going to wake up back in a cage, finding that this was all just a dream after all—a small reprieve from the hell I've endured these past several months. My thoughts drift to my crew, and I shudder inwardly as I conjure all sorts of horrors of what may have happened to them. I've got to find them, somehow.

He gives me a concerned look. "What is wrong, Liana?"

"I was just thinking about my crew."

"How many of you were there?"

"There were seven of us total. I'm the commander." A wistful smile crests my lips. "We were on our way back to Terra from Mars. We went into stasis for the journey, and I..."

Clenching my jaw, I lower my gaze to the floor, struggling to push down the maelstrom of emotions swirling within.

When I finally lift my eyes to Soran, he gives me a sad look. Anger fills me. I don't want his pity. I don't deserve it. "It's all my fault this happened."

His brow furrows deeply. "Why do you blame yourself?"

"I was the commanding officer. It was *my* job"—I place my hand to my chest for emphasis—"to make sure everything was working properly before we went into stasis. I... There must have been something I missed, something I forgot. I just don't understand how we were taken without the ship waking us up. It's supposed to alert us when something is wrong."

I close my eyes briefly, and the painful memories rush in. Subconsciously, I reach up to touch behind my left ear, wincing slightly when my fingers trace over the small piece of metal that rests just on top of the skin from the embedded translator the Zovians gave me.

"What is that?" Soran reaches for me, but I jerk away quickly. After so many months of beatings and shock sticks, it's hard to not flinch when he tries to touch me, and a short puff of air escapes my nostrils in frustration. I'm stronger than this.

He quickly retracts his hand, and the smooth, shimmering red scales on his face darken slightly. "I will not harm you. I would sooner end my own life than ever hurt you. I swear to the Creator."

His eyes stare deep into mine; his words sound sincere. The look on his face is nothing short of wounded, grief-stricken that I fear him.

But I'm not afraid of him. He and his brother have been nothing but kind to Tr'lani and me since our escape. I meet his gaze evenly. "I believe you, Soran."

I reach back and twist my long auburn hair and pull it over my shoulder to one side, turning my head slightly so he can see behind my left ear. I take his hand in mine and place it lightly over the small metal nub protruding from the skin.

His touch is soft—light as a feather—as if he's being very careful not to hurt me.

"I think it's some sort of translator. When they put it in, it hurt like hell, but I think it's the only reason I could understand them...and probably the only reason I can understand you now. I've had a couple of headaches since then but..." I frown. "Don't you have one of these?"

His eyes are wide with concern. "How did you survive this?"

"What?"

"That is a Cerdolion translator. They have a high implantation death rate."

Already a closet hypochondriac, his words send me into full-blown panic mode. "Could it still kill me?"

He shakes his head. "Tr'lani would surely have already detected any issue when she scanned you. I do not believe you are still in danger, but we will have another Healer check you once we arrive at my home world. Perhaps we can have a V'loryn Healer assess you since you are so similar to their species."

Although his words aren't entirely reassuring, it's enough that my entire body sags in relief. "Wait a minute." My head snaps up to meet his gaze. "I'm not speaking Terran Common, am I?"

"No, you are speaking Mosauran—the Draken dialect."

"What?"

"Your translator enables you to speak my language without real-izing it."

"I. Am. Speaking. Mosauran." I punctuate each word deliberately, listening carefully to how it sounds as it leaves my mouth. Closing my eyes, I concentrate and speak again. This time I make sure to speak in Terran Common. "Can you understand me now?"

He cocks his head to the side, blinking several times in confusion. "I do not understand your words. Is that your native tongue?"

"Yes. Why can't you understand it?"

"Your language is not programmed into the translator because your species is unknown."

"What does that have to do with it?"

He explains. "Adding a new language to the translation database is a great undertaking. That is why first contact with any new species can be difficult. It often takes many cycles for teams of translators to ensure the new species' language is properly converted into each and every language the embedded translators are programmed for."

"And...everyone uses these embedded translators?"

He shakes his head. "The V'loryns do not use them."

"Why not?"

"The 'legal' ones"—he makes sure to emphasize the word legal —"are a Mosauran design. The V'loryns do not trust us, and therefore do not trust the translators. Besides, their people are very adept at assimilating languages. And every species in the known universe speaks V'loryn because almost everyone trades with them for their L'sair crystals."

"What are L'sair crystals?"

"A type of mineral used for fuel. They power ships and, in many cases, entire planets. It is the most efficient, clean energy in the known universe, and they only exist in the V'loryn planetary system."

I sink back in my chair, filing this information away in my brain for later use. The realization that there's so much I need to learn about this part of the universe is daunting, to say the least. But I've always been the kind of person who enjoys a challenge.

Deciding to start with something basic, I look to Soran. "So, there's more than one Mosauran dialect?"

"Yes, there are three, but the one we are speaking is the most common. Does your language have multiple dialects?"

"Yeah, but everyone learns the common tongue. More than a century ago, Terra experienced great earth shifts and drastic climate changes. They could have been more devastating, but all the Terran governments got together and formed one United Planetary Government with a common language—Terran Common—so we could work together to stabilize our planetary ecosystem."

Soran leans forward a bit in his chair. "Your world sounds...interesting."

"It's beautiful, actually." A wistful smile curves my mouth as my thoughts turn to home. "My mom is a botanist, so she always has a huge garden year-round, you know. Half of it is organized into long, neat rows full of edible plants, while the other half is wild, full of vines and all these vibrant, blooming flowers." A sharp pain stabs at my chest as I picture my mother's face. "She always wanted me to follow in her footsteps."

He cocks his head slightly to the side. "Was she upset that you chose to become a pilot instead?"

A short huff of air escapes me as a smile crests my lips. "How could she be? She always said I was more like my dad. And"—I shrug—"I guess she was right."

He smiles his devastatingly handsome smile again, and I feel an answering blush warm my cheeks.

"Your father is a pilot as well?"

"Yeah, but he only does planetary transports now. No more trips back and forth to Mars Colony." Tears swim at the edge of my vision as I think of him, but I blink them back. "He can't stand to be away from my mom for very long."

Soran tips his head slightly to the side. "They sound very close, your parents."

"They are. What about yours?"

Something akin to sadness flashes briefly behind his eyes and he lowers his gaze. "My parents were very close before my father was killed." His voice is thick with emotion.

My heart clenches at the visible pain in his expression. "How did he die?"

I regret the question as soon as it leaves my lips. Despite the fact that I want to know more about this man who has haunted my dreams for years, it's none of my business and I shouldn't have asked. But now that I have, I cannot take it back.

He continues. "One of the other Great Houses betrayed us. They stormed the palace, intent upon murdering my family as we slept. My father died protecting us."

I reach out and place my hand on his forearm. "I'm so sorry, Soran."

With a slight clench of his jaw, he nods. "Thank you. It was many cycles ago. We were very young when it happened."

Silence settles in the space between us a moment before he lifts his gaze again to mine. "Your species...they have close attachments to their mates and offspring?"

My thoughts turn to my sister's worthless ex-husband. "Most of us do."

He gives me a puzzled look. "What do you mean, 'most'?"

I shrug. "Well, my older sister's husband...I mean, her mate—" I correct myself, using the proper term he'll understand. "He left her and their daughter almost three years ago. He just decided one day that he didn't want a family anymore, I guess."

His eyes widen in shock. "He abandoned his family?"

"Yeah."

"Does this...happen regularly among your people?"

"I don't know how regular it is, but I know it happens. That's why we try to be really selective about our mates. We want someone who is not only compatible, but who is as invested in the relationship as we are, you know?"

His brow furrows deeply. "He did not deserve them. At least he had the basic decency to stay long enough to guard the egg."

I look up at him in confusion. "Egg?"

"Their fledgling," he explains. "Your niece. Before she hatched."

My eyes go wide. "Your people lay eggs?"

He gives me an incredulous look. "Yours do not?"

I blink several times in shock and then shake my head. "No. Terran women...our babies gestate inside us before they are born."

His jaw drops, and all the color drains from his face. After a moment, he snaps it shut and clears his throat, studying me as if *I* were the alien here. Which...I guess, technically, I am.

"Do you have a mate?" he finally asks.

My thoughts drift to Jeff. "Sort of. I mean, we were friends, but it was turning into something more."

He cocks his head to the side.

"It's...complicated. He was on the ship with me."

Closing my eyes, I can still picture their faces asleep in the stasis pods. I was their Commander, and I failed them. I look to Soran, meeting his gaze evenly. "I have to find my crew. They're out there somewhere, and it's my job to find them and bring them home safely."

~

**Soran**

My heart clenches when she mentions her mate. From the devastated look on her face, I can tell that she must care for him very much. Unbidden jealousy rises in my chest, but I push it back down. How can I be jealous? I barely know her, and...she is not mine.

It is decided, then. I will not tell her anything about the fated bond. She has already made her choice, long before she met me, and I will not try to persuade her to change her mind.

# CHAPTER 6

LIANA

After we finish eating, Soran leads me down the hallway to crew quarters. Stopping in front of one of the rooms, he instructs me to place my open palm on the plate to code it to recognize me. When we step inside, my jaw drops at all of the space. A large bunk in one corner, a desk and chair in the other. There's even a sofa and a set of storage lockers along the other wall and a small door across the way.

"I apologize for how small these quarters are," he says. "But this is only a glider. They are designed for stealth, not comfort."

Everything has a sleek, minimalist look to it, but then again, he did say this glider was built for efficiency, so I wasn't really expecting plush furnishings or soft touches here. I arch a brow at him. "If you think this is small, you would be absolutely claustrophobic on a Terran ship."

He darts a quick glance around the space as if he can't believe what I've just said. After a moment, he gives me a teasing grin. "Until we find your home world, I will just have to take your word for it."

I laugh. I like how he says, "until we find your home world," as if he's completely confident that we'll find my planet.

Inhaling deeply of the clean air, I smile as I take it all in. I move to the center of the room and extend my arms. Tipping back my head I close my eyes and spin once in a slow circle, marveling at the fact that I can stretch my entire body and not touch cold metal bars. I've lived in a cage so long, I almost forgot what it felt like to be free--to have a space that's all my own.

When I open my eyes, I look to the small door on the far side of the room. "What's through there?"

He opens it and moves aside for me to enter. "Each cabin has its own cleansing room."

Anxious for a bath, the idea of a shower sounds amazing. But when I step inside, the space is completely bare, and my gaze sweeps the room in confusion. "Where is everything?"

Soran's head jerks back slightly in surprise. "You have never used a cleansing room before?"

"Not like this." I gesture at the empty area.

He presses an opaque crystal near the door. I watch in wonder as a sink and what I can only assume is a toilet come out from hidden panels in the wall.

He frowns. "What are Terran ship cleansing rooms like?"

"We have the basic stuff, but none of it magically comes out of the wall like this."

"Magic?" He smirks and then arches a condescending brow. "Your people must be far more primitive than I thought."

Instantly offended, I snap. "What? We're not primitive. Just because we don't have things that slide out of the wall, doesn't mean —" I stop abruptly at the slow grin that spreads across his face.

He laughs. "I was only teasing you."

I narrow my eyes, and he laughs even louder. "For one so small, you are very fierce. A creature of fire. Like my sister, Caryn."

His words catch me off guard. I'm not sure how I feel about the "fire" comment, but I am very curious about his family. "You have a sister?"

"Yes."

"Where is she?"

"Back home on Mosaura." He smiles. "I believe the two of you will get along well."

His expression falters a bit on the last sentence, and I wonder what's wrong, but he quickly changes the subject, showing me how to activate the shower and everything else in the room.

When I ask him about a change of clothing, he leaves briefly and then returns with a small bundle of surprisingly soft fabric. He gives me an apologetic look. "It is an emergency shirt, meant for one of my people. I wish I could offer you something better, but at least this will cover you. If you need anything, I'll be on the bridge."

I wait until he's out of the room and the door whooshes closed behind him before peeling out of my clothing and making use of the shower.

As the warm water flows over me, the tired muscles of my neck and shoulders begin to unknot. I haven't felt this good in a long time.

When I'm done, I pull the clean shirt over my body. The soft fabric falls just below my knees, and the arms are so long they extend past my hands. I roll the sleeves up to my elbows. My auburn hair slips over my shoulders to fall around my face. Reaching up, I run my fingers through the long, dark strands, releasing a sigh of contentment now that I'm clean and my hair is no longer a tangled and matted mess.

When I sit on the edge of the bed, my exhaustion hits me like a giant wave. This mattress is soft and inviting; a luxury I haven't had in a long time. Laying down, I pull the blankets over my body and curl up on my side, cocooning myself beneath the warm fabric.

Today was a good day with Soran. Reaching up, I touch my mouth. It's been so long since I smiled this much that the muscles of my face are tight, but I welcome the discomfort. As I think of all I've been through, I repeat my vow that I will not let it break me. I'm alive, and I *will* find my crew and my home world. There is always hope, and I choose to hold on to it with both hands.

For the first time in a long time, I know that I'm safe as I allow myself to drift off to sleep.

～

*I'm surrounded by darkness. Long tendrils of fear unfurl and wrap around my spine. Cold fills me as the sickening sharp clicks of Zovian speech echo nearby. A dull thump sounds along the metal floor, followed by the electric hum of a shock stick. My heart stops and then begins hammering in my chest.*

My eyes snap open, and I bolt upright in bed, panting heavily. I look to the viewscreen; the stars blur by, reminding me of where I am. Scrubbing a hand across my face, I draw in a deep breath and focus on clearing the dark memories from my mind.

I swing my legs over the side of the bed. Unable to still my trembling hands, I curl them into fist and press them into my lap to stop their shaking. After a moment, I stand and then walk to the viewscreen.

Wrapping my arms tightly around my form, I fight back tears. Anchoring myself in this moment, I repeat my mantra aloud. "I am a Garza, and I come from a line of strong women. I am the Commander of the *Navis*, and I will never give up. I will find my crew and my planet or die trying."

I'm so tired it should be easy to sleep. But I can't. I don't want to close my eyes and fall back into my nightmares. As crazy as it sounds, I miss sharing such a small space with Tr'lani. It was comforting knowing she was nearby.

On the long flight between Terra and Mars, the crew is awake for at least a week each way before we enter the sleep pods for the longest part of the journey. It's a safety to make sure everything is running smoothly with the ship before we go into stasis and then again before we approach our final destination.

Whenever I couldn't rest during that time, I'd go to the command center. Something about sitting at my station, monitoring the ship's functions was relaxing. I'm a pilot, after all, and the bridge is my second home. When Soran briefly showed it to me earlier, I realized that it's the one place in this entire quadrant that feels even remotely familiar.

Stretching my arms up over my head, I yawn loudly and then start for the door. It's going to be a long night.

# CHAPTER 7

SORAN

Rowan's expression is a mixture of relief and pity when I tell him that Liana already has a mate—a male that was part of her crew.

"Then that settles it," he says firmly. "She cannot be your Ashaya."

Frustration burns through me. "That settles nothing. It doesn't change what I feel in here." I place my fist to my chest, directly over my heart. "Do you not understand?"

Worried eyes meet mine. "What are you going to do?"

"I'm going to help her find her missing crew and her home world."

He shakes his head. "She is probably going to Aerilon. When Tr'lani sent out the message to her family, she mentioned Liana, requesting that they accept her into their clan because she has no home and no protection."

I frown. "That is almost unheard of for an Aerilon clan—especially one of the High Clans—to accept an outsider as one of their own. Do you think they will?"

"Once her clan receives the message, I have no doubt they will accept Liana. She claims Liana kept her alive, that she took many of the beatings from their masters that were meant for her because she knew Tr'lani would not live through them."

My mouth drifts open in shock. Liana is so much smaller than Tr'lani. How did she survive beatings from the Zovians *and* the Anguis? They are known to be especially brutal. As I think of Liana's Terran form, I am ashamed that my first impression of her was that she was fragile. "She is much stronger than I realized," I whisper, more to myself than to him.

Rowan nods in agreement. "Tr'lani owes Liana a life debt and has claimed her as her sister. I believe her family will not hesitate to accept the Terran into their clan."

He opens his mouth to speak again, but the doors to the bridge whoosh open, revealing Liana.

Her worn and tired appearance is concerning. "Are you feeling unwell?"

A pained smile tugs at her lips as she takes a seat at the empty station next to mine. "No, I...I couldn't sleep. On my ship, whenever I had trouble sleeping, I'd come to the bridge. It may look a bit different from what I'm used to, but *this*"—she runs her hands across the smooth glass of the control panel—"feels familiar." She lifts her gaze to me. "Will you show me the controls?"

I dip my head in a subtle nod. "Of course."

I tap her display to activate it, and she frowns as she examines the menu. "I can't read any of these glyphs."

Rowan turns to her. "An unfortunate consequence of your language not being programmed into the translator. It can allow you to speak our language, but it has no form of reference to help your brain translate our writings."

She studies the display and determination sets in her features. "I'm a fast learner. Teach me the symbols."

"You don't need to concern yourself with—" Rowan starts, but I shoot him an irritated glance, stopping him abruptly.

He's very possessive when it comes to the glider. It's his personal ship—customized and built to his exact specifications. It took at least three months of coaxing before he agreed to allow me to pilot her.

And the way he fusses over every little scratch on the outer hull and is constantly polishing the control panels so that they shine like new, you'd think it was his own fledgling instead of a flying chunk of metal.

She turns to him. "I don't know how long it will take me to find my planet, or if I'll *ever* find it. But I need to learn how to survive here. I need to be useful at something. I can't just sit in my quarters all day. I'm a pilot. *This* is what I do." She gestures at the controls. "*This* is what I know. And I have to start somewhere. Even if I never find Terra, I have to find my crew. And the only way I can do that is if I begin by learning how to pilot one of your ships."

Rowan sits back in his chair, crossing his arms over his chest. It's obvious from his expression that he's reluctant to allow her to "learn" how to do anything on his precious glider.

As if she can read his mind, Liana meets his eyes evenly. "Look, I can tell this ship means a lot to you. Pilot to pilot, I promise to be really careful with her." She gives him a small smile. "What do you say?"

Instead of answering, he stares at her with an unconvinced expression and her smile begins to falter.

Annoyed by his ridiculous attachment to his glider, I elbow his ribs, startling him so much he nearly falls out of his chair.

His nostrils flare as he shoots me an angry glare, straightening himself back in his seat. With a heavy sigh, he purses his lips before reluctantly nodding. "Fine. But be careful with her. *This* one"—he points to me—"decided it would be a good idea to go through an asteroid field the very first day he piloted her, to shave a bit of time off our trip." Closing his eyes, he inhales and exhales deeply. "I shudder just recalling all the damage he did to the outer hull."

I wave a dismissive hand at him. "It wasn't that bad. Stop being so dramatic. It was only a few minor scratches."

His eyes go wide. "Minor scratches?" His voice rises in pitch. "An entire outer panel had to be replaced."

Sighing heavily, I shake my head. "It was cosmetic damage. Nothing more."

He gives me an incredulous look. "It was more *than* that. The damage was so severe, I'm surprised the entire ship didn't decompress and shoot us both out into space."

I open my mouth to reply to his ridiculous recounting of events but stop abruptly when I hear a startling sound.

Both of us turn to find Liana doubled over, her body shaking so hard with laughter that tears begin leaking from her eyes. "Oh my gosh," she wheezes. "You two are hilarious!"

Glad to see her laughing so much, I grin at Rowan, who appears less than amused at first, but after a moment, I notice the smile that tugs at his lips.

When she finally stops, she looks at my brother and grins. "So...that's a yes? You'll teach me how to pilot the ship?"

He draws in a deep breath as if dramatically steeling himself to the idea before he nods.

She gives him a beaming smile, and his cheeks flare deep reddish-orange as he returns her expression with a wide grin of his own.

I recognize that awestruck look on his face. It's the same one he gives to any attractive female that looks his way. As if sensing my jealous thoughts, he darts a nervous gaze toward me, and I narrow my eyes at him.

Her small hand grips my forearm, drawing my attention back to her. "So." She smiles brightly, and my cheeks flush with warmth because now *I'm* completely mesmerized by her beautiful smile as well. "Where do we begin?"

We spend half the night taking turns showing her the various menus and teaching her the Mosauran symbols to navigate the controls. Because she is a pilot, it doesn't take long for her to get the hang of it. I'm impressed not only by her piloting skills but also her intelligence. She has already committed more than half the glyphs to memory.

I ask her to give me a return demonstration of how to prep for FTL, and when she mixes up one of the symbols with another that is very similar, she growls low in her throat.

Rowan and I instantly sit up in our seats at attention. My blood heats as my entire body flushes with warmth. Is she trying to initiate the mating ritual?

I share a confused glance with my brother.

Liana's brow furrows softly. "What's wrong?"

"Were you..." I hesitate, unsure how to delicately ask this question. "Were you growling?"

"Yeah," she replies casually.

Rowan's jaw drops.

Noticing his shocked expression, which I'm almost certain is mirrored on my own face, she gives us a puzzled look. "What is it?"

The scales of his cheeks flush a deep red-orange hue as my brother clears his throat. "You might not want to do that around a Mosauran."

Her head jerks back slightly in surprise. "Why?"

"That particular pitch of growling indicates that you are interested in initiating a mating."

Her eyes go wide. "What?"

Wondering if the translator is misinterpreting something, I decide to break it down into a simpler explanation. "It is what a female does when she wishes to initiate the mating ritual and shav-rhokan."

"'Shav what?" she asks, her voice rising in pitch.

I open my mouth to explain the mating battle that ensues after such a declaration, but she puts her hands out to stop me, shaking her head. "Never mind. I don't really need to know all that right now." She meets my eyes evenly. "But trust me when I say that is *not* what I was doing. I repeat. I was *not* trying to initiate any kind of mating ritual. I would *never* do that. All right?"

I nod. From not only her words, but the expression on her face, it is obvious that such an idea is repulsive to her. Whether it is an aversion to my facial scar or my overall general alien appearance compared to her own, I do not know. I only know that the way she is staring at my brother and I right at this moment is enough to deflate any warrior's pride.

~

Despite her obvious fatigue, she refuses to go back to her quarters. I think she avoids returning to them because she does not wish to be alone. With Tr'lani already resting in her own quarters, Rowan and I are the only other people to keep her company.

When she finally closes her eyes and curls up in the chair, I stare down at her small form, uncertain what to do. I do not wish to wake her, for she needs rest. Who knows how long it has been since she was able to sleep like this.

I remember what it was like those first few months after Rowan had rescued me. Haunted by the nightmares of my traumatic memories, it was often disorienting—terrifying even—waking up alone. I do not want that for her. I look to my brother and drop my voice to a low whisper, "I'll stay with her on the bridge until she wakes."

He gives me an understanding nod before leaving for his own quarters. This chair isn't exactly comfortable, but I've slept in worse places. I run a quick check of the controls to ensure the cloaking shield and autopilot are functioning normally.

Gently, I drape a blanket over her in case she gets cold. Careful to retract my claws, I tuck it around her shoulders. Lying partially on her side, her long silken hair falls back from her face, exposing the delicate curved shell of her ear. Dark lashes fan across her cheeks—the many small spots across the bridge of her nose only adding to her charm.

I wonder if her skin is as soft as it looks, and my hands flex at my sides with want to touch her. But I dare not. Not unless she asks. Who knows how many have touched her against her will; I would never do that to her.

Settling back in my chair, I close my eyes and drift off to sleep.

# CHAPTER 8

SORAN

small yawn startles me awake, and when I open my eyes, Liana gives me a sleepy smile.

"Good morning."

"Good morning," I reply in the standard Terran greeting.

This has been our routine for the past week and a half—waking together on the bridge at our stations. She does not use her quarters for anything but bathing and dressing. And ever since she joined our crew, neither do I.

The rest of her time is spent either here on the bridge with Rowan and me, learning more about the ship, or with Tr'lani.

It took three days before the haunted look finally left her face. Now that it has, she smiles at me often, and I treasure each one as if it were as precious as L'omhara.

"Where are Rowan and Tr'lani?" she asks.

Almost as if her question has summoned them, the doors whoosh open, and they enter the bridge.

A wide smile breaks out across her face as she looks to her friend. "There you are. We were just talking about you two."

Tr'lani hums in greeting to my Ashaya before she speaks. "Have you eaten yet?"

Liana shakes her head. "No. Have you?"

Tr'lani's eyes dart to my brother before she answers, and I don't miss the pronounced deep red-orange coloring that creeps across his cheeks. "You two fell asleep here on the bridge again, and I didn't want to wake you. We just finished breakfast. We're going to try sending another message to my family. I still have not heard anything back from the earlier transmission we sent. Maybe this time"—she gives Liana a pained smile—"we'll reach them."

To my great surprise, Rowan places a reassuring hand on Tr'lani's shoulder. "Even if we do not, I will escort you to Aerilon myself. I give you my most solemn vow as a warrior of Mosaura. I will do all that I can to reunite you with your clan."

My eyes widen. He's giving her his most solemn vow? Perhaps I'm not the only one with feelings for one of our passengers.

After speaking more with her friend, Liana looks over her shoulder at me. "Feel like grabbing a bite?"

A smile twists my lips as I think on this odd Terran phrase: "grabbing a bite." It is one of many that she has taught me over the past several days. This is how she asks if I wish to consume a meal with her.

"Of course." I arch a brow, deciding to tease her a bit. "I was thinking that perhaps we could soften the nutrient bar enough for your pitifully tiny fangs to chew, by soaking it in the liquid protein you enjoy so much."

Wrinkling her nose, she makes the cutest disgusted face I have ever seen. I laugh as she narrows her eyes. "If you dare try it, you'll be sorry."

My brows shoot up to my forehead in mock surprise. "You would challenge a Mosauran warrior to combat over a nutrient bar?"

The edges of her lips curl up in a barely suppressed grin. "I would but...you're a nice guy, Soran." She shrugs. "I wouldn't want to hurt you."

A wide smile spreads across my face. "Well then, I will endeavor to please you so as not to incur your wrath."

She laughs, and the sound is so enchanting it fills my heart with warmth.

Knowing how much she enjoys my teasing, I make sure to do it often. I love making her laugh.

She calls over her shoulder as she steps into the hallway. "I'll meet you in the crew mess in thirty minutes."

I remain locked in place, staring at the closed doors with what I'm sure is a lovestruck grin on my face.

Rowan's gaze darts to mine, sadness flashes briefly behind his eyes. We've discussed this many times. He's afraid I'm going to get hurt. Liana already has a mate, and even if she did not, it is forbidden to take a mate outside of our race.

It is hard to be so often in her presence and know she can never be mine. Every day, I learn something new about her—more of who she is. And I have seen how she suffers from nightmares and dark memories, but she does not let it break her. Instead, she spends every day learning whatever she can to help her survive. To forge a new path in this unfamiliar part of the universe.

All these things speak to a strength of heart and will that is equal to that of a Mosauran warrior. She is intelligent, strong, brave, and kind. Even if she were not my Ashaya, I would still desire her as mine, for she is all the things I could ever wish for in a mate.

But she is not mine, and she never will be. While my mind has accepted this, my willful heart still refuses. In the end, I know it will break me when she leaves, because I am too far gone now. The damage is already done; I cannot distance myself from her any more than I could will Mosaura to cease its rotation around Drakonus.

But I do not believe she feels this way for me, and I find that it does not matter. What she needs is a friend. And I want nothing more than to be whatever she needs.

~

## Liana

Sitting at the table, I wait for Soran to hand me my sawdust brick as I've affectionately dubbed the nutrient bar.

"Voila," he says, using one of the Terran words I've taught him as he slides it toward me.

From his excitement, you'd think we were at some amazing and delicious restaurant instead of the crew mess to have a sawdust brick and, in his case, liquid sludge.

Closing his mouth over the straw that sticks up from his protein pack, I wrinkle my nose as he takes a long swig. I still can't believe he can drink that stuff without gagging.

His sharp, ridged brow creases in confusion as he puts his packet down. "What do you normally have for breakfast, Liana?"

"Usually some oatmeal with fruit or some toast with coconut oil slathered on it."

"I...do not know what any of those things are. Your breakfast sounds...interesting," he says thoughtfully.

My mouth begins to water. Who knew I'd be craving something as simple as oatmeal and toast? Soran is watching me closely, studying my expression—the dreamy look I'm sure is on my face right now at the thought of real food.

I tap my communicator and hold up the display to him. "I checked our nav charts. It looks like we'll arrive at Le'ro in a little over twenty-two hours."

Le'ro is a trading planet we'll be stopping at to refuel and pick up some supplies. I'll admit I'm a bit apprehensive about leaving the safety of the ship, but the thought of real food, new clothes, and breathing fresh air is too tempting to pass up. Besides, if this is my new reality now, I need to learn to deal with my fears.

He nods. "I'll need the measuring scans from you and Tr'lani so I may purchase your clothing. I'll get a sampling of various foods for you to try as well since we do not know what may or may not agree with your system. Rowan will remain on the glider with you both in case—"

I put my hand up to silence him, giving him an incredulous look. "What? I'm not staying on the ship. I'm going with you."

His brows shoot up to his forehead. "You are not afraid to leave the glider?"

"Of course, I'm afraid. I'd be stupid not to be. But I can't let my fears rule me. For better or worse, this is my life now. And the sooner I start learning how to survive here, the better."

He gives me a hesitant look. "I...do not think it would be wise for you to leave the ship. This trading post is one of the nicer ones in this sector, but there is still risk."

"There is always going to be risk. Nowhere is completely safe, Soran. Just look at Tr'lani. She wasn't even in the neutral zone. She was on one of the Aerilon system's core planets when she was taken."

From the shocked expression on his face, I'm guessing she hadn't shared with either of them the exact details of how she was captured. "I still do not think—"

I cut him off. "Look, I appreciate what you're trying to do, but you can't protect me from everything."

He huffs his displeasure at my words, but I continue. "This part of the universe is all new to me. The only way I'm going to be able to find my crew and my planet is if I learn how to survive here." I place my hand on his forearm and meet his gaze evenly. "And I would appreciate you teaching me how to do that, Soran."

With a slight clench of his jaw, he nods. He knows I'm right. "Fine. Follow me to the training room. We will continue your sparring lessons and then practice some more with the blaster and dagger."

A slow smile curves my lips. "I'll try to remember to set the blaster to stun for our practice," I tease.

He laughs, but a hint of worry lingers behind his eyes. I almost caught the ship on fire the first time we practiced when I unknowingly had the blaster set on kill instead of stun. To be fair, I had no idea there were different settings for the weapon, so it technically wasn't my fault.

I know Soran doesn't like the idea of me going with him, but at least he recognizes and respects my reasons for wanting to go. I appreciate his attempt to shield me from danger, but I'm strong. I don't know what the future holds, but I know I need to be prepared to face whatever challenges await me.

# CHAPTER 9

SORAN

Liana hugs Tr'lani tightly as we stand at the airlock. "Are you sure you don't want to come with us?"

Tr'lani nods and grasps both of Liana's hands in her own. "It's safer on the glider. I wish you wouldn't go. You should stay here with me and Rowan."

Liana gives her a reassuring smile. "I'll be fine. Besides"—she darts a glance in my direction—"I have a big, strong Mosauran warrior with me. Nobody's going to bother us."

Thrilled by her appraisal I straighten my back, standing a bit taller as I tilt up my chin and puff my chest out with pride at her words.

A smile twists her lips as she looks over at me. "All right, all right." She laughs. "Don't let my words go to your head."

I tilt my chin up even more and arch a teasing brow. "Why would they 'go to my head?' Your words are truth. I *am* a big, strong Mosauran warrior." I flex my arms to show off the muscles built from years of training, and she laughs even louder.

Rowan rolls his eyes—a Terran gesture we've all seemed to pick up over the past several days. "It's too late. You have created a monster," he says, using one of the many Terran idioms Liana taught us as he hands her a blaster and laser knife. He claps me on the shoulder and repeats her words in a mocking tone as he passes me my weapons. "Here you go, 'big, strong Mosauran warrior.'"

I smirk. "Jealousy is not a healthy thing, Rowan. Besides," I touch his bicep. "Your muscles may be much smaller than mine but—"

He punches at my arm. "I'm not jealous of you, you maltak. And everyone knows I'm stronger than you anyway."

I laugh and I'm about to tease him when his expression suddenly turns serious. "Check in with me every hour, so I know you're all right."

Rowan is a good male. Although I am older than him, with the way he constantly worries about me, you'd think that he was the elder brother. "We will," I promise.

As soon as the airlock door opens, we're assaulted by the bright, blinding light of Le'ro's sun. Liana squints her eyes against the glare before they finally adjust. Her mouth drifts open as she takes in the landscape around us.

Since it was her first time landing the glider, she chose a remote spot at the far side of the landing zone, near the edge of the thickly forested area surrounding the city. She is an excellent pilot, but she wanted a "buffer" I believe she called it, in case she had problems with the touch down.

My gaze sweeps over the dozens of other ships in varying shapes and sizes nearby. I suspect many of their owners are mercenaries or mid-level traders by the look of their vessels. With rusted and patch-work-covered hulls, it's a wonder many of these are even space worthy.

But I also know that corsairs can be extremely clever. Several of these vessels may simply be made up to appear dilapidated—concealing weapons and engines that are actually equal to or better than Rowan's glider. This type of deception is often done to lure others into believing they are easy prey, when in fact, *they* are the predators.

I glance back at Rowan, his sharp gaze scanning the ships with slightly narrowed eyes. I'm certain he's thinking the same thing as I, and I'm glad he spared no expense on the glider's defenses. No one can even get near her without the ship's system alerting him.

When I turn back to Liana, I watch in rapt fascination as she spreads her arms wide and tilts her head up, closing her eyes as she revels in the feel of the sun's warmth upon her skin. Drawing in a deep breath, a smile curves her mouth.

Le'ro is known in this sector for its majestic forests and soft pink skies. Only a few trading posts exist on this planet, the rest is still wild and uninhabited land. I walk up beside her. "What do you think?"

Sea-green eyes bright with tears stare up into mine, and her voice is thick with emotion when she speaks. "It's beautiful." Her gaze drifts out to the forest again. Inhaling and exhaling deeply, her saddened expression disappears just as quickly as it surfaced, and she masks her pain behind a warm smile as she turns back to me. "In the entire time we were held, we went from one space station to another, but I've never been to an alien planet before. Let's go exploring, shall we?"

I incline my head.

As we walk through the trading village, I scan the area around us for any potential threats.

Although I'm certain she is capable of defending herself, I have to force my mouth to remain shut even as everything inside me wants to demand that she return to the glider. Not that she would ever listen. Liana is both fierce *and* stubborn—a lethal combination in any female. A small puff of air escapes my lips as I smile to myself. I could no sooner make her do something she didn't want than I could get the planets to change their rotation around Mosaura's sun.

~

**Liana**

As we wind our way through the streets, people watch us with curious expressions. I try to ignore it, but it's very unnerving. I look up at Soran. "Why are they staring at us?"

His eyes don't leave the crowd as he continually scans our

surroundings, on alert for any threat to our safety. The only indication I have that he's heard me is when he answers. "Because of our close proximity during our sparring session earlier, you carry my scent. As a result, many of them probably believe we are a mated pair," he replies matter-of-factly.

Remembering the feel of his strong muscular arms wrapped around me in the Drogev hold, my entire body flushes with warmth as my heart stutters an erratic beat.

When we practiced, he leaned down to whisper in my ear, instructing me to calm my breathing and focus on freeing myself. For a moment, I'd thought he was going to kiss me.

Recalling the memory, I subconsciously reach up to trace my fingers softly over my lips. That moment keeps replaying in my mind. Imagining the taste of his warm mouth, I know I wouldn't have hesitated to return the kiss if he had.

Shaking my head, I push down my errant thoughts. After everything I've been through, I need to be focusing on finding my crew and getting back home. The last thing I need is to get involved with someone. Especially an alien. I can just imagine the look on my parents' faces if I brought Soran home to meet them. Scales, claws, fangs, wings, and all.

He looks over at me, flashing his handsome smile, and warmth spreads across my cheeks. I know without a doubt he'd win them over, and my parents wouldn't care about his alien appearance.

Softly biting my lower lip, I return the smile, and his becomes even brighter.

Yeah, they'd definitely love him.

As we walk along the crowded thoroughfare, I'm struck by just how much this reminds me of a Terran marketplace. The cobblestone streets are lined on either side with rows of small shops, while straight down the center dozens of open and shaded carts overflow with what appears to be various food and craft items on display. With tails, fangs, feathers, horns, scales, and wings, aliens of all shapes, sizes, and colors make up the crowd, many of them openly staring at us as we pass.

One thing strikes me as curious and I turn to Soran. "There are several mated pairs," I use his terminology to get my point across, "that appear to be mixed species. Why do they look so concerned about us, if they think we're together?"

Scanning for any hint of danger, he is ever vigilant, and his eyes continue to search the people around us. "Two reasons," he replies in a rather clinical tone. "First, they probably believe you are V'loryn, and it is well known that our species barely tolerate each other. And second, I am a big, strong Mosauran warrior." A teasing grin spreads across his face as he gives me a smug look. "A very impressive male indeed."

I roll my eyes and laugh heartily. "You're not going to let that one go, are you?"

My heart stops as his silver eyes meet mine and a devastating smile curves his mouth. "Never," he winks. "Because it is truth."

A soft puff of air escapes my lips as I grin and roll my eyes again. "Okay then, big, strong Mosauran warrior, how about we find me some proper clothes?"

He grins, gesturing to a shop two doors down. "That is where we are headed to first."

As soon as we enter the clothing store, a feather-covered alien guy that looks similar to a large green and red version of a peacock moves from behind the counter immediately. He bows low to Soran, spreading his wing-like arms out to display the row of deep crimson feathers that line each one. "Oh, great Mosauran Warrior, how may I help you today?"

Although his tone and expression are pleasant, I notice the tense set of his shoulders and the fearful look in his eye as he stares up at Soran. Tr'lani was right. Everyone fears the Mosaurans.

Soran motions to me. "We are shopping for her today."

The man cocks his strange feathery head to the side, studying me curiously. He waves a small scanner around my body, careful not to touch me. His green eyes are huge, like some kind of over-exaggerated cartoon character, but at least his face looks friendly, and I don't get any creepy vibes from him.

"I have all the latest V'loryn fashions," he tells me proudly as he points to a vid display overhead.

An entire lineup of muted-colored tunics and leggings appear on the screen. Tapping my finger to my lip, I stare at the selection but don't see anything I really like.

Sensing my hesitation, he offers, "We have Aerilon fashions as well."

Soran hands him the scanning chip with Tr'lani's measurements. "We will also need some Aerilon clothing for another female who is traveling with us. A full wardrobe," he adds.

The man's jaw drops a moment before he quickly snaps it shut. "A"—he clears his throat—"*full* wardrobe, you say?"

"Yes," Soran replies. He gestures to me. "And for my companion as well, once she finds something that is to her liking."

His eyes go as big as saucers before he gives us a beaming smile. This must be similar to someone on Terra getting a big commission from a sale.

The display changes to present a selection of brightly colored garments that appear to be made entirely of beautiful, shimmering silk. Like something straight out of a fairy tale and fit for a princess.

I pick out several items for Tr'lani but don't really find anything that calls out to me, except for a bra. Apparently, they're one of the few species that have any need for them. While Aerilon clothing is undoubtedly beautiful, I don't want something for aesthetics. I need clothes that are durable and easy to move in. My gaze drifts to Soran, and I scan him appraisingly. I want the warrior look too. "Is there a selection of Mosauran attire?"

The man's eyes dart to Soran and then back to me. "Yes, I apologize. I did not realize you'd wish to match your mate."

My cheeks heat, and I start to correct him but stop when he spins to go to the back of the store. "I'll just gather the Aerilon items while you peruse the Mosauran selections," he calls out over his shoulder.

I choose my entire wardrobe from the Mosauran clothing, and I love it. The fabric looks just like Soran's—the same kind of dark metallic material. According to Soran, it's incredibly strong and resilient. Once I try it on, I find it's also surprisingly comfortable. These are the softest pants and shirt I've ever owned in my life. My boots make me a few inches taller, and they're really light instead of clunky like I'd expected.

Once I'm fully dressed, it doesn't escape me how Soran's eyes travel discreetly over my form more than once. If he were Terran, I'd definitely think he was checking me out. But, he's Mosauran, so I cannot be sure. Maybe it's merely curiosity that someone so V'loryn-appearing is wearing Mosauran attire.

After Soran pays the clothier, I watch as a drone takes all our packages to fly back to the glider.

Satisfied that I have new clothing, I walk a bit taller as we continue through the streets. It feels good to wear something that doesn't look like an oversized nightgown. As we pass a mirror, I do a quick scan of myself, and a smile tugs at the corner of my lips. I look fierce in this outfit, and I absolutely love it.

Without warning, something large bumps into my back. I spin to find a mass of writhing green tentacles attached to what could almost pass for a Terran male's upper body. His eyes are wide with yellow, horizontal slit pupils that expand as he looks down at me.

My mouth drifts open in shock. A cold, thick, slimy rope wraps around my knee, squeezing tight, and I cry out in alarm when I realize it's a tentacle.

Fear and anger rush through me as I draw my laser knife and slice at another one snaking up my thigh.

The alien shrieks and jerks away as his now-severed appendage slaps to the pavement with a sickening squelch.

Soran spins to face me, his eyes quickly scanning the scene. His reaction is almost instantaneous as a primal roar rips from his throat, and he charges, slamming the male back against the wall.

"Please, Mosauran Warrior, I did not realize she was yours. I would never have touched her if—"

His words are cut off as Soran's large hand tightens around his throat. With a terrified expression on his face, he tries to speak, but only a wet gurgle escapes his open mouth. Writhing in panic, his tentacles frantically flex and extend but I notice he doesn't dare wrap them around Soran's body.

Soran's scales flush a darker gray hue, and feral rage burns in his eyes as he glares at him, baring his sharp and deadly fangs. "Even if she were not mine, it does not give you the right to touch her without her consent."

A sudden sting stabs my right shoulder, and I cry out in surprise. "Ow!" I look to the site and find a small dart. Shocked, I immediately pull it out, and my jaw drops when I notice the long, sharp needle dripping with blood.

Soran spins to face me. "What happened? Are you—" The words die in his throat as his gaze lands on the dart in my open palm. His eyes go wide in alarm. In one fluid motion, he throws the alien off to the side, grips my forearm, and pulls me behind him, shielding me with his fully extended wings.

Warmth spreads through my body, and the world begins to spin. My mind floats in a dream-like haze of pure bliss.

A low growl rumbles from somewhere nearby, and it should be terrifying, but I find I don't really care. My vision blurs as darkness creeps in around the edges. I want to reach out and touch Soran's wings, but I can't feel my limbs.

The air swirls around me, kicking up dust and debris. A loud and primal roar fills the air as I fall to the ground. I blink again. A giant silver-gray dragon stares down at me, its beautiful iridescent scales glinting in the sunlight.

"Wow, a real-life dragon," I manage to whisper before I close my eyes and fall away into darkness.

# CHAPTER 10

LIANA

I'm surrounded by warmth, and a strong and steady rhythm beats beneath my ear. It's so soothing and comfortable, I don't ever want to wake. A small sigh of contentment escapes me as I stretch my arms and legs. I open my eyes to pitch-black nothingness, and my blood runs cold.

I jerk up but stop abruptly as strong arms tighten around my form. A terror-filled cry rips from my throat as I thrash against my captor.

"Liana. It's me. Soran."

Instantly, I still.

His warm hand cups my chin, and he brushes his thumb softly across my cheek.

Relief washes through me, and I blink several times, trying to make out his shape in the darkness.

"Can you see anything?"

"No," I barely manage to speak through my fear. I hate the dark. "Why—why can't I see? Where are we? What happened?"

"An Anguis slaver shot you with a breaking dart."

"A breaking dart?"

"It instantly immobilizes its target. Slavers use it to capture and 'break' their new slaves. It is mostly used on gladiators. It takes away your vision, making it difficult to fight against the masters."

Panic coils tight in my chest as I realize what he's saying. A slave that cannot see is almost completely helpless, making it easier for the masters to break them. "Will I"—my voice catches—"get my vision back?"

His warm hand gently cups the side of my face, and he hesitates a beat before he responds. "You should. It is not meant to be permanent."

Although his reply is no doubt meant to be reassuring, I notice the words he doesn't say: I'm Terran, and he doesn't know how my body will respond to this toxin. It shouldn't be permanent, but it could be.

Realizing I cannot do anything but wait, I clench my jaw and push down my fear, swallowing against the lump in my throat. A cool breeze brushes against my skin, carrying the scent of forest and earth on the wind. Instinctively, I press myself closer against Soran's warm body.

"We're not on the ship, are we."

He runs his hand soothingly across my back. "No. But we are safe. I flew us out into the forest. I've contacted my brother. He will come for us as soon as it is dark. The Krulta was working with the Anguis who shot the dart." His voice is a low rumble of displeasure. "He was a distraction to pull my attention away from you so they could hit you with the dart. They are both dead now, but I doubt they were here alone. And if we are being watched, it is better to wait for nightfall for Rowan to retrieve us."

Breathing in and out through pursed lips, I focus on trying to remain calm. *As soon as its dark.* That means it's still light outside, and I'm completely blind. Fear and worry twist deep in my gut, but I force myself to ignore it. Panicking won't help anything, and neither will tears.

*We are safe.* As I repeat these words in my mind, my body begins to believe it. The tense muscles of my neck and shoulders slowly unknot as I relax in Soran's arms. The strange, dream-like image of a silver-gray dragon floats through my mind, and Soran's statement comes into sharp focus. I sit up, turning my head as if to stare at him even though I still cannot see. My brow furrows in confusion. "What do you mean, you flew us into the forest?"

"I had to shift into my draken form to kill the Anguis and his partner and then fly us away from danger."

My jaw drops as I picture the giant winged dragon. I thought it was just a drug-induced dream. "That was you?" I ask, unable to hide the shock in my voice that I'm pretty sure is also visible in my expression. "You're a dragon?"

"Draken," he corrects, emphasizing the hard *K* sound. "My battle form."

My jaw drops even lower. "You can change forms?" My voice rises in pitch on the last word.

"Of course. Many species can," he says as if it's the most obvious thing in the world.

"So, why haven't you ever shifted before now?"

"There is no need to shift on the glider. And my draken form is much larger than my current one. Too large for me to risk shifting on most space stations." His voice carries an air of regret as he continues. "I'm certain I destroyed all the vendor stands around us when I shifted, but at least no one was harmed besides our enemies."

Gently, he tightens his grip around my form as he leans back a bit, pulling me with him. I'm sitting on his lap with my legs across his thighs, and the fact that he's relaxed reassures me that his words are true. We are safe. For now. And that's enough for me to allow myself to melt into his embrace.

His strong arms are wrapped around me, and it feels like the most natural thing in the world. I rest my cheek against his chest and breathe in his masculine scent—a strange mixture of earth and spice, something close to ginger. It's only now that I realize his top is bare. I pull back slightly. "What happened to your tunic?"

"When I shifted into battle form it shredded all my clothing."

"Oh," I reply, mildly shocked that he's not wearing any clothes. But, it's not like I can see anything. Besides, it doesn't matter. It's Soran, and I trust him. With a small nod, I allow myself to relax back against his chest. "Thank you for saving me, Soran."

"You should not thank me." His voice is thick with regret. "It is my fault you were almost taken. I...I was distracted. I should have been more vigilant."

I gently place my hand to his chest. His heart beats steadily beneath my open palm in a reassuring rhythm. "You shouldn't blame yourself. You saved me. That's all that matters."

He gently covers my hand with his. "Rest if you are tired. I will keep watch."

Knowing that he can shift into draken form in an instant, I have complete faith in his ability to defend us from danger. I shake my head, thinking of how wrong it all could have gone. "Thank god they didn't hit you with the dart as well," I add.

"It would have taken more than one to knock me down and affect my vision."

"How do you know that?"

"The masters used breaking darts on me several times...in the beginning. The first was so they could implant the chip to prevent me from shifting into my draken form to escape them."

My mouth drifts open slightly before I quickly snap it shut. "You were a slave?"

"Yes. I was a gladiator in the arena for three cycles before Rowan rescued me."

A heavy silence settles around his words, and I trace my hand up his arm to gently cup his face. I heard horror stories from many of the other slaves about the sheer brutality of the gladiator rings. I run the pad of my thumb lightly across the sharp ridge of his left cheek. "You should have told me, Soran."

He shakes his head. "It... What happens to slaves is unspeakable. And I did not want to burden you with my painful memories because I know that you carry your own."

His words strike a chord in my heart, and I squeeze my eyes shut against the tears that would come if I let them. A reply forms in my mind but is quickly discarded before it reaches my lips. How inadequate is speech in describing my pain? Raw emotion like this is felt deep in the soul, understood at the most primal core of one's being in a way that the highly evolved part of the brain can barely manage to comprehend.

I understand his pain, and now I know that he understands mine. He tightens his arms a bit more around me as he rests his chin lightly atop my head.

"How did you get taken?" I ask softly.

He's silent for so long, I wonder if he will answer. When he finally does, his voice is thick with emotion. "The night my father died saving us, I stayed behind with him to fight our attackers. I loved my father and I knew he did not stand a chance alone. We held the door as long as we could while my mother, Caryn, and Rowan escaped on the transport. When our enemies finally forced their way in, we fought until we could fight no more. There were too many of them. They executed my father in front of me." Deep sadness fills his tone. "Before he died, he begged them to spare my life. They sold me to slavers but lied to my family, telling them I'd been killed along with my father."

"How did Rowan find you?"

With my hands on either side of his face, I can feel the hint of a smile that curves his lips beneath my fingers. "My brother is the only one who never believed I was dead. He insisted that he would have felt it if it were true. After my mother regained her throne, they captured one of the original assassins who had been sent to kill our family. Rowan tortured him until he gave up the truth."

Warm tears slip down my cheeks as I imagine all he went through. To see his father murdered before his eyes... "I'm so sorry."

He wraps his arms a bit tighter around me. "Thank you," he whispers softly.

We sit together in shared silence. My upper body moves with each gentle rise and fall of his chest. This closeness between us is neither awkward nor uncomfortable. I trace my hand down to his shoulder and arm, my fingers gliding over the smooth, silken texture of his scales.

I've often wondered how they would feel. Perhaps my lack of vision is the reason I'm not nervous to explore, because I cannot see his expression as I study him, learning him through touch. "Your scales are much softer than I thought they'd be," I whisper, more to myself than to him.

He surprises me by giving my hand a gentle squeeze before lightly brushing the tips of his fingers across my cheek. "You are soft as well."

His heart beats beneath my ear as my thumb traces a lazy circle on his forearm. A small smile tugs at my lips. "Dragons are myths on my world, you know. When I was a child, my mom used to read me a story about a princess and her dragon."

"Dragon." He repeats the word, drawing out the G. "That is the Terran word for my draken form?"

"Yes."

"Strange that it is so similar to the word used by my people," he says, and I notice the slight hesitance in his voice. "Tell me more about these myths."

I shrug. "Well, dragons were these ancient—" I hesitate a moment, not wanting to say the word, but finally realizing that I don't want to hold anything back from him either. "Monsters."

He stills.

I continue. "In one of the stories I remember from my childhood, the dragon wanted the princess, but her parents, the king and queen, hid her away from him, fearing for her safety. So, he burned the castle and the entire village to the ground before one of the knights—a warrior"—I make sure to use a term he'll understand—"finally slayed him."

He's quiet for so long, I start to worry that I may have offended him. I decide to tell him a different variation of the fairy tale. "My favorite version of the legend, however, was the one my mom used to tell me often."

"And what was that?" he asks.

"In that story, the dragon was in love with the princess and she with him. He rescued her from the evil knight that wanted to force her into bonding. And they lived happily ever after high up in the mountains in the dragon's cave."

His muscles tense beneath me.

Panic skitters up my spine. "What's wrong?"

"The ship is almost here."

Holding my breath, I strain to listen for any sounds but hear nothing. "I don't hear—" I start to say, but stop abruptly as a faint, rumbling noise fills the air.

It grows louder, moving closer to our position. Even though I cannot see, I turn my head in the direction of the sound while holding tightly to Soran. "Is that the glider?"

"Yes."

The wind whips up around us, kicking up dust and debris. Soran twists, shielding me with his larger form.

A low thud sounds, and the ground trembles slightly beneath us as the glider touches down on the forest floor.

Soran carefully lifts me back into his arms as if I weigh nothing, cradling me close to his chest. I wrap my arms around his neck, blinking my eyes as if that will somehow magically clear my vision.

It doesn't, of course, so I use my other senses to tell me what's happening around us.

His footsteps echo loudly up the ramp. The sharp click and subtle hiss of the airlock opening is quickly followed by Tr'lani's cry. "Thank the Creator you're all right! Can you see anything?"

I squeeze my eyes shut, saying a silent prayer in my mind, but when I open them again, there's still nothing but darkness. I shake my head. "The toxin hasn't worn off yet."

Rowan pats my shoulder, and I only know it's him because he says, "Do not worry, Liana. You are safe, and your vision will return soon."

"Yes," Tr'lani adds. A low electric hum buzzes lightly around my head, and I realize she must be scanning me as we speak. "It shouldn't be more than a few hours now."

Hope fills me. "You're sure?"

The scanner chimes loudly to indicate it's done. "Yes," she replies, and I smile at the complete confidence in her voice.

"You're certain you weren't tracked here?" Soran asks, a slight edge to his tone. "Why didn't you wait until dark?"

"We need to get off this rock as soon as possible," Rowan replies. "Tr'lani and I scanned the channels while we waited on the ship. An A'kai cruiser is on its way here to refuel, and I don't want to risk being here when they arrive."

Once we're back in space, I don a headset and continue to scan and flip through the channels, listening for any sign of the A'kai. I don't want to risk being caught unaware. After a few hours, Soran's voice cuts through the static noise in my ear. "We're far enough away from Le'ro. If they were tracking us, we'd know by now."

Despite his reassurance, I'm reluctant to quit, worried I may have missed something. "I'm just going to cycle through the channels once more to be sure."

I can't pilot or check our nav course because I'm still blind. Since listening to the channels for any sign of our enemy is the *only* thing I can do at the moment, I'm going to make sure I'm thorough, leaving nothing to chance.

By the time I'm finished, the static hum in my ears has gone from annoying to being one of the most pleasant sounds I can imagine because it means we're safe.

Tr'lani helps me to my quarters and waits outside the cleansing room while I shower. When I'm done, she brings me a set of nightclothes that came with my new wardrobe. The shirt and pants are soft as silk against my skin.

She sits beside me on the sofa, and a loud yawn escapes me as I lean against her. "Why am I so tired?"

"It's the effect of the dart wearing off."

My eyelids are heavy, and I allow my head to fall back against the sofa.

Tr'lani moves away from my side and gently guides me to lay down on the cushions. A whisper of fabric glides over my body as she covers me with a blanket. When I turn onto my side, her voice is soft in my ear. "You should rest, Liana. The toxin will metabolize faster that way. And when you wake, you should have your vision again."

Even though I don't like the idea of being alone, in the dark, I'm too tired to reply. I close my eyes and fall away into sleep.

# CHAPTER 11

LIANA

L ying on the soft blanket of grass, I stare up at the stars.

"Can I go with you next time, Aunt Liana?" a small voice asks, and I smile as I turn to find my niece Elizabeth beside me.

Reaching across, I take her small hand in mine, giving it a gentle squeeze. "Maybe when you're older, my angel."

Thunder rumbles loudly overhead. A streak of lightning flashes as dark clouds twist and roll across the sky, blocking the light from the stars.

"We need to find shelter."

I sit up and blink in surprise as the image falls away. "Elizabeth?" I call out, but she isn't here, and no one answers.

Jumping to my feet, I turn and inhale sharply when I see Talel stalking toward me.

Obsidian eyes lock onto mine with a predatory gaze as long, sharp fangs extend from his mouth.

Knowing his inhuman speed makes him far too fast for me to even think I'd have a chance if I ran away now, I stand my ground. My hands tremble at my sides as I curl them into fists, bracing for his attack. Clenching my jaw, I meet his gaze evenly. I will not be killed without a fight.

*With an explosion of movement, he lunges forward. I cry out as my body instinctively reacts in defense. Strong arms wrap around me, and I thrash and struggle against his hold. "No!"*

"Liana, wake up!"

My eyes snap open to pitch-black nothingness.

"Liana, you're safe." Soran's voice cuts through the darkness. "It was a nightmare. You're safe."

Panting heavily, I place a hand over my chest as if to still my rapidly beating heart. "Lights on," I call out, but nothing happens. "Lights—"

He touches my arm. "They are already on."

Inhaling sharply, I bring my hands to my face. My fingers trace over my eyelids as they flutter open and closed. "I still can't see." My voice quavers as I struggle to contain my panic. "Why can't I see?"

His warm hands cover mine, pulling them gently from my face. "You were only asleep for half an hour. Your sight will come back," he says softly. "Just give it some time."

Shakily, I nod. I've never felt so vulnerable before. "How long have you been here?"

"I came as soon as Tr'lani left. I wanted to be here when you woke up, in case you needed something or if your vision was not yet returned."

Carefully, I reach out toward the sound of his voice. His hand finds mine a moment later, and I move closer to him on the sofa.

His body stills as I lift his arm and wrap it around my shoulder before I nestle into his side. I drop my head to his solid chest as an unbidden tear escapes my lashes and rolls gently down my cheek. Emotions lodge in my throat, and I'm unable to speak.

We sit together in shared silence and it is neither uncomfortable nor strange. Soran makes me feel safe. I relax, allowing myself to melt against him.

After a moment, he shifts so that my head is tucked beneath his chin. His warm breath blows softly through my hair with each exhalation.

When he finally speaks, his voice is a low and pleasant rumble above me. "For several months, after Rowan rescued me, I would have nightmares of my captivity almost every time I closed my eyes. I would avoid my sleeping chamber because I was afraid to fall asleep and experience my trauma all over again."

I tip my head back to face him. "What did you do?"

He continues. "In the palace common rooms, it is easy to hear activity throughout the rest of the household. If I slept there, when I woke, the familiar sounds would remind me where I was. I would often find Rowan sleeping in a chair beside me. After a while, I realized he did this so that I might wake up to a friendly face and know that I was safe."

Swallowing against the lump in my throat, I think on all the times I've awakened to find him either asleep in his chair or working at his station, monitoring the glider's controls. Gently, I trail my hand down his arm and entwine our fingers in the Aerilon gesture of gratitude. "You do this for me every time I fall asleep on the bridge, don't you?"

He doesn't speak, but he doesn't have to. His silence answers for him--confirming what I already know to be true. He understands my pain because he went through this too. I'm not weak and never have been. My first instinct would usually be to pull away because I'm strong; I've never needed anyone. But I trust Soran. Something about him makes me want to stay in his arms.

Maybe it's because he's one of the only people I know in this godforsaken part of the universe, or perhaps it's because he's kind. Or maybe it's because for once in my life, I don't feel like being strong right now.

I feel like being held.

# CHAPTER 12

SORAN

It's been three days since Liana regained her vision. We sit together on the bridge, and I watch in awe as her hands fly deftly across the control panel. She maneuvers the ship through a small asteroid belt as if she's been piloting a Mosauran glider her entire life.

Sensing my gaze upon her, she turns to me, and her lips curve into a stunning smile. "Can you show me the shortcut to pull up the nav system again?"

With a quick nod, I move from my seat to lean over her shoulder. She is so close that the heat radiates from her body to mine, and I can tell by the flush of her cheeks that she finds our close proximity appealing.

I raise my hand. "Will you allow me?" Although I do not know the full extent of the abuse she went through during her time as a slave, I can only guess how horrible it was.

She allows me to touch her now, ever since the day she lost her sight, but I always ask because I never want to presume. Her trust is a gift that I will never take for granted.

I take great care to announce my presence and avoid any sudden movements around her. Although she would never outwardly show her fear, sometimes I can smell the acrid scent of it when she's surprised.

Tr'lani is even more skittish than her. She was a slave for roughly two cycles before they met, and I shudder to think of the abuse she must have endured being held for so long.

"Yes." She nods.

Cautiously and ever so gently, I take her hand and guide it across the control panel until we reach the nav system shortcut menu. Pulling it up, I show her the correct motion to move through the floating display options until we find the ones we need.

My nostrils flare as I discreetly inhale her delicious scent deep into my lungs. Detecting the faint hint of arousal, I relish in the knowledge that my Ashaya likes the contact of our hands. Fierce possessiveness, unlike anything I've ever known, rushes through me and I long to gather her in my arms. Instead, I force myself to step back and give her space.

She mumbles something, and I smile when I hear her pronunciation of words in my language. Although she has a translator, she often turns it off so that she may use the language modules to study my native tongue. I do the same as I try to learn Terran, encouraging her to teach me. She has an exceptional ear for linguistics, and I wonder if this is a skill her species is known for or if it is something unique only to her. She does not wish to rely on her translator forever, she says, because technology can always fail. She is wise, my Ashaya.

"So, where did you find me?" she asks, gesturing at the nav display.

Moving my hand over the screen, I point to the upper left corner. "There. That is Vylax station."

Inhaling and exhaling deeply, she maximizes the image and stares at it for a moment, nervously chewing on her bottom lip in the way that she does when she's trying to puzzle something out. And I'm mesmerized, as I always am when she does this. It is a habit she claims to have picked up from her mother.

She turns to me. "Where is V'lora from there?"

I point to the star that is V'luna and the second planet orbiting it. "There."

"And you think Terra might be close to V'lora?"

I nod. "You look so similar to them. There may be some common evolutionary thread that exists between your people and theirs."

"Do you have any pictures of V'loryns?"

Running my hands over the console, I bring up an image of a V'loryn male from the ship's database.

"Wow," she whispers. "I know you said they're distantly related, but the A'kai look more like demons, and these guys look just like elves."

"Elves?" I ask, pulling her gaze back to mine.

"They, uh, on my planet, they're these attractive, mythical beings with pointy ears."

A sharp stab of jealousy spears through me. It doesn't escape me that she included the word "attractive" to describe the elves that she says the V'loryns resemble so closely. I flex my fingers and crack my knuckles before cutting the picture off.

"Hey!" she cries out. "I was still looking at that."

Forcing my expression to remain neutral, I lie. "We have a limited amount of fuel and taxing the computer so you can look at images all day is a waste of resources."

She narrows her eyes. "Are you—" She cocks her head slightly to the side as she studies me, and a slow smile curves her mouth. "Are you jealous? Of a picture?"

I tilt my chin up to feign indifference. "Why would I be jealous?" I flick a small crumb off my console. "The V'loryns are a dishonorable people who hide their true intentions behind their stoic masks."

Her head jerks back in surprise. "What?"

I cross my arms in front of my chest and lean back in my chair, angling my head back slightly to expose my jaw in the way she has told me looks very distinguished. I'm not sure what she means by that, but the way she said it made it sound like a good thing, and I want her to look at me with the same awestruck wonder she had when she looked at the V'loryn male. I quirk a teasing brow. "To use the Terran vernacular that you are so fond of, they suck."

She bursts into laughter, doubling over and clutching at her sides.

~

**Liana**

It takes me a moment to catch my breath, and I reach up to brush away tears of laughter. Shaking my head, I grin and tease him. "You *are* jealous, aren't you?"

He gives me an imperious look, staring down his very regal nose at me. "Of course not. Everyone knows Mosauran males are much more attractive than V'loryns."

My jaw drops at his arrogant statement, but I quickly snap it shut. A wide smile spreads across my face as a witty remark sits just on the tip of my tongue, but I pause as my gaze rakes over his form.

With his chiseled jawline, beautiful reflective silver eyes, shimmering silver-gray scales, and those massive muscular biceps crossed in front of his broad chest, he's right. He definitely has no reason to be jealous of the V'loryn male. Even the facial scar that he's so self-conscious of suggests a slight hint of danger that only adds to his appeal.

His remark about the V'loryns bothers me though. "So, what would your people think of me if they dislike the V'loryns so much? I mean, you said I look a lot like them and—"

He cuts me off abruptly. "You are more like a Mosauran."

I've seen images of Mosauran females, and I know for a fact that I look nothing like them. "How's that?"

Reflective eyes stare deep into mine. "You have the heart and will of a warrior."

I look away from him. "Don't say that, Soran. I'm not a warrior."

"Yes, you are," he states firmly.

I meet his gaze evenly. "No, I'm not." I hate what I've become— someone who can't even sleep in their own quarters for fear that they'll have another nightmare. Angry at myself, I bite my bottom lip to keep it from quivering pathetically as I struggle to contain my emotions. "True warriors are brave. They don't fear monsters that can no longer hurt them."

He leans forward, his brow creased in a deep frown. "Why do you doubt the strength in your heart? I knew you were a warrior the first moment I saw you, when you fought the Anguis and the A'kai to protect Tr'lani."

The memory of Talel's invasion of my mind sends an involuntary tremor through me. I curl my hands into fists, pressing them into my lap to still their shaking.

Soran's voice rips me from my thoughts. "Liana? Are you all right?" His eyes are full of concern.

"I'm fine." After all the time spent pushing down my emotions when I was a slave, the practiced lie leaves my lips easily. "I don't want to talk about it anymore."

He opens his mouth as if to speak but then closes it again and gives me a reluctant nod.

Neither of us speak. The mood between us is strained now, and it's all my fault. After a moment, I stand and excuse myself from the bridge.

I keep it together long enough to reach my room. Once I step inside, I lean back against the door and slide down to the floor, wrapping my arms around my knees as my breath comes in quick, shallow pants. I squeeze my eyes shut against the dark and painful memories, holding in my tears. My chest tightens, and I feel like I can't breathe. Clenching my jaw, I slam my fist against the cold, metal floor, raging against the maelstrom of emotions swirling within.

Despite my best efforts to blink them back, unbidden tears escape, but I quickly brush them away. I can't break down now. I have to be strong. If I'm not strong, I'll never make it back to my family.

My eyes snap up to the viewscreen and the streaks of white light that fly past it. My crew are out there somewhere, and I have to find them. They're counting on me.

The door chimes loudly as someone requests entry. I drop my head in my hands and take a deep breath. "Enter," I call out.

The soft whisper of metal as the door slides open is quickly followed by Soran's voice. "Are you all right?"

Locking down my emotions, I give him a brief nod but refuse to meet his eyes. I don't want him to see me like this.

He stands there a moment before carefully lowering himself to the floor beside me. Close enough that I can feel the heat radiating from his body, but he doesn't touch me. Instead, we just sit quietly together.

A dull ache settles deep in the center of my chest as I think of my family, and devastation washes through me anew. Stifling a sob, I quickly brush away the tears that fall as I draw in a shaking breath.

His voice is soft when he finally speaks. "I am sorry if I upset you, Liana. It was not my intention to do so."

I nod and then turn my gaze back to the viewscreen. "I know, Soran." As I watch the stars blur past the window, an image of my father fills my mind. A wistful smile ghosts my lips at his memory. "My dad taught us to love the stars. On cool, clear nights, he'd spread this huge blanket out over the grass for us to lay on, and we'd stare up at the night sky while he told us all about the constellations."

Even without turning to face him, I can feel Soran's eyes on me as he waits patiently for me to continue.

"On Terra, our ancestors used to navigate by the stars, you know. My dad told us that if you learn the stars, you will never be lost." I turn my attention back to the viewscreen, staring out at the distant and foreign points of light against the black void of space as unbidden tears slip down my cheeks.

Soran gently puts his hand on my forearm. "Liana?"

Emotions lodge in my throat, but I somehow force the words past my lips. "But I don't know these stars, Soran. They're not mine." I look down at my hands. How do I describe the despair that threatens to overwhelm me every time I think on all that I've lost?

I lift my gaze to find sadness reflected in his silver eyes as he stares down at me. "Sometimes I feel like I'm broken. Like I'll never be whole again. And I'm trying so hard to find my way, but I still feel so lost." The admission leaves my mouth before I even realize I've said it aloud.

Soran says nothing. A pained expression mars his handsome face. What *can* he say? He was a slave, too, and I know he understands my pain. He lifts his hand and holds his upturned palm out to me.

I stare at it a moment before placing my hand in his and entwining our fingers.

He gives me a solemn look. "Not all warriors come back from a battle intact. Just because their scars are not visible does not mean they are not there." He pauses. "When my people fight, we do so in teams so that when one becomes injured, his fellow warriors are there to carry him."

I'm silent as I wait for him to continue.

"In battle, your team is only as strong as the weakest warrior among you. We vow to one another that if one of us falls injured, we will carry them to victory or to death. We will not leave them behind."

His gaze drifts down to our joined hands before he lifts his silver eyes back up to meet mine. "I will carry you, Liana of House Garza, to victory or to death. I will not leave you behind. We are bound to one another, and if you are broken, so am I."

He continues. "I understand what it is to feel broken. You are lost from your past and the only life that you have known. The things you have suffered—the nightmares you relive in your memories—they will never completely go away. But you will learn how to carry them. There will be some days that are easier than others, but many will still be hard. And every day, you choose the light and resist the darkness that threatens to consume you, you become much stronger. I know you are lost, but you have also been found. You are not alone in your sadness, and I promise to do everything I can to help you to heal. I give you my most solemn vow as a warrior of Mosaura."

His eyes stare deep into mine with an intense emotion I cannot discern—a strange mixture of pain and devotion. Although he comes from a race of warriors, he understands my trauma, and he doesn't find me weak because of it. His words touch something deep inside me and I know that I'm falling for this man—this alien dragon warrior—despite my attempts to shield my heart from him, knowing that eventually, we will be parted.

Reaching up, I cup his face. Something about the way he watches me draws me closer. My eyes drift down to his perfect, full lips, and I wonder what it would be like to kiss him. As if sensing my thoughts, he leans in. The warmth of his breath fans across my face—the scent of spice and ginger is a heady mix, and I'm already imagining the taste of his mouth as we drift closer.

Tr'lani's voice comes over the speaker, startling us both, and I pull away quickly.

"Liana, come to the bridge. Quickly," she says. "I have the most wonderful news."

Hot embarrassment burns through me, and I'm unable to meet Soran's eyes as I reply. "I'll be right there."

As soon as we enter the bridge, a wide smile lights Tr'lani's face, and she embraces me warmly. "We've had a message from my brother. He's going to contact me once they're in range so he can come for us."

Us. She said the word "us." I'm happy for her. I really am. And I love knowing that she wants me to go with her. In fact, she expects it. But when I think of saying goodbye to Soran, a deep ache settles in my chest like a heavy stone.

Strange how I've grown so close to him in such a short amount of time. I understand that shared trauma can bond two people very quickly, but it's more than just that. He's easy to talk to. And even on my hardest days, he somehow finds a way to make me smile. He understands me in a way that no one else ever has.

When Tr'lani pulls back, my gaze drifts to his. His lips curl up in a faint smile, but I notice the sadness that flashes briefly behind his eyes. Maybe he's dreading being parted from me as much as I dread the idea of being parted from him.

# CHAPTER 13

LIANA

Time is a vague concept in space without the rising of the sun at the start of a new day. So, when a gentle knock on my door startles me awake, I'm mildly disoriented and still half-asleep when I leave the bed to answer.

When Soran greets me with his beaming smile and asks if I want to join him for breakfast, I realize it must be the equivalent of morning here on the ship, and I readily agree.

Although this is our usual routine, I can feel his eyes on me as we eat. It's almost like he's nervous about something, but I don't know what. He's never this anxious.

Perhaps it's that we've been confined to the glider for so long. Maybe it's because there's four of us here, and it feels crowded to him after it had only been just he and his brother before Tr'lani and I came along.

"Liana?"

His soft voice breaks me from my thoughts. "Yes?"

"I have something I would like to show you."

There's a gleam in his eyes that I've never seen before. It's that edge, that anticipation of...something.

"Lead the way."

I follow him down the hallway, and he stops in front of a door. I've been here before and know that this leads to a vacant room. "Where are we going?"

He motions for me to enter. "You will see."

When we walk in, I notice the entire space is empty except for a single clear glass globe on a pedestal directly in the center.

Curious, I study it a moment. "What is this?"

He smiles before reaching back for a folded blanket on a table I hadn't noticed off to the side.

Carefully unfolding it, he grabs two corners of the quilt and allows the rest of it to fall open, gently lifting it so that the fabric billows up for a moment before settling on the floor next to the pedestal holding the globe.

His reflective silver eyes flick up to meet mine. "If you would please lay down," he says, motioning to the blanket.

My heart begins hammering as I sit, and he settles down beside me.

As soon as I lay back, the room goes black. Panic grips me as dark memories begin to surface from the hidden recesses in my mind. I close my eyes, breathing through pursed lips as I remind myself that I'm not still in a cage.

Soran's warm hand covers mine, and I startle.

He immediately retracts his hand. "Liana, it's all right," he whispers. "Open your eyes."

Drawing in a shaking breath, I open my eyes to a field of bright stars overhead.

My jaw drops as I stare in awe at the starry night sky. I raise my hand as if to touch one of the brilliant dots of light and smile as it begins to glow even brighter. "What is this?"

"It is a projection of the night sky as it can be seen from Mosaura," he replies. "My people used to be explorers—ancient cartographers. They were fascinated by the stars and mapped every system they could find, storing all the information in the Ancient Archives on my home world. This one"—he points to a star just above us—"is the tip of Kilena's sword. It is one of the stars my ancestors relied on for navigation." The constellation begins to grow brighter at his touch.

"This"—he points to a star just below it—"is the edge of Tormin's shield. The constellation glows brightly. Kilena was the First Empress of our people, and Tormin was her bonded one. When they died, the Creator gave them a place in the heavens, where they will always be able to look over our people and guide them. When you align these two stars together, you know that your navigational bearings are true."

As Soran continues pointing out the various constellations, tears gather in the corners of my eyes as I realize what he is doing. He's teaching me about the stars that surround Mosaura so I won't feel so lost.

*If you learn the stars, you'll never be lost.* My father's words echo in my mind, and I draw in a shaking breath.

"Liana, have I upset you?"

His face turns toward me, and even in the darkness I can see the concern that flashes behind his eyes.

I reach across and take his hand in mine. Emotions lodge in my throat, but I somehow manage to speak through them and whisper softly. "Thank you."

A warm smile crests his lips before he turns his attention back to the stars and begins pointing out another constellation.

As I listen to his deep, velvet voice, I become lost in his words. I'm falling in love with this man—this dragon warrior from my dreams. Now that I've found him, I don't want to leave and go to Aerilon. If I do, I may never see him again, and that thought is almost unbearable.

He turns back to me and flashes another one of his devastating smiles. "I have a projection of the stars surrounding Aerilon as well, but would you like to see Telvo Station first?"

"What is that?"

"The next station we will be stopping at."

"Sure."

"Immerser, display Telvo Station," he commands as he moves to his feet. He looks down and offers me his hand. "You may wish to stand for this."

He pulls me up beside him. My eyes go wide as the room turns into a bustling station filled with all kinds of aliens of every shape and size. In the midst of the large crowd, however, I notice plenty of Mosaurans.

"Wow!" I stand there with my mouth gaped open. The Mosaurans are stunning. Differing shades of gray, silver, gold, charcoal, red, and tan with yellow, purple, green, orange, and red highlights to their brows and cheekbones. Each one is different, and their scales all shimmer with a brilliant iridescent glow as they move beneath the lighting. "Your people are beautiful, Soran," I whisper more to myself than to him.

He cocks his head slightly to the side to regard me.

I hope I haven't insulted his masculinity by calling him beautiful. Men can be so weird about stuff like that.

A small Mosauran child, maybe two to three years old by Terran standards, passes us, and I smile brightly.

"Oh my gosh. He's so precious!" I coo at the cute little Mosauran as his family walks past us.

~

**Soran**

My eyes widen as she begins making what I assume are maternal sounds for her species. She is very enthralled with the fledgling before her, and I fear that her mating heat may be quickly approaching. I know she already has a mate, but if she challenges me to the mating battle, I doubt I would be able to refuse her. My desire for her is too strong not to accept. I would be honored if she chose me as hers.

Her eyes are alight with wonder, and I smile to myself, imagining showing her my home world. Watching her fuss over the fledgling, I imagine her holding our offspring. Although, I wonder if we are even compatible in that way.

But as soon as the thought surfaces, I dismiss it immediately. She already has a mate. I cannot claim her as mine. Besides, to do so would make me Outcast from the Empire, my family, and everything I have ever known.

And yet...when she turns to me and her lips curve into a stunning smile, I know that if she wanted me, I would give up everything for her.

Part of me doesn't want to know, because I cannot bear the thought of her with another, but I ask anyway. "Your mate. Does he want fledglings too?"

A pink bloom spreads across her cheeks, and she averts her gaze as if embarrassed. "No, he doesn't like the idea of fledglings. And it hadn't really come up because we were never..." She pauses a moment as if trying to find the right words before she finally says, "fully mated."

My mouth drifts open in shock. "You and your mate never...mated?"

She shakes her head. "I...it was complicated between us. We were still just dating...courting," she corrects. "We hadn't decided to bond yet."

Hope fills me, and I want to roar my happiness to the stars. She is unbonded. Now, I must show her that I am worthy to be hers, and perhaps she will choose me as her mate.

# CHAPTER 14

SORAN

Liana sags forward in relief at her station as yet another A'kai
cruiser moves out of range of our glider. Although they
should not be able to detect us with the cloak, it is still
greatly unnerving to know that there are so many searching for our
vessel. Talel is relentless in his pursuit of my Ashaya.

She shakes her head. "I don't understand. Why do they want me so
badly? What makes my blood so special?"

I meet her gaze evenly. "The wound I gave Talel was a mortal one.
Of that, I am certain. When he tried to stop us from leaving the
station, he claimed that your blood is the reason he survived—that it
had healed him."

Tr'lani steps forward. "I have wondered about this as well. And I
remember that there was a rumor on Aerilon before I was taken—that
the A'kai are fighting a plague that is devastating their population."
She looks to Liana. "If your blood healed him from a mortal wound, it
would be the most valuable substance to them in all of the known
universe. Especially if they believe it might be the key to finding a
cure for their illness."

Cold fills me. All the color drains from Liana's face as she stares at the display and the blinking green dot on the map, indicating yet another cruiser is nearby. She lifts her gaze to us. "If Talel makes the connection that his mate's people have made contact with mine..." she doesn't finish her sentence, but she doesn't have to. We already know what she means to say.

She meets my eyes evenly. "Maybe we should risk traveling without the cloak. The sooner we reach Mosaura and Aerilon, the sooner we can begin searching for my people...for my home world. Time is against us, and we're wasting it hiding from the A'kai. This ship is fast. We have a good chance of—"

I cut her off abruptly. "No."

"Why not?"

"Because if we fail, he will have you. And that's exactly what he wants. He will search your mind and find your home world."

She shakes her head. "He can't find my home world even *if* he searches my mind. I'm a pilot, and *I* don't even know where it is. My people have never ventured beyond our solar system."

"But his beloved knows where Terra is," Rowan says grimly. "All he needs is enough information extracted from your thoughts and he will put the pieces together and your planet will be enslaved."

Fire burns in her eyes as she runs a frustrated hand through her hair. "We have to take the risk and decloak so we can travel at full speed. We're running out of time."

My heart clenches at the desperation in her voice, but I cannot bear the thought of her being taken by the A'kai. "I understand what you're saying, but I also know that if we're caught, the fate of your world will be decided that much sooner. At least this way, we still have a chance."

Moving closer, I place my hands on her shoulders and meet her gaze evenly. "I know you fear for your people. I do too. Together, we will find them, and we will either save your planet, or we will die in the attempt. But whatever we do, we cannot risk Talel capturing you again."

The fire leaves her eyes because she knows I am right. But the frustration behind her gaze remains. She sighs heavily. "You're right. I'm sorry."

I dart a quick glance to my brother before returning my attention to Liana. "When we reach Mosaura, I will ask my mother, the Empress, to commit some of our forces to finding your people and your home world. Once it is located, perhaps an alliance can be formed between our two races to ensure the protection of your planet from an invading force."

Tr'lani turns to her. "My family is of the High Clan of Al'ani. My people will help you as well, Liana. Of this, I am certain."

My Ashaya is quiet as we eat dinner. Normally she is very talkative, but I understand the things that weigh heavily on her mind. When we are finished, she reaches behind her ear to turn off her translator like I've taught her.

"Care to continue our lessons?" she asks in broken Mosauran.

I know she does this to distract herself from thinking about the A'kai. But I cannot help the smile that tugs at my lips as her tongue struggles to wrap around the Mosauran words that come so easily to her when she is using the translator. She's been utilizing the language modules every evening to study Mosauran *and* Aerilon. I'm surprised at how quickly she is picking up both dialects. Her goal is to be able to learn them well enough that she can add her spoken and written language to the translator program. She does this so that when she finds her crew, they will be able to integrate more easily into our societies.

It is both noble and selfless to undertake such an enormous project, speaking to a strength of character that continues to amaze me. Many in her position would wallow in despair, but she chooses to reach for hope while also preparing for the hard reality that she may never find her planet or her people again. I often wonder if it is a characteristic of her species. Are they a strong people? Or is it specific to just her?

I follow her down the hallway, believing we are going to her quarters to converse, but she turns instead into the training room.

I cock my head to the side. "You wish to spar?"

She smiles and steps onto the training mat, spreading her feet apart in the defensive stance I taught her. No sooner do I step into the circle, she rushes toward me, and I barely duck in time to avoid her attack. She grins as I regain my footing, and we begin to circle each other.

She spent two years in the Terran military, and her defense training must have been very similar to Mosauran Drokar because she is indeed a worthy sparring opponent. It has not taken very many lessons for her to become efficient in my people's style of fighting.

At first, I was very careful with her because I feared that her size made her weak. But she uses it to her advantage, forcing my center of gravity to shift in a way that challenges everything I know.

She jumps, spinning and kicking out with her right foot, and I barely miss taking a direct blow to the face. Horrified that she almost hit me, she stops, and I use her hesitation to rush toward her and take her in a Drogev hold, instantly immobilizing her. With one arm banded around her waist and arms from behind and the other around her neck so that my hand cups her jaw firmly to keep her still, I lean down and whisper against the curved shell of her ear. "Never let your guard down when facing an opponent."

Her green eyes are full of defiance as she turns her head to look back up at me, gritting her teeth as she tries to free herself. "But I almost hurt you."

"I'm fine," I state firmly. "Never feel sympathy for your opponent. They will use it against you. Now. Concentrate. Do you remember how to break this hold?"

She struggles, growling in frustration. "My *opponent*," she emphasizes the word, "is a close friend, and I did not want to hurt him." The sound of her growl, combined with the slight struggle as she tries to break free, remind me of the shav-rhokan, and my body instinctively responds.

Desire burns through me like flame. Subconsciously my arms tighten around her form, like they would if I'd subdued a Mosauran female and won the mating battle. Instinct wars within me and I want nothing more than to claim her as mine and take her as my mate. But I quickly force myself to release her and step away, not wanting to scare her with my reaction.

She gives me a confused look. "Why'd you let go? I thought you were going to show me how to break the hold?"

As she moves toward me, my nostrils flare as I take in her delicate scent. It's always stronger when we spar like this, and my want of her is so great it threatens to overwhelm me. Although it is difficult, I force myself to focus as I push down my longing, reminding myself that her life may well depend upon her training someday. "I am your friend, but you must treat me as if I were the enemy when we practice. I want you to be prepared for anything if you must fight."

A smile tugs at her lips as she stares up at me through dark lashes. "I know. But it's hard because it's you, and I care about you. I don't want to hurt you, Soran."

My heart clenches as I stare deep into her sea-green eyes. I long to take her in my arms and promise her that I will be her shield and her protector. That she will always be safe, and no harm will ever reach her. But I understand, more than most, that the universe is a dangerous place. And because I love her...I must prepare her as best I can to face any dangers that may await. "You would only hurt me if you were harmed because I did not train you well, Liana. I would shield you from all danger if I could, but I might not always be with you. I want to make sure that no matter what you may face, you are prepared."

Her lips curve into a stunning smile before she turns her back to me. "Then take me in the Drogev hold again. I think I remember what to do."

I bite back a groan as I wrap my arms around her once more, reveling in the feel of her body flush against mine. So distracted by the sensation, I'm unprepared when she twists from my grasp and spins to disable me, slamming her fist against the underside of my jaw.

My head whips back, and the world tilts and spins. In the small part of my brain that is still functioning as I fall backward, pride fills me at how well my Ashaya delivered such a devastating blow.

# CHAPTER 15

SORAN

When I open my eyes, I find her sea green ones staring down at me in concern. I'm lying in my bed, and she's seated beside me, holding my hand in her own.

"Soran!" She leans forward and presses her lips softly to my cheek. "Oh, thank God you're awake."

"What—" I start to ask what happened but stop abruptly when Rowan's smirking face fills my vision.

"Oh God. I'm so sorry," Liana says, drawing my attention back to her. "I didn't mean to hit you so hard."

It all comes back to me as I sit up. Tr'lani steps forward and runs the scanner over my face as I open my jaw, surprised that it doesn't hurt. "I gave you something for the pain," she says, "but I suggest you try to rest."

My mind is still a bit hazy, so I'm not going to argue. A smile crests my lips as I turn to my Ashaya with pride. "That was amazing. You completely disabled me with one solid hit just like I taught you."

Her jaw drops. "Are you serious?"

Because my thoughts are still foggy, I start to nod but then stop when I realize that not only was there shock in her voice, but also a subtle hint of anger.

She continues. "You're going to praise me for knocking you out cold? I thought you were dead!"

Despite her obvious irritation at my words, the smile doesn't leave my face. I'm so proud of her. She's a warrior.

"You think this is funny?" she asks incredulously. "I could have killed you."

Rowan rolls his eyes behind her. He's hurt me far worse when we have sparred before, but she doesn't need to know that.

Tilting my chin up to expose the regal jawline she loves so much, I puff my chest out with pride. "I'm a big, strong Mosauran warrior. We are not so easily killed."

She lets out an irritated huff, but I can see the hint of a smile that curves her lips at my teasing. "You're not invincible, Soran."

Intending to show her that I am well, I swing my legs over the bed to stand, but she puts a hand to my chest to stop me, pushing me back onto the mattress.

The aggressive gesture as she pins me back on the bed stokes the flames of my desire. Intense need burns through me like fire as my body responds to her as if she were a Mosauran female challenging me to the shav-rhokan. It takes everything I have to suppress the low growl of arousal that rumbles deep in my chest.

"Are you crazy? You just woke up. You heard Tr'lani. She said you need to rest, so you're *going* to rest."

I'm completely mesmerized by the fiery edge dancing just behind her eyes as I stare up at her beautiful face. And although I want to argue that I'm well, I don't because I love that she is so concerned for my well-being. "And what will we do with our time?" I grin, delighted to know that she is so protective of me. As if we were already a mated pair.

"Want to play some kartu?"

I cock my head slightly to the side. "Where did you learn how to play kartu?"

Her gaze darts to Rowan, and jealousy stabs at my chest.

I narrow my eyes at him before returning my attention to her. "If he taught you this game, then it is not a good idea for me to play you."

She gives me a confused look. "Why?"

I smirk. "Because you learned from an inferior player, and I will beat you in less than five hands."

She crosses her arms over her chest. A smile tugs at her lips. "I'd like to see you try."

I grin. "Is that a challenge?"

"That depends."

"On what?"

"What do I get if I win?"

Her eyes sparkle with mischief, and when her small tongue darts out to lick her lips as she waits for my answer, I forget whatever response I was going to give her.

With a sly smirk, she cocks her brow up slightly. "Well?"

Mesmerized, I ask. "Well, what?"

"What do I get if I win?"

"Oh, that," I reply. I want to tell her that I wish to be her prize. I am hers to do with as she pleases. She is fierce and determined and brave. And she has bested me in combat. What male wouldn't want to be hers? "Will my undying devotion suffice?" I ask, only halfway teasing because I would give anything to be her mate.

She laughs. "I suppose that will do."

A slow smile curves my lips. I'll let her win every hand. "Then, I am yours...*if* you beat me."

Rowan clears his throat. I was so enamored of my Ashaya I'd forgotten he and Tr'lani were still here.

Liana smiles at him. "Want to play with us?"

He looks back at the door a moment as if torn between playing and returning to the bridge. And when his gaze darts to mine and I give him a signal to please leave, that decides it. "I...appreciate the offer, but I think I should monitor the ship for a while."

My brother loves kartu, and I recognize how difficult a decision this was for him to turn down the chance to play. Poor Rowan. He's a

125

terrible player, but it's his favorite game. I decide I'll let him win every hand from now on for this favor.

Tr'lani smiles at him. "I'll help you."

The lovestruck grin he gives her in reply tells me he's not *that* sorry he'll miss out on this game. I know he relishes the time he spends with Tr'lani just as much as I do with Liana.

Time seems to pass quickly as we play several rounds of kartu. Liana laughs heartily each time she draws a winning hand, smiling triumphantly. At first, I was letting her win, but now we're almost evenly matched. Although she has a tendency to tease and joke, it has often been muted in the past compared to now. This is the first time I feel like I'm seeing a glimpse of the person she was before she was taken.

"Do your people play any games like this?" I ask.

Studying the kartu fanned out in front of her, she looks over at me. "Yeah, it's how we pass the time on long cargo runs when we're not in stasis." She looks back down to study her hand, a wide smile forming across her face. "Ah-ha!" She spreads her kartu on the table before me as her eyes light up with joy. "A full span! If we were playing strip kartu, you'd already be naked," she teases.

Her words catch me completely off guard. "What?" I ask, wondering if I've heard her right. "What is strip kartu?"

She laughs and gives me a small shrug. "I just made it up. On Terra, people sometimes play a game similar to kartu, where you have to strip off an item of clothing for each losing hand you play. The first person to become completely naked, loses."

My jaw drops as I imagine her naked before me. A disturbing thought hits me, and I narrow my eyes. "Have you played strip kartu with Rowan?"

She looks down at her hand, studying her kartu as she answers matter-of-factly. "Yes. Your brother is a really good player. I've lost to him several times."

I freeze, and then a series of murderous thoughts fill my mind as I think on my brother, picturing him gazing at her naked form. But the instant she grins, I realize that she is only teasing, and I immediately relax.

"Actually," she adds, "I've never played the 'strip' version of any game. But I know it's a thing some Terrans do." She slaps her kartu on the table. "Ha! I win! So that means you're all mine," she declares triumphantly.

My heart stops. Although I know her words are in jest, the primal part of my brain responds and my body flushes with warmth as she announces her claim to me.

"Yours," I barely manage to reply, and I watch, enchanted, as a beautiful smile lights her face.

When she stands and her gaze darts to the door, disappointment rushes through me when I think she's going to leave. Instead, she surprises me by asking if I'd like a cup of tea.

I nod because I want her to return to my quarters. As she disappears into the hallway, I jump up and race to the shower, cleansing and changing into soft knit pants and a sleep shirt before she returns.

From what I've observed, her people must be obsessed with cleanliness, because she uses the shower every evening and sometimes even twice a day. Terrans must have superior scent receptors, and I do not want her to ever think that I smell bad. Because of this, I've taken to showering daily instead of every other day like I used to, buffing my scales to a fine sheen.

Rowan complained that he only lost our sparring session yesterday because he was blinded by the brilliant light reflecting from my shimmering scales. He is simply jealous because my scales are now more attractive than his.

When Liana returns, she sits on the small sofa beside me and hands me a cup. She takes a small sip of her tea and stares up at me over the rim. Setting it down in her lap, she leans forward. "That was fun. I haven't laughed like that in—" She stops, sadness flickering briefly across her expression before she retrains her face into an impassive mask. "A long time," she finally finishes.

I wait patiently for her to continue, but she remains silent. Her gaze drifts to the window on the far wall, and I recognize that although she is here with me, her mind has returned to the dark thoughts that plague her.

"Liana, what is wrong?"

Shaking her head softly, she turns to me. "I just...I can't stop thinking about my crew. I keep wondering if they're safe, if they've found good people like you and your brother or if they're..."

She doesn't finish her sentence, but I already know what she means to say. It is far more likely her crew are slaves, like she and Tr'lani were.

"Sometimes, I feel guilty because despite everything...I'm happy here." Her sea-green eyes stare deep into mine. "With you."

My heart stutters.

Slowly, she leans forward and lifts her hand to my face. The tips of her fingers brush lightly across my cheek. Heat blooms in their wake as her eyes search mine. She touches the top of my scar, and I start to turn from her hand, but she stops me. Her gaze is full of concern. "Does it hurt?"

"No," I reply, but that isn't entirely the truth. The pain from this scar is not a physical one. It is a reminder of all I endured during my slavery.

She cups her hand to my cheek. "You don't have to be ashamed of your scar. You're beautiful, Soran."

I lower my gaze, but she places two fingers under my chin to tip my head back up to her.

A teasing grin lights her face as she arches one brow. "Would it be better if I said 'handsome' instead of 'beautiful'?"

Tilting my chin up even more, a smile tugs at the corner of my mouth as I puff my chest out with pride. I've taken great care to preen myself for her, to look my best. She is appraising me just as a Mosauran female would, and I am glad she does not find my appearance lacking.

A soft huff of air escapes her in a breathless laugh. "You're such a showoff, you know."

I open my mouth to make a witty reply, but at just that moment, she leans in and presses her soft lips to mine. I'm so stunned, I go completely still.

When she pulls back, a pink bloom spreads across her cheeks. She tucks a stray tendril of hair behind her ear. "I'm sorry. I—I shouldn't have done that."

Uncertain how to respond, I search her eyes. "I don't understand what—"

The doors to my quarters whoosh open, revealing my brother, who has the absolute worst timing ever. "How are you feeling?" he asks.

She stands and gives me a nervous smile. "I'll leave you two to visit."

"Liana, wait."

As she steps out into the hallway, she calls over her shoulder. "I'll be back to check on you later."

Rowan gives me a puzzled look. "Is everything all right?"

Lowering my gaze to the floor, I sigh heavily. "I do not know."

# CHAPTER 16

LIANA

After what happened with Soran last night, I decide to take my bridge shift with Rowan. I glance across at him, sitting at his station. He looks so much like his brother, they could almost pass for twins.

I turn my attention back to my display, listening intently to my headset as various ships speak to one another on the different channels. Although I don't hear anything unusual, I'm still not sure it's safe. "I say we continue on this course a few more hours just to be certain. What do you think?"

"Agreed," Rowan replies, not taking his eyes off the viewscreen.

Usually, he's really chatty when we're on the bridge like this, but not now. Today, he's all business, and I know it's because of the two A'kai ships that passed us less than an hour ago. We altered course in response. This will add an extra day to our trip to Telvo Station, but it's better to avoid the A'kai if we can. Even with the cloak, there is still a risk they could detect our FTL signature.

Since the mood is somber anyway, I decide to ask my burning question. "Why is Soran so sensitive about his scar?"

Rowan gives me a hesitant look before answering. "Because that scar cost him everything."

"What do you mean? How?"

"He had a betrothed at the time of his capture. Maina. We all grew up together. She is the daughter of Lord Argona, who is like an uncle to us. And it only made sense to ally our Great Houses officially through bonding. Maina already called Soran her 'Chosen one.' She promised she would take no other as her mate but him. I already considered her like a sister, and I know Caryn did as well."

"What happened?"

"After I rescued him...as soon as we got close enough to Mosaura, he contacted her. The moment she saw him in the viewscreen, her expression faltered, and I knew." Sadness fills his expression. "I do not think he did, however, because he was surprised that she was not there to greet him when we landed."

Tears sting my eyes, but I blink them back. How horrible for him to have survived all those years thinking of her, and she wasn't even there for him when he returned home.

Rowan continues. "When she finally arrived a few days later, Soran thought for sure she had come to claim him as her mate as they'd discussed many times before he was taken. But, to my great and utter shock, she turned her back to him and chose me instead. Challenging me to the shav-rhokan—the mating battle. I refused her, of course, but Soran was completely devastated."

Anger fills me. "She refused him because of a scar?"

Nodding, he lowers his gaze. "She said it would be too painful for her to look at every day. To be constantly reminded that he had been a slave."

"That's ridiculous! She couldn't have loved him if she rejected him like that."

"I agree. Maina is a very attractive female, desired by many. But she is also very vain. Most Mosauran females are. I do not believe she truly ever cared for him beyond his appearance. If she had, the scar would not have mattered." He pauses. "She wanted the prestige and power that would come from a formal bonding with our House, and it mattered not to her, in the end, which of us she bonded with to gain it."

I turn to Rowan. "And...what happened to Maina? Did she—"

Already having anticipated my question, he nods. "Although it is not the one she originally desired, she received a title anyway. She is bonded to our cousin."

My mouth drifts open in shock and my heart breaks for Soran. I can't even imagine the pain of watching the woman you love choose someone else, all because of a scar. No wonder he's so sensitive about it.

And I decide, in this moment, that it's my favorite thing about him. Because without it, he would already be bonded to someone else, and I would have met the man that I love too late.

# CHAPTER 17

LIANA

It's only been two days since Soran was injured...and two days since I kissed him. But he hasn't mentioned it, and neither have I. My cheeks heat in embarrassment when I think of how he went completely still when I pressed my lips to his. I don't know what I was thinking. I doubt he even finds me attractive. After all, he says I look similar to a V'loryn, and his people find them appalling. He's my friend. And a good one at that. I don't want to ruin that between us by trying to initiate something he may not even want.

His deep velvet voice snaps me back from my dark thoughts. "Shall we continue our sparring lessons?"

I want to, but after what happened last time, I'm afraid I'm going to hurt him again. "How about we just practice the different holds instead of full-out sparring?"

He agrees, and we go through several different movements. The problem is, one thing leads to another, and soon we're sparring when I'd originally wanted to just kind of take things easy.

It's my fault because I'm very competitive. When I couldn't break out of that last hold, I wanted to prove to myself I could take him. So I challenged him to spar as soon as he released me.

Breathless and panting, we circle each other a moment before he rushes me. Grabbing me from behind in the Drogev hold with his arm banded around my waist and his other hand holding my neck and chin, my back is pressed firmly against his front.

So close to him like this, I take in his delicious masculine scent. His lips graze my ear. "The secret is to never surrender. Remember that."

Oh, but I want to surrender right now in his arms as the sound of his rich, warm voice sends a wave of desire straight through me. The muscles tighten in the pit of my stomach, and a breathless moan escapes my lips as I lean my head back against the solid wall of his heavily muscled chest.

And then I feel it. The swell of his long, hard length—his stav, as his people call it—pressing insistently against my backside. I know little of Mosauran anatomy, and I've often wondered if we're physically compatible, but now it seems that my concerns were unfounded.

He lowers his head to the curve of my neck and shoulder. A warm puff of air hits my skin as he scents me, no doubt able to sense my aroused state as easily as I can sense his.

Overwhelmed with sensation, I desperately want to touch him, but I'm still locked in the hold. "Soran, let me move, I want—"

He drops his arms and steps back so fast I almost lose my balance. I spin to face him. "Why did you let go?"

His silver eyes stare at me intensely. The muscles ripple just beneath the surface as he stands across from me, looking every bit like it's taking all his control just to stay away. "We should stop," he rasps.

I don't know if he means stop sparring or stop what's potentially happening between us, but I ask the question anyway. "Why?"

He drops his gaze to the ground. With a slight clench of his jaw, he speaks in a voice so low I barely catch it. "My mating heat approaches."

"Your...mating heat?"

His eyes flick back up to mine. "Yes."

I frown. "What exactly does that mean?"

"Our females are only fertile every three cycles. As I've explained before, that equates to roughly three of your...*years*." He accentuates the word "years" as if it's hard for him to wrap his tongue around it.

"What does that have to do with anything?"

"If a female we find attractive becomes fertile, our bodies respond by going into mating heat. We then present ourselves as suitors, hoping she will declare the shav-rhokan—the mating battle."

His gaze travels over my form, and my jaw drops as I realize the implications of his statement.

"Are you saying you're attracted to me?" The words come out a bit higher in pitch than I'd intended, but it's only because I can't believe this handsome draken warrior is interested in *me*. I don't look anything like a Mosauran female; I'm surprised he finds me desirable. While this is definitely welcome news, I'm a little bit concerned about the "mating battle" because it doesn't really sound all that romantic.

He nods but doesn't say anything further.

We stand there a moment in awkward silence before I ask, "And...you're afraid you'll mistake our sparring sessions for this 'mating battle,' am I right?"

"Yes." His silver eyes stare deep into mine with an edge of fire and hunger visible in their depths. "Although I know that would not be your intent, I do not trust myself to spar with you until this passes."

Feeling bold, I take a small step toward him. "What exactly *is* 'the mating battle?"

He gives me a confused look. "Do Terran females not challenge males to fight to determine if they will be a worthy mate?"

My jaw drops. *What. The. Hell.* "Uh...if there's any fighting involved between Terran mates, it's usually because they're mad at each other or there's some kind of abusive situation going on."

He cocks his head to the side. "Then how do Terran females pick their partners? How do they know a male will give them strong fledglings if she doesn't know that he can defeat her in battle?"

A surprised laugh escapes me, but my face quickly falls when I realize he's serious. "Wait. What?" I ask, thinking I've misheard him. "Explain this shav—" I pause, trying to recall the rest of the word.

135

"Rhokan," he finishes my sentence. "After the last great plague, our males outnumber our females twenty to one. When a female is interested in taking a mate—usually during her mating heat—she will challenge a group of males, or sometimes one male, by announcing shavrhokan. If the males are interested in becoming her mate, they will fight her. Whichever male is able to defeat her, he then gives her his mark, and she accepts him into her body, and they become a mated pair."

*She accepts him into her body.* His words repeat in my mind, sending another ripple of warmth down my spine to melt my core.

His nostrils flare, and he stares at me with a hungry gaze.

He's definitely attracted to me. That much is obvious, judging by the large bulge beneath the confines of his clothing. But does he love me like I love him, or is this just some weird biological compulsion of his species?

And I *do* love him. At first, I thought it was just fascination because of my dreams. But the more I've gotten to know him, the harder I've fallen. How could I not? I can't stop thinking about that day when he showed me the stars so I wouldn't feel so lost. But does he love *me*?

The only way I'll know is if I ask. And I need to start with the truth and tell him about my dreams. He watches me intently, and there is a flicker of uncertainty behind his gaze as I step forward and take his hand in mine. "Soran, I have to tell you something."

His eyes search mine as I entwine our fingers. "It's something I should have told you a long time ago, and—"

The doors whoosh open to reveal Tr'lani, excitement lighting her face. "Rowan received a signal from an Aerilon ship. He's trying to contact them now. Come with me to the bridge."

I'm reluctant to release his hand. "We'll talk later?"

He nods and then I turn to follow her.

# CHAPTER 18

SORAN

It's been several hours, but Rowan has finally made contact with the Aerilon ship. I only left a few minutes ago to join Liana and Tr'lani in the crew mess but now we're all racing back to the bridge.

As soon as the doors whoosh open, my jaw drops when I notice an Aerilon male's face on the viewscreen. His golden eyes narrow slightly as he looks past me to Tr'lani and Liana. He inhales sharply. "Tr'lani?" His voice is a mixture of hope and disbelief; a deep vibrational hum emits from his throat. "I was so afraid we'd never find you, my beautiful sister."

His eyes are bright with tears as he raises his open palm to the display as if to touch her, and Tr'lani does the same.

They stare at one another as if afraid to look away. A broken sob escapes her, and a tear rolls down his cheek.

"All this time," he barely manages. "We never gave up searching. How did you escape?"

The answering hum from Tr'lani fills the bridge before she turns back to us. "Prince Soran and Prince Rowan of Mosaura saved us from the A'kai. But"—she takes Liana's hand in her own—"Liana is the one who kept me alive before that."

He studies Liana a moment before bowing deeply. "You have my deepest gratitude. Have you been able to contact your people--the V'loryns?"

Liana opens her mouth to answer, but Tr'lani interrupts. "She's not V'loryn, Al'aneo. She's Terran."

He leans closer to the screen, his sharp gaze scanning her from head to toe.

Tr'lani continues. "She was taken from her ship by the Zovians while she was in stasis. She doesn't know where her home world is. I wish to bring her into our clan, so she can become an Aerilon citizen and have the same rights and protection of our people."

Al'aneo's golden eyes turn to Liana. Lifting his hand to the screen, he extends his first three fingers to touch the display as if reaching out to her. Liana and Tr'lani copy the gesture. "For all you've done for my sister, I shall be proud to welcome you into Clan Al'ani as in'ari."

Clan Al'ani is one of the Ruling High Clans of Aerilon. Tr'lani and her brother are royalty like us. Their acceptance of Liana as in'ari not only makes her Aerilon, it also means she is now a member of the royal family.

Liana gives Al'aneo and Tr'lani a watery smile. "Thank you. You have no idea how much it means to me."

My chest tightens. Does this mean she's going to leave with them?

Al'aneo's image begins to distort. "We're traveling near a binary system. It's interfering with our signal. We are en route. I will see you in five solars, and I'll contact you again tomorrow," he says just before the viewscreen goes dark.

**Liana**

Tr'lani gives me a warm smile. "I told you my family would accept you."

My heart is full as I stare at my friend; my sister in all ways but blood. Despite my best attempts to speak clearly, my voice quavers with emotion. "Thank you."

She wraps her arms around me, hugging me tightly. "Now that you are of Clan Al'ani, I'm certain the rest of the High Clans will vote in favor of searching for your people and your home world."

Her words fill me with hope.

Rowan looks to me. "When the Aerilon contact us again, I will transmit everything you told us about Talel and his associate discussing your home world."

Tr'lani nods. "In the meantime, you can live with me on Aerilon."

I have nowhere else to go. My people are unheard of in this region of space, and without any formal alliances between my government and theirs, I'm blessed that Tr'lani's clan has offered to take me in. But I wonder how well I'll be able to integrate into their society.

Noticing my hesitance, Tr'lani gives me a concerned look. "What's wrong?"

"I just—I'm concerned about how I'll live on a planet full of people who fly. I mean, I certainly don't have any wings."

A flicker of sadness crosses her face as her broken wings flutter softly behind her.

Almost immediately, I curse myself for my careless choice of words. "I'm sorry, Tr'lani. I didn't mean to remind you of—"

She gives me a pained smile. "It's all right. I have to accept the fact that my wings may never be repaired."

Rowan interrupts. "We will find someone to help you and we will not give up until we have exhausted every possibility."

I'm struck by the look of intense devotion on his face as he regards her.

Gently, she places a hand on his forearm as her golden eyes stare deep into his. "Thank you, Rowan."

After coming up with a tentative plan of where to meet Tr'lani's brother, she and Rowan leave to grab something to eat, leaving Soran and me alone on the bridge. As I sit at my station, I pull up the nav charts. Waving my hands, I scroll through the display like Soran taught me. We'll reach Telvo Station to refuel in roughly three hours. It's five solars until we reach Tr'lani's brother and then six solars more to Aerilon Prime.

Soran sits at his station beside me, scanning the display as he checks the ship's readings. We were interrupted a few hours ago, but I want to continue our conversation.

I take a deep and steeling breath and then turn to face him. "Soran?"

His head snaps toward me, his reflective silver eyes staring at me intently. "Yes?"

"I—" I lower my gaze a moment, uncertain how to begin. Softly biting my lower lip, I realize it's now or never. "I wanted to continue our conversation...from earlier."

I'm surprised by how earnest he responds. "I do too." He reaches across to gently place his much larger hand over mine. "Liana, I don't want you to—"

The doors whoosh open, and Rowan enters the bridge.

Startled, I quickly pull my hand away from his.

With a serious expression, Rowan takes his station and pulls up his console, studying the display. "I'll do one more sweep for enemy vessels before we decloak." He turns to me and grins. "You want to dock the ship when we reach Telvo?"

I smile widely at Rowan's vote of confidence in my piloting skills. He loves his glider, and he wouldn't trust me to do this if he didn't think I was capable. How do I know this? Because I was the same way with my ship. I wouldn't let anyone even near the controls if I didn't have complete faith in their abilities. "Yeah, I'd love to."

Soran's jaw drops and then he turns to Rowan, crossing his arms over his chest. "Why do you never trust *me* to dock the ship?"

Rowan arches a condescending brow. "Because you suck at docking."

I laugh, and Rowan joins in too as Soran stares at him with narrowed eyes.

Now that I've taught them the Terran expression "you suck," it has become one of their favorite colorful expressions.

I shake my head and then laugh even harder. What's my contribution to the vast Mosauran Empire? The spread of the Terran expression "you suck."

# CHAPTER 19

SORAN

*A*lone. The thought fills me with dread. This is our last stop to refuel before we meet with Tr'lani's brother. My Ashaya will leave with them soon, and I doubt I'll ever see her again. My chest tightens as I study her out of the corner of my eye.

My mind drifts back to the memory of her soft lips pressed to mine. My people do not do this, and when I tried to ask her what it meant, a dark flush spread across her cheeks, and she apologized for having done it in the first place. I suspect it means something more than gratitude or friendship, but I was unwilling to press her further. That she gifted me her touch in the first place humbles me. Especially after all she has been through.

Seated at her station, her expression is serious as she stares at the nav display. Her fingers move deftly across the control panel as she charts our course safely around another asteroid field. Small chunks of debris hit the outer hull, echoing loudly through the ship's metal walls. She chews nervously on her lower lip. "We're still hitting some of the smaller pieces."

"It is unavoidable," I reply. "You are doing well. It is only the larger formations we need to avoid, and your course takes us around all of those."

Turning her head, she smiles brightly at me, and I cannot help but smile widely in return. Her smiles are as brilliant as the night blooms of the silari—as beautiful as they are rare.

The glider's proximity alert sounds just as a large black ship appears in the viewscreen. Her smile disappears, and all the color drains from her face.

Quickly scanning the image, I determine it is a Lycaon ship. They are very similar to A'kai cruisers, and I know that's why she's afraid. I hate the worried look on her face. I wish I had killed Talel every time fear crosses her expression. I should have put the blaster to his head instead of his chest. Pressing the controls, I magnify the display. "It is not an A'kai vessel. Notice the design." I point to the rear engines. "It's a Lycaon ship. Very similar to the A'kai cruisers."

Her shoulders visibly relax. "What are Lycaons? I don't think I've ever seen one before."

I perform a quick search on the computer and pull up an image from the ship's directory. A Lycaon male fills the screen. It changes from humanoid form to lycan form and back.

She inhales sharply.

"What's wrong?"

"They...when they change form," she whispers, her eyes are wide as she stares at the image, "they look just like werewolves."

"Werewolves?"

"Monsters of ancient Terran myth." Swallowing thickly, she turns her gaze to mine. "Are they bad?"

Rowan waves a dismissive hand at the Lycaon ship. "They are a mostly nomadic race that travel in packs. They fear our people."

"He's right," I add. "We have not had many dealings with them since the last Great War."

Seemingly satisfied with our answer, she turns her attention back to Telvo station. "Do you know if there are any slavers here?"

I clench my jaw, wishing I could reassure her completely, but I cannot speak an untruth. "It is possible, but we're so close to

Mosauran space. It is highly unlikely anyone dealing in"—I pause a moment; the word "flesh" is sitting on the tip of my tongue, but I cannot bring myself to say it, not after what she's been through—"illegal contraband would be there."

## Liana

The Lycaon ship moves out of range as we approach the station, and I'm glad. Their cruiser reminds me too much of the A'kai, and they look like werewolves when they shift. Werewolf and vampire stories always terrified me when I was a child.

Focusing on my task, I begin my docking checklist to prepare the glider as we move closer to Telvo. "I've got this," I say out loud, giving myself a miniature pep talk. Surprisingly, I feel as confident piloting this vessel as I did the ones I used to fly for the Terran space program.

A dull thud echoes along the outer hull as the docking clamps align with our ship. The display lights green a moment later, alerting me that we have a good connection. When I look over at Soran, he's already smiling at me.

Rowan gives me an approving nod. "You are an excellent pilot, Liana."

I'm practically beaming. "Thanks. You two are pretty good instructors."

"We only taught you the basics. The rest is *all you*," he adds, using the new Terran lingo I've been teaching him. He gives me a thumbs up. "You've got this."

Tr'lani waves over her shoulder as she disembarks with Rowan. They're off to see a Healer he found. Hopefully, she can repair Tr'lani's damaged wings.

I step onto the ramp, and a wave of panic rushes through me. The last time I left the safety of the ship, we were targeted by slavers. I'm worried that this time won't be any different, and my heart begins racing as fear coils tight in my chest.

I turn back to the glider. Everything inside me wants to run back through the airlock and seal it behind me. Closing my eyes, I take a deep breath and will myself to calm. I cannot let my fears control me. If I do, then I'm lost, and I'll never find my crew, my family, or my home.

*I am a Garza, and I come from a line of strong women. I can do this.*

"Ready?" Soran's voice snaps me back into focus, and I open my eyes to find his silver ones staring back at me intently.

Drawing in a deep and steeling breath, I push down my fear and anchor myself in this moment. I'm alive. I survived because my will is stronger than the evil that tried to break me. And I have hope that I'll find my planet and see my family again. I've got this. "Let's go."

# CHAPTER 20

LIANA

As we make our way through the promenade, I stare in awe at everything around me. The station is amazing. All glistening metal and glass, everything is so brightly lit it feels like we could be standing under the sun instead of artificial lighting. This place is a definite upgrade from the seedy stations Tr'lani and I were taken to as slaves. Everything is so clean and shiny, even the metal floor and wall panels reflect our images with sparkling clarity as we pass.

The station is much larger than I first realized. Each level is a concentric ring lined with dozens of shops and restaurants. Aliens in every possible shape, size, and color stroll among us, but it's the Mosauran females that draw my attention.

Most of them are at least half a head taller than the males, their muscular build putting even Soran and Rowan's exceptional forms to shame. Now, I'm really curious about the shav-rhokan—the mating battle—because it looks like it would take at least two Mosauran males to best a female in a fight.

Soran smiles across at me. "Where would you like to go first?"

I arch a teasing brow at him. "I believe I was promised a gourmet meal."

"So you were," he grins. "And that is exactly where we are heading right now."

I follow Soran through the throng of people, and after a few minutes, he points up ahead. "There it is."

My stomach growls with renewed vigor at the sight of our target. As we get closer, the air grows thick with exotic spice. The rich scent reminding me a bit of my favorite Indian restaurant I used to visit frequently back home.

We approach the counter, and my eyes go wide as I take in the kitchen behind it. One of those octopus-type aliens—a Krulta, I believe Soran called them—appears to be the chef. With a tentacle going in almost every direction, I marvel at how he's able to keep track of everything.

One stirs food in a pan, while another grabs what looks like a starfish. The starfish wriggles against its hold, and I gasp in horror as the Krulta's whip-like tentacle flings it into a steaming pot. A pitiful, garbled squee fills the air as it thrashes in the boiling water before going completely still and silent.

My jaw drops. I think I'm going to throw up.

"What do you—" Soran starts to ask, but stops abruptly, his eyes widening in alarm as he looks down at me. "Are you all right?" He leans down, his silver gaze studying my expression in concern. "You look ill. What's wrong?"

I open my mouth to speak, but the Krulta ladles the starfish out of the pot, slapping its body onto the counter just before another tentacle brings a knife down to bear. It slashes the pitiful thing open, using another tentacle to rip out the entrails. The neon green and yellow gloop slides off the counter onto the floor with a wet slap against the metal.

Closing my eyes, I swallow against the bile rising in my throat as I turn away from the horrendous scene. Now, I think I understand why my friend, Amanda is a vegetarian.

"Liana?" Soran's voice pulls me back from my thoughts. His entire face is a mask of concern as he stares down at me. "Your color has changed. You look...green. Is this normal for your species? I've never seen you do this before."

I straighten, standing a bit taller, smoothing my hand over my hair to compose myself. Purposefully, avoiding looking back at the kitchen, I meet his gaze evenly. "I'd like a vegetarian dish."

He blinks several times in confusion. "This word is not translating. What is 'vegetarian'?"

"You know," I start, "plant-based instead of animal-based?"

He nods and turns his attention to the menu. After a moment, he points to a few different items. "What about those?"

I look down at the selections, unable to make heads or tails of the glyphs that I can only assume are the descriptions of each dish. Lifting my gaze to his, I shrug. "I don't know. Um...maybe something that isn't too spicy?"

His gaze sparkles with barely restrained amusement as he gives me a slight smirk. "We should also take into account your pitifully tiny fangs...choose something you will be able to chew easily."

I roll my eyes in mock frustration, and a teasing smile tugs at my lips. "My fangs are just fine like they are, thank you very much."

At that moment, an Aerilon man walks up behind the counter. As soon as he sees us, his wings shoot out to his sides, and I gasp. They're so beautiful—like something straight out of every a fairy tale I've ever read about the fae. He smiles widely at me. "How can I help you, enchanting one?"

Soran visibly stiffens beside me.

From what I've seen, Tr'lani's people are strikingly handsome, and this guy is no exception. My eyes drift once more over his sparkly wings, and I'm practically mesmerized.

The Aerilon eyes me appraisingly, and my cheeks flush under the scrutiny of his intense gaze, but I force myself to stare directly at him. "My...friend"—I gesture to Soran—"was helping me pick something out."

He grins and then turns to Soran, but the smile quickly falls from his lips at the thunderous expression on my normally friendly Mosauran's face.

Soran's nostrils flare, and he looks more intimidating in this moment than I've ever seen him before. "She'll have the zalari." His voice is a low rumbly growl. "And I'll have the rotuska."

*What the hell is wrong with him?*

The Aerilon narrows his eyes, but when he turns to me, a bright smile lights up his face, and he bows his head slightly. "Your order will be ready shortly."

I thank him, and as soon as we're far enough away that I don't think anyone can hear us, I spin to face Soran. "What was *that* about?"

He looks down at his wrist comm, pretending to study something on the display. "To what are you referring?"

"Don't play dumb," I snap. "Why were you rude to that Aerilon? That's one of Tr'lani's people. What's wrong with you?"

His eyes flick up to meet mine. "He was displaying his wings."

"What's so bad about that? They're beautiful."

"*That* is the point," he grits through his teeth. "He was preening for you."

My head jerks back in surprise at his attitude and sharp tone. "What the—" I start, but stop talking when Soran shoots another murderous glance at the Aerilon.

My jaw drops. I recognize that expression. I've seen it on Jeff's face several times. Every time he thought someone was showing some interest in me, he'd give that same possessive, angry look to whoever he perceived as a rival.

"Soran?" I lean forward, drawing his attention back to me. I meet his eyes evenly, trying to gauge his reaction to what I'm about to ask next. "Are you...jealous?"

His cheeks flush a dark, red-orange hue, and he looks down, his brow creasing into a deep frown as if my question troubles him and he doesn't quite know how to answer. With a slight clench of his jaw, he finally lifts his gaze back to mine. "What if I was?"

I study him a moment. I want to believe that it's because he has feelings for me beyond some strange biological impulse of his species.

That his jealousy is not merely some weird quirk of his DNA that will pass once his mating cycle is over. Despite my fear of rejection, I need to know. "Would you feel this way even if you weren't—"

"There is something I must tell you, Liana." His words cut me off abruptly.

"What is it?"

∾

**Soran**

She stares at me with a questioning look, and I swallow nervously. I love Liana. That's why I'm jealous of the Aerilon's attentions toward her. She is as intelligent as she is beautiful, and I know once she reaches Aerilon, she will have her choice of any number of suitors. The Aerilon are not like my people. They do not frown upon mixed-species pairings. I don't want her to leave with Tr'lani and her brother. I want her to stay with me. I want her to choose me as hers, and I have to tell her before it's too late. "Liana, I—"

"Are you Terran?" a small voice calls out, interrupting me.

Liana and I turn toward the direction of the voice but find no one. We're all the way at the back of the restaurant. I'd purposefully chosen this secluded section to enjoy our meal so we wouldn't be disturbed.

My gaze sweeps the area, but there is only a stack of crates on a hover sled along the back wall. "Where are you? Come out from where you are hiding," I command, half-expecting someone to appear from behind the boxes.

To my great shock and horror, a hand reaches through a small opening haphazardly carved on the side of one of the crates. "Please help me," the voice says. "Please, I'm so scared."

# CHAPTER 21

SORAN

Before I can stop her, Liana rushes toward boxes, falling to her knees when she reaches them. She takes the offered hand in her own.

I rush to Liana's side and kneel beside her. An audible gasp comes from the container as I peer inside. My jaw drops. A Terran female with golden hair and green eyes wide with alarm meet mine. She scrambles away, her body slamming against the back of the crate in a panicked effort to put more distance between us.

My nose wrinkles as the sour scent of her fear fills the air. If I had never seen a Terran before, I'd easily mistake her for V'loryn.

Trembling, she cowers in the far corner. "Please, don't hurt me. I didn't mean to misbehave. I'm sorry. It won't happen again. Please, don't tell my master."

I shake my head. "I mean you no harm."

"It's okay," Liana adds. "This is Soran. He's one of the good guys. He saved me. My name is Liana. What's yours?"

The female slowly lifts her head, and I see the same tempered hope in her eyes that I saw in Liana's when we rescued her. "My name is

Abby. Please help me. Master is taking me to a Healer to abort my child before I'm delivered to my new owners."

Liana inhales sharply, covering her mouth with her hand in response to the Terran female's words.

"Please," she begs. "Please don't let him take me. I don't want to lose my baby."

Abby moves forward, holding one hand over her stomach. My eyes widen as I notice the large swell of her abdomen. She's heavy with child. Liana told me her kind carry their young like this. I've heard the V'loryns do as well, but I have never seen it before.

"We will help you," I vow.

She reaches her hands out to both of us, covering them with hers. "Please, hurry. Master is getting food, but he'll be back shortly."

Spinning toward the restaurant counter, my eyes narrow as they rake over the line of patrons. Which one is "Master," I wonder, because I want to make sure I do not kill the wrong male. We're close, but not quite inside Mosauran space, and I haven't seen any patrols on the station. It is a mandatory death sentence to traffic slaves, so it appears I will be the one to enforce the law here today.

"Which one is your master?"

"The Zovian." She points to the only Zovian in line at the counter. I crack my knuckles and extend my claws, eagerly anticipating the opportunity to deliver the sentence for his abhorrent crimes.

My gaze sweeps back to Abby, watching her master with wide-eyed fear. Before I kill him, I need to free her from this crate.

"Move back," I tell her. "I've got to force this open."

She nods and scoots to the far side of the container. Pulling my knife from my belt, I use the laser blade to slice through the locking mechanism. With an audible snap, the device clicks open. Gripping the panels on either side, I waste no time and pull the lid away.

She lifts one delicate hand to shield her eyes, squinting against the bright lights of the station. With sunken cheeks and pale skin, she looks like she has not been fed a decent meal in weeks.

I extend my hand to help her up, but as she tries to stand, her knees buckle beneath her. Reacting quickly, I wrap both arms around her, catching her before she falls. Gently, I lift her small form from her prison.

Anger roils through me as I scan the interior of the crate. There was barely enough room for her to move in there, and it sickens me that she was kept in something not even fit for an animal to be transported in.

As I carefully set her feet on the ground, Liana takes her arm to steady her. The Zovian spins. With a frantic clicking of his mandibles, he rushes toward me. This male must be a fool to run straight toward his death. "Unhand her! She is my property!"

I step in front of Abby, spreading my wings wide, shielding her and Liana from his view.

He skids to a stop and then begins to scramble backward.

Faster than him, I lunge forward and wrap my hand around his throat to pull him toward me. Enraged, I bare my fangs as I squeeze his neck, using just enough pressure to leave him desperate for air but not so much that he cannot speak. "Do you have any others that look like her?"

He thrashes wildly against my hold. "No! No, I do not! I swear!"

His attempts to free himself are futile. He is no match for my strength, and now he will die for his despicable crimes.

"Don't kill him!" A soft hand touches my other arm, and I glance over my shoulder at Abby, shocked that she would plead for this disgusting creature's life. "He sold my mate less than an hour ago. I need to know who he gave him to. Maybe we can find him."

A loud gasp draws my attention to one of the restaurant patrons, and I realize that if we don't move to a more secluded location, we're going to draw a crowd. And that's the last thing I want to do.

I look back to Liana and Abby. "Follow me."

Dragging the Zovian to the back door of the restaurant, I force it open and usher everyone out into the service hallway, pulling it closed behind us. We don't need an audience for this.

I slam him against the wall. "Who did you sell her mate to?" I growl.

He opens his mouth, but only a pitiful whimper escapes him. I loosen my grip just enough to allow him to answer. His mandibles click frantically. "Please, Mosauran warrior. I beg you. Do not kill me."

"Tell us where we can find her mate. Now!"

His antennae shift forward, and he screeches in pain when I pull him up higher and then slam his back against the wall again with more force. He barely manages to speak. "Only if you agree to spare my life."

I narrow my eyes. "The punishment for your crime is death. I will only promise you a quick one if you tell me what I need to know. Otherwise, you will suffer before you die. I swear it to the Creator."

His large compound eyes seem to dim slightly as he lowers his head, accepting his fate. "I sold the Lacerta to an Anguis captain in Docking Bay 24. The ship is called the Kurmar."

I turn to Liana and Abby. "Wait here while I—"

"Look out!" Liana cries out.

I spin back to the Zovian as he slashes a laser blade at my torso. I drop him, raising my arm to shield myself from his attack, just as a bright arc of light zips past me, hitting him square in the chest. Bright orange goo explodes from the cracked shell of his torso. I look up in shock to find Liana still pointing the blaster at the Zovian's dead body, her eyes burning with anger. "You won't hurt anyone ever again, you disgusting piece of shtak."

I blink several times as I stare in awe at the hardened expressions on Abby and Liana. Terran females may be small, but what they lack in size, they make up for in their ferocity.

Abby lifts her gaze to me. "Please. We have to hurry and find Grex before it's too late."

I freeze. "Grex, the Lacerta, is your mate?"

Tears gather at the corners of her eyes. "Yes," she barely manages. "Please, we have to find him before they sell him to someone else."

Grex and I were once owned by the same master many cycles ago. We fought together, in pairs, many times in the arena. Like me, he never mated with any of the female "prizes" we were given because he was an honorable male—something I'd never before encountered among those of his race. My eyes drift down to her swollen abdomen. "You carry his child?"

She lowers her gaze to the floor as a tear slips down her cheek to her trembling jaw. "I...I was given to many gladiators against my will. I don't know if it's his."

All the color drains from Liana's face at her words, and I still. My hands curl into fists at my sides, angered by all the abuse Abby must have endured. I know what happens to slaves in the gladiator circuits. When I close my eyes, I can still hear the panicked cries of the females who were given to me as a prize for winning a fight. They were terrified that I'd force-mate them like so many others had done before me.

Liana's voice rips me from my dark memories. "I sent a message to Rowan and Tr'lani. They are on their way to get Abby."

Abby gives her an indignant look. "What? No! I'm going with you to find Grex."

"Neither of you are going with me," I interject. "You're both going back to the ship with my brother. I will find Grex and bring him back to you or die trying. I swear it to the Creator."

"No," Abby protests.

Liana looks down at the Terran female's swollen abdomen, heavy with child. "You have a baby to think of. You can't risk getting hurt or taken. Your mate wouldn't want you to endanger yourself like that."

Abby's eyes are bright with tears as she turns to me. "Bring him back to me. Please."

I open my mouth to answer, but Liana beats me to it. "We will do everything we can to get him back. I promise."

Placing my hands on her shoulders, I meet her gaze evenly. "You cannot go with me."

Her eyes burn with defiance. "I'm not leaving you, Soran. You need backup."

My nostrils flare. Why must she argue with me? "You're staying here." I point firmly to the floor for emphasis. "I will not risk you. If I fall, you could be taken again."

She tilts her chin up defiantly. "You're not going alone, and that's that."

My Ashaya is brave.

"I will not take you with—"

She puts her hand up to silence me. "We're not arguing about this, Soran. I don't care what you say, I'm going with you."

Brave *and* stubborn...unfortunately for me.

Drawing in a deep breath, I bite back my frustration. "Fine."

I tap a message out to Rowan, not bothering to wait for his response. As soon as my comm blinks to show that he's received it, I look up at Liana.

She puts a hand on Abby's shoulder. "Wait here. When you see a guy that looks like him"—she points to me—"and a woman who looks like a beautiful fairy princess, you'll know that's Rowan and Tr'lani."

Abby nods, and Liana turns back to me with a determined look. "Let's go."

## CHAPTER 22

SORAN

As we approach the ship, my eyes scan the area. I do not sense anyone nearby, but I could be wrong. I don't know what we're going to find here. This vessel could be crawling with slavers. I cannot bear the thought of Liana being captured again. Unable to quell the panic inside me, I spin to face her. "Why are you doing this? Why did you insist on coming? On placing yourself in danger?"

She lifts her gaze to mine, and despite the worry etched in her features, she stares at me as if my question is absurd. "Because I care about you, Soran. I was worried about you doing this alone. I've already lost too many people. I don't want to lose any more."

"You're worried about *me*?" I ask incredulously. "What about you? I love you, Liana, and I would sooner die than see you taken by slavers again. I am a warrior of Mosaura. I—"

She presses a finger to my lips, silencing me abruptly. Something— an emotion—flickers briefly across her expression, but it is gone too quickly for me to know what it was. Her gaze holds mine as she takes a small step toward me. Stretching up on her toes, she twines her arms around my neck. Her sea-green eyes search my own. "You love me?"

Wrapping my arms around her, I pull her close. Gently I rest my forehead against hers as I speak the truth deep in my soul. Taking her hand, I place her open palm against my chest. "I love you, Liana Garza of Terra. You are my heart."

I stare deep into her eyes, searching for any sign that she feels the same about me. Her gaze drifts down to my mouth. She leans forward and presses her soft lips to mine.

My heart pounds as she molds her perfect form against me. Her tongue darts out to trace along the seam of my lips, and I open my mouth to grant her entrance. Her taste is exquisite, and I groan low in my throat as her smooth tongue curls around my ridged one.

Completely lost in the sensation of her body against mine, I'm reluctant to pull away, but I know that we must. She whispers against my lips. "I love you too, Soran."

Happiness blooms in my chest. I gently skim the tip of my nose alongside hers as I breathe in her delicious scent, committing this moment to memory.

It takes all my strength to force myself to step back just enough to meet her eyes. We must get this done. Quickly. So that we may return to the glider that much sooner. "I will go in first."

Her eyes dart to the ship and then back to me. "I'll be right behind you."

Cautiously I make my way up the ship's ramp and knock loudly on the airlock door, hoping to gain their attention. An Anguis face appears in the small window only a moment later.

His dark yellow pupils expand and then contract into a thin vertical slit as he studies me warily through narrowed eyes. His voice is a muffled hiss as he speaks through the door. "What business do you have here, Mosauran warrior?"

"I'm interested in purchasing one of your gladiators."

He bares his fangs. "Your people do not deal in flesh."

This male is smart. He suspects my ruse for the trap that it is. I only hope the promise of credits will override his sense of caution. "I am not like most Mosaurans," I reassure him.

His gaze darts behind me, and I know the moment he spots Liana because his eyes go wide with a look I recognize well from my time as a slave. He wants her. Badly. He turns his attention back to me. "Is that one yours?" He motions to Liana, and I nod.

The airlock door slides open. The Anguis stands with his blaster pointed directly at me.

Although he tries to portray otherwise, his fear is evident in the slight trembling of his hand as he holds out his weapon. My nostrils flare as I scent the air that escapes his vessel. Four distinct scents, including his own, waft from the ship. All of them are male, and I dare not make a move against him until I know exactly what we're up against.

He stares at me warily before his eyes light up when they drift to Liana behind me. "How much for the V'loryn?"

Anger twists deep inside me. I palm the hilt of my knife, ready to activate the laser blade at a moment's notice. "She is not for sale. Now, how much for one of your gladiators? And how many do you have onboard?"

"I have three for you to choose from."

Relief floods my system. He is the only slaver on the ship; we will not have to fight our way through others.

His yellow eyes rake over Liana's form with a lust-filled gaze. "But I will trade you two of them for her."

He reaches forward to touch her, and I react instinctively. Lightning fast, I rip the blaster from his grip with one hand and slash his throat open with the other.

Obsidian blood gurgles from his throat, streaming down his front. His eyes meet mine in shock as he puts his hand to the deep cut as if to stem the bleeding of his mortal wound. His mouth opens, but only a choked sound escapes his lips before he sinks to his knees and collapses to the floor.

I turn back to Liana about to apologize for the gruesome display of violence but stop when I notice no sign of fear or disgust in her expression. Instead, her sharp gaze scans the door behind me. "Do you think there are more slavers on board?"

"No. I only scent him and the three gladiators."

Her eyes meet mine. "Good. Let's hurry."

As we head for the cargo area, I consider the other two slaves being held with Grex. I am hesitant to free any strangers. Especially gladiators. Many of them are lethal...dangerous, and I wonder what species the other two are.

When we enter the hold, Liana's expression betrays nothing of her fear, but my nose wrinkles at the acrid scent of it. She and Tr'lani were kept in a place like this for many solars, and I'm certain it calls forth dark memories. I wrap a possessive arm around her waist, both to comfort as well as keep her close to my side.

The stale smell of sweat and blood fills the air, growing more pungent as we move toward the cluster of rusted metal cages. Dim lights cast sinister shadows from the row of slave collars and sharp instruments made to torture and break that line the racks along the wall. A hint of death lingers here as well, and I shudder inwardly as dark memories swim to the surface of my thoughts. But I push them back down as we approach the cells.

Something moves in the shadows, and Liana tenses against me.

"Soran? Is that you?"

I smile when I recognize the voice of my friend. For so long, I believed he was dead. "Yes."

The shocked look on his face is quickly replaced with panic as his nostrils flare, no doubt scenting his mate on our clothing. "Where is Abby?" The concern is evident in his voice as his yellow, reptilian eyes scan the space behind us, as if expecting her to be there.

"She is safe. We came to free you, my friend."

"What about us?" A low and menacing voice draws my attention to the shadows of the other two cells.

Liana takes a curious step toward the nearest cage, searching for the owner of the disembodied voice.

I follow beside her with my hand lightly resting on her forearm, reluctant to break contact with her body and ready to pull her behind me at a moment's notice.

Two large, scaled hands with three claw-tipped fingers and a thumb wrap around the bars of the cage. Glowing lavender eyes stare at us, unblinking, with a predatory gaze. The click of its claws against the metal floor echoes loudly in the silence as it steps forward.

My protective instincts surge, and I pull Liana behind me as I glare unflinching at the Garkol.

Known throughout the quadrant as one of the most dangerous and lethal species, they are a race of formidable warriors. One of the few that is evenly matched to my own people. Their skin is the color of stone and almost as impenetrable. This makes them prizefighters in the arenas, for they are difficult to kill.

Large sweeping horns curl back from his head, making him appear even taller than he already is as he stands at full height, staring down at my Ashaya. The muscles of his square jaw tic slightly before he opens his mouth. "Will you free my brother," he darts a glance at the cell on the other side, "and I?"

Bravely, Liana steps forward. "We're here to free all of you."

A sinister grin spreads across the Garkol's face, revealing two sharp, elongated fangs. The other Garkol approaches the bars in the cage beside him, watching Liana with a curious and unnerving gaze.

Garkols almost always fight in pairs in the ring. The crowd pays more to witness the cruel but effective brutality they inflict upon their opponents.

I look down at my Ashaya. "They are too dangerous to be released. They are Garkols and might turn on us."

She gives me a disapproving look before walking toward the first one's cell. "I don't believe that anyone should ever be subjected to slavery, to be treated as if you were nothing."

The Garkol cocks his head to the side as he regards her, and I struggle to resist the urge to pull her back to my side.

She stares him directly in the eye. "Give me your word as a warrior that you will not harm us if we release you."

"My word?" A look of shock flitters briefly across his features. His nostrils flare. "I can scent your fear, and yet...you would take my word?"

She straightens her stance and tips up her chin, holding his gaze. "Yes. I met one of your females. We were both slaves. She was kind to me. She told me that your people are honorable, but no one believes it because of your"—her eyes travel over his large and imposing form —"appearance." She pauses. "I met a man whose appearance was so similar to my own people, and that alone would have made me inclined to trust him if I'd met him under any other circumstance. But he was crueler than I could have ever imagined."

My hands curl into fists at my side as she speaks of Talel.

She continues. "I understand now that appearances mean nothing. Now, give me your word, and we will release you."

To my great shock, he and his brother drop to one knee, bowing their heads before her. "You have our most solemn vow that we will not harm any of you if you free us."

"Good." She spins to face me and gives me a subtle nod.

Drawing in a deep breath, I clench my jaw and hesitantly press the release on the control panel. The sharp snap of the cells as they unlock fills the silence. Fierce protectiveness rushes through me, and I spread my wings to shield Liana behind me as the first Garkol steps from his cage.

With a threatening glare, he approaches. My muscles tense in response, ready to attack if I must. Grex stands by my side to face him —the two of us forming a protective barrier between the Garkols and my Ashaya. The other one moves to the left as if to flank us. My low growl of warning stops him abruptly.

The first one speaks, staring around me to Liana. His deep voice rumbles in his chest. "If ever we can repay this debt, we will. You have our vow as warriors of Garkolna."

Liana pushes between Grex and me to step forward, extending her hand in the greeting that is customary of her people. The Garkol's skin shimmers with color, from bright red to orange, and the venomous spines of his arms and tail slap against his skin as they retract before he slowly reaches out to her. I watch with great anxiety as his much larger hand swallows her own, and they perform the "Terran handshake," I believe she calls it.

He cocks his head to the side, and his sharp gaze travels over her form. "What are you?"

She smiles. "I'm Terran. My name is Liana. What's yours?"

He bows low before her. "I am Zuran, and this is my brother, Ulin. I have only seen a very few of your females in the slave circles. My brother and I helped free one not long ago." His gaze shifts to the other Garkol. "We were caught, but our brother, Orun, escaped with her. We received word that she is under the protection of our clan back home on Garkolna. No one will dare come for her there."

Liana's eyes widen in shock. "What did she look like? What was her name?"

"Amanda of House Knight."

She gasps, and tears brighten her eyes. "Amanda Knight? She's my best friend and the doctor on my ship. Was she—did she have a dog with her?"

"A...dog?"

"An animal...covered in golden fur, walks on four legs."

"I am sorry. I did not see any creature like that."

She looks down, nodding grimly before lifting her gaze back to him. "Please, give Amanda a message." Her voice is thick with emotions. "Tell her that Liana of...House Garza is so glad she's alive."

He crosses his arm to his chest. "I vow to deliver your message."

I place my hand on her shoulder. "We should go."

She looks to Zuran. "How will you get home?"

His expression softens at her concern. I did not know Garkols were capable of empathy. "Do not worry for us. We will find our way." He steps toward her and extends his hand again. "Only a few of my people have the gift of foresight. I am one of them. If you would permit me?"

Liana gives him a questioning look but offers him her hand once more. When he takes it, he closes his eyes, and his skin shimmers from orange to dark green and back again. "You will find your home and your family. You are one of the great Uniters foretold in the

Ancient Tomes of the Saraketh. You will bear four children, each of them as noble and brave as their mother."

His eyes flick up to meet mine for a moment before returning to hers. "And you are wrong, Liana Garza of Terra. You are braver than you know. Bravery is not courage in the absence of fear. Bravery is having courage despite your fear."

He and his brother bow low before her and step back. "I am honored that the Creator allowed us to meet. I know I will see you again."

Zuran and his brother exchange a knowing look, and then turn to us. "We will escort you. You will need our help to make it back to your ship."

# CHAPTER 23

SORAN

Z uran's words about us needing his help to get back to the ship are ominous, and my chest tightens with worry. I alert Rowan that we are returning with Grex and receive a message that our engines are already primed for FTL.

As we make our way to the glider, several people watch us warily. Two Garkols, a Mosauran, a Lacerta, and—as far as they believe—a V'loryn walking through the station together must be a strange and perhaps even a disturbing sight. My eyes sweep over the crowd of people, scanning for any possible threats.

Liana looks back to tell me something, but stops abruptly. All the color drains from her face as her gaze fixes on something over my shoulder.

She rushes toward me, and I turn my head, following her line of sight as she cries out. "No!" Grabbing my forearm with a strength I didn't know she possessed, she pulls me off balance just as two bright lights shoot past me, narrowly missing my chest.

The world shifts into slow motion as my eyes meet Talel's across the promenade. Flanked by several of his men, he fires again, and I cannot move fast enough as another blast races toward me. Raising my hand in futility, I cry out in panic as my Ashaya throws herself over my body to shield me with hers.

Just as the light is about to reach her, Ulin jumps in front of her, sacrificing himself and taking the full brunt of the blast. His back explodes in a mass of burned tissue, and he drops to the floor.

Zuran cries out and rushes to his brother.

Chaos erupts on the station as people panic, frantically running in every direction in their attempt to escape the blaster fire.

The mob blocks the path between the A'kai and us, giving us time to drag Ulin behind a nearby low wall.

Zuran rolls him onto his stomach, and Liana stares wide-eyed at the wound, the tissue already knitting together as it heals. She reaches out to touch the charred flesh and then looks to Zuran. "How is this possible?"

He darts a quick glance over the wall before answering. "Garkols are not easily killed." His eyes shift to mine. "Get back to your ship. You must hurry. We will hold them off."

Liana protests. "You have to come with us. We can't just leave you here."

His glowing lavender eyes meet hers evenly. "The Creator crossed our paths for a purpose. And I believe it was to help you escape."

She starts to protest, but he cuts her off abruptly. "I assure you. My brother and I will not die today. We will hold them back for as long as we can, but the three of you need to go. Now! Before it's too late!"

Scooping Liana up in my arms, Grex and I break into a run. Racing as fast as we can to the glider, I don't dare look back over my shoulder for fear that they follow us. Talel had at least a dozen A'kai Centurions, and I doubt we could take them all on if we had to.

Grex looks to me. "We're not going to make it. We need to hide."

He's right. Just up ahead, three A'kai round the corner, stopping us in our tracks. Before they can notice us, we turn down a side hallway.

I press my comm to alert Rowan there's danger. It's a system we've had since we were children. A flashing red light should blink in a preset pattern on his unit. He'll understand exactly what it means without me risking sending a message that I'm certain would be intercepted.

Weaving through a crowd of people, I curse myself for my care-lessness. I should have been more alert. I thought that since we were so close to Mosauran space, this station would be better protected, that they wouldn't allow A'kai scum in here. Guilt and shame wash through me at the knowledge that I've placed my Ashaya in danger. I should have insisted she stay on the ship.

Scanning the shops along the promenade, I search for a place to hide. A flash of gray skin catches my eye—another Mosauran—and I motion to Grex. "This way. Follow me!"

He nods, and we race to the shop. I slam the door shut behind us, and reflective green eyes snap up to meet mine in a questioning look.

I dip my chin in a quick nod of greeting. "Brother of Mosaura, may we shelter with you?"

His sharp brows crease in confusion as he looks to me, Liana, and Grex. Without saying a word, he motions for us to follow him to the back.

Shutting the door behind us, his eyes go wide as Liana removes the hood of her cloak. "My Prince," he says, having recognized me. "I'm surprised to see you travel with a V'loryn."

"She's not V'loryn." I meet his gaze evenly. "Please. I ask that you help my Ashaya return to our glider." The moment the word "Ashaya" escapes my lips, I curse myself for saying it aloud. I still haven't even explained it to her.

He visibly stiffens in surprise at my words. None of my people have ever bonded or found a fated mate outside of our race.

"She is your...Ashaya?"

"Yes."

Liana's eyes meet mine, a question behind their sea-green depths, but she doesn't speak it aloud.

He stares at her in wonder. "I did not know it was possible outside of our species."

"Can you help us get to our ship?" I cut him off, hoping he won't have any more questions.

He nods. "Of course."

~

After trying once again to contact Rowan and Tr'lani, I get no answer. I suspect Talel has somehow jammed station communications while he searches for us. Surely Rowan got my message and understands why we're not there. That he'll wait for us, I have no doubt, but I do not want him to worry.

Turning to Liana, I place my hands on her shoulders. "Do you remember the way back to the glider?"

"Yes."

"You must go. I will follow as soon as I can."

She shakes her head. "No. I won't leave you."

"You must."

"No."

I take both her hands in mine and lean forward to gently press my forehead to hers. Closing my eyes, I draw in a deep breath. "You have to. We are more likely to be caught if we travel together back to the ship." I open my eyes to find concerned-filled green ones staring deep into mine. "Please do not be so stubborn," I whisper. "You know I am right."

Grex and the Mosauran shopkeeper watch us closely, but I do my best to ignore their curious stares.

I wrap my arms tightly around her, running my hands over her long, silken hair as I hold her against my chest. "You are my heart, Liana. If you travel with me, they will find you for sure. They are looking for the two of us together." Placing two fingers beneath her chin, I tip her head up to mine. "Besides." I give her a teasing grin. "I am a big, strong Mosauran warrior. I will be fine."

Despite the worried look in her eyes, a nervous laugh escapes her. "I can't believe you're joking at a time like this."

I'm worried too, but I do my best to smile. I meet her eyes evenly. "You are as fierce as a Mosauran warrior, and I do not doubt your ability to make it back to the glider without difficulty. Trust that I am capable of the same, and we will be reunited shortly."

Her gaze holds mine as a small smile curves her mouth. Stretching up on her toes, she presses her soft lips to my own once more. She feels so perfect in my arms, I'm reluctant to release her.

She cups my cheek. "Be careful, my love."

"I will."

When she pulls away, I struggle against the want to gather her back in my arms. I don't want her to leave. She's so concerned for me when *she* is the one who is truly in danger. If she is caught... I shudder inwardly at the memory of her going still beneath Talel's hand as he violated her mind in the R'ugol.

The shopkeeper steps forward, holding out a cloak. "Wear this."

She drapes it around her shoulders, tying it firmly in place before pulling the hood over her head. She gives him a warm smile. "Thank you for your kindness. I will not forget it."

He bows low before her. "Ashaya are sacred in our culture—a blessing from the Creator. It is my honor to help you in any way I can."

Her gaze flicks to mine, and it is easy to read the question behind her eyes before she turns her attention back to him. "Thank you." Without another word, she exits the store, stepping out into the crowded plaza. I hold my breath until she disappears from view.

The shopkeeper wastes no time turning back to me. "Why do the A'kai hunt you? Is there unrest between our two races?"

Talel and his men pass in front of the store as I stare through the glass, my hands curling into fists at my side. My sharp claws dig into my palms, drawing blood as I struggle to contain my rage, resisting the urge to charge at them now. I want nothing more than to kill Talel for what he's done to Liana. "Her people—their blood is special," I explain. "The A'kai hunt her and her kind."

His eyes widen, and Grex stares at me in shock. "Then my mate is not safe either," he whispers, and I give him a grim nod.

My gaze returns to the plaza, the last spot I was able to still see her. At least, if Talel's here, he's not wherever she is by now, and I try to take comfort in that. Grex places a hand on my shoulder. "I didn't think I'd ever see you again. How did you find me?"

I relay the story to him and the shopkeeper; my eyes never leave the A'kai as I track their movements along the promenade.

It isn't long before Talel and his men move on. The plan was for Grex and me to remain here at least thirty minutes before making our way to the ship, but the wait is agonizing. With each second that ticks by, I worry that she's been caught.

Anger burns through my veins. I will kill them if they dare touch her.

Fear for my Ashaya makes me impatient, and I turn to Grex. "I don't want to wait any longer."

From his expression, I can tell we are of the same mind in this regard. "Agreed."

I look back at the shopkeeper. "Thank you for your help."

He bows low. "My family fought on the side of your House during the last Civil War. May the Creator guide and protect you."

"May the Creator guide and protect you as well," I reply solemnly.

Dipping my chin in a subtle nod to Grex, we carefully slip out of the shop and into the crowd.

The journey back to the glider is brief, as I don't have to hide my appearance. We Mosaurans and Lacerta all look alike to the A'kai. The one they're looking for is Liana. Not Grex and me.

As soon as we step onto the ship, I call out her name, but there is no answer. Rowan and Tr'lani rush to greet me.

I look to my brother. "Where is Liana?"

He gives me a confused look. "We thought she was with you."

Panic tightens my chest. "She should have been here by now. She left before we did."

Tr'lani pales as she stares over my shoulder at the door, despair easily read in her features.

My heart begins to race, and despite knowing it is foolish to search for her, everything inside me is urging me to go. I cannot stand the thought of her alone and in danger. Palming my blaster, I turn for the door. "I have to go back out there. I have to find her."

A heavy hand clamps down on my shoulder, stopping me in my tracks. I spin to face Rowan, roughly shoving him away. "Do not try to stop me!" I snap.

Grex steps directly in my path. "Just give her a moment. She may have taken a different route than we did."

Angry and impatient, I meet his gaze accusingly. "Would you wait if it were Abby?"

He opens his mouth as if to speak but quickly snaps it shut, confirming the answer to my question.

When I push him out of the way, he doesn't resist because if our roles were reversed, I know he'd do the same.

Slamming my hand to the control panel, the door slides open, and my breath catches in my throat when I find Liana standing on the other side.

Relief floods my system. I gather her into my arms and back us into the glider, quickly sealing the airlock shut behind us. Hugging her tight to my chest, I send a silent prayer of thanks to the Creator that she made it here safely.

I pull back, and my eyes rake over her form, appraising her for injury. "I was so scared something had happened to you. What took you so long?"

She removes the hood of her cloak and unfastens the clasp at her neck, allowing the thick material to slide back from her shoulders and drop to the floor.

I stare in shock at the obsidian blood that mars her clothing. Panic spikes through me before I realize it cannot be hers. Her people bleed red, not black.

Her eyes flick up to meet mine. "I'm fine. But I was almost caught. I killed one of Talel's men to get away."

My gaze travels over her form, and I place my hands on her shoulders, sliding them down her arms as if to reassure myself she is unharmed.

She continues. "The blast drew the attention of his fellow soldiers, and I had to take a longer route to get back here. The entire station is crawling with A'kai. We need to leave. Now."

Rowan's voice calls out behind us. "She's right. We should hurry."

We rush to the bridge, and Rowan slams into his chair. He's already punching our destination into the computer as Liana and I take our stations.

Rowan looks to me. "Take over weapons." His eyes dart to Liana. "You've got control of the ship. I'll double-check our coordinates."

Her jaw is set in determination as she focuses on the viewscreen. "I'm on it. I've got this. Everyone, hold on."

Effortlessly, she begins the engine startup sequence, her fingers deftly flying across the control panel. I'm glad she's such a skilled pilot. I doubt we'd be able to pull this off so quickly on our own.

Panic coils tight around my spine; I won't be able to relax until we've put some distance between the A'kai and us. The ship groans loudly as the docking clamps release. Liana maneuvers the glider away from the station, and I hold my breath while we wait to be cleared to spin up for FTL travel.

A Hawkan male appears in the viewscreen. He narrows his eyes as he looks to my Ashaya.

I go still. This is it. They've caught us.

Liana is frozen in her chair, staring at the screen. Her entire face goes pale; her hands grip the control panel so tightly her knuckles turn white.

"You are clear for FTL," the Hawkan male says, shutting off the display.

Without a word, she skillfully completes the sequence. Within seconds, the ship's engines launch into FTL travel, and the stars begin to blur outside the viewscreen.

As soon as Rowan confirms our course heading, Liana wastes no time activating the cloak and the autopilot before she turns to Tr'lani. I'd been so nervous, I wasn't even aware she was on the bridge with us. "Was the Healer able to do anything for your wings?"

Tr'lani's golden eyes dim slightly as she looks to her friend. "The Healer said they will have to be rebroken...and then perhaps they can be mended by the MRU. But she was uncertain it would work."

I notice the slight clench in my brother's jaw at her words. "There has to be another way," he says.

Tr'lani gives him a pained smile. "You were there, Rowan. You heard what she said just as well as I did."

He crosses his arms over his chest. "I don't believe it. You shouldn't have to go through all that pain again. We *will* find another way."

*We.* I look to him, and when his eyes meet mine, I know for certain. He has feelings for the Aerilon.

Liana puts a hand on her shoulder. "When we reach your people, they might know of another way to repair your wings. We can't give up hope."

Tr'lani's eyes are bright with tears as she nods in agreement. "You're right." She takes a deep breath and swallows thickly before lifting her gaze back to Liana. "I'm going to check on Abby. Would you like to come with me?"

"Yes."

# CHAPTER 24

LIANA

When we enter the med bay, Abby is lying on the bed with Grex seated in a chair beside her, holding her hand. Covered from head to toe in light-green scales, the scarred warrior looks so big and intimidating next to her smaller form. His long, tapered tail is curled around her baby bump as if cradling the child that she carries. Gently, he runs the claw-tipped fingers of his other hand through her long, blonde hair. He leans forward and brushes his lips across her forehead, whispering soothingly to his mate while Tr'lani picks up the scanner and waves it over her abdomen.

Tears stream down Abby's face while she waits for the results.

Soran and Rowan enter behind me, and I step closer to see if I can make out anything on Tr'lani's screen.

Grex whispers softly in her ear. "Please, Abby, do not be so distressed, my cherished one. What happened to you is not your fault. Even if the child is not mine, I will love it just as if it were because half of the child is you, my beloved."

I draw in a shaking breath as Tr'lani studies the scans. Without thinking, I take Soran's hand as we wait to hear what she's discovered about the baby.

Tr'lani lifts her gaze to Abby. "The tests are conclusive. Half of the baby's genetic material comes from Grex and the other half from you." She smiles brightly.

Abby puts her hand to her mouth as she cries tears of joy.

Grex pulls her into a tight embrace, and I'm so keyed up from everything that's happened, that a tear of happiness slips down my cheek before I quickly brush it away.

"Is the baby healthy?" Abby asks. "Can you tell if it's a boy or a girl?"

With a flick of her wrist, Tr'lani projects an image of the unborn child on a floating screen before us. She grins. "It's a girl."

My breath hitches in my throat, and I stare in awestruck wonder as the display shows what she'll look like as she gets older. She's beautiful. She has many of Grex's features, appearing more like a Lacerta than a Terran with her light-green scales and long tail.

But she lacks the sharp ridges that define his brows and cheeks, seeming to favor Abby's softer Terran facial features. She is also missing the sharp spikes that run from the top of his head and down his back and tail, having slightly rounded nubs instead. And where Grex is completely hairless, she has a full head of blonde hair and striking green Terran eyes, inherited from her mother, instead of the vertical slit pupils of a Lacerta.

Abby looks to Grex. "If we ever find my home world, I hope my parents are still alive to meet their granddaughter."

Confused, I ask. "Why are you worried they might not still be alive?"

She turns her attention to me. "When they brought me out of stasis two years ago, one of the Healers that scanned me...they somehow estimated that I'd been asleep in suspended animation for at least thirty to forty years before I was awakened. Maybe more."

My mouth drifts open in shock. "What? How? I don't understand." I go still as everything clicks into place. Cold fills me as her green eyes stare into mine, and I realize why she looks so familiar. My mind rebels against the idea even as I know, deep down, that it's true. "You're Abby Worthy, aren't you?"

"Yes."

I shake my head softly in disbelief. "No," I barely manage, "you can't be her."

"Liana, what's wrong?" Soran's voice is in my ear.

Tears gather at the corners of my eyes. My bottom lip quivers, and I clamp my hand over my mouth to stifle the pitiful sob that escapes me.

It takes me a moment to compose myself, and when I finally do, despite my best efforts, my voice quavers as my eyes travel over Abby's face. "I knew you looked familiar. You disappeared twenty years ago. I learned all about you and your crew in school when I was just a child. There are so many theories of what could have happened to your ship and now...I know."

Tears stream down her face. "My parents...do you know what happened to my parents?"

Swallowing against the lump in my throat, I force myself to continue. "Every year, they visit the launch site. All the families of your crew...they leave flowers in remembrance." My voice catches and I close my eyes, picturing my family, wondering if they do the same for me now. "They thought your shuttle had been destroyed because they never found any trace of it. If you were asleep for that long, how many years was I in stasis? How many years have passed on Terra since I was taken?"

All this time, I thought it had only been months that I've been gone. It could have actually been years...decades even. My entire family and everyone I love, could be dead.

Soran's voice pulls me from my despairing thoughts. "The Healers could have been wrong. They've never seen your species before. They may have misinterpreted their readings when they scanned Abby."

Tr'lani chimes in. "He's right. There's so much I don't understand about your anatomy. Your people are very close to V'loryns, but there are still many differences between you." She looks to Abby. "The fact that your people can procreate with other races is something I've never heard of any other species being capable of. Mixed-species pairings have never resulted in the natural creation of offspring. It has always been impossible...until now."

Grex nods. "That is why most of the races do not condone such pairings. They consider it unnatural. Many societies condemn them as Outcasts...my people included."

Tr'lani stares at the display, cocking her head to the side as she studies it. "According to these readings, Terran genetic material is highly adaptable." She looks to Abby. "Perhaps that's why you were able to conceive a child naturally with Grex."

Soran's expression is full of worry and he wraps a protective arm around me, pulling me close to his side. "If the other races discover this, Terrans will be in even more danger than they were before."

Grex gives him a grim nod. "He's right. Slaves that can be bred will fetch much more on the markets. Once other races find out about Terrans and the fact that they may be breeding compatible with other species..."

I turn to Abby. "How were you taken? Do you remember anything?"

She shakes her head. "I went into stasis on the *Intrepid* and woke up in a cage on an Anguis slave ship. I was alone; I don't know what happened to the rest of my crew."

~

**Soran**

As Abby and Liana discuss the similarities of the events surrounding their abductions, it conjures many painful memories for them both. Grex wraps a protective arm around his mate, and I do the same. Tr'lani eyes us discreetly, but it is Rowan's gaze that falls heaviest on me. I see the concern etched in his features. He doesn't want me to be Outcast any more than I do. But I love Liana. Even if she were not my Ashaya, I would love her still.

She is stronger than anyone I have ever met. It is well known that R'ugol breaks the mind as well as the body. That's why it is such an unspeakable crime...because the victim rarely, if ever, recovers. That she survived and still pushes forward speaks to a strength of will and determination I've never seen in anyone before. A smile tugs at my lips as I think of the fire behind her eyes when she is determined to do something. She is brave. And also very stubborn. Both excellent qualities in a female. If she chooses me and agrees to become my mate...I will give up everything for her.

Without warning, the ship's proximity sirens begin blaring.

Worried sea-green eyes find mine. "We have to get to the bridge!"

As we race through the corridor, Rowan pulls ahead of me. He's always been the faster of the two of us, and he slips through the bridge doors before Liana and I are even close to reaching them.

As soon as we enter, ice fills my veins. The large black hull of an A'kai cruiser dominates the viewscreen.

All the color drains from Liana's face. "Can they see us?"

Rowan shakes his head. "No."

Liana's fingers fly over her control panel as she checks the glider's systems. The scent of her fear is strong, but her stoic expression betrays nothing as she works at her station. My protective instincts surge, and I desperately wish I could gather her in my arms and reassure her that she is safe. The A'kai cannot see us while we are cloaked.

Silence fills the bridge as we watch the A'kai cruiser become smaller and smaller in the viewscreen. After what feels like an eternity but I'm certain was no more than half an hour, the ship disappears completely into the black void of space.

I reach across and take Liana's hand. She gives me a small smile, but the dark circles under her eyes tell me she's exhausted.

"You should rest," I whisper softly.

She shakes her head. "I'm not that tired, but I could definitely use a shower." She stands from her chair. "I'll be back in about twenty, and I was thinking...maybe we could talk then?"

I give her a quick nod before she turns and leaves the bridge.

As soon as the doors slide shut, Rowan looks to me. "Terrans must have an exceptionally heightened sense of smell. She bathes every day...sometimes even twice," he adds.

I turn my head, flaring my nostrils to scent myself.

He arches a questioning brow. "What are you doing?"

"Do I...smell bad to you?"

He wrinkles his nose. "Well, now that you mention it, you could definitely benefit from a shower."

Horrified, my mouth falls open. Oh, Creator. Terrans have sensitive noses, and if Rowan believes I smell, Liana definitely must have thought so as well. Anxiety ripples through me. "Do you think she noticed my odor?"

A smile tugs at his lips as barely restrained amusement dances behind his eyes.

"You maltak! I thought you were serious."

He doubles over with laughter.

"You think it is fun to tease me like this?" I ask incredulously, and his laughter grows even louder. "I am already nervous enough as it is...wondering if she will decide to claim me as hers."

His laughter dies, and his expression quickly sobers. "You have decided then?" he asks.

I meet his gaze evenly. "I love her, Rowan. I...do not wish to be without her."

He glares at me accusingly, but it is easy to see the hurt in his eyes. "And what about your family? What about me? You would give up everything? Become Outcast for her?"

I shake my head. "You know I don't want to lose you or our family. I do not want to become Outcast."

"Then, the answer is obvious," he snaps. "You cannot take her as your mate."

"It's not that simple."

"Yes, it is," he counters.

I give him a pointed look. "I've seen you with Tr'lani. You *know* it is not that simple."

With a slight clench of his jaw, he looks away but says nothing.

"What is your plan?" I press, knowing from his expression that I've hit a nerve. "You will just tell her goodbye once we reach her brother's ship? Never see her again?"

"She doesn't want me," he replies in a voice so low I almost miss it.

My head jerks back slightly in surprise. "She said that?"

He shakes his head. "She didn't have to. I overheard her brother mention a male that she was supposed to be joined to before she was taken. Apparently, he has waited for her return all this time."

"And she wants to be bonded to this other male?"

"I didn't ask...I couldn't bring myself to."

"Then, how do you know she still wants him?"

He gives me a defeated look. "I am Mosauran. Her people are handsome and they are known for their beauty." He gestures to himself. "I look nothing like the males of her species. Why would she desire me when it is clear—from the interested glances she received from nearly every Aerilon male that we passed on Telvo station—she could have any male she wants?"

I put my hand on his shoulder. "Why don't you speak with her? Tell her how you feel?"

He lifts his gaze to mine. "Because to pursue her, no matter how much I may wish to, would mean that I would become Outcast. I cannot betray our family when they need me." His eyes stare deep into mine. "Mother and Caryn need us, Soran. The Civil War may be over, but we both know how easily such truces are broken and the devastating consequences of lowering our guard."

His words strike a chord in my heart, and a hollow ache burns in the center of my chest at the memory of House Caladan's betrayal and the assassination of our father. "I don't want to lose you, Rowan. I don't want to become Outcast. But I love her. I cannot deny what I feel in here." I place my hand to my chest.

"It is the fate bond making you feel this way."

"No," I reply quickly. "At first, I thought so too. But now that I know her, I cannot imagine ever taking another as my mate. I would desire her as mine even without the pull of the bond. Mother will understand. I believe the Council will too."

He gives me a sad look. "I hope you are right."

I stand from my chair.

"Where are you going?"

"To shower so my beloved does not find my scent unappealing."

Crossing his arms over his chest, Rowan rolls his eyes. "I've never seen you preen as much as you have ever since Liana came onboard. If you continue to buff your scales every day instead of once a week as most normal people do," he teases, "eventually you'll begin glowing in the dark...possibly even blind everyone the moment the sun hits your scales as you step off the transport when we reach Mosaura."

I laugh. "Jealousy is a terrible thing, brother."

He rolls his eyes again, but I can see the smile that tugs at his lips.

# CHAPTER 25

SORAN

After a quick shower, I head straight for Liana's quarters, hoping she'll still be there.

When she opens the door, she greets me with a stunning smile. Stretching up on her toes, she wraps her arms around my neck and leans forward to press her soft lips to mine.

When she pulls back, I lift my hand to touch my mouth, still tingling from the intimate contact. "What is this called?"

A smile lights her face. "It's a kiss."

"Kiss." I repeat the word to store it in my memory.

She tilts her head to the side. "Your people do not kiss?"

I shake my head. "No."

She gives me a hesitant look. "Do you...like it?"

"Very much."

A beautiful smile curves her mouth. Slowly, she leans in to press her lips again to my own. It feels amazing—this Terran kiss.

Her lips are warm and softer than the finest silkara, and I'm already addicted to the taste of her mouth. Completely lost in this delicious sensation, my every nerve ending is on fire as she seals her mouth over my own. Her tongue finds mine, curling around it, and my mind...stops...functioning.

Delicate fingers dip beneath the hem of my shirt to knead and caress my chest, sending small ripples of pleasure down my spine.

Desire courses through me like fire as I wrap my arms around her, lifting her off the ground. She wraps her legs around my hips. The feel of her body against mine calls forth the instinct to claim her as I press her back against the wall.

My stav lengthens and extends, hard and erect, seeking the heat of her center. She inhales sharply when I roll my hips against hers, and the scent of her arousal grows stronger.

Primal instincts surge through me, and I run my hands through her hair. Gripping the long strands between my fingers, I tip her head back, revealing the elegant column of her neck. Skimming the tip of my nose along her delicate skin, the scent of her need is strong—a heady and delectable mix.

She desires me as much as I desire her. I only need for her to say the words—to declare shav-rhokan—to say she chooses me.

As she moves her hips against mine, my entire body trembles with need. I long more than anything to claim her as my mate. *"Choose me, Liana Garza of Terra. Choose me, and I will show you that I am worthy to be yours,"* my mind whispers to hers.

She recoils as if my touch were fire, pushing against my chest for me to back away.

Confused, I quickly lower her to her feet and step back to give her space.

Her eyes are wide with fear. Guilt and shame rush through me as I realize what I've done. "I'm sorry, Liana. I never meant to scare you."

She shakes her head softly. "You don't have to apologize. You didn't do anything wrong. It's just...after what happened with—" She stops just short of speaking Talel's wretched name.

Placing her hands on either side of my face, her sea-green eyes stare deep into mine. "I trust you; I know you would never hurt me, Soran."

Her gaze holds mine as I brush the hair back from her face before cupping her jaw. "You are my Ashaya. I would die before I would ever harm you. I swear it to the Creator."

"What is 'Ashaya'?" She stares up at me in confusion. "I don't know this word in your language, and my translator doesn't recognize it either."

Pulling her close, I gently rest my forehead to hers. "I have to tell you something."

A small line of worry creases her brow. "What is it?"

"I knew the moment I first saw you that you were mine. 'Ashaya' means—"

A loud explosion splits the air, rocking the ship to one side, and I barely manage to catch her in my arms before she falls.

She gives me a panicked look. "We have to get to the bridge."

We race down the hallway, and as soon as the bridge doors open, I see Grex with Abby, one arm wrapped protectively around his mate.

Tr'lani stands beside Rowan as his hands fly across the controls. "It's an A'kai Cruiser. They've found us."

"How?" I snap.

Rowan's eyes remain glued to his monitor. "I don't know, but that hit knocked out our cloak, and I can't get it back online." He slams his fist down on the panel in frustration. "Talel is on that ship. He's demanding our surrender."

Tr'lani is visibly shaking. All the color drains from my Ashaya's face, but from the slight clench of her jaw and the determination that burns in her eyes, she is every bit like a Mosauran warrior as she jumps into her chair and studies the viewscreen.

Rowan barely avoids another hit from their canons.

"Can we outrun them?" she asks.

Glancing at the display, I curse under my breath. "No."

"Their ship may be faster," she says, "but ours is much smaller, more easily maneuverable." Her eyes light up, and she points to the screen. "There! I'm taking us into that asteroid field."

In silent agreement, Rowan and I exchange a quick nod before I give Liana full control of the glider while Rowan, Grex, and I take the weapons controls.

"Go to the storage locker," she calls out to Tr'lani. "We each need a blaster."

Tr'lani quickly disappears down the hallway. The engines groan in protest as the ship rolls to the side, and Liana punches the accelerator controls, racing into the dangerous asteroid field.

My stomach lurches each time the glider makes a sudden turn, but the answering explosions—so close that they shake the entire vessel—are far more threatening than the floating debris that surrounds us.

Another blast rocks the ship, and the engines spin down with a high-pitched whine, followed by a deafening silence. My pulse pounds in my ears as the dark metallic hull of the A'kai cruiser fills the viewscreen.

Liana brings her fists down on the display in frustration. "That last hit took out our engines and weapons. We're running on emergency power only." She spins to face me. "I need to get to the engine room."

A shockwave ripples along the hull, and the sound of metal grating metal echoes loudly through the ship.

Ice fills my veins. "It's too late. They've already latched onto our airlock."

Rowan's wide eyes meet mine. "They mean to board us."

The scared whimper that escapes Abby makes my heart clench. Tears stream down her face as she trembles in Grex's arms.

Liana stands and takes Tr'lani's hand. She lifts a determined gaze to me and pulls the blaster from her hip. "We'll go down fighting if we must, but we won't be taken again."

Panic coils tight in my chest. I don't know how many A'kai there are, but I know that their cruisers carry too many for us to take on at once. I will die before I let them touch my Ashaya. I look to her and Rowan. "I'll set the ship to self-destruct. We can use the escape pods to get clear of the blast."

My gaze travels over everyone in the room, and it is clear from their expressions that we are all in agreement.

Quickly, I punch in the codes, setting the glider to a silent countdown. The A'kai and their ship will be blown apart before they even realize what's happening.

My pulse pounds in my ears as we race from the bridge to the escape pods. Alarms blare throughout the vessel as the airlock is forced open, followed immediately by shouts and heavy bootsteps that echo loudly down the hallway.

"We go in twos," Rowan whispers, ushering Grex and Abby into the first pod and Tr'lani into the second.

He turns back to me. "Brother, I—"

There is no time, and I wrap my arms around him in a firm embrace. "May the Creator be with you." Pulling back, I grip his shoulders and meet his eyes evenly. "We will find each other again, in this life or the next."

His gaze holds mine as he repeats the warrior's vow. "In this life or the next."

He steps into the pod with Tr'lani, and the door seals behind him as they strap in. With one last look at my brother and Grex, I give them each a firm nod before pressing the release to eject them into space, sending a silent prayer to the Creator to protect and preserve them.

I spin toward Liana to find her staring at the second seat of our pod with a worried expression.

She points to the red blinking light above the harness. "What does that mean?"

Despair fills me. "It must have been damaged when we were hit." I clench my jaw and look over my shoulder to the empty hallway. Bootsteps thump heavily against the metal floors as the A'kai storm through the ship, searching for us.

There are no more escape pods. This is intended to be a four-person glider. The extra pod was a redundant system in case of failures like this one. At least one harness still functions. Liana will survive, and that's all that matters now. "You must hurry," I tell her, motioning toward the entry hatch.

She shakes her head. "What about you?"

"The harness is damaged. I must stay behind."

She grabs my forearm, trying to pull me into the pod, but I don't budge. "You can't expect me to just leave you here, Soran!"

I place my hands on her shoulders, staring deep into her luminous green eyes before pulling her close to my chest. "There's no choice, Liana." Running my hand through her silken hair, I close my eyes and gently nuzzle the top of her head, inhaling deeply of her delicate scent, knowing it is the last time I will ever hold her. "I won't let you die."

She holds tightly to me. When she lifts her gaze to mine, her eyes are bright with tears. "I—I can't leave you here. I won't!"

Glancing over her shoulder, I watch the other two escape pods drift farther out into space. They will live, and now...I'm determined that my Ashaya will too.

"Go," I tell her, ushering her through the door.

Turning back to me with a speed I did not know she possessed, she stretches up on her toes and wraps her arms around my neck, pressing her soft lips to mine. I gasp in surprise at the sudden and unexpected contact, but my body instinctively responds to her touch.

Pulling her close as I claim her mouth, seconds pass like an eternity, and I'm reluctant to let her go. But I know I must. At least I'll die with the memory of her kiss burned into my mind.

When she finally pulls away, she stares up at me. "I'm sorry, Soran. I hope you can forgive me."

My brow furrows. "For wha—"

I stop short as she raises the blaster to my chest. A deafening sound splits the air. Sharp pain rips through me, knocking the breath from my lungs, and I fall back against the wall. Paralyzed by the stun setting, I slide helplessly to the floor.

*She shot me. I can't believe she shot me.*

She hooks her arms up under my shoulders, grunting in frustration as she tries to drag me to the pod. I'm too heavy; it won't work.

Loud voices cry out, and I know the A'kai are close. She's wasting time trying to save me. She'll die if she doesn't get far enough away before the ship explodes. Anger burns through me, but all I can manage is a low, rumbling growl in the back of my throat as she kneels beside me, pushing the full weight of her body against mine to roll me to the side just enough that she's able to pull my legs into the hatch.

"Don't you growl at me," she snaps. "You left me no choice." She moves to my back and grits her teeth, straining to push my upper half into the pod.

"Why"—she groans—"do you have to be"—she slams her body against my side—"so damn heavy."

I narrow my eyes. I swear to the Creator, if we live through this, we need to have a serious conversation about trust.

"Don't give me that look," she says. "I'm not leaving you behind, and that's that."

The A'kai voices grow louder, and my body trembles as I struggle to move.

She jumps in the pod and grabs my forearm, bracing her feet on the side wall. Her limbs shake as she struggles to pull me inside. After a moment, I finally tumble through the opening onto the floor. She scrambles out from under me and slams her hand on the hatch panel, sealing it shut just as two angry green faces appear in the window.

"Open this hatch! Now!" one of them cries out. "Lord Talel wants her alive!"

Haphazardly wrapping the harness straps around us both, Liana tucks her body close to mine and pulls the release.

With a loud rush of air, the pod violently ejects, spinning away from the ship.

Liana cries out as my body slams into hers, pinning her against the wall as we tumble away in the dark void of space. A blinding yellow-orange flash fills the viewscreen as the glider and the A'kai cruiser explode in a brilliant display of light.

Still paralyzed, I grit my teeth, waiting for the shock wave to hit us, unable to brace myself or Liana as it approaches. The wave crashes against the outer hull. The pod shudders turbulently, throwing us back against the metal bracing.

Liana's pained cry and the sudden silence that follows stops my heart as her body goes limp behind me.

Alarms blare through the speakers. My eyes dart to the computer readout. Our pod took heavy damage from the explosion; we won't last very long in space. I scan the screen as the nav control autopilot searches for the nearest habitable planet.

The computer locks on the closest rock, and I clench my jaw in frustration as information scrolls across the display. Freezing temperatures and conditions just barely suitable for habitation fill the screen. If we manage to somehow survive entering the atmosphere and landing, I don't know how long we can survive there. Terran physiology is not as resilient as V'loryns or Mosaurans—they are unable to regulate their body temperatures as effectively as most other species.

The hull groans loudly as rough turbulence shakes the pod. A wall of flame flares brightly outside the viewscreen as we begin our descent into the upper atmosphere. The computer flashes a warning of damage to structural integrity. Panic fills me as the interior begins to heat to near boiling temperatures. If we don't break through the atmosphere soon, we'll burn up before we even reach the planet's surface.

"Liana." I somehow manage to speak, but she doesn't answer. She remains completely still behind me, and I cannot move my paralyzed limbs to turn and check on her condition.

Staring transfixed at the viewscreen, the icy landscape races toward us. The hull scrapes the top of a snow-covered peak, and I squeeze my eyes shut, bracing for impact.

The pod shakes violently as we crash through the trees, rushing to the valley below. A deafening boom explodes throughout the cabin. I pitch forward, slamming against the wall as we hit the ground, and my vision goes dark.

# CHAPTER 26

LIANA

My head is pounding as my mind slowly trickles back into awareness. With a low groan, I twist onto my side and open my eyes to total darkness. I freeze.

*Oh God. Am I back in a cage?*

Shakily, I extend my hand, and my fingers graze the solid, metal floor beneath me. Memories rush back like a tide to the shore as panic skitters up my spine.

"Soran?"

He answers with a low moan, and relief floods my system. He's alive. I blink several times, trying to adjust my eyes to the darkness, but it's no use. I can't see anything. I reach up to trace my fingers over the harness, searching for the release. As soon as I find it, the restraints retract, and I fall forward.

Sharp pain stabs at my left side when I hit the floor. Each movement is agony as I drag myself across the cabin. Sweeping my hand out in front of me, I frantically push aside any fallen debris as I feel for Soran's body.

Another low groan fills the cabin.

"Soran?"

Extending my right arm toward the direction of the sound, my skin brushes across the smooth, warm scales of his forearm. I grip him tightly and move closer. Thankfully I don't feel any cuts or abrasions as I trace my fingers up to his shoulder and neck to touch his face. I run my hands over his skull and along the hard, bony V that spans the top of his head, skimming through his short dark hair to feel of his skull beneath. Finding no obvious injuries, I cup my palms to either side of his face, tilting it up to mine. I gently press my forehead to his.

"Soran?" Despite my attempt to keep my voice even, it quavers as his name leaves my lips. Closing my eyes, I send a silent prayer to whoever may be listening to please let him be all right.

He doesn't answer, but his warm breath fans across my face, and I take comfort in the knowledge that he's still breathing and alive. I skim my hands down his arms and neck, then down the hard planes of his chest and abdomen as I continue to check him for injuries.

A sudden puff of air blows through my hair, and I jerk my head up in surprise.

"Liana," he draws in a ragged breath, "are you all right?"

I'm so relieved he's talking that I struggle to blink back tears. "I'm fine. Are you?"

He shifts beside me and inhales sharply.

"What's wrong?"

"My right leg," he barely manages. "I think it's broken."

Swallowing down my panic, I quickly run my hands along his thigh and down to his lower leg, stopping when I feel the strange angle that I recognize shouldn't be there.

Carefully, I roll up his pants to expose his calf. He hisses in pain as my fingers trace lightly along the injury. "We'll have to set it with something."

"There's a bone mending device in the emergency bag."

His body shifts, and his breathing quickens as he struggles to sit up. "The med kit," he bites out, "should be in that compartment."

Confused, I blink several times as if that will somehow help me see in the dark.

"Can you not see?" An edge of panic bleeds into his tone.

A rush of air moves back and forth across my face, and I can only surmise that he's waving a hand in front of me to test my vision.

"Not in the dark like this."

He cups my chin and tips my head up slightly as if studying me, tucking a stray tendril of hair behind my ear with his other hand. "This is...normal for your species? This night blindness?"

I shrug. "That's a strange way to put it. But...yes."

"I knew you did not like the dark, but I didn't know you were unable to see in it."

"How well can Mosaurans see in the dark?"

"Almost as well as we can in the daylight."

Okay, so that would be a really helpful genetic trait to have right now. "Are there any emergency lights in the pod that I could use?" I ask, hopeful.

"No."

That makes sense. Why would a species that can see in the dark need flashlights? Great...just great.

A muffled grunt followed by a sharp hiss of pain tells me he's trying to get up again. "I think I can retrieve the med bag."

I stand. "No. Just direct me. Be my eyes. I'm not useless, Soran."

With a loud thud, he settles back on the metal floor. "All right," he reluctantly agrees. "Just keep walking straight. Three steps."

I nod and do as he says. "Now what?"

"Turn right and reach up."

I turn and reach up along the smooth wall until I feel an indentation. "Here?"

"Lift and pull on the handle," he instructs.

Standing on the tips of my toes, I brace one hand on the wall for leverage. I struggle to lift up before the small door finally swings out. I sweep my hand inside and bump against something immediately. My fingers brush against course fabric. I grasp it tightly. "Is this it?"

"Yes."

Cautiously, I slide the bag out and hold it to my chest as I retrace my steps back to Soran. He takes it from me. A rustling sound fills the cabin as he searches for the bone mending device.

I'm thankful we're alive, but angry at myself. Of all the things I learned about the glider, I should have familiarized myself with the emergency med kits. Any pilot worth their wings knows how important it is to be prepared. I can't believe I didn't think of this. And now, my ignorance could mean the difference between life and death out here. Wherever "here" is.

"Here it is," he says.

I nod even though I can't see what he's talking about and reach out my hand to take it from him. "You'll have to tell me what to do."

"I must wrap this around my leg," he explains as if I can actually see what he's doing. "It will inject a sedative before it starts to work. I should only be—" He stops. A short puff of air escapes his nostrils the way it does when he catches himself just before saying something he thinks will upset me.

"You should only be what?" I ask, encouraging him to continue.

"I'll be unconscious while it works because of the pain medication. Hopefully, it won't be more than a few hours." His warm hand gently takes mine as I stare unseeing into the darkness. "Please stay in the cabin until I'm awake again. It is completely dark out there. We're safe in here. We do not know what may be outside."

Fear skitters up my spine at the realization that he can see out the viewscreen of the pod, and it's so dark outside that it's pitch-black. What if we've landed on a planet of perpetual night? I struggle to push down the painful memories that surface and float to the front of my mind, of my time spent in the cages; kept in the total darkness.

Clenching my jaw, I shake my head to clear my thoughts. Soran needs me; I have to focus. "Okay," I reply, trying to keep my voice even despite my fear. Up to this point, I'd been so focused on him I hadn't even considered the possible dangers outside. But now that I have...my mind is imagining all sorts of horrors.

After a few moments that consist of him hissing and grunting in pain, followed by a few words that my translator doesn't quite pick up because I'm fairly certain they're Mosauran curse words, he takes my hand in his own and places it atop something cold and smooth like glass.

"Press here to activate the mender when I tell you, all right?"

"Okay."

Even with the chill in the cabin, a bead of sweat trickles down my spine as I wait for his signal.

"Liana?"

"Yes?"

"I'm going to kiss you."

Despite all my anxieties, a short puff of air escapes me as a small smile curves my mouth. His warm hand cups my cheek. He presses his lips to mine in a tender kiss. He pulls back just enough to skim his nose alongside mine as he whispers, "You are my heart."

"And you are mine," I reply softly.

He draws in a deep breath. "Now."

Pressing firmly against the glasslike surface, it vibrates softly as it turns on, filling the cabin with a low hum. Soran's body slumps beneath me, and I swallow down my panic.

"Soran?"

He doesn't answer, and my waiting begins.

# CHAPTER 27

LIANA

While he sleeps, I search the cabin, attempting to make a mental map of the space to familiarize myself with everything. In the same cabinet as the medical bag, I find a blanket and drag it back to Soran, covering him as the air inside the pod grows colder. If it's cool in here, I can only imagine how cold it must be outside.

An image of a winter wonderland fills my mind, but I quickly dismiss it. The nav computer picked this place because it was habitable. So, it can't be all that bad out there, right?

Okay. *One thing at a time, Liana.* A wistful smile tugs at the corner of my lips as I remember my father's words when he was teaching me how to fly. Tears sting my eyes, and I quickly blink them back. I'm not going to cry. Swallowing against the lump forming in my throat, I inhale deeply and breathe out through pursed lips to center myself as I mentally run through my checklist.

Every good pilot has a checklist for any number of situations. Whether it's for preflight, landing, course adjustment, or in this case, a crashed landing. My first priority is to make sure the transmitter is working. It's comforting to know that even an alien ship has one of these. Nobody wants to be stranded without any means of transmitting a distress signal for rescue.

Since I have no way of determining who might respond to our beacon, I'll have to wait to activate the transmitter until after Soran wakes up. We'll need to place it somewhere far enough away from the pod that nobody can find us without our knowing it, and yet close enough that we can see who responds before we approach them.

Because we don't know what's outside, and our vessel is intact, this will make a better shelter than anything we could construct ourselves. Once the transmitter is activated, hopefully it won't be too long until a nearby "friendly" ship detects us. I'd make an inventory of our supplies, but I still can't see anything. My blaster is tucked in my belt, and I run my hand over it for reassurance. If anything tries to get in here, I'll at least be prepared for that.

All that's left is to wait for Soran to wake up. I'm tired, and there's nothing else I can really do at this point. I lift the edge of the blanket and lie down beside him. He's so warm, it's not long before I succumb to the urge to nestle against his side, draping my arm across his chest. Resting my head on his shoulder, I listen to the even sound of his breathing. His exotic scent clings to his clothes. A pleasant yet masculine mixture of spice—I love how he smells. I smile to myself as I wonder if all his people have this scent or if it's specific to my big, strong Mosauran warrior. If I have to be stuck on a strange, alien planet, I'm glad, at least, it's with him.

As I lay here, my mind drifts to Tr'lani, Rowan, Grex, and Abby. I hope they're okay, wherever they are. Their pods left several minutes before mine and Soran's. Maybe they got picked up by a ship, and they're looking for us even now. The thought fills me with hope as I struggle to stay awake.

After what feels like an eternity, I finally close my eyes and allow myself to drift off. I'm sure Soran will wake me when he's up.

# CHAPTER 28

LIANA

My eyelids flutter open as a twinge of urgency in my lower abdomen startles me awake. Blinking several times, it takes my vision a moment to adjust to the low light coming in through the viewscreen. Soran's outline is just barely visible with his face turned to me.

I reach across and lightly touch his cheek. "Soran?" I whisper, but he doesn't stir.

The ambient hum of the bone mending device reminds me the machine is still working. The break must have been worse than he let on because, surely, it's been more than a few hours at this point.

I roll to the side, and the urgent discomfort of my body demanding that I relieve myself reminds me why I'm awake. Now that there's some light in the cabin, my eyes drift to the lever of the hatch door. Feeling again for the blaster at my belt, I stand and quietly pad across the floor.

Taking a deep breath, I activate the release mechanism. The metal groans loudly as I push the door open. I shiver against the sting of cold that assaults my skin as the outside air rushes into the cabin.

Poking my head out, goosebumps pebble my flesh as I take in the winter wonderland that surrounds us.

A dark gray and overcast sky looms overhead as a sharp wind howls around the pod, carrying small flurries of snow that dance wildly in the current. The ground is covered in a thick blanket of white. The cold air burns my lungs with each inhalation. Why couldn't we have landed on a tropical island instead? That would have been nice.

We've landed in the middle of a clearing surrounded by a heavily wooded area. Turning to look at the downed line of trees near the edge, I recognize the path of our descent. We're lucky to have survived this crash at all. Thankfully, our pod was able to land in one piece.

A sea of trees surrounds us. Towering up toward the clouds, they remind me of the extinct, majestic sequoias of Terra. Covered in red pine needle leaves, the trunks are varying shades of gray. They're so thick, the only thing I can really see beyond them are large imposing snow-covered mountains in the distance.

I went to Alaska once with my dad. We flew up there just after I qualified for my pilot's license. It was a celebratory flight; I'd always wanted to see the wild and untamed nature that everyone always raved about when they spoke of that part of the world. I remember how beautiful everything was. It was amazing, but terrifying as well.

Any pilot can tell you that there is no room for error when flying through those mountains. Even one mistake can be catastrophic—the sharp edge that exists between life and death. That knowledge alone lent a breath of thrill and adventure to the trip. To be in the midst of nature at its most raw...to recognize and accept that there are forces much stronger than anything created by Terrans was both a humbling and exhilarating experience.

This place reminds me of that. We can survive here, but it is not going to be easy.

I scan the terrain for any hidden dangers, including wildlife. I don't see any alien animals nearby, so I cautiously step out of the pod and gently close the door behind me. I don't want to risk anything going in to find Soran while he's asleep.

After finding a nice spot just a few meters from the door and away from the pod's viewscreen, I quickly relieve myself and then go about studying our surroundings. A glowing pair of yellow eyes catch my attention, and I freeze. My heart begins to thunder as the menacing gaze holds mine a beat before disappearing back into the forest. Whatever that was, it had the eyes of a predator. I can only hope it was just curious about us and has decided to move on.

Turning, I look again at the several downed trees from our crash. From the scattered and splintered wood, I could probably build a fire, but I worry that would only draw unwanted attention. I can't risk it while Soran's still so vulnerable.

When I go back to the ship to open the hatch, I'm struck by how close the door is to the ground now. I'm certain it wasn't like this before. In fact, I remember practically having to climb out, and now I can easily just step inside.

Kicking aside a patch of loose snow next to the hull, my mouth falls open when I notice a fine web of fissures splintering across a layer of ice beneath my feet.

My heart stops. We've landed on an iced-over lake.

That explains the clearing.

Cautiously, I open the door, and a series of sharp cracks slice through the howling wind; the hatch lever drops another couple of centimeters as the pod sinks farther into the icy water below.

Fear coils tight in my chest. I have to get Soran out. Now! I can't wait for him to wake up.

I rush back inside, crying out his name. "Soran! Soran, wake up!"

He doesn't move, and he doesn't respond. The bone mending machine continues to hum, and I curse under my breath. I drop to my knees behind him and bend down to wrap my arms up under his shoulders. Standing, I lift and pull with all my might, barely managing to move him a few centimeters if even that.

Frantic, my breath comes in short, clipped pants as panic threatens to overwhelm me.

Taking a deep breath, I close my eyes and concentrate on my

breathing...just like my father taught me. "*One step at a time, Liana,*" his voice echoes in my mind. I can do this. I just have to focus.

Opening my eyes, I scan the room for something, anything that might help me to move him. My gaze falls on the blanket covering his body. Kneeling next to his sleeping form, I pull off the blanket and roll it, laying it along the length of the opposite side of him. Placing one hand on his shoulder and the other on his hip, I groan in frustration as I try to maneuver him onto his side, but he's too heavy. Working quickly, I shove as much of the material under his body as I can. I move to his other side and barely manage to pull it underneath him the rest of the way until his entire form is on top of the blanket.

Moving to his head, I gather the top corners of the fabric in each hand and stand, pulling him across the floor. He's still heavy, but this makes it so much easier to move him, and he practically glides over the smooth metal until we reach the hatch. Now, I just have to figure out how to get him up over the step.

Straddling his abdomen, I curl my arms up under his shoulders, lifting him into a sitting position. I brace the med bag behind his back to keep him upright as I move back behind him. Grabbing his arms again, I step outside the ship and pull. Every muscle screams in protest, but I somehow manage to drag him through the opening. Once his upper body is on the ground, I grab the blanket again to pull him the rest of the way out. It's much harder to slide him over the ice and snow, but at least it's doable. I drag him far enough away from the pod that I don't have to worry about him sinking with it if it goes down.

I scan the forest, checking for any other watching eyes before darting back into the ship and quickly throwing out all the supplies. A low groan echoes along the hull as the ice shifts around the vessel.

Searching for anything else of value, a green blinking light on the display reminds me I haven't detached the transmitter. Without that, no one will ever find us.

I grip the control panel firmly to pry it off, but it won't budge. Clawing at the casing, I dig my nails into the seal and grit my teeth as

I force it open. It peels back just enough that I can reach my hand in while holding the warped metal open with the other.

The pod drops suddenly, and I lose my grip, trapping my hand in the casing. A pained cry escapes my lips as sharp metal slices the top of my forearm just above my wrist. Icy water slowly pours in through the open hatch.

Despite my anxiety, I push down my fear. My father warned me that people die when they allow panic to overwhelm them. It clouds their thoughts so much they can't concentrate on doing the things they need to ensure their survival. *One thing at a time, Liana. One thing at a time.*

I reach inside the panel and grip the transmitter, forcing it loose from the connectors. Grasping the metal casing with my other hand, I hold it open as much as I can while I wrap my fingers around the device firmly. I've got to do this, no matter how bad it hurts. I have to pull it free, or else we'll never get off this frozen rock.

More water rushes into the pod, so cold it's like a million tiny needles stinging my skin, numbing my legs from my calves to my feet. Panting heavily, I steel myself and begin to count.

*One. Two. Three.*

Jerking my arm, I rip the transmitter from the casing and scream as the warped metal slices my skin. Blood pours from my wound and drips into the water below. The freezing air offers a temporary reprieve from the pain as I hold tightly to my hard-earned prize. I look down at the ice water filling the pod. My legs feel heavy and numb, but I push myself to move.

Sloshing through the cabin to the open hatch, I slide the transmitter toward Soran. If I don't get far enough away from the pod before it sinks, at least he'll have it when he wakes up. Water pours inside the vessel as I grip the edge of the ice and pull myself up and over until I'm free of the opening.

Frozen and shaking, each inhalation of cold air stabs at my chest as it fills my lungs. I dig my nails into the ice and drag myself forward. The urge to curl into a ball and allow darkness to take me is so tempting, but the memory of predatory yellow eyes flash through my mind, and I force myself to keep going. I have to protect Soran. He's still unconscious, and he'd be easy prey for whatever is lurking in the forest.

When I finally reach him, I wrap my arms around his body just as a loud bubble erupts near the side of the pod. My jaw drops as the top of the vessel bobs up and down a moment before the water boils with activity, swallowing the entrance completely. As it sinks from view, I turn back to Soran and hug him tightly to me. That could have so easily taken us with it.

Although I'm cold, I'm grateful for our Mosauran attire. Already the strange, resilient fabric is dry despite being wet only moments ago.

Two sets of large menacing yellow eyes appear in the forest, and ice-cold fear floods my veins. Gathering my strength, I manage to stand and position myself in front of Soran. If they think he'll be an easy meal, they're gravely mistaken. I feel for the blaster tied to my waist and grip the handle for good measure, ready to blast anything that tries to charge us.

After a rather tense couple of minutes, the glowing eyes disappear from view, and I drop my gaze to Soran's unconscious form again. "Don't worry, I've got this," I whisper, placing a quick kiss to his forehead. "I'll keep you safe."

I dig through the med bag, searching for something to treat my injured hand. I don't know what half of this stuff is in here, but I manage to find a bandage. Gritting my teeth, I wrap it tightly around my injury to stop the bleeding.

Running my fingers roughly through my hair, I twist it back and tie it into a loose knot to keep it out of my face. Now, I just have to find some shelter. I turn back to Soran, his eyes still closed.

"Lucky for us," I tell him, "my dad loved to camp. He taught me and my sister how to survive in the wilderness."

I'm silent a moment, searching for any sign that he's heard me, but he remains unmoving. A short puff of air escapes my nostrils, and a small smile forms on my lips. We're alive, and we have hope. "Well, we'll just pretend we're camping, all right?"

I roll my eyes when I realize I'm still expecting him to answer.

My sister Angela would laugh if she were here. She always used to make fun of me for talking to myself. I can't help it. It's one of my coping mechanisms for dealing with a stressful situation—talking myself through it.

Shaking my head, I look down at Soran. I still have to figure out how to get him and our supplies away from here. There has to be something I can use to move him off the ice. We can't stay here; we need to find another shelter before nightfall, and I'm certainly not going to leave him alone while I search for one.

My gaze drifts to the fallen trees and the long, broken branches scattered nearby from our crash. I pick out two of the straightest ones I can find and lay them out beside him. My left hand throbs in agonizing pain, but I do my best to ignore it as I tie the four corners of the blankets to the two solid pieces of wood and pile our supplies near his feet, atop the fabric. Moving around to his head, I grip the top of the limbs, one in either hand, grit my teeth, and stand. I lift Soran so that his upper body is partially suspended while the bottom of the long branches drag along the ground—forming a makeshift sled of sorts.

He's really heavy, but it's not impossible to move him this way. I'm definitely going to pay for this later though. My muscles haven't had a workout like this in a long time, if ever.

I scan the alien landscape before me. The closest mountain formation is straight ahead, and if the mountains here are anything like the ones on Terra, chances are I can find some sort of cave we can shelter in. It doesn't look far, but I know looks can be deceiving.

Giving myself a quick pep talk, I head for the base of the mountain. I can do this. I just need to find somewhere to shelter for the night, and we'll figure out the rest from there.

My dad not only made sure I knew how to survive in the wilderness, he taught me how to fly before I could even drive. To be a good pilot, you have to be able to adapt to new situations—to keep your mind focused even when everything else is chaos all around you. I glance over my shoulder at Soran's unconscious form.

"Lucky for us, I'm a damn good pilot," I tell him. "Don't worry. We're going to be okay. I've got this."

He doesn't answer, of course. But he doesn't have to. Just knowing that he's here is enough. He's alive and we survived. I didn't make it this far to die on some frozen wasteland of a planet. We're going to make it through this.

The cold wind stings my exposed face and whips around my body, but I've been through worse. I survived all the terrible things my masters did to me, and I'm not going to die here. I'll find Terra, and I *will* see my family again. As Soran would say, "I swear it to the Creator."

When we enter the forest, the canopy is so thick that what little light we have from the gray sky overhead barely penetrates through the trees. It's so cold the breath puffs from my lungs like smoke with each exhalation.

I keep my eyes trained on the woods around us. This planet is harsh and unforgiving, and I cannot afford to let down my guard. Soran's counting on me.

My arms and legs burn with effort as I pull him and our supplies steadily over the snow-covered terrain. Sweat dampens my hair and trickles down my back, chilling the clothing against my skin. I'm so tired, I want to collapse. And I'm tempted to rest, but I know if I stop now, I'll never get going again.

Concentrating on putting one foot in front of the other, it feels like I've been walking for hours. I'm thankful for all the sparring practice sessions I've had with Soran on the glider. If this had happened right after Tr'lani and I were freed, my muscles would be nowhere near as strong as they are now.

As we approach the base of the mountain, the forest begins to thin. Light filters through the trees, casting a warm reddish glow on the ground around us from the red leaves as the sun rises higher in the sky.

My body is aching, and I'm on the verge of collapse, but we're almost there, and I refuse to quit now.

As we draw closer, I notice the yawning mouth of a cave carved into the side of the rock base, and a smile tugs at my lips. I glance over my shoulder at Soran, still asleep. "You see that?" I jerk my chin toward the cavern. "I think we've found shelter."

I drag him behind a large boulder near the opening and carefully lower him to the ground. Kneeling beside him, I place my hand atop his.

His head turns toward me, and even though his eyes remain closed, just that small sign that he's aware of my presence brings a smile to my face. "Here's the plan," I tell him, hoping he can somehow hear me. "We can't risk just blindly walking in there. I'm sure we're not the first ones here to seek shelter in this cave. I'm going to have to go check it out. But first"—I study our surroundings—"I'm going to have to have some light."

This is an ice planet, and I'm hoping that a fire is a universal deterrent to anything unfriendly. Grabbing a small limb from the closest tree, about as long as my arm and less than half the width of my wrist, I snap it from the trunk. A sap-like substance oozes from the exposed end. On Terra, pine sap is extremely flammable. Maybe this stuff is too.

When Soran was teaching me how to use the blaster, I remember one of the targets caught fire after I hit it with the highest setting.

Gathering a few smaller branches, some twigs, and dead leaves, I pile them together and then clear the ground around it. I don't want to catch the entire forest on fire when I try this.

Turning up the blaster to the kill setting, I carefully aim for the direct center of the pile and press the trigger. After a moment, a wisp of smoke rises up but disappears almost instantly. I place my hand over the spot. It's warm but not hot enough to catch fire. Disappointment rushes through me. I need something more flammable to use as tinder.

A cool breeze whips through the forest; a wisp of hair tickles my nose, and a wide grin spreads across my face. Plucking several hairs from my head, I nest them in with the twigs and leaves. Aiming the blaster again, I focus on the center, and sure enough, my hair ignites, creating a small flame that quickly turns into a fire.

Suppressing the urge to jump up and down with joy, I focus on the task at hand. Removing my bra, I grab my torch limb and reluctantly wrap the material around the end. It's the only piece of clothing I could bear to part with. I can't afford to lose anything else. It's too cold on this planet.

Before I light my new torch, I drag Soran closer to the fire, hoping that will be enough to keep any predators away. I lean down and press a quick kiss to his cheek, watching a moment to see if he'll awaken.

When he doesn't, I take his hand and give it a gentle squeeze. "I'll be right back, okay? I have you near the fire so that nothing will bother you while I make sure the cave is clear."

Tears sting my eyes, but I blink them back. He's so strong, but right now, he looks so vulnerable it breaks my heart. I'm so afraid to leave him here alone, even for a moment. But I have to. I can't risk taking him into the cave without making sure it's safe first. Swallowing against the lump forming in my throat, I press my forehead gently to his.

"Don't go anywhere, okay," I whisper. "I'll be right back. I promise. I love you."

Sticking the end of the limb into the fire, it catches quickly, and I move to the entrance of the cave. Torch in one hand and blaster set to kill in the other, I cautiously walk inside. It's much deeper than I thought, and the ceiling is high enough that Soran shouldn't have any problems standing in here. Silver metallic ore lines the walls, shimmering as they reflect the flame. The sound of dripping water is music to my ears. I'm so thirsty, I could drink a gallon right now. Hopeful, I head toward the sound, and my eyes light up when I find two small pools at the back of the cave.

A low hiss stops me short, and I freeze in place when I notice something that looks like a cross between a rabbit and a porcupine the size of a Labrador backed against the wall. This creature is something straight out of a nightmare. Large, blood-red eyes stare at me menacingly as it bares huge razor-sharp teeth, dripping with saliva. Long, sharp quills quiver and extend straight out from its back as it growls low in warning.

Slowly stepping back, I move to put some distance between us. "Good rabbupine," I say in a soft and friendly voice as if I'm talking to some kind of cuddly creature instead of this monstrosity. "I'm not here to hurt you. I just need somewhere to shelter for the night. You feel like sharing this cave? Maybe?" I keep speaking as I ease my way backward.

The hairs rise on the back of my neck, and I still as another low hiss sounds over my shoulder. Fear skitters up my spine. I don't have to look to know there's another one directly behind me. Cautiously turning so that I can look back and forth between the two, I hold out the blaster to one and the torch to the other. The one on my left snarls and gnashes its terrifyingly large teeth as it stalks toward me.

I lower the torch to place the flame directly between us. It hisses low in displeasure, and out of the corner of my eye, I see the one on my right advancing on me.

With my best attempt at a threatening growl, I take a chance and lower my head to lock eyes with it. Instead of causing it to back down, this only makes it more aggressive. Its body bristles with anger.

A sharp sound slices the air, and I turn just in time to avoid a quill as it shoots past me, barely missing my thigh. Acting on instinct, I throw the torch at one and fire the blaster at the other. The walls echo loudly with their screeching cries as they race past me out of the cave. I rush to the entrance, and watch as one collapses, dead, while the other runs in the opposite direction of Soran, disappearing into the forest.

Eager to get him under shelter, I grip the top end of his sled. With a loud groan of effort, I somehow manage to lift it despite my exhaustion and drag him into the cave.

I'm so tired, I can barely move, but I force myself to go back out to the woods. Gathering more fallen twigs and branches, I stack them together at the entrance just inside the cave and make a new fire using the flame from the first one.

As soon as I'm satisfied that it has plenty of fuel to burn for at least a few hours, I collapse next to Soran. My left hand feels numb except for a dull throbbing sensation, and the bandage is almost completely soaked through with blood. Breathing heavily, I roll to my side and place my other hand over his chest, feeling his heart beat reassuringly beneath my palm. I lean forward and place a gentle kiss to his cheek.

"I hope you wake up soon," I whisper. "I miss those gorgeous silver eyes and the sound of your voice."

# CHAPTER 29

LIANA

As if on cue, his eyelids flutter and open. His reflective gaze stares up into mine, and a smile crests his lips. I pepper his face with kisses. "Thank God you're awake!"

He smiles back, but his expression quickly morphs into confusion as he notices our new surroundings. "Where are we?"

I relay the entire story to him.

When I'm finished, his brows shoot up to his forehead in shock. "You dragged me all the way here?"

"Yes."

His jaw drops a moment before he quickly snaps it shut. "But I am at least two times heavier than you and much taller. How did you manage this?"

"It's simple physics. The angle of the sled, the distribution of your weight. It was hard, but"—I sweep my arm around the cave for emphasis—"not impossible."

He frowns as he reaches up to touch his lips a moment before staring at me accusingly. "You *kissed* me." He narrows his eyes. "And then you *shot* me."

I give him an incredulous look. "Are you really mad about that? I couldn't just leave you behind. I had to distract you so I could save you."

His lips form a tight thin line. "We need to have a discussion about trust."

Exasperated, I roll my eyes. "Well, that's just going to have to wait. I'm too exhausted to talk about it right now. We need to gather more wood for the fire, or those rabbupines or something even worse are going to come back."

Lifting the rabbupine quill to his nose, his nostrils flare as he scents the sharp tip. "Poison," he growls low in his throat. "These creatures are dangerous." He turns back to the cave entrance and surveys the landscape outside as if searching for any new threats. "I will kill anything that tries to harm you. I swear it to the Creator."

Well, he must not be *that* mad about me shooting him to say something like that. And something about his declaration makes my heart swell as his silver eyes rake over my form.

His expression morphs into concern, and he reaches for my injured hand. "You're bleeding. What happened?"

"When I pulled the transmitter out of the casing, my hand got caught."

"Why didn't you mention your injury before now? It needs tending."

Practically frantic, he rifles through the med bag. After a moment, he pulls out a small tube and reaches for my hand. Carefully, he unwraps the bandage, and I inhale sharply when it tugs at my flesh as he removes it. Sharp pain shoots through the site as fresh blood pools over the wound. Tears spring to my eyes, but I manage to hold them back.

His nostrils flare as he studies the shredded skin. "How did you drag me all that way with this injury?"

"I didn't have a choice. I wasn't going to leave you behind."

His eyes meet mine, his expression a strange mixture of tenderness and guilt. "I'm sorry. This will sting, my beloved, but only for a moment."

I draw in a deep breath, bracing for the pain. "I'm ready."

Soran squeezes the thick, clear gel-like substance from the tube, and places it on two of his fingers. Gripping my forearm firmly to hold me in place, he rubs the gel over my wound with his other hand. The moment it touches my skin, intense pain sears along every nerve ending of my injury. I cry out, struggling to pull away from his grasp. Dark memories of the Zovians cutting deep into my flesh fill my mind.

Desperate to escape the burning sensation, I reach up to wipe it away with my free hand, but he catches my wrist and pulls me to his body to keep me still. "You have to let it work."

I writhe in agony against his hold, but he doesn't budge. In the small part of my mind that's still functioning, I realize now just how much of his strength he's held back when we're training.

After what feels like an eternity, the burning subsides, and he releases his grip. Trembling with the echoes of remembered pain, I look down at my hand, and my jaw drops when I notice the perfect skin. Not a single mark remains.

Tenderly, he brushes the hair back from my face and cups my cheek. "Are you all right?"

"Yes, but...why did that hurt so much?"

"It's a rapid tissue regenerator," he says, as if that explains everything.

I glance down at my hand again, flexing it experimentally to make sure it's still okay. Cold wind whips through the cave, and I immediately revert back to survival mode. I meet his eyes evenly. "Tomorrow, we need to find somewhere to set up the transmitter. We'll rest tonight, but we need to make sure to keep the fire going."

He nods. "It is a good plan. I will gather more wood." Without another word, he strides to the entrance, and I stare up at him, my mouth gaping.

He gives me a confused look. "What is wrong?"

"It's just...your leg was broken. Badly. And I still can hardly believe you're up and walking like nothing. It doesn't hurt?"

He arches a brow. "How primitive is your world that you are so shocked by the basic medical technology of an emergency supply bag?"

Instantly offended, I glare up at him and open my mouth to argue but quickly snap it shut when I notice the teasing smirk on his lips. I narrow my eyes as I try, but fail, to suppress a smile. "You love teasing me, don't you?"

He grins.

I hate to admit it, but these "basic medical technologies" are pretty advanced compared to what we have back on Terra.

He turns his gaze back out to the surrounding forest. "I will scout the area to check for any hidden dangers and gather more wood."

"Wait!"

Stopping abruptly, he spins to face me, tilting his head to the side in a questioning look. "What is wrong?"

"We don't know what all may be out there. What if you get hurt?"

A devastating smile curves his mouth. "I promise you, Liana, nothing will try to harm me now that I am awake." He flexes his impressive biceps and puffs his chest out exaggeratively before giving me a wide grin. "I am a big, strong Mosauran warrior."

I suppress the urge to roll my eyes even as a smile twists my lips. Rowan's right. I've created a monster. He's never going to let that one go.

"All right," I concede. "Just be careful, okay?"

He laughs softly as he steps out into the snowy landscape.

While he's outside looking around, I take stock of our inventory and walk to the back of the cave to check out the pools I'd been meaning to investigate before the rabbupines made their presence known.

Side by side, the smaller one is slightly elevated compared to the other. Water trickles from the ceiling, feeding into it first, and then flows in a steady stream to fill the larger one below it. This is good. It means we can bathe in one without contaminating the other to use for drinking water. If it's safe, that is.

Staring at the water, I'm surprised to notice a fine mist of steam rising from the surface. Curious, I kneel and place my open palm to the floor near the pools and smile as the subtle heat radiating from the stone warms my hand.

My gaze turns to the larger pool. Big enough to fit at least four people and shallow enough that I can see straight to the bottom. Oh my God. I'd love to strip right this second and wade in. But I really don't want to be naked and exposed if those rabbupines decide to come back.

When Soran returns, he piles the wood at the entrance to the cave. Feeding some of the new fuel into the fire, it's not long before it turns into a roaring flame. Exhaustion hits me like a giant wave, and I yawn, unable to ignore my tired and aching muscles any longer.

"You should rest."

My gaze drifts longingly toward the two pools. "I'd really love to have a bath first. Is there anything in the emergency kit that can check the water to make sure it's safe for bathing and drinking?"

He nods and begins to search the bag. After a moment, he returns with a device that looks like a ruler. Dipping it into the water, a floating display pops up from the top of the instrument. With a thoughtful expression, he studies the series of symbols before him.

"Here"—he points to the first glyph—"is the universal symbol for safety. Memorize it, and I will teach you the rest."

**Soran**

We are fortunate to have a readily available water supply. My nostrils flare as I detect the lingering scent of many creatures. I suspect they must visit this cave regularly for this reason. I will have to be extra vigilant for any unwanted visitors. "I will keep watch while you bathe. Nothing will disturb you. I swear it to the Creator."

She smiles, and a pink bloom spreads across her cheeks before she moves behind a large boulder to undress. My Ashaya is very shy about her body. I don't understand this. Is she worried I will find her strange? Or is it that she's been so abused, she still has lingering fears?

I hear her quietly undressing behind me. In this modesty she has, her species is much like the V'loryns. They are very private about their bodies. When my people shift back from draken form, we are completely nude because our clothing cannot shift with us. So, our society has learned to be more accepting of nudity than hers, apparently.

A small splash tells me she's entered the water, and when a sigh of contentment escapes her, it's the sweetest and most enticing sound I've ever heard. I clench my jaw in frustration as need burns through me. Gritting my teeth, I shake my head. She is exhausted and does not want my touch right now. If she did, she would initiate contact like she did in her quarters.

I force my attention to the fire, adding more wood to ensure it burns for several more hours. Night is falling, and already the wind has picked up and the air grows colder.

When she emerges from the pool, she wraps herself in one of the emergency blankets and comes to sit by the fire. Her hair glows with a reddish-brown hue in the firelight, and as she turns her gaze to mine, my breath hitches in my throat. My Ashaya is the most beautiful female I have ever seen.

Her people may closely resemble V'loryns, but I've never found their females to be attractive. Their impassive expressions and neutral stares make me uncomfortable. But Liana is nothing like them in this respect. Her face is very expressive. I've spent enough time with her that I've learned the meaning behind almost every facial expression she makes, but it is her smile that is my undoing. I would do anything to coax one from her lips. From what I've learned of her past, I imagine she must have used to smile often. If she chooses me, I will try to make sure that she smiles every day.

"It's getting colder, isn't it?" she asks, interrupting my thoughts.

"Yes. And I do not know how long the nights are on this planet."

She looks down a moment before flicking her eyes back up to meet mine. "Are you going to bathe too?"

My nostrils flare as I discreetly attempt to scent myself. I do not believe that my odor is sour, but she must think so if she's asking if I will bathe. "Yes."

I practically race to the back of the cave and quickly peel off my clothing. As I settle into the water, I lament the fact that there is nothing in the emergency bag to buff my scales with. Then again, I supposed preening for one's potential mate is not something one normally does in a survival situation.

"Feels good, doesn't it?" her small voice calls out.

"Yes. It's perfect." And it is. It would be even more so if she were in here with me, but I do not believe she is ready to claim me yet.

As soon as I'm finished, I step out of the water and smile when I find the emergency blanket she left for me. I dry off and pull my pants over my hips, leaving my torso bare. It is cold, but not unbearably so for me. My Ashaya, however, is shivering despite her nearness to the fire.

I move beside her to stack more wood on the burning pile and stoke the flame to ensure it will burn evenly. Reaching into the emergency pack, I pull out another blanket and drape it over her form. I tuck it tightly around her shoulders.

"Aren't you cold?" she asks.

I love that she thinks of me. "I am fine. My people are able to regulate our body temperatures to adjust to almost any climate."

She moves closer and extends her arm to wrap the blanket around us both.

*Is this it? Is she challenging me to the shav-rhokan?* Sometimes Mosauran females will wrap their wings around a potential mate to initiate the battle. Every muscle tenses in preparation as I wait, hoping to hear the words leave her lips, for her to tell me that she has chosen me to be hers.

Although as she relaxes against my side, I remember that she is Terran, and their ways are very different. My body doesn't realize this though. I'm not certain how claiming one's mate is done among her people. She said that Terrans court one another to determine compatibility before making a final decision to bond. I hope that her kisses and declarations of love mean I am now hers, but I do not know for sure.

The feel of her against me and the soft scent of her skin is intoxicating. Nervous anticipation flows through me. I desire her more than anything. Instinctively, my body begins to respond to her nearness. I need to get my reaction under control before we lay down. The last thing she needs is to be afraid as she sleeps. Her mind may know that I would never hurt her, but I know from my time in the arena that the body does not always listen to the mind; I do not want her to recoil from me in fear.

"Before we go to sleep, I'd like to check the area around the cave. Make sure there's nothing that could pose a threat nearby."

I do not scent any predators close to our new shelter. I'm almost certain they are able to recognize instinctively that I am something that they need to fear. A few minutes alone to focus on this task will give me enough time away from her to get my body under control.

Worry flickers across her expression. "You want me to come with you?"

I smile at her concern and shake my head. "I will be swift."

She steps closer and takes my hand in her own, giving it a gentle squeeze. "Please be careful."

Knowing how much nudity bothers her, I move behind a large boulder several steps from the cave to remove my pants and shift into draken form. I breathe a deep sigh of contentment as my body begins the change. My draken form is always ever ready just beneath the surface, like a wild and untamed thing awaiting to be freed. To shift is one of the greatest joys imaginable.

A thrill runs through me as I breathe in the fresh, cold air and spread my wings. The deep stretch as they unfold from my body is a feeling unlike any other. Staring up at the gray and overcast sky, I lift off and climb above the trees.

From up here, I can just make out the tracks that show how far she dragged me from the escape pod, and my eyes widen in shock. How was she able to carry me over such a great distance?

Scanning the terrain, I see no signs of any cities or settlements nearby. Perhaps this planet is devoid of any kind of sentient species. My heart sinks when I realize that if our companions do not rescue us, our chances of being found are very slim. From what I can tell, there are no moons rising as the anemic sun begins to set. So, when night falls, there is nothing but pitch-black darkness. And while this is not a problem for me, it is a definite problem for my Ashaya, since her people are essentially blind in the dark. I wonder if a fire is a good idea after all. I do not wish to draw attention to us.

My eyes track movement in the woods below, and I swoop down to get a closer look. If there is danger here, I must find it before it finds us.

# CHAPTER 30

LIANA

Soran's been gone a while, so I step just outside the mouth of the cave and scan the surrounding forest for any sign of him. Finding nothing, I call out his name, but he doesn't answer.

I dress quickly and palm the blaster at my hip before I leave the cavern to search. Following his footsteps in the snow, I gasp when I reach the end and find four monstrous animal footprints in the ground beside his. Panic fills me for about three very long seconds before I remember he's able to shift into a draken.

The first time I saw it, I was drugged by the breaking dart, but if I remember correctly, he was enormous in this form. Not that he's not already huge and more muscular than any man I've ever seen while in his humanoid form, but it was even more so when he was a draken.

Despite the two blankets wrapped around me, goosebumps pebble my arms and legs, and I shiver as the cold wind whips through my hair. I miss the fire. Logically, I know he can take care of himself, but I still worry. This is a strange new planet that we know nothing about. I glance up at the gray, overcast sky, wondering if I can spot him from here.

A branch snaps on the ground nearby, drawing my attention away from the clouds and to the forest around me. I turn and then freeze. A pair of yellow eyes stare menacingly at me from deep in the shadows. This is the same type of predator that watched me when I dragged Soran to the cave.

Fear twists in my gut as sweat beads across my brow. Raising the blaster, I keep my eyes trained in the direction of the creature. It studies me with a hungry gaze.

As it moves closer, I can just make out the shadow of its large form. At least three times my size and covered in a thick hide of white fur that perfectly matches the snow all around us, this predator looks like a wolf—but much larger than any that exist on Terra.

I'm far enough from the cave, that if I run, I might not make it.

Its lips are pulled back in a feral snarl as it stalks toward me, revealing a row of sharp fangs at least half the length of my forearm and dripping with saliva.

Adrenaline courses through my veins and my hand tremors slightly as I keep my blaster trained on the wolf. The hairs rise on the back of my neck as a chorus of howls echo loudly in the forest. Just like the wolves of Terra, these things must hunt in packs. The soft crunching of snow alerts me to four more sets of hungry yellow eyes approaching behind the first one.

In the small part of my brain that's still able to think rationally, I make a mental note to carry a knife from now on, in addition to my blaster. Two weapons are better than one, and seeing as how I'm outnumbered, I could use any advantage I can get right now.

At my feet are two deep grooves in the snow, left behind by the makeshift sled I used to pull Soran and our supplies here. As if by divine intervention, a large flat stone with a knife-sharp edge juts up from the ground. I lower myself just enough to sweep my hand over the freshly tilled earth. Keeping my eyes focused on the wolf, I wrap my fingers around the rock and grasp it firmly. Now, at least, I have two weapons. Hopefully, I'll just have to use one.

Rising back into a defensive stance, blaster in one hand and sharp rock in the other, I breathe heavily through my nostrils as my heart hammers in my chest.

The wolf growls and lowers its head as it stalks closer, readying to attack as the others move to flank my sides.

Fear gives way to blinding anger as primal rage burns through me. I didn't make it this far to be some creature's meal—to die on some unknown planet.

I hold its gaze evenly and grit through my teeth. "If you think I'm going to die today, you're wrong. I *will not* be your prey. You'll be mine."

A deafening roar thunders overhead, shaking the ground beneath us. The wolves look just as stunned as I am as they lift their eyes skyward, crouching into a defensive stance. Limbs twist and snap above us as something breaks through the trees, felling two enormous trunks. I roll to the left to avoid the one that lands beside me, sending tremors through the earth with its fall.

A feral cry of terror echoes through the forest, followed by a sickening crunching, and then absolute silence. The scent of blood hits the air. Bitter and metallic, I can almost taste it on my tongue. My body shakes as my pulse pounds in my ears. Whatever this is, I cannot outrun it. I'll have no choice but to fight where I stand.

Undeterred by whatever is lurking nearby, three pairs of yellow eyes continue to stare at me through the darkness. A long snout with two rows of razor-sharp teeth snarl threateningly at me, and despite knowing that I'm outnumbered, I do the only thing I can. I aim the blaster at the nearest one, readying to fire.

A deep and threatening growl, behind me, sends a jolt of fear down my spine.

The three wolves flee quickly, and I spin to face this new foe, prepared to defend myself.

My jaw drops and I'm frozen in place as I stare gaping at the creature before me. An enormous, towering dragon covered in dark silver-gray shimmering, iridescent scales flicks its long, tapered tail in agitation as its eyes follow the retreat of the wolves. After a moment, it lowers its massive horned head. A large, silver reflective iris contracts and then expands as it meets my stunned gaze. Its nostrils flare, drawing in my scent before it releases a quick huff of air, nearly knocking me down. A nervous laugh escapes me. "Soran?"

Tipping his head slightly to the side, he cocks one big ridged brow, and it looks so ridiculous, I double over with laughter.

He narrows his eyes in mock irritation, and I place my hands on my hips as I tease him. "Don't look at me like that. I just got a condescending look from a dragon. How many people can say *that*?"

He rolls his eyes, and I laugh again. After a moment, I cautiously reach out and touch his snout. He nuzzles against my palm. A quick puff of air escapes his nostrils, and a black curl of smoke tickles my skin.

A smile curves my lips as I run my fingers along the soft, smooth scales up to his cheek, watching in wonder as the reddish-orange color there darkens even more beneath my hand. His silver eyes stare deep into mine.

"You're beautiful," I whisper in amazement.

I had expected his dragon scales to feel rough, like sandpaper. Instead, they are smooth and soft like a fine layer of silk, just as they are when he is in his other form. I gently trace the familiar scar of his cheek that comes down from his brow, and he closes his eyes and tilts his head into my touch, as if relishing the contact of my skin upon his.

A sudden rush of air whips around me, forcing me to close my eyes. When I open them, he's back in his humanoid form, standing naked before me. My jaw drops, and before I can stop myself, my eyes travel down his nude body.

Row upon row of thick, corded muscle covers him entirely. My entire body flushes with warmth. He is masculine perfection incarnate, like something carved from stone that is too perfect to be real. My mouth goes dry as my eyes move lower. I'm shocked when I don't see the typical male anatomy below his waist. In fact, I don't see anything at all. I could have sworn I felt something when we made out, but maybe I was wrong. How's that supposed to work if we...?

Softly shaking my head, I force my gaze back to his face. I don't care if he looks...not like what I expected. I'm just so glad we're both alive and those wolves are gone. I rush forward and wrap my arms around him.

He returns the embrace, and when I finally pull back to stare up at him, I notice a small smile tugging at the corner of his lips.

"I am different than your Terran males. My appearance is not what you expected," he says this as a statement, but I know it's more of a question.

My cheeks burn with embarrassment. "Well, you are an alien, right?"

He arches a teasing brow. "*I'm* the alien?"

I laugh because he's right. I guess *I'm* the alien to him.

He continues. "We are not like V'loryns. Our stav does not extend from our bodies until we are ready to mate."

My jaw drops at his blunt words, and a small squeak escapes from the back of my throat before I close my mouth and swallow nervously. "Oh," is all I manage to finally say.

He cups my face and runs the soft pad of his thumb gently across my cheek. "I did not mean to frighten you with my draken form. I apologize if I scared you."

I start to answer, but something moves in the darkness, and his eyes dart in the direction of the sound. When he turns back, all traces of his warmth and teasing are gone as he gives me a firm look. "You should not have been outside the cave. It's not safe. This forest is full of predators. How could you be so reckless? What were you thinking?"

Mad that he's upset with me, I snap back. "I was looking *for you*. I was worried because you'd been gone for so long."

He cocks his head to the side. "I promised that I would return to you."

Rolling my eyes, I huff. "I know, but I'm tired, and I panicked. I forgot about your draken form and thought you were taken by something."

His brow furrows. "How could you forget about my draken form?"

I sigh heavily. "Because sometimes I forget that you're not Terran."

He looks down at himself as if my statement is ridiculous. After a moment, his expression turns solemn. "I saw how far you had to drag me. You are strong. Much stronger than I realized. You should not worry. Even if something happened to me, I do not doubt you would be able to survive on your own."

Stunned by his words, I feel a swell of pride knowing a brave dragon warrior has so much confidence in me. But that's not why I was so concerned. I wasn't worried for myself. I was worried because I love him. I open my mouth to tell him this, but he keeps talking.

He continues. "But strength is not enough, Liana. You must also use your mind."

Crossing my arms, I shoot him an irritated look. "I *know* that, Soran. I panicked, though, because I thought something had taken you."

He puffs his chest out and tilts his chin high. "Nothing would dare attack a Mosauran warrior in draken form."

I roll my eyes at his overly confident declaration. "How was *I* supposed to know your draken form was that big?"

His brow furrows in confusion. "You saw me on Le'ro when I killed the Anguis."

Crossing my arms over my chest, I purse my lips. "I was drugged by a breaking dart, remember?"

He pulls me into his arms. "Forgive me. I was not thinking."

As glad as I am that he has such faith in my survival skills, I don't like that he believes he can take chances with his life because he thinks I'll be okay without him. I stare deep into his silver eyes. "I know I can survive, Soran, but I love you. I don't want something to happen to you. Just because you can shift into your draken form, it doesn't make you invincible."

Gently, he drops his forehead to mine and runs his fingers softly through my hair. "Until we know more about this planet, we will stay together. Always."

"Good," I agree.

"Are you hungry?"

"Actually, I'm starved," I reply, turning to glance back at the cave and imagining the sawdust brick that awaits me for my meal.

He motions for me to wait a moment

Curious, I watch as he walks around a nearby thicket. He returns and my jaw drops when I notice what he has in his arms. Dropping the large carcass to the ground at my feet, I recognize the yellow eyes and razor-sharp teeth as one of the wolves that tried to attack me.

"You want to eat that?" I ask incredulously.

He frowns. "Why not?"

I gesture at the bloody carcass. "It's raw, for one thing."

"Easily fixed," he replies before another rush of air swirls around me, and he's back in draken form...and literally blowing fiery flames out of his mouth to show me what he means.

My eyes go wide. But after a moment, I shake my head. Why am I surprised? *He is* an alien, after all.

Soran's ability to breathe fire is definitely a good thing on this frozen planet. And since we don't know how long we'll be here, he's right. We shouldn't waste anything. Although the thought disgusts me, we could use this creature's hide to make clothing or an extra blanket and dry the meat for extra rations. All the times my dad stressed the importance of learning how to survive in the wilderness, I'm glad I actually paid attention.

"Let's drag this thing back to the cave."

He nods just before he shifts back into humanoid form. Uncaring of his nakedness, he carries the dead animal as if it weighs nothing, dropping it just beside the entrance.

My jaw goes slack as I stare appreciatively at his muscular and very naked backside. His entire body is covered in layers of thick, finely sculpted muscle; he moves with a grace that belies his massive form.

He turns back, and I snap my mouth shut. "Do you want me to burn it?" he asks.

It takes me a moment to respond. "No."

Reaching into the emergency pack, I retrieve a knife and turn back to find him staring at me with a questioning look. I hold up the laser blade. "If we're going to be here a while, we're going to have to make our supplies stretch."

He watches me curiously. "What do you intend to do with that?"

"I'm going to remove its pelt. We can strip the meat and use the fur for more clothing or a blanket...something to keep us warm."

His brows go up in an expression that's a cross between amusement and disbelief. "What kind of planet is this Terra? Your people skin animals to make clothing?"

I roll my eyes. "You've never had any survival training?"

He tilts his chin up. "Of course, I have."

"Well, how would you make more blankets or clothes, then?"

He frowns. "My body is able to adjust to variations in the temperature." His sharp gaze rakes over my covered form. I'm wrapped from head to toe in so many layers, I probably look twice my normal size at this point, and I'm still a bit chilled. "*And*...your species is unable to do this as effectively as mine..." His voice trails off. "I suppose it makes sense that you would learn to make clothing in survival situations," he adds under his breath.

"You sure you're not cold?"

"A little, but it is nothing I cannot handle."

My mouth drifts open. It literally feels like we're in Alaska in the middle of winter right now. "Well, I'm freezing to death, and I'm going to need some heavier clothing or blankets if we're going to be here for a while."

He gives me a panicked look. "You are dying?"

**Soran**

As soon as the words leave her mouth, alarm bursts through me. Lifting her into my arms, I rush inside the cave and set her near the fire. I shove my discarded clothes at her. "Put these on," I say quickly. "I do not need them."

She looks up at me in confusion. "What?"

"You just told me you were freezing to death."

"I didn't mean that *literally*."

I cross my arms over my chest. "You cannot retract your words now. I know you...and you are not prone to complaining. You would not have said you were 'freezing to death' unless it were so."

She opens her mouth to protest, but I wrap another emergency blanket tightly around her, making sure to cover her face and her small button nose loosely so she may still breathe. I throw several more pieces of wood on the fire.

She gives me an incredulous look. "It's just a figure of speech." Her voice comes out muffled between the layers of fabric.

I shake my head firmly. "I will not allow you to die, Liana."

"But, I—"

I narrow my eyes and give her my best stern look.

She laughs. "Don't give me that face."

A heavy sigh of frustration escapes my lips as I stare across at her. My Ashaya is very stubborn. "Then do not protest when I am trying to help you." Before she can say anything else, I quickly move behind her, setting her in my lap. I unfold and extend my wings from my back, wrapping them around her figure. "This should help warm you."

She gasps, and I worry that I've hurt her. Afraid I may be holding her too tight, I immediately loosen my grip. "What's wrong?"

"Your wings," she says, and I loosen them even more in case they are too constrictive. "They're so beautiful."

Confused at first, I cock my head to the side to regard her. She smiles as she stares down at my wings wrapped tightly around her small form, and my chest fills with pride. "You like my wings?"

The petal-soft skin of her hands trace delicate patterns along one of the dark-gray, leathery folds. "Yes. I mean...I knew you had them, but you always keep them tucked into your back. They're amazing."

I look down at them. They are nothing special. In fact, my coloring is rather drab compared to most other Mosaurans. I've always thought it a blessing that I can blend against most backgrounds, but I also worried this would hurt my chances of attracting a potential mate. Mosauran females appreciate a male with vibrant markings and colors. But as Liana stares at my very dull-colored wings with a look of awestruck wonder, I realize now that this is obviously not going to be a problem for us.

If we return to Mosaura, however, I'll have to hope her head isn't turned by the more colorful males of my species. Just thinking about it makes me tighten my wings around her even more as possessive jealousy ripples through me.

She relaxes against my chest, idly tracing her fingers along the folds of one wing. "I'm glad it's you," she says softly.

"What do you mean?"

"If I have to be stranded on an alien world," she whispers, "I'm glad it's with you, my love."

I tighten my arms and wings around her. "I feel the same."

We lay down next to the fire, and she turns in my arms to face me. Striking green eyes stare into mine, and I'm completely mesmerized. She nestles closer and drapes her arm across my chest. "Is this all right?" she asks.

My heart pounds. It is more than all right. It is complete and utter bliss. "Yes."

Resting her head on my shoulder, she closes her eyes. "So tired," she mumbles softly.

I press a kiss to her forehead. "Rest, Liana. We are safe for now."

It doesn't take long before the sound of her breathing evens out, and she drifts off to sleep. It is no surprise she is so exhausted. My Ashaya dragged me a long way. She is braver than anyone I know. If not for her, I'd be dead right now. She risked her life to save me, both from the glider and the escape pod. She asked me what Ashaya means, and I have not yet told her. I shudder inwardly at the thought that I could have passed from this world to the next without giving her my truth—without explaining what she is and how much she means to me.

Now I will wait no more. Tomorrow, I will tell her.

# CHAPTER 31

SORAN

When morning comes, she's still asleep in my arms and wrapped tightly in my wings. Last night I caught the scent of several predators in the forest. The same kind that tried to attack her. They were careful to stay well clear of the cave entrance but were still close enough that I know there are many of them. My protective instincts surge, and I tighten my arms and wings around her. I breathe deeply of her delicious scent and gently nuzzle the top of her head.

Her eyelids flutter open and she looks up at me through a half-lidded gaze. She gives me a sleepy smile.

With a small sigh, she nestles even closer. I know she can survive on her own and is fully capable of defending herself, but protective instincts for one's mate are heavily embedded in my people's biology.

"Soran?" Her tired voice rips me from my thoughts.

"Yes?"

"Good morning."

She presses a quick kiss to my lips and then stretches her body out. The soft hiss of pain she makes as she does this does not escape me. I cup her cheek, lifting her gaze to mine as I stare at her in concern. "Are you hurt?"

She shrugs. "My muscles are just a bit sore. That's all."

Guilt fills me as I remember how far she had to drag me from the pod. "You should rest some more, Liana."

A warm smile curves her lips as she shakes her head softly. "We have a lot to do today. We need to set up the transmitter, or we'll never get off this frozen rock."

"You are certain it will work without the pod?"

She grins. "I was a pilot, remember? If you can't troubleshoot a transmitter, you might as well forget any chance of being rescued. Any pilot worth their wings knows that."

A laugh rumbles in my chest. She is brilliant.

As she sits up, I allow my wings to fall away. She shivers slightly as she meets my gaze, tucking the emergency blanket around her shoulders. "We'll eat breakfast, and then we'll search for a location to set up the signal. After that, I'll make the repairs, and we'll set it to transmit."

"It cannot be repaired here first?"

She shakes her head. "No. I don't want it to accidentally start transmitting from here and compromise our location. We have no way of knowing who may respond. And if it's the A'kai, we don't want to give away our position."

I nod. She is right. My gaze drifts down to her hand—the one she injured retrieving the transmitter—and pride fills me. My Ashaya is strong, brave and brilliant. If not for her, we would have no chance of being rescued.

As I move around the cave, I notice her eyes travel discreetly down my form. A flicker of confusion flashes briefly across her expression before she lifts her gaze back to mine. She did this the first time she saw me unclothed as well. My appearance must be too different from that of the males of her species. She is disappointed in my body, but there is nothing I can do about this, and I can only hope that, eventually, she sees past it.

After breakfast, we step outside the cave and I turn to face her. "Are you ready?"

She nods and I shift into draken form.

## Liana

Soran extends his leg and looks at me expectantly. I don't know why the thought of riding on his back makes me nervous, but it does. Maybe it's because I'm so attracted to him. Even in this form, the way the powerful muscles flex and move beneath his scales makes me think of his humanoid form—pure masculine perfection.

He tilts his massive head in my direction, arching one eyebrow in a questioning look as he waits for me to climb on. *"Second thoughts?"*

The words arc through me like lightning, and my entire body tenses, but I quickly force myself to relax. This is Soran, and I hate that I react to him like this.

As if sensing my distress, he gives me a pained look.

I reach out to rest my hand lightly on his jaw. "I'm not scared of you. I trust you. I just can't help my reaction sometimes. When you speak in my thoughts, it reminds me too much of..." I swallow thickly against the pain-filled memories of Talel's invasion of my mind. Closing my eyes briefly, I shake my head as if to clear them away. "I'm fine. I promise."

I do my best to give him a reassuring smile, but from the look on his face, I know it falls short.

Pushing down my fear, I climb up his leg and onto his back.

He's still as I settle over his shoulders and grab onto a few of the hard spikes protruding from the back of his neck. My eyes widen when I realize how sharp they are. "Uh...no sudden stops, okay? I don't want to get skewered." I give him a nervous laugh, only halfway teasing because it's definitely a valid concern.

His spikes snap flat against his back just before his huge body shakes beneath me, sending small tremors through mine as he laughs. Turning his head, he grins and winks in a very Terran gesture, and it looks so ridiculous on his fierce dragon face that I double over with laughter.

He turns his attention back to the forest, walking along the edge between the mountain and the thick canopy of trees.

I'm about to ask why he hasn't taken off yet, but it occurs to me that he's probably giving me time to get adjusted. Every good pilot knows you need to familiarize yourself with a ship before you start flying, and I suppose this really isn't that much different.

Taking advantage of this moment before we take to the sky, I run my hands over his smooth scales. Brilliant bursts of iridescent color reflect off their surface as he moves beneath the light filtering in through the trees. "Beautiful," I whisper under my breath.

He stops and tilts his chin up, puffing his chest out with pride at my words.

I laugh heartily. "*Now*, you're just showing off," I tease.

His body shudders and another wisp of smoke escapes his nostrils as he laughs.

I shake my head in mock annoyance as we continue on. "*My big, strong Mosauran warrior,*" I think to myself.

"*Yours,*" he agrees. Something about the way he says it makes my heart stutter.

Desire coils deep in the pit of my stomach as a low vibration begins to thrum through his body, melting my core. But it stops just as suddenly as it began when he unfolds his massive wings. Powerful muscles flex beneath me as they extend and then begin to flap, lifting us from the ground. Swirling snow and debris kick up from the sudden blast of wind, and I squeeze my eyes shut as the world falls away.

Cool air whips around my form, in sharp contrast to the comfortable warmth of his body as we soar above the tree line. With a sudden dip, he catches a current that lifts us even higher.

I gasp at the stark but beautiful landscape beneath us, and my mouth drifts open in wonder. "This is amazing, Soran."

I've always loved flying, but it's never felt as invigorating as this. Rapturous, all-consuming adrenaline burns through my veins. It is complete and utter freedom. An intense and heady rush, this is the high that every pilot chases when they take to the sky.

Strong wind claws at my form, threatening to rip me from his back. But I flatten myself against his spine and hold on tight. His entire body shakes as several violent gusts push against him, and he struggles to align himself with another current. Tucking his wings, he slips into the stream, and the pressure is suddenly gone.

Spreading his wings again, he glides effortlessly above the gray clouds. I scan the horizon, watching in awe as the dawning sun sets the snow-covered landscape on fire below us in brilliant shades of red, orange, and yellow.

A wistful sigh escapes my lips. "The very first time I flew with my dad...that was it, Soran. I knew then and there that I wanted to be a pilot when I grew up. It was early morning like this. The sun was just coming up, and he pointed toward the horizon." I smile at the memory. "'There it is,' he told me. And I'll admit, I wasn't quite sure what he was talking about."

I can feel Soran listening, as if he's holding his breath and waiting to see what comes next.

"Confused, I asked him what he meant, still not sure what I was supposed to be seeing. He pointed at the horizon. The soft, warm glow of the sun's early morning rays just barely peeking over the gentle curve of the earth below us. He called it the 'beautiful edge.'

"And when I piloted my first ship out into the black void of space, I —" My voice catches. Tears sting my eyes, but I blink them back and continue. "It was the most amazing thing I'd ever done in my life. Terra was just below me in the viewscreen, and it looked so incredible. More beautiful than anything I could have ever imagined. My dad had told me about this, but until you see it for yourself, you can't picture just how breathtaking it is. Something so raw and perfect...created by the stars long before we ever even existed..." I smile as I hold onto the image in my mind. "He said pilots in the Terran space program call the round curve of our planet, 'the edge of it all.' He told me I'd be overcome with emotion when I first saw it— that even the most stoic pilots can't help but be moved by its beauty." The smile falls from my face as sadness starts to creep in around the perfect memory. "He was right."

As if sensing my pain, Soran's voice whispers in my mind. *"I will do everything I can to help you find your family, Liana. I swear it to the Creator."*

Emotions lodge in my throat, but I somehow manage to speak around them and whisper, "Thank you."

Turning my attention back to the landscape, I notice we're just above the mountain's highest peak. "As close to the top as you can, all right?"

He nods as he scans the terrain below us. Circling a few times, he extends his wings, allowing the air to catch them, the sails billowing out as he carefully drifts onto a ledge near the mountain's peak.

Given the size of his form, I brace myself for a jarring landing and am surprised by how lightly he manages to set us down.

The wind is much stronger up here, and I hold tightly to his neck, afraid I'll get blown off as he walks away from the edge to a small, level clearing. The bitter cold air stings my exposed skin as Soran kneels and extends his leg for me to climb down. I shiver as soon as I leave the warmth of his body and stand upon the solid ground.

When I turn back, I stare up at him expectantly, waiting for him to shift, but he doesn't. I wonder if he feels more comfortable as a draken. I'm about to ask when the wind carries a chorus of distant howling. He looks to me, darting his gaze briefly in the direction of the sound before nodding slightly, as if to indicate that this is the reason he keeps his draken form—to protect us.

Biting back my discomfort, I pull the transmitter from my pack and place it in the center of the clearing. My hands shake with the cold, and it takes all my effort to hold them as still as possible while I carefully study the components.

A large shadow falls over me, and the air around me goes still. I look up to find Soran curling himself around me, one wing extended directly overhead to offer shelter against the freezing wind. "Thank you, my *big, strong Mosauran warrior*," I tease as I stroke his ego. "Your draken form comes in handy sometimes."

His chest rumbles slightly as dark smoke escapes his mouth in his "draken laugh."

Turning my attention back to the transmitter, I carefully piece together the frayed bits of wiring that came lose when I ripped it free of the console. It's not damaged beyond repair, but it's going to take a while to get everything reattached.

After what feels like an eternity, but I'm sure was probably no more than thirty minutes at most, the low temperature takes its toll, and my hands begin shaking. Carefully, I set down the transmitter and turn to press my hands against Soran, tucking myself into the warmth of his body.

He curls his tail tight around my back as he covers me with his wing. His heart beats a steady rhythm beneath me, and I sigh in contentment. Enveloped in his warmth, I'm reluctant when I have to push away, but I know I need to keep going. Our lives depend on this.

As the temperature steadily drops, my breaks for warmth become more frequent. Off in the distance, the sun sits low on the horizon. The day is almost gone. I can't believe I've been working this long. I wish I could have done most of this back in the cave, but I couldn't risk accidentally activating the beacon there. I learned enough in my time as a slave to know we cannot assume that someone responding to this distress signal would do so purely for benevolent reasons.

It's so cold my teeth are chattering. Oh god, I hope Grex and Abby didn't get stuck on this frozen rock also. This definitely wouldn't be good for her *or* the baby.

Soran gently nuzzles my shoulder to get my attention.

His silver eyes study me with a piercing gaze. He's worried about me. It's strange how much emotion his eyes can convey even in draken form.

A smile tugs at my lips. This is why he's so bad at kartu—he doesn't have a poker face.

"I'm all right." I do my best to reassure him. "Besides, I'm almost done."

He gives me a subtle nod, and I go back to my work.

When I'm finally finished reattaching the mangled wiring, I look up to find him watching me intently. I smile. "This is it."

I press the button to activate the transmitter and watch in triumph as the lights blink rapidly before turning solid green. I let out a whoop of excitement. "Thank god, it worked."

His head jerks back slightly in shock. *"You doubted that it would?"*

Despite the cold, warmth spreads across my cheeks. I nervously tuck a stray tendril of hair behind my ear. "I didn't want to worry you, but the transmitter was in pretty bad shape after I ripped it out of the console."

He narrows his eyes. *"You know how I feel about deception."*

"Deception?" I ask, staring up at him in confusion.

His gaze drops down to my lips, and I realize he's talking about when I kissed him as a distraction to stun him and force him onto the escape pod.

I roll my eyes. "You're *still* upset about that?"

He sighs heavily as his lips form a tight, thin line.

Placing my hands on my hips, I let out a frustrated huff. "I already said I was sorry. You know I wouldn't have done it if I'd had any other choice. Can you please get over it already? You turned out all right, didn't you?" I gesture at his massive form. "Besides, you keep reminding me that you're a big, strong Mosauran warrior."

He lifts his chin and looks down at me with a teasing smirk. *"You're the one that called me that first."*

I laugh. "All right, all right. And you're never going to let me forget it, are you?"

He arches a brow and dips his chin in a subtle nod.

A smile crests my lips. Yep. He's definitely never going to let that one go.

The wind gusts, and an involuntary shiver moves through me.

His gaze darts briefly to the horizon where the last of the sun's rays spread out across the snow. He stares down at me in concern. *"Are you ready to leave?"*

I reach back to rub my neck, my muscles sore and achy from sitting hunched over the transmitter all day. The cold only makes it worse, and I can hardly wait to return to our warmer cave.

Starting toward him, I stop abruptly, as the realization hits me.

"Hey." A slow smile curves my lips. "You've been talking in my mind and I... It didn't make me react...badly."

A dozen emotions flash behind his eyes before he lowers his head to gently nuzzle my side. He curls a wing around me, pulling me closer as he shields me from the freezing wind. It feels so good, reminding me of the way he held me last night. Just the thought makes me shiver again, but this time it's not from the cold. I'm ready to get back to the cave for more snuggle time with my big, strong Mosauran warrior.

He pulls back just enough to look at me, tilting his head to the side. *"What is 'snuggle time'?"*

My jaw drops as my cheeks burn red hot with embarrassment. "Can you hear everything I'm thinking?"

He looks up with a thoughtful expression as if considering his answer before lowering his gaze back to mine. *"I do not believe so. Would you like me to try?"*

I shake my head emphatically. "No." If he only knew all the thoughts I have about him, his cheeks would be the ones turning bright red right now.

When I climb onto his back and settle over his shoulders, he makes sure I'm secure before turning into the wind. My hair whips behind me, and I flatten myself against his back, holding tight to his warm body. Without warning, he breaks into a gallop. I lift my head just as we reach the edge, and my heart slams into my throat as we drop off the side. My stomach lurches, and everything shifts into slow motion as we begin to fall.

Just when I think I'm going to throw up, he extends his wings. Our descent halting so abruptly, I nearly lose my grip from the sudden force. Somehow, I manage to hold on. His wings catch the wind, and we slip into the current, gliding effortlessly through the stream.

Exhilaration rushes through me. I let out a whoop of excitement as he folds his wings and dives through the clouds. The sharp thrill of adrenaline floods my system, chasing away all my fears. "This is incredible!"

Sailing on the wind, we race over the forest. I haven't felt this free in a long time. His powerful muscles flex beneath my thighs as he flaps his wings to make a giant arc over the woods. I lean to the side and extend one hand to skim the tops of the snow-covered trees, watching in wonder as the caps explode in a rain of white powdery dust that trails along behind us.

He makes another low pass over the forest before circling back to our cave. His wings snap open, and he carefully drifts down, landing with an audible thud that shakes the earth beneath us. Throwing my leg over the side, I slide off his back and gasp in surprise when I sink hip-deep into the snow.

With a sudden rush of wind, Soran changes behind me and scoops me up into his arms. I start to protest because I can walk by myself, but he's so much taller, and the cold doesn't seem to bother him like it does me.

As if he senses my hesitation, his sharp gaze meets mine. "Please do not protest my help, Liana."

Wrapping my arms around his neck, I relax against his chest and grin. "I wasn't going to. Believe me, the last thing I want is to get frostbite."

"Frost...bite?"

"You know...where your toes or fingers lose circulation from the cold and eventually fall off?"

His face pales. "You are never leaving the cave again."

I roll my eyes. I'm not going to let him do all the firewood gathering. I'm not some helpless damsel in distress. I arch a questioning brow. "Hey. What happened to your belief that I can take care of myself?"

Probably anticipating an argument, he gives me a pointed look. "That was before you told me about..." He frowns as if trying to find the words, before he finally continues, "Frostbite."

When we reach the entrance, he gently lowers me to the ground, and a small wave of disappointment washes over me at the sudden loss of contact between us.

# CHAPTER 32

SORAN

As soon as I set her down in the cave, she starts for the pools at the back.

"If you are thirsty, I will bring you some water if you want to sit by the fire," I offer. Now that's she's told me about this "frostbite," my concerns for her well-being have increased exponentially, and I need to make sure she is warm.

She gives me a quick glance over her shoulder. "I'm hungry, I'm tired, and I'm thirsty. But what I want most right now is a nice, relaxing soak in the pool."

I turn my back to her, giving her privacy while she enjoys her bath. Fixing my gaze on the forest outside, I scan the area for any predators lurking just beyond the light of our fire. The scent of the wolves still lingers in the woods.

They are cunning predators, and they seem to prefer to hunt in packs. We will need to keep this flame going every day to discourage them from approaching our shelter.

When Liana is finished bathing, she sits by the fire. Wrapped in the emergency blanket for additional warmth, I notice her slight shivering despite being so near the flames. I gather more wood and throw it onto the pile, hoping the extra fuel will warm the cave that much quicker.

She tracks my movements with heavy-lidded eyes and gives me a tired smile. "Thank you, Soran."

Longing to touch her, I extend my wings and embrace her smaller form. I've wanted to do this all day. "I will hold you again as we sleep. It should help keep you warm."

Her cheeks redden slightly. "I'd like that."

Happiness blooms in my chest as we lay down. She nestles into my side without hesitation. She feels perfect in my arms, and I wrap my wings tightly around her. A small sigh of contentment leaves her lips as her entire body relaxes against mine.

She trusts me. Completely. And I am honored that she does so.

We lay there in silence, her eyelids drifting open and closed as sleep tries to claim her.

I study her face and the many small dots that cover the bridge of her nose and cheeks. She has told me she loves me, but she has not declared her intent yet to claim me as her mate. If she chooses me, I wonder if our fledglings will look more like her or myself. I hope they take after her, for she is perfect.

My thoughts drift to the Garkol who read her future. Four children. The thought both excites and pains me in the same measure. I cannot bear to think of her with another mate. I pray that the children he saw in her fate were also my own.

It doesn't escape me that I would have had an answer to this question and an end to my agony if I'd only thought to ask him if those children he saw in his vision had wings.

Curling my arms around her small form, I breathe deep of her delicate scent as I lightly skate my fingers up and down her arm, marveling in the soft, smooth texture of her skin. So different and fragile compared to mine and yet so soft, I am already addicted to touching her.

Moving to her back, my fingertips drag over a strange pattern of thick, irregularly textured flesh. I inhale sharply and go still. These are her slave markings. Rage fills me, and I clench my jaw as I think of the ones who did this to her. I wish I could kill everyone that ever touched her against her will.

Her brow furrows slightly as I trace a jagged scar across her shoulders. I tilt my head to gently nuzzle the top of hers, wanting to comfort her even as she drifts in the place between wake and dreams. My protective instincts surge, and I hold her tightly. If anyone dares try to hurt her again, I will end them without hesitation.

As if realizing how much I wish to study her striking green eyes, her eyelids flutter and open, and she gazes up at me sleepily. A soft smile curves her lips.

"You're awake," she whispers.

"Yes."

A brilliant smile greets my words. She shifts in my arms to face me, molding her form completely against mine.

"Is this 'snuggling'?"

A pink bloom spreads across the bridge of her nose. "Yes."

I wrap my wings tighter around her. "I like this 'snuggling.'"

She reaches up, gently tracing her finger across my chest. My nostrils flare slightly as I breathe in our combined scent, and fierce possessiveness rushes through me. I want more than anything for her to claim me, but first...I must tell her the truth.

I open my mouth to speak, but she begins instead.

She cups my cheek. "Today was one of the best days I've ever had."

I frown. "But you were so cold and miserable up on the mountain. I wanted to convince you to return to the cave for warmth because I could barely stand to see you suffering so much." A short puff of air escapes me as a smile tugs at my lips. "But you are stubborn, and I knew you would not listen to me anyway."

Her jaw drops. "I am *not* stubborn," she protests, staring at me with mock offense.

I arch a brow at her.

She laughs. "All right. Fine." She rolls her eyes and then grins. "Maybe just a little."

She is more than a "little" stubborn, but I know better than to say this.

She continues. "Of course, I was cold, but when we were flying...I felt like myself again. I remembered who I was"—her voice catches —"before I was taken." She turns her gaze to the wall, a far-away look on her face. "I used to be so fearless. I never backed down from a challenge, and I had this...this fire in my soul that burned so bright I felt like I could do anything. And now?" Her eyes brighten with tears. "I'll never be that person again."

A dull ache centers in my chest. I recognize this pain. "After Rowan rescued me, I found it difficult...impossible to return to my old life as if nothing had happened. And as much as I knew my family loved me, they did not understand what I had been through. How could they?"

"What did you do?"

"I traveled to a small village high in the Liral mountains. It is home to a sacred temple. I made the excuse that I wanted to go there to honor the Creator. I hoped that with time spent in deep reflection, I would somehow find myself again...to become the person I had been before I was taken."

"What happened?"

Dark memories return to the surface of my mind, and I close my eyes briefly against the pain. "I realized that the person I had been— that version of me—no longer existed, and never would again. I had survived horrible things, but that was the cost of my survival—the loss of who I was...before."

A tear slips softly down her cheek. "Sometimes I feel like I'm broken, Soran. As if I'm a stranger even to myself. And, I wonder if...*when*," she corrects herself, "I find my family again...if they'll even recognize me. I'm not the same person I was when I left."

The resignation in her voice fills me with pain, and I wrap my arms tighter around her. "All the Great and Lower Houses have swords that have been passed down for many generations. Each one unique and engraved with the sigil and words of their House; many even have symbols that represent their owners and the wars they have seen.

"These blades have been wielded over thousands of cycles in defense of the Empire...many of them broken on the field of battle." I run my fingers lightly through her hair and down her back. "Even when they are broken, they are never discarded. Instead, they are repaired with L'omhara. Each line of this ore in the blade tells a story, rendering each and every piece unique. The sections that contain the repair will never break again—having been strengthened in the firing process of binding the two separate metals."

I cup my hand to her cheek as I meet her gaze evenly. "They are stronger and more beautiful for having survived the damage wrought from war." I stare deep into her sea-green eyes, brushing her tears away with the soft pad of my thumb. "We are as the blades that defend the Great and Lower Houses. We are not broken, Liana. We are transformed into something stronger than we were before."

She reaches up and gently cups my face.

"There is something I must tell you," I whisper. "Something I should have told you long ago."

A crease of worry mars her delicate brow. "What is it?"

"You asked me what 'Ashaya' is." I take her hand in mine and entwine our fingers. "It means you are my fated one."

A question lingers behind her eyes, and I am silent as I wait for her to ask.

"Is that why you saved me? Why you love me?"

From her expression and her tone, it is clear something about my admission displeases her, so I do my best to explain.

"This bond is very rare among my people, and never has it been found outside of our race."

I pause, allowing the weight of my words to settle in the space between us. Cupping her chin, I tilt her face up to mine and marvel at her luminous gaze. "You are a creature of fire—as fiercely brave and intelligent as you are beautiful. I see the flame that burns deep inside you, just behind your eyes. You asked why I saved you. It is because my soul recognized the fire in yours, and I could not bear the thought of it being extinguished."

I press my forehead gently to hers. "It is also why I love you and how I know that I would love you even without the fated bond."

A dozen emotions flicker across her expression, and I wait with bated breath for her to speak. "I dreamed about you almost my entire life, Soran. Even this"—she reaches up and lightly touches the scar at the top of my brow—"was familiar to me." She trails her delicate fingers along the jagged mark and then cups my cheek.

I place my hand over hers. "I don't understand."

Her sea-green eyes stare deep into mine. "I don't understand it either, my love. But I have seen you in my dreams since I was a child. And even though my parents tried to convince me you weren't real...deep down, I always knew that you were."

She shakes her head softly. "I don't know why I have this connection to you. I only know that I love you and this"—she places my hand over her heart—"feels right in a way that nothing else ever has." She lowers her gaze. "But you are a warrior of Mosaura. Your females are strong. And I am not. You think I am strong and brave, but deep down, I'm still scared. I worry that I'll be taken again, that I'll never find my people or my home world. And my biggest fear"—her voice quavers and breaks on the last word—"is that I'm not who I was before. I feel like I'm broken, Soran. You need someone who is whole, not damaged."

I take her hand in mine and guide it to the scar along my face. "I used to believe this was a curse." I search her eyes. "But now I know that if I did not have this mark, I would not be the warrior that stands before you now. We both have scars, Liana, because we are survivors. Some of them are visible, and others are buried deep inside us. But they have made us who we are."

A tear slips softly down her cheek.

Placing my hands on either side of her face, I force her gaze to mine so she may see the truth in my soul. "Who you are now is the *only* version of you I have ever known. And I love *her*. I love *you*...just as you are. You are fierce, intelligent, strong, and brave. Every quality that I could ever have hoped for in a mate. Do not push me away because I will not go. I will never leave you. The ways of your people are different than mine, and I will wait for however long it takes for you to choose me. You are my Ashaya. And I feel it here"—I place my hand on my chest—"because it is truth. And I will give up anything and everything just to remain by your side because you are my heart."

I wrap my wings tightly around her and press my forehead again to hers, running my fingers through her long, silken hair. "Choose me, Liana. I long to be yours."

She leans forward and presses a soft kiss to my scar. She trails her hand lightly down my shoulder until she finds mine, entwining our fingers. Lifting our joined hands to her chest, she stares deep into my eyes. "I will carry you, Soran of House Mosaura, to victory or to death, but I will not leave you behind. We are bound to one another, and if you are broken, so am I. We will be broken together...and together, we will heal."

Overwhelming emotions surge through me, and I capture her mouth with my own.

*Mine.*

"I want nothing more than to be yours, my Ashaya. To walk by your side until the end of our days. Tell me," I whisper against her lips, "do you choose me, Liana?"

Anxiety wars with anticipation as I wait for her to answer. Wrapping her arms tightly around me, she leans forward to give me a gentle kiss. "I do."

Intense joy rushes through me, brighter than a thousand stars, and I want to roar my happiness to the sky.

I crush my lips to hers but am confused as she pushes against me and moves from me to stand. I stand too, wondering what I've done to make her reject me. Perhaps I was too aggressive with my affections.

"Liana, what is wrong?"

∼

**Liana**

I dip my chin as I keep my eyes trained on his, trying my best to appear as fierce as a Mosauran female. "Shav-rhokan."

He stills, the pupils of his eyes dilating until just a sliver of silver remains around the edge. He drops his chin to stare across at me through heavy brows. His gaze is both predatory and filled with desire, every muscle is tense as if it is taking everything inside him to hold on to his control. "You are certain?" he rasps.

Circling him, I tilt my chin up and move closer. Close but not quite touching, the very air around us seems charged with electricity. A short puff of air escapes his nostrils, parting the hair on top of my head as he scents me. A low rumbling growl vibrates deep in his chest, sending small ripples of pleasure straight to my core.

Heat radiates from his form to mine as he positions himself behind me. My body hums in awareness of him as my heart beats wildly in my chest. I bite my lower lip in anticipation of what happens next. He told me about this. I won't fight. I'll struggle, but it will only be for show. I want to be conquered by him.

One arm snakes around my waist while the other bands across my chest as he pulls me back into a solid wall of muscle, every inch of his body pressed against the back of mine. The delicious vibrations of his growl move straight through me as he dips his head, lightly skimming the tip of his nose along my temple, down to my jaw. As he scents along the column of my neck, my heart races, and my every nerve ending is on fire at his touch.

His grip is firm but it does not scare me. This is Soran, and I trust him completely.

His warm breath whispers across my skin as he opens his mouth just above the curve of my shoulder, and a rush of heat moves through me. Something sharp touches my sensitive flesh, and I try to twist in his arms, putting up a mock form of the struggle he would expect if I were a Mosauran female.

He stills, and the sharp sting on my skin lifts away. I tilt my head back to look up at him. His reflective eyes are wide with concern. "Have I hurt you?" he whispers.

I'm not afraid. I want him. "I'm fine. Don't stop."

His silver eyes dilate once more into obsidian orbs as his lips pull back to expose sharp fangs. He removes my tunic, and then slips his fingers beneath the waistband of my pants, pushing them down my hips.

His hands possessively trace back up my form, claiming my body as his. He bands his arms tightly around my waist and chest to pin back me against him, locking me in his embrace.

He lowers his head, and with just enough pressure to not break the skin but still keep me in place, he clamps down on the curve of my neck and shoulder as his hands travel over my form.

I'm bare and pressed against him as one large palm cups my breast. A low moan escapes my parted lips as his thumb brushes over the peak until it stiffens into a sensitive bead. His touch is fire and I push back against him, wanting more.

*"You are mine, Liana Garza of Terra,"* his voice whispers in my mind.

Desire pools deep in my core as he wraps his wings around me, molding my body to his. "I'm yours."

Something hard presses against my hip, and a small shiver of anticipation runs through me. I want to see him, I want to kiss him. Reaching back, I take his length in my hand, and he groans. He's so large my fingers cannot wrap entirely around his stav.

His deep, velvet voice whispers against the shell of my ear. "Am I as you expected, my Ashaya?"

Breathless with anticipation, I turn in his arms. Heavy-lidded eyes meet mine before I lower my gaze to stare down at his bare form. Much larger than a Terran male and covered with a line of thick ridges, his stav is hard and fully erect. Silver liquid beads from the slit at the top, and when I run my thumb over it, the breath hisses from his throat.

He captures my hand and then moves my thumb to trace it across my abdomen, marking me with his scent.

He stares at me with a hungry gaze. Hard planes of muscle ripple just beneath the surface as his chest rises and falls with ragged breaths. I stare deep into his eyes. "You are more perfect than I could have ever imagined."

Cupping his neck, I pull him to me. I press my lips to his and he opens his mouth, deepening our kiss. He tastes of earth and spice.

Slow at first, he finds a sensuous rhythm. The delicious ridges of his tongue move expertly against mine, and I'm lost in sensation.

His large palm gently cups the soft globe of one breast as I slowly caress up and down the hard ridges of his length. I clench my thighs together, wishing he were already between them; imagining how he will feel deep inside me.

He pulls back, and I know he has heard my thoughts through our connection. His nostrils flare as his eyes meet mine. One arm wraps firmly around my back as the other moves lower to cup my mound and the soft folds of my center. Retracting his claws, he holds my gaze intensely. I gasp as one finger parts the soft lips.

His thumb brushes over the small bundle of nerves at the top, and I inhale sharply as electricity arcs through me.

He pulls me closer and leans down to close his mouth over my breast, growling low in his throat as the peak hardens beneath his delicious ridged tongue. He moves to the other, giving it the same attention before kissing a heated trail down to my stomach.

Dropping to his knees, he places his hand over my mound and looks up at me through a half-lidded gaze. "May I kiss you here?"

Breathless and panting, I barely manage to whisper, "Yes."

His eyes burn with desire as he pulls at me gently, guiding me down onto the blanket spread out on the cave floor. His warm hands trail along my inner thighs before he gently pushes them apart, opening me to his gaze. He lowers his head to place a soft kiss to my mound.

"You are perfect," he whispers.

When his ridged tongue slicks through my folds, I gasp. I've touched myself before but it has never felt like this. When he circles the sensitive nub at the top, my every nerve lights up with pleasure. I reach down and run my fingers through his hair, reveling in the delicious sensation of his mouth on my body.

A soft moan escapes my lips as he continues to tease the sensitive bundle of nerves. He dips one finger inside the entrance of my core and I cry out and arch up against him, wanting more.

He growls low in arousal. "Soran please." My words escape in a breathless whisper as I writhe beneath his tongue. I want him inside me so badly. I long to take his stav deep in my channel; to know what it feels like to be completely connected to him in all ways. Banding one arm across my hips, he holds me in place as he continues to lap at my sensitive flesh.

Desire pulses through my veins as pleasure builds deep in my core. My entire body goes taut as his mouth closes over the sensitive nub. When he swirls his tongue across it, blinding heat rushes through me and I'm swept away into oblivion. I cry out his name as he continues to taste me, prolonging my pleasure as wave after wave washes through me; until I'm breathless and panting beneath him.

He lifts his head to look at me and I reach down, placing my hands on either side of his face. I pull his lips back up to mine, opening my thighs to cradle his hips between them. He stares down at me intensely. "You are my heart, Liana Garza of Terra. I vow to always and only be yours."

I smile up at him. "I love you, Soran of House Mosaura. I vow to always and only be yours." Repeating the sacred bonding words, I watch as a handsome smile lights his face.

He leans down to capture my mouth in a hungry kiss. I wrap my arms and legs around him, holding him close as he positions his stav at the entrance of my core.

A loud boom shakes the ground, and he stills above me. Sitting back on his knees, he pulls me with him, cradling my body against his chest as he looks out the mouth of the cave.

The forest falls eerily silent, and my skin prickles with fear.

"What was that?" I whisper.

He pulls on the blanket and wraps it tightly around me. "Dress quickly," he says, his gaze trained on the woods outside. "I think it's a ship entering atmosphere."

Hurriedly pulling on my clothes, I notice he doesn't bother covering himself. He moves to the cave entrance and then turns worried eyes to mine. "Wait here. I will make sure it's safe."

"What are you—" I start to ask, but he shifts, and before I can say another word his powerful wings are already lifting away, swirling snow and debris beneath him as he takes off into the sky.

How could he leave like that? He doesn't know that it's safe. I thought we agreed to stay together? Anger rushes through me, and I vow that the minute he returns we're going to have that discussion about trust that he's wanted to have ever since I shot him on the glider.

Pacing back and forth in the cave, I palm my blaster at my side as if to reassure myself that everything's going to be okay.

A deafening roar echoes through the forest, and my heart stutters and stops as the hairs rise on the back of my neck. I recognize that sound. It's Soran.

Grabbing the blaster in one hand and a torch in the other, I race through the woods toward the clearing. If a ship landed nearby, it has to be there.

# CHAPTER 33

SORAN

A deafening roar escapes my throat as intense heat rips through my side from the blast. My wings falter, and I crash to the earth, writhing in unbearable pain. Unable to maintain my draken form, I shift. Twisting onto my side, I band my arm across my torso, holding pressure over my wound as I struggle to catch my breath.

Gritting my teeth, it takes all my strength to stand as someone emerges from the ship.

It's a Mosauran transport. I do not understand. Why would they attack one of their own? I call out. "I am Soran of House Mosaura! Why do you fire on me?"

A moment later, Talel steps off the platform, a sinister grin on his face as he stalks toward me with his blaster in hand. His sharp gaze scans me from head to toe before sweeping out toward the forest. His expression becomes enraged. "Where is the female?"

Behind him, the ship's image shimmers and distorts as the guise of the Mosauran transport falls away to reveal an A'kai glider. I curse myself. I should have been more careful. I had no idea his people possessed this type of technology.

"Your ship exploded with the glider. You should be dead," I grind out. "How did you survive?"

Instead of answering, he raises his blaster. Without warning, bright light erupts from the barrel and races toward me. I lunge to the side but not fast enough. Warmth explodes through my chest, forcing the air from my lungs as I fly backward, slamming again to the ground.

Dazed, my eyelids flutter open and closed as I stare up at the overcast sky. In the part of my mind that's still functioning, I realize the blaster was not set to kill, or else I would already be dead. It must be on one of the lower settings. I'm able to move, but just barely. I groan as I twist onto my side, struggling to sit up, but it's no use. The world tilts and spins around me, and I collapse against the earth.

The crunch of his bootsteps through the snow as he approaches fills me with dread. My muscles quake in protest as I desperately try to push myself back up. I have to kill him. If I don't, he will find Liana.

He kneels beside me, baring his fangs, "Where is the female?"

With the last of my strength, I jerk my arm up and catch him by the neck.

His eyes go wide with fear as my fingers tighten around his throat.

Something sharp stabs my neck. Searing pain blooms from the site, causing me to relinquish my grip.

Reaching up, I pull a large dart from my flesh. Crushing the vial in my hand, shards of glass fall beside me, and the bittersweet scent of the breaking dart toxin fills the air.

I release a bellowing roar, cursing Talel to the Creator. From the size of the vial, and the way it's already starting to affect me, he must have given me at least three times the usual dose. The edges of my vision begin to darken, and my limbs feel heavy and numb as the poison spreads through my body. I tilt my chin up defiantly and meet his gaze. "She died in the crash."

He narrows his eyes and leans forward, flaring his nostrils. "You lie." He tips his head to the side. "I thought Mosaurans didn't believe in mixed-species pairings and yet...I can smell her delicious scent all over you."

Rage fills me. "You will not touch her again."

A wicked grin spreads across his face. "Yes, I will, and you will watch as I do."

Anger burns through my veins as my vision goes dark.

Completely blind, my ears twitch as the sound of crunching snow alerts me of movement off to the side. My nostrils flare as I scent two more A'kai.

Strong hands roughly grab at me, binding my arms and wings. A sharp sting on my side is quickly followed by Talel's dark voice.

"Try to shift, and the chip I placed inside you will explode."

Enraged, I snarl. "I will kill you if you harm her."

"You forget," he says. "I watched you fight in the arena. I know all of your tells and can anticipate your every move. Don't worry. We'll find your female, and you'll be reunited with her soon."

Gritting my teeth, I bare my fangs. "I will rip you apart until there's nothing left for your brother to mourn if you dare touch her. I swear it to the Creator."

Talel's men drag me through the snow and up onto the glider. The floor is cold as ice against my skin. The scent of blood, sweat, and death is thick in the air, telling me that many have met their end on this vessel.

A loud groan of metal echoes through the ship as a door swings open. Talel's men relinquish their grip a moment before forcefully pushing me forward. Unable to catch myself, I slam into a wall. The sharp clank of the cell sealing shut is a familiar one, stirring dark memories of my captivity.

I lift my head as an unexpected scent touches my nostrils, and a voice calls out.

"Soran, is that you?"

"Tr'lani?"

"Yes, it's me," she replies, panic laced in her tone. "Where is Liana? Does Talel have her?"

"No. She is safe."

Rowan's voice cuts through the darkness. "Brother, are you injured?"

"They stunned me with a blaster and injected me with breaking dart poison."

Tr'lani gasps.

"But I will regain my function shortly...and when I do," I growl, "I will kill them all."

"Agreed," he replies solemnly.

**Liana**

My heart stops when I reach the edge of the forest and see Talel and his men standing next to a glider, Soran's limp form on the ground beside them. I place a hand over my mouth to stifle a gasp and watch as two A'kai drag him into the ship. Oh God, what happened?

Talel turns his gaze out to the woods, seeming to stare directly at me. Ice-cold fear floods my veins, but it's quickly replaced with blinding rage. I'll kill him for hurting Soran.

"Find her!" he snaps at his guards, and I know he's speaking of me.

Quietly, I slip back into the forest and the shadows. I have a blaster, but there's two of them, and I cannot guarantee I'll be the victor in a firefight. Soran's counting on me; I can't afford to be captured.

An idea forms in my mind, and I race back toward the cave. When I finally reach the dead rabbupine's body near the entrance, I carefully grasp one of its quills and jerk it free from its lifeless corpse. Lifting the end to study it, hope fills me when I notice the poison glistening on the tip.

Soran said the tips of these quills were dangerous. I just have to pray that it's enough to do some damage to the A'kai. Quickly, I pull out three more. It won't take Talel's men long to locate me with the fire going.

My skin prickles in awareness as a low growl sounds from somewhere behind me. The wolves are watching, but they're far enough away that I don't have to worry about them just yet. And I may be able to use them.

Positioned behind several large boulders just outside the cave mouth, I cover myself with the wolf pelt I made, hoping it masks my scent from the A'kai.

It doesn't take long for Talel's men to arrive. Stomping around our shelter in frustration, one of them snarls. "She's not here!"

Concealing the quills up my sleeves, I step out from behind the rocks and raise my hands as if in surrender. "Please. Take me to Soran. I'll go with you if you will just take me to him."

One of them sneers. "Of course, you'll come with us."

I walk up between them. "I promise I won't fight. I just want to be with my mate."

"Mate?" one of the guard's eyes widen in shock. "Mosaurans do not take mates outside of their species." He lifts his head, his nostrils flaring. "You carry his scent, but he has not mated you. Yet." His gaze darts menacingly to the other guard as he steps toward me.

He reaches out and grabs a lock of my hair, lifting the strands to study them between his thumb and forefinger. "Just like silkara," he whispers. His glowing sinister green eyes meet mine. "Is your skin as soft as your hair, I wonder?" he asks, moving to touch me, but I jerk away.

His companion's gaze fixes on me as he speaks to his friend. "Let's wait to take her back. Talel says her blood is exquisite, and I would like to have a taste before we take her in."

The other guard nods in agreement, and they begin to circle me. Their green eyes swirl into obsidian orbs as their vampire fangs extend.

Like predators readying to pounce on their prey, their towering forms loom over me, and fear twists deep in my gut.

Lightning fast, I jab two rabbupine quills each up under their chins, piercing the skin below their jaws. They howl in surprise before snarling and ripping the quills from their bodies, throwing them off to the side.

Their nostrils flare in anger, and I slowly back away, raising my blaster to point it at the closest one. If I need to, I'll use it, but first, I want to see if this poison works. It's essential to my plan.

Fury burns in their eyes as they stalk toward me. Without warning, the closest one rushes forward with blinding speed and knocks the blaster from my grasp. His hand clamps around my throat in a crushing grip.

Gasping for air, I claw at his hand, struggling to escape his deadly hold.

Suddenly, his expression falters. His glowing eyes register shock and then disbelief as his hold on me loosens, and I drop to the ground.

He and his companion fall to their knees and collapse in the snow as paralysis sets in.

I pull their blasters from their belts to disarm them and glance over my shoulders to find several pairs of yellow eyes in the woods behind me, observing with great interest.

Fear mars their features the minute they notice the wolves.

I don't know why they haven't attacked yet, but I can only guess it is because Soran's scent is so strong here both in the cave and on me. These creatures are intelligent, remembering what he is and how easily he killed one of their brethren.

Stepping farther back from the two guards, I watch as the first wolf stalks toward them, passing me by as if I weren't even there.

"Enjoy your meal," I whisper.

Pulling another four quills from the dead rabbupine's body, I conceal them in my sleeves and head back for the clearing.

Snarls and muffled screams echo loudly through the forest, and then fall silent. I feel no remorse for the deaths of those men; I'm only relieved that they're dead. Satisfied that they will no longer be a problem, my thoughts turn to Talel. Gripping one of the blasters in my palm, I set it to kill. I will make sure he can never hurt anyone the way he hurt me, ever again.

When I return to the edge of the forest, I conceal myself behind one of the large tree trunks. From here, I can see the ship and get an accurate headcount on how many men Talel has left. If he keeps sending them out into the woods, that will work in my favor. After all,

I know this place better than they do. They have no idea the dangers or what waits for them when they come after me.

His vessel is small, no bigger than a transport. The larger ship must be in orbit above the planet. I estimate the glider only carries maybe six people at most. I've already taken care of two. Now, I just have to wait for him to send more.

He does, and after disabling two more of his guards and leaving them to be found by the wolves, I return to the edge of the clearing to look for Talel. He'd be a fool to send more men, especially since he probably only has two left, but I also know he believes I'm weak. So, I wait to see if he or more of his people emerge from the ship.

The sun dips low on the horizon, casting long shadows across the forest floor as I crouch behind a large trunk. My eyes struggle to adjust in the growing darkness. If I wait any longer, I won't be able to see anything. I'm going to have to try to sneak onto the glider to rescue Soran.

A branch snaps behind me, and I spin toward the sound. The hairs rise on the back of my neck as I scan the dark woods. A pair of glowing green orbs float toward me in the blackness.

A low growl fills the air, and I inhale sharply as they blink. Lightning fast, I raise my blaster and fire but miss as Talel twists to the side, avoiding the hit.

Rushing toward me with inhuman speed, he wraps one hand around my throat and lifts me into the air. Pain explodes across the back of my skull as he slams me against the tree.

The world spins around me, and I blink several times, struggling to remain conscious as darkness dances at the edge of my vision. My skin crawls when he leans forward to scent me, his nose skimming along my neck.

He jerks back in disgust. "You stink of the Mosauran. I'll have to clean you before we can play, my pet." An evil grin lights his face. "And then you can tell me where your home world is. My people are very interested in finding yours now that they know what your blood can do."

My nostrils flare as I glare at him in defiance. "I'll never tell you, you monster."

His lips twist up in a feral snarl and sick delight dances behind his eyes as he stares at me. "I'll tear your mind apart if I must. But make no mistake, I will find this information. But that will have to wait until we get back to the glider. I promised your Mosauran he could watch as I take you in front of him."

Rage fills me, and I kick out with my left leg, making contact with his chest.

My triumph is short-lived when he hits me with a shock stick, jamming it into my side. Electricity arcs through my body, and my mouth opens in a silent scream as my eyes roll up in the back of my head, and I fall away into darkness.

# CHAPTER 34

LIANA

When I open my eyes, my vision is blurry. Blinking several times, it slowly comes into focus. Panic tightens my chest when I realize I'm suspended in a force field, unable to move and dressed in only a paper-thin gown.

An Anguis moves in front of me, his long, sinuous tail coiled behind him as if readying to strike. The nearly transparent inner lids sweep across his obsidian eyes. The yellow vertical slit pupils expand as his forked tongue snakes out, scenting the air. "Excellent," he hisses. "You're awake."

Despite my fear, I force my gaze to remain locked on his but say nothing. I already know from my time as a slave that pleading and tears won't solve anything.

I scan the room for anything that might help me escape. A large metal table off to the side is lined with various sharp instruments. A few syringes sit on the end, filled with dark yellow liquid that looks just like the sedatives used by the slavers. Hope fills me. If I can somehow distract the Anguis, I might have a chance.

The doors whoosh open, drawing my attention across the room to find Talel. My pulse pounds in my ears as he walks in, a sinister grin on his face as he approaches. "Release her," he snaps at the Anguis.

"But, my Lord, she has not been sedated."

He turns a dark gaze to the Anguis who cowers before him. "Yes, Lord Talel."

As soon as he presses the release, I drop like a stone to the floor. I move to stand, but Talel's words stop me abruptly.

"Remain on your knees," he commands.

Clenching my jaw, I do as he says. Without a weapon of some sort, I have no hope of disabling him to escape. So, I hold my hands up in mock surrender and use the only weapon available to me in this moment: Deception.

Lowering my head into a subservient pose, I speak in a soft and trembling voice. "I give up. Please just don't give me back to the Mosauran, and I'll do whatever you want."

He's silent, and when I cautiously lift my gaze to his, glowing green eyes meet mine. "You will do whatever I want anyway, my pet."

Remembering how much he loved to force my submission, I bow low as he stands before me. My gaze darts briefly to the syringes on the table beside him. If I can, at least, immobilize him, the Anguis will be easier to take down.

He inhales sharply, and I hold my breath as he steps forward. Placing a hand on my hair, he gently runs his fingers through the long strands. "It appears you missed me," he says in a voice tinged with awe and disbelief.

I remain silent.

"Look at me," he snaps, and I immediately lift my eyes to his, feigning submission.

"Please don't give me back to the Mosauran," I practically whimper. "I'll do anything. Just please, don't give me back to him."

His eyes widen in shock. "You fear the Mosauran more than you fear me?"

I nod quickly.

Talel steps forward and gives me a curious look. This is what he wants: to be adored despite his cruelty. I discovered this in his thoughts when we were connected. "If this is a trick, I will know once I touch your mind."

Despite his even tone, it is easy to recognize the hope in his voice. He wants to believe that I would actually submit to him of my own accord. "It is not a trick. I swear."

Moving purposefully closer, I lift my chin to stare directly into his eyes and turn my head slightly to the side as if offering my neck.

His glowing green eyes swirl into pitch-black, obsidian orbs as he stares at me with a hungry gaze, his fangs extending in anticipation as he steps toward me. He snaps at the Anguis. "Leave us!"

My heart hammers as he drops to his knees before me, placing his hands reverently on my shoulders, staring deep into my eyes. "You are my special one." Cupping his hand to my cheek, he runs the pad of his thumb lightly across my skin in a gentle caress. "Your blood healed my mortal wound. You and your kind will be both savior and servant to mine. You will save your Masters, and you will adore us as gods."

Wrapping his arm around my body, he drags me closer while his other hand moves to my hair. Grasping the long strands, he forcefully pulls to tip back my head, exposing the column of my neck. Fear coils tight around my spine as he drops his head to the curve of my neck and shoulder, inhaling deeply.

"The scent of your blood calls to me even now."

I shudder inwardly as his tongue snakes out, and he licks the flesh over my artery. My eyes dart again to the syringe on the table beside us, almost even with his shoulder. "I will drink of your blood and enter your mind. I will fill you with longing and desire for my touch. And you will adore and worship me as the god that I am and will be to your people."

Panic beats at my chest, but I force myself to remain still. The A'kai are fast, much faster than Terrans. If I reach for the syringe now, I won't stand a chance.

The sharp tips of his fangs graze my skin, and I choke on a scream as he sinks them deep into my flesh. The suction and pull as he drinks my blood is excruciating agony, and I can feel my body growing weaker as he feeds.

The hard press of his erection against my abdomen fills me with disgust, and when he drops one hand to fumble with the clasp of his pants, I take advantage of his distraction. In one swift motion, I grab the syringe and plunge the sedative deep into the side of his neck.

He jerks back, his eyes burning with anger as crimson blood drips from his fangs and chin.

In a blur of movement so fast, I barely have time to register it, the back of his hand connects with my jaw.

My head whips to the side, and pain explodes through my body as I slam to the floor.

He bares his fangs, and a thunderous roar rips from his throat.

I scramble away, but he grabs my ankle and jerks me back toward him. Clamping his hand around my throat, he begins to squeeze. "How dare you try to deceive your god."

Digging my fingers into the flesh of his hand, I open my mouth, gasping for air as he holds my neck in an iron vise.

Darkness creeps in around the edges of my vision as I fight to remain conscious. I cannot give up. I have to find Soran.

Talel's dark gaze burns into mine as a low growl rises from his chest. "I will teach you obedience."

Like a sharp blade, his consciousness stabs through mine. My eyes roll up in the back of my head under the assault of his rage. Dark tendrils unfurl and snake through my mind as his voice echoes deep inside me. *"Give me the name of your home world."*

*"Mars."* I throw up the lie, creating a wall between us, and brace myself to defend it from invasion.

His grip loosens, and his mind recedes from mine as the sedative begins to take hold. "What have—" he mumbles, falling to the side. His eyes are wide as he stares up at me in shock. "What have you done to me?"

His hand falls away from my neck, and I gasp as oxygen floods my burning lungs. Rolling onto my side I cough, struggling to draw in several deep breaths.

Weak from blood loss, my head swims, and my movements are sluggish and uncoordinated. Shaking, I barely manage to get to my feet. Freeing the blaster from Talel's belt, I click the setting to stun and shoot him three times for good measure. Enough to make sure he stays down.

Anger fills me as I stare at his body. I'm tempted to set the blaster to kill and end him right now, but I need him alive so I can find out who his beloved is. She's the key to discovering the location of my home world.

But first, I need to find Soran.

Stumbling, I make my way toward the doors. I slam my hand on the access panel, and they whoosh open. A noxious stench hangs thick in the air, and an intense wave of nausea rolls through me. Swallowing against the bile rising in my throat, I scan the hallway and notice a long row of cells. Several pairs of eyes of varying shapes and colors meet mine with shocked expressions visible in their alien features. This is too large to be the glider. We must have been transferred to a bigger ship.

Several voices cry out, fear and desperation in their tone. "Help us! Please! Release us from these cells!"

Groggy and weak, I force myself to continue forward.

"The controls are on the far wall," another voice yells. "Hurry!"

"Liana!" Soran's voice calls out, and I turn to see him in one of the cages. "Open the cells before they come back! Quickly!"

Tearing my eyes away from him, I limp toward the control panel.

"Hit the display twice for release," someone says.

Struggling to keep my eyes open, I force myself to focus on my task. Foreign symbols light up the screen, and I tap my fingers twice in the center.

Sharp clicks echo behind me as all the cell locks snap open. When I turn to find Soran, the world tilts and spins around me, and I collapse to the floor in a boneless heap.

"The V'loryn saved us. Help her," someone says behind me.

Warm hands touch my face before a low and threatening growl sounds overhead. "Release her," Soran's voice fills my ears. "She is mine."

≈

**Soran**

The Lacerta steps back, and I scoop Liana's unconscious form into my arms.

Her eyelids peel open just enough for her gaze to meet mine. She reaches up to cup her hand to my face. "Soran," she whispers, barely managing a faint smile before her head lolls back, and she stills.

Panic races through me when I notice the puncture marks on the side of her neck. Although they are not bleeding, crimson stains trail down her skin from the site. My nostrils flare as I scent Talel, and my blood boils with rage.

Flashing red lights fill the hallways as loud sirens blare through the speakers. People scramble and rush past us in their hurry to escape. Holding Liana, I turn my attention to the display and quickly scroll through the menus to access the ship's systems. It doesn't take much effort to disable security.

After that's done, I pull up a map of the facility and then spin back to the crowded hallway, scanning for Rowan and Tr'lani as we race toward the docking bay.

They are here somewhere; I just need to find them. Pushing past the throng of people, I hold Liana tight to my chest as we run through the corridors.

When we reach the docking bay, I'm surprised to see not only smaller transports but several large and expensive ships. Anger floods my veins when I realize these must belong to prospective buyers that are here to purchase slaves or partake of their services.

"Soran!" I hear my brother's voice cry out.

I turn toward the sound. He holds tight to Tr'lani as they push through the crowd to reach us.

Rowan's eyes go wide as he looks down at Liana's still form in my arms. "What happened?"

My eyes dart to the two puncture wounds on her neck, and Tr'lani gasps when she follows my gaze. "Talel attacked her," I explain before

263

turning my attention back to the rest of the escaped prisoners. "Have you seen Grex or Abby?"

She shakes her head. "Not since the escape pods."

Rowan scans the bay and then motions off to the left. "We must hurry. We need a ship."

We race toward the closest one and rush up the ramp, sealing the door shut behind us. When we reach the bridge, Rowan spins up the engines while I strap Liana in a chair next to Tr'lani. Just outside the viewscreen, chaos reigns as the rest of the former slaves frantically board the other ships and gliders in an attempt to get away.

I don't know where Talel is hiding, but we don't have time to look for him now. This ship is large and crawling with Anguis and Zovian slavers. We need to get as far away from here as possible.

We lift off, and Rowan carefully maneuvers our vessel toward the exit, careful to avoid colliding with the dozens of other ships that are escaping too. As soon as we pass through the force shield, our consoles light up, and alarms begin to sound with a proximity warning. My jaw drops as a massive cruiser comes into view.

Tr'lani cries out excitedly. "That's my brother's ship!"

Rowan looks to her. "You are certain?"

"Yes."

He nods and spins back in his chair, typing into the console to send out a hail.

Within moments, Al'aneo appears in the viewscreen. His eyes go wide as they meet his sister's. A low hum of greeting sounds in the back of his throat.

Tr'lani answers him with her own. "Thank the Creator you are here, Al'aneo."

He opens his mouth as if to reply but quickly snaps it shut as someone approaches behind him, whispering in his ear. His gaze darts off to the side, a slight frown tilting his lips as he studies something we cannot see from our viewscreen.

He turns his attention back to us. "Stay where you are. We are sending a team to take care of the slavers so that we may liberate their cargo." He narrows his eyes. "Their executions will be swift. When we are finished with them, you may dock with us.

He leans forward to cut off the viewscreen, but I stop him abruptly. "Talel, brother of the First Prime of A'kaina is on that ship."

Surprise followed quickly by anger flashes across his expression. "It matters not who he is. He was trafficking slaves, and he *will* meet the same fate as the others."

"We need him alive."

Fury burns in his eyes. "Why?"

I gesture to Liana's still form in my arms. "Because he has information that could help us locate my Ashaya's home world. Once we extract it from him, I will kill him myself. I swear it to the Creator."

Drawing in a deep breath, Al'aneo gives me a quick jerk of his chin. "Fine. But only because he has information about my sister's home world."

His reply catches me off guard, and it takes me a moment to realize he is speaking of Liana. They truly do consider her part of their clan.

He reaches forward, and the screen goes blank.

# CHAPTER 35

LIANA

When I open my eyes, it's to a brightly lit room. Sterile walls and the faint hum of a scanner at the head of my bed tell me I'm in a med center, but I don't know where. My gaze travels over my surroundings, and I find Soran asleep in a chair beside me. His large, hulking form barely fits in the seat. He looks terribly uncomfortable, and I wonder how long he's been there.

As if sensing I'm awake, his eyes open, and a wide smile spreads across his face. He stands and leans over me, pressing a quick kiss to my forehead as he stares down at me with a strange mixture of panic and devotion. "You're awake." He takes my hand gently in his own. "How do you feel?"

"I'm fine," I whisper. "Thank God you're all right."

"Of course, I am." He gives me a teasing grin. "I am a big, strong Mosauran warrior."

Rolling my eyes, I shake my head softly and a short puff of air escapes me as I laugh.

He presses his lips to my mouth in a brief kiss. When he pulls back, his eyes search mine in concern. "Are you thirsty? Hungry? Do you need anything?"

I'm surprised that I'm neither thirsty nor hungry. But there is something that I need to know. "Where are we, and what happened to Talel?"

"We are safe and on board Tr'lani's brother's ship. The Aerilon have Talel in a holding cell."

I stare up at him in confusion. "How did we end up here?"

He explains everything that happened after I passed out, including how Grex and Abby were the first ones found by Al'aneo's ship. I need to speak with Talel, but before I can say anything else, Tr'lani's brother Al'aneo enters the room. He begins to hum in friendly greeting. "My sister. It is good to see you are well."

Tr'lani steps forward and takes my hand before leaning down to wrap her arms around me. "I'm so glad you are awake," she whispers in my ear.

I'm so happy to see her, it's difficult to hold back tears of joy as I return her embrace. "I was so worried about you. What happened? Where did you and Rowan end up after the glider?"

Pulling back, she gives me a warm smile. "You should rest. We have plenty of time to talk about it later. We are almost to Mosaura, and it is only a few solars travel after that to Aerilon. Your new home," she adds. "I'll let Abby and Grex know you're up. They came to check on you less than an hour ago."

Al'aneo moves to her side and I catch his attention. "I need to speak with Talel."

He and Tr'lani are twins, and it is easy to recognize the warmth in his expression. "We will arrange it. But right now, you must rest. I will take you to him first thing in the morning."

"No, I need to speak with him now. He's the only chance I have of finding Terra."

He gives me a pitying look. "If Talel knows the location of your home world, the A'kai have probably already conquered your people."

I shake my head. "He doesn't know where my planet is, but he knows someone that does."

His brow furrows deeply in confusion. "Who is it?"

Soran interrupts. "Liana overheard Talel speaking with his mate, and while she did not see her face, their conversation made it clear she is not A'kai. She mentioned a city on Liana's home world. Her people have made contact with theirs. Because the female did not see Liana and never mentioned her planet by name, Talel is unaware of the connection. He does not realize how close he is to finding Terra."

Al'aneo looks to me again, his golden eyes studying me intently. "Is there anything you can tell us about your home world that might help us locate it?"

"My people have never ventured beyond our planetary system. Terra is the third planet of eight orbiting a yellow dwarf star. We call our galaxy the Milky Way. I scanned many of the stellar maps on the glider, but so far, nothing looks even remotely familiar to me."

He rests a hand on my forearm and gives it a gentle squeeze. "Do not give up hope, Liana. We will not stop until we find your planet. But as for Talel...you are still recovering. Our people are already interrogating him. We will find out who his mate is. Please rest so that you can regain your strength. I promise you may see him in the morning."

Tr'lani takes my hand. "He's right. You should rest. We are almost to Mosaura." She darts a glance at Soran. "We will continue on from there to Aerilon."

Soran's gaze drops to the floor, and I open my mouth to speak to him, but Al'aneo interrupts me. "Tr'lani told me you are a pilot. That you were interested in seeking similar employment on our world."

"Yes, I did talk to her about that." I glance at Soran, but his expression is unreadable. "Would you mind if I had a moment alone with Soran?"

"Of course," they reply and quickly leave the room.

Sadness flashes briefly behind his eyes as he stares down at me. "You still wish to go to Aerilon?"

"I don't know. I thought I did, but now with you—"

Abby and Grex walk in, interrupting us. Abby rushes toward me. "You're awake." She smiles brightly and takes my hand in her own.

I smile back, but my eyes drift to Grex pulls Soran aside. "Your mother, the Empress, has contacted the ship. She is waiting to speak with you."

Soran turns to me. "I will be back as soon as I can."

My first instinct is to ask him to wait—to stay and tell me why he's acting so strange. Does he think I'm going to go to Aerilon without him? While that may have been the plan before, everything has definitely changed now that we're together. He told me he was mine and I was his. Now, we need to discuss what happens next. Once we've figured that out, we'll talk to Tr'lani and Al'aneo.

The words are just on the tip of my tongue, but I cannot force them past my lips. Despite how much I want to know why his eyes look so sad, his mother is waiting to speak with him. I don't want to keep him from his family. How long has it been since he talked with her?

He and Rowan had already been away from Mosaura at least a week on their journey to V'lora to negotiate a new trade agreement for L'sair crystals for the Empire. Several weeks have passed since then, and so much has happened.

We won't arrive at Mosaura for a few days. We'll have lots of time to discuss all this later. I nod. "All right."

With a subtle inclination of his head, he leaves the room.

I sit up in the bed and turn my attention to Abby.

She lovingly cradles her hands over her very pregnant belly. Grex's tail wraps protectively around her abdomen as his large palm settles over hers. My heart melts when he presses a tender kiss to the back of her head.

"How's the baby?"

She's practically glowing as she answers. "The Healer says she's perfectly healthy."

"What happened to you two after the escape pods?"

"We landed on this amazing world with pink sandy beaches and lavender oceans." She shrugs. "After everything we've been through, it was almost like a mini-vacation."

I have to force myself not to purse my lips. *Of course*, they landed on a beautiful tropical island while Soran and I were struggling to survive in the alien version of Alaskan winter. But as my eyes drift to the large swell of her abdomen, I'm grateful they didn't land on the same planet we did. Although it was nice, it still must have been terrifying for them to be alone, especially with a baby on the way.

She continues. "There were these strange dolphin-looking creatures, and they would jump out of the water...they were so friendly. It was amazing, Liana. And—it didn't take long for Tr'lani's brother to find us."

"Al'aneo found you?"

"Yes. They came looking for us." She pats Grex's arm around her waist. "They even offered to allow us to make our home on Aerilon. They said the same for you and Soran, since he's going to be Outcast now."

My eyes snap up to hers. "Outcast?"

Her brow furrows. "He didn't tell you? His people—the Mosaurans —they don't believe in mixed-species pairings. Any who take a mate outside their race become Outcast from their society, and they cannot return home."

I look to Grex. "And—your people? The Lacerta?"

"The same," he replies with a grim expression. "But I'm not like Soran. After the last war, I don't have any family to return to. Abby and our child are all I have left."

His words settle like a heavy stone in the pit of my stomach. Soran would be Outcast if he stays with me. He would lose everything. His home, his family, his title, his people. I can't let him give all that up. I know what it's like to be separated from the ones you love. It's the worst pain imaginable.

It's decided then. I'll go to Aerilon with Tr'lani and Al'aneo. I won't let Soran give up everything for me. I love him too much.

# CHAPTER 36

LIANA

T r'lani leads me from the med center and down a long
hallway. I'm surprised at how beautifully decorated the interior is. This ship feels more like a home than a military
cruiser.

Elegant trim and crown molding carved in intricate nature designs
line the corridors and rooms. Soft glowing light filters down from the
panels above. Thick, plush brown carpet covers the floors, and the
walls are a comforting shade of light green. In several areas, flowering
vines spill over from containers above to drape down the walls in
fascinating curtains of bioluminescent purples, reds, blues, and
greens.

So fascinated by the design of the ship, I almost run into Tr'lani's
back when she stops in front of a set of doors, motioning to them.
"These are your quarters."

She leads me inside, and my jaw drops as my eyes scan a cabin that
looks much too large and opulent to be aboard a ship. "Tr'lani," I
whisper in amazement, "this is gorgeous."

A smile lights her face. "I wanted you to be comfortable. These quarters are reserved for members of the family. Since you are now part of our clan, they belong to you too."

Emotion wells up inside me, and my voice is thick as I hug her tightly. "You'll never know how much it means to me that you've welcomed me into your family."

"You will always be part of our clan, my beautiful sister."

"Thank you."

She pulls back and gives me a warm smile. "I am in the room just to your left down the hall. The cleansing unit is through these doors"—she motions off to the side—"and I've already had clothing placed in there for you." She puts her hands on my shoulders and gives me a pointed look. "You lost quite a bit of blood, and you need to rest while your body replenishes from the injection I gave you. I know you wish to speak with Talel. But rest assured that our people are doing everything they can to gather information from him."

Because the Aerilon know that he trafficked in slaves, I can only imagine the torture being inflicted upon him to give up said information, but I certainly don't feel sorry for him. Not in the least. I just hope he's still able to speak by the time I get a chance to interrogate him myself tomorrow. But first, there is something more pressing that I need to ask.

"Tr'lani?"

"Yes?"

"Did you know about the Mosaurans? That they become Outcast if they take a mate outside their race?"

From the sadness that flashes behind her eyes and the expression on her face, she doesn't have to speak, because I already know the answer. Lowering her gaze from mine, she nods. "It is an old law. One that my people used to follow as well before we became more...enlightened."

She takes my hands in her own, giving them a gentle, reassuring squeeze. "You and Soran are welcome to live with us. Despite the long history of mistrust that exists between our two species, I do not doubt that he will be accepted into the clan if you take him as your mate."

I swallow against the lump in my throat and meet her gaze evenly.

"I can't do that to him. I can't ask him to give up everything for me." I place my hand over my heart. "I know how much it hurts to be separated from your family, and I wouldn't wish that kind of pain on anyone...especially not on him. I love him too much."

Expecting her to argue, I'm surprised when she doesn't. "I understand. As much as I—" her voice catches, and she lowers her gaze as a tear slips down her cheek. Brushing it away, she continues. "As much as I care about Rowan, I couldn't let him become Outcast for me either."

Her words stun me, and my mouth drifts open in shock before I quickly snap it shut. I wrap my arms around her, and she returns the embrace. "Sometimes," she whispers, "the most selfless thing you can do for someone you love...is to let them go."

Unable to speak through my emotions, I nod against her.

When she finally pulls back, she reaches forward to tuck a stray lock of hair behind my ear as she gives me a pained smile. "If you need me, I am just down the hall."

"Will you please tell Soran where to find me? I need to...speak with him."

She nods.

As soon as she's gone, I explore the room, trying to occupy my mind so I don't think on what I must do. These quarters are larger than anything I've ever stayed in. Tr'lani's family must be really important...unless this is just the status quo for their people. She told me that Aerilon value jewels and precious metals, and it's definitely reflected in not just the décor on the ship, but also in all the elegant furnishings in the rooms.

The large floating bed near the far wall has an intricate metal and wood pattern on the frame depicting an elaborate nature scene. Aside from the fact that it's suspended above the floor by some kind of invisible force, it looks like something that belongs in a castle, straight out of a fairy-tale book.

Allowing myself to fall back onto the puffy cloud-like comforter, everything here seems to be designed not just for aesthetics, but also for comfort. From the plush, thick rugs to the soft, stuffed cushions of the furniture. The window takes up half the outer wall. It's larger than the viewscreen of any ship I've ever been in, and as the stars blur past us outside, it's nothing short of stunning.

Although much larger, the cleansing room is similar enough to the one on the glider that I don't have any trouble making use of the shower. Despite the warm water, my every muscle is still tense as I slip on the silken lavender gown Tr'lani laid out for me. It's soft on my skin, but also so short and low cut, it leaves almost nothing to the imagination. I'm glad when I notice the long, matching robe lying next to it and quickly wrap it around my shoulders.

Laying on one of the plush sofas, I stare out at the viewscreen and the myriad stars blurring past. The heavy weight of my exhaustion tries to claim me, but I fight it back. Reaching up to touch my lips, I close my eyes, remembering the feel of Soran's mouth on mine. Sadness fills me, and I shake my head softly. I have to let him go.

The door chimes, ripping me from my thoughts. "Enter," I call out.

Soran steps inside. He walks toward me and his eyes go wide as they drift down my form. "You were sleeping." He says this as a statement, but I know it's meant as a question.

"I laid down for a bit, but I was waiting for you."

He gives me a hesitant look. "What is wrong?"

"Grex told me about your people. About you becoming Outcast if you take me as your mate." I search his eyes. "Is it true?"

Lowering his gaze, he nods. "It is truth. I wanted to tell you, but I needed to speak with my mother first to see if an exception could be made."

From his expression and his tone, I already know what her answer must have been.

I shake my head. "Why didn't you say anything before now?"

He kneels in front of the sofa. Gathering me into his arms, he runs his fingers through my hair as he presses a soft kiss to my forehead. "Because I didn't want you to be hurt, Liana, if my mother didn't accept you."

"You were worried about *me* being hurt?" I ask incredulously.

"What about *you*? You're the one who would be giving up everything. I can't let you do that, Soran. Not for me."

He stills and gives me a wary look. "What are you saying?"

"I'm going to Aerilon with Tr'lani and Al'aneo. I won't let you become Outcast from your people."

His eyes search mine with a mixture of grief and confusion. "You do not wish to be my mate?"

Tears swim at the edge of my vision from his devastated expression. "It doesn't matter what I want, Soran. I won't let you give up everything for me."

Placing his hands on either side of my face, he forces my gaze to his. His silver eyes practically burning as they stare deep into mine. "It is not your decision. It is mine. You are my mate, and you chose me to be yours." He takes my hand and places it to his chest. "You are my heart, Liana. I cannot be without you. No matter the cost to myself."

His words make my breath catch in my throat, and before I can say anything else, he pulls me into his arms and seals his mouth over mine in a claiming kiss.

I'm breathless as he lifts me from the sofa and carries me to the bed.

Gently, he lays me down beneath the blankets and moves in after me. He pulls me close until there is no space between us. He captures my mouth, pressing his lips to mine with an urgency that makes my heart pound.

His large dark-gray wings wrap around and enfold me, molding my body to his.

I gaps as he rolls me beneath him. He settles between my thighs and I moan as his stav presses insistently against my center. With only the thin barrier of his clothing between us, desire pools deep in my core and I long to take him inside me.

His nostrils flare as he draws in my scent, and when his eyes meet mine, the same hunger reflects in them that he had in the cave. "Tell me that you still love me...that you desire me to be yours," he whispers. "Tell me, my Ashaya."

Tears sting my eyes. "I can't let you give up everything for me, my love."

He presses his soft lips to mine. "It is not your decision. It is mine," he whispers between kisses. "And I cannot be without you." He pulls back just enough to stare deep into my eyes. "You are my heart. Tell me that I am yours as well."

I reach up and cup my hands to his face and meet his silver gaze evenly. "You are my heart, and I am yours."

He crushes his lips to mine with an intensity that leaves me breathless and panting with want. Pressing a line of kisses along my neck, it is the most exquisite sensation as he rolls his hips against mine and wraps his wings even tighter around me.

I run my fingers through his hair and whisper softly in his ear, "Shav-rhokan."

He stills for a beat and then captures my mouth in a branding kiss that steals the air from my lungs.

I unfasten the clasps of his shirt and slide it back from his shoulders, running my hands over the layers of corded muscle of his powerful form. Like fine silk stretched over hardened steel, he is masculine perfection and he is all mine.

Careful of my skin, he extends his claws and slices a sharp line down the fabric of my gown, leaving me bare beneath him. His eyes travel over my body. "You are more beautiful than anything I have ever seen," he whispers in awe-filled reverence.

Gently, I slide my fingers beneath the waistband of his pants and push them down over his hips. I want no clothing between us now. All I want is him.

He stares down at me with an intense gaze of love and devotion. "You are my heart, Liana Garza of Terra."

Lost in the depths of his silver eyes, I trace my fingers along the deep scar that runs from his brow to his cheek as if reminding myself that he's real and he's here. I've dreamed of him for so long and now he's finally mine. I cup my hand to his neck and pull his mouth down to my own. Tender at first, he groans low in his throat as his tongue curls around mine and he deepens our kiss.

I run my hands through his hair and then trace them down his neck to his shoulders, kneading the powerful muscles along the length of his back. They ripple and flex beneath my fingers. With his bare skin against my own, warmth floods my body as I wrap my legs around him, holding him close. His stav is a hard brand against my inner thigh as he moves his hips against me.

With one arm braced to my side to keep the bulk of his weight off my form, his other hand cups my jaw before he gently trails his fingers down my neck and farther until he reaches the gentle slope of one breast.

Palming the soft globe in his hand, he teases the peak into a hard-beaded tip as he rolls it between his thumb and forefinger. I gasp and arch beneath him and he swallows my cries with a kiss.

He shifts and his stav moves between my slick folds. A low groan escapes him, and he closes his eyes as if reveling the sensation before he claims my mouth like a man possessed.

He's larger than any Terran male could ever be, and as I reach down and wrap my fingers around his thick, ridged length, he growls low in arousal as I place his tip at the entrance to my core. Desire pulses deep inside me; I long to join my body with his.

His gaze holds mine and the breath stutters from my lungs as he slowly enters me. Tight heat blooms deep within, and I gasp at the small twinge of pain as he pushes through my barrier, filling me completely. It only lasts a moment as my body adjusts to his.

He moves his hips, and my head falls back as sensation ripples through my body; the ridged length of his stav creating the most delicious friction between us.

A low moan escapes my mouth as he shifts his hips and then sinks even deeper. With his wings wrapped tightly around my form in a possessive and claiming embrace, he moves in a slow and steady rhythm.

His silver reflective eyes stare deep into mine with a look of intense claim and devotion, and I've never felt so safe and loved as I do in his arms at this moment.

I reach up to trace the hard line of his jaw and stare at him in wonder, lost in the sensation of my body joined with his.

Cupping the back of his neck, I pull his mouth back down to me. "I love you," I whisper against his perfect lips. I wrap my arms and legs tighter around him, drawing him impossibly deeper.

The small muscles of my channel flutter around his length as I adjust to the overwhelming fullness of his stav completely sheathed inside me. He groans low in his throat and then begins to move faster. "Mine," he growls, staring deep into my eyes as he claims my body in long, deep strokes.

"Yours," I breathe. We move as one until I'm only aware of him and him alone. Nothing exists outside of this joining of our bodies. His intense silver gaze holds mine as every movement of his body brings me closer to the edge.

My mouth falls open as desire burns through me. All-consuming and overwhelming. Each thrust of his hips becomes more forceful and deeper, and I arch my body to meet his. A tight coil of pleasure builds deep within my core and I'm breathless and panting beneath him.

He drops down low and wraps his arms beneath me, holding me closer. With his chest pressed against mine, I gasp as this new angle makes everything more sensitive. His entire body is trembling as if it's taking all his strength to keep from losing control. "I want to be gentle with you," he rasps.

"You won't hurt me. I promise." Wrapping my legs tighter around him, I whisper against his lips. "I am the bondmate of a Mosauran warrior. I've chosen you as mine, and I want all of you."

He captures my mouth in a branding kiss. A low and feral growl escapes his throat and each movement of his hips becomes deeper and more powerful.

I twine my arms around his neck, holding tight to his heavily muscled form as the fire of his passion consumes me. The ridges of his stav move deep inside me, creating delicious heat and friction.

His silver eyes stare down at me, all fire and possession as he claims my body with each and every stroke. The muscles of my channel clench tightly around his stav. My body goes taut. Blinding heat sweeps through me and I cry out his name as wave after wave of pleasure moves through my entire form.

"You. Are. Mine." He growls and then clamps a strong hand on my hip. Holding me in place, his strokes become more forceful. I open my mouth as another orgasm rushes through me, in the wake of the first one; more intense than anything I've ever felt before.

I gasp and cry out in overwhelming pleasure as he makes one final thrust, burying himself impossibly deeper and pinning me in place. My vision goes white as his stav pulses deep inside my core, filling me with delicious warmth as he roars above me. "Mine!"

He collapses on top of me, but makes sure to keep most of his weight on his elbow at my side. I run my fingers gently up and down the length of his back. His heart beats wildly against mine as he nuzzles my neck. "You are mine," he growls low in my ear.

With our bodies still joined, he stares down at me and I already know what is coming. A softly glowing light centers on his chest and begins to grow brighter. He places his palm directly over the spot, and when he pierces his chest with his claws, the light begins to pulse. Extending his hand to my chest, directly over my heart, the tips of his claws lightly pierce my skin. A small hiss of pain escapes my lips at the sharp sting, but he captures my mouth in a kiss, replacing my discomfort with pleasure.

Although he explained this to me when I asked about shav-rhokan, nervous anticipation fills me as he lowers his body so that his chest is completely pressed against mine. Heat sears my skin directly beneath his beating heart, but he swallows my gasp with another kiss.

Intense warmth blooms from the site and across my entire body, filling me with a delicious heat. I close my eyes, lost in the sensation— as if it is wrapping around my very soul. A wave of pure bliss moves through me.

I open my eyes in sudden awareness as our hearts sync, beating in time as one. "You are my heart," he whispers before pressing a tender kiss to my lips.

Skimming the tip of his nose alongside mine, he wraps his arms and wings possessively tighter around me. With his stav still buried deep and hard inside me, he cups one hand to my breast, and then angles his lips over mine. And I don't think we're going to sleep anytime soon.

~

### Soran

I try to let her rest, but I cannot stop kissing her soft, warm skin and gazing at her in wonder. She is perfect, and when she opens her sea-green eyes to stare up at me, that is my undoing. I have to have her again. We mate several more times throughout the night and into the morning. I am reluctant to release her from my arms when she says she wants to bathe, but I remember how obsessed her people are with bathing, and I join her in the shower.

I run my hands over her beautiful form as I kiss a trail down her jaw to the curve of her neck and shoulder. She gasps lightly, and I lift my head to look up at her.

Her face is flushed, and her hair is slightly disheveled as it spills over her shoulders in long auburn waves. Her lips are still red and swollen from our Terran kisses and, unable to stop myself, I press my mouth hungrily to hers, whispering passionate words between each breathless kiss, losing myself in her touch once again.

~

### Liana

As we lie in bed, Soran tightens his wings around me, holding me close as he runs his fingers through my hair with a pensive look on his face.

"What's wrong, my love?"

His silver eyes meet mine. "When I was a slave, I thought the Creator had abandoned me. My despair was so great that I thought it might consume me entirely. But then, I met another warrior of Mosaura, named Markus.

"We were both owned by the same master for a while, and forced to fight in pairs in the arena. In all that time that I knew him, he never once lost his faith. He is the reason I did not give up hope."

I cup Soran's cheek. "What happened to him? Did he get rescued as well?"

He nods. "Shortly after he was sold, he escaped and went to Rowan. He is the one who told my brother that I was alive. I owe him a life debt that I can never repay."

"What do you mean?"

"Markus and his crew disappeared five cycles ago while patrolling our borders. The Empire would have counted the among the dead if not for my insistence that we not give up hope. I have ordered our military to be ever vigilant for any sign of their vessel. Something inside me tells me that they are still alive, and I trust this instinct. If they are lost out there somewhere, we will find them."

I take his hand in mine, squeezing it gently. "What made you think of him, my love?"

Gently, he touches my face as he stares deep into my eyes. "It made me realize that he was right. The Creator is the great architect of our lives. If not for Markus, I might never have been rescued. I could have died in the gladiator pits. And I would never have known such happiness as I do now that I have found you, my Ashaya."

# CHAPTER 37

SORAN

When we reach Talel's holding cell, Liana's hand grips my forearm to stop me.

"I want to speak with him alone first."

Clenching my jaw, I reluctantly nod.

The look in her eyes is one of fierce determination. Although I know my Ashaya is strong, she has been through more than most, and I dislike the idea of her being alone with that monster. "I would like to be in there with you."

Expecting her to put up some sort of resistance to my request, I'm surprised when she doesn't. Two Aerilon soldiers stand sentry on either side of the entrance to his cell and incline their heads respectfully as we pass.

Talel's dark gaze practically bores into Liana's. If she is afraid, her expression betrays nothing as she glares across at her previous master. "Who was the woman you were speaking to? The one that thinks you're her beloved?"

He narrows his eyes. "Why do you want to know?"

"Tell me," she demands.

He cocks his head to the side and studies her a moment. "I've had much time to think while in this cell. I've wondered why you kept me alive when you so clearly wished me dead. I thought perhaps, it was a lingering effect of the R'ugol—an attachment to the one who shared your delicious mind so intimately. But that was not it, was it?" He tilts his head to the opposite side. "I tasted your exquisite blood, and I know you are not V'loryn. No. You are something different. Something we have not seen but have heard of before. In the archives of my people, there are stories of a planet of creatures similar to yours, whose blood was said to taste finer than any other and possessed exceptional healing powers."

His gaze shifts to me. "When you shot me, I should have died. I knew the instant I was hit that it was a mortal wound. Resolved to my fate, I lay on the floor, waiting for death to claim me." A far-away look crosses his face as if reliving the memory. "But something miraculous happened. My body healed completely. Blood has always had restorative powers for my people, but never to that extreme—a mortal wound mended and closed." His eyes return to Liana. He bares his fangs and licks his lips. "What an infinitely precious commodity your blood would be if my people possessed a ready supply of it."

Lightning fast, Liana steps toward him and jabs the shock stick through the cell and into his side.

Talel's mouth opens in a silent cry as his body twists and writhes on the ground in agony.

When she pulls back, his hand moves to his wound, and he hisses in pain.

"Tell me who the woman was. Now."

He stares up at her in disbelief. "You dare to use that on me?"

She raises the shock stick, readying to strike him again if he doesn't answer.

Fire burns in his gaze as he grits through his teeth. "When I break free, you will pay dearly for that."

"This"—she hits him again with the shock stick—"is nothing compared to what you did to me. What you've done to who knows how many victims," she grinds out.

When she steps back, Talel is panting heavily. His head drops to hang against his chest as he draws in big gulping breaths.

"Hurts, doesn't it?"

He lifts a dark gaze to her. "Yes."

"Who is your beloved? Give me her name."

A low rumble of evil laughter starts deep in his chest as a sinister grin spreads across his face. "Now, I understand. It has all become clear." He narrows his eyes. "You think to use my beloved against me. You believe she will tell you what I will not in exchange for my life. She would never jeopardize our plans by revealing any of my secrets to you."

"Tell me who she is!"

She shocks him again, and he cries out in agony as electricity arcs through him. When she pulls back, he bares his fangs in a twisted snarl. "I will not. My Beloved and I will build an Empire greater than any that has come before. And when the A'kai find Mars, we will bathe in the blood of your people. I swear it to the Ancient Blood God, Gwaedara."

Anger burns in her eyes as she stares down at Talel. "You won't live long enough for that to happen."

He gives her a murderous gaze. I step toward his cell and meet his cold eyes evenly. "Our Healers have ways of extracting information, but I doubt it's something you'll enjoy."

He huffs. "Am I to believe you would spare my life if I tell you what you wish to know?"

I growl low in my throat.

He gives me a dismissive look. "You think I do not have allies on your world, Soran?" He chuckles softly. "Trust me. I will not be held for long."

I curl my hands into fists at my side. "I doubt that."

"My brother is First Prime of A'kaina. Would you really risk starting a war between our two races by murdering his own flesh and blood?"

"You harmed my mate; you broke our laws. Your brother has no recourse to deny us our justice."

He sneers. "You think my brother cares about your laws? Do you know how many slaves *he* keeps?" He leans forward. "Dozens for his own personal pleasure." Shaking his head, he settles back against the wall. "No. My brother does not care for your laws, and he certainly does not obey them. Sleep well before we reach your home world, Soran. Because once you arrive, I suggest you take great care with who you trust. The A'kai are allies with many Mosaurans that would see the fall of your House. And when it falls"—his eyes shift to Liana —"I will take your mate as my concubine and partake of her body and her blood every night for my pleasure."

Covered in armor from head to toe for exactly this reason, I hit the control panel and open the cell. Grasping Talel by the throat, I jerk him up and slam his back against the wall. Frantically, he claws at my hand, but it's no use. His claws cannot pierce Mosauran armor. His face turns from light green to dark as I tighten my grip around his neck, choking the air from his lungs.

Fury burns in his eyes, and he bares his teeth in a show of aggression. Drawing back my other arm, I pound my fist into his face over and over until I loosen his fangs, and they fall to the floor. Releasing my grip, he crumples to the ground, dark blood dripping from his mouth and his nose.

When I step back, I stare at him in shock. Already his bruising fades as he begins to heal before my very eyes. Rage consumes me when I realize it's because of how recently he's had Liana's blood—the potent effects still lingering in his system and allowing for rapid healing.

He laughs darkly, and I clench my jaw as I notice the pointed tips of his canines. The fangs already beginning to grow in place of the ones he lost.

He reaches up to touch them, baring them aggressively as soon as they're fully regrown. "If you kill me, Mosauran, you'll never get any answers."

Panting heavily, my hands curl into fists at my side.

With a half-mad look on his face, he laughs as if to taunt me further.

Liana's soft touch on my arm forces my attention back to her as she pulls me out of his cell, sealing it shut behind us. She takes my hand, twining our fingers together. "Let's go."

Rage twists in my gut at the thought of all she has endured by his hands. Unable to speak through my anger, I nod and allow her to lead me back to our quarters.

As soon as we enter, I pull her into my arms, nuzzling the top of her head. Guilt and shame wash through me as I whisper into her hair. "Please forgive me, Ashaya."

She lifts a confused gaze to me. "For what?"

"I should have killed him that day I fought him in the arena. I could have ended him then, but I didn't." I swallow hard against the lump in my throat, and my heart clenches as I look down at her beautiful face. "If I had, he would never have touched you."

Placing a delicate finger to my mouth to silence me, she quickly replaces it with her soft lips. "Stop," she whispers. "You cannot blame yourself for what he did to me."

But I do. And I always will. I know that I cannot change what is, but it doesn't absolve me of my guilt. Just as I cannot change the fact that my people will never accept her as my mate, and we will both be Outcast from my family and the Empire.

We will reach Mosaura tomorrow. After everything she has been through, she deserves better than the prejudice I am almost certain she will face from many of my people. I only hope that my mother and sister will treat her with kindness even if this is the only time they will ever meet.

# CHAPTER 38

LIANA

Staring out the viewscreen, my jaw drops at the beauty of the planet before us. Mosaura. Varying shades of green and black are the dominant colors of this world. So different from the blues and greens that dominate Terra; it's more beautiful than I could have imagined.

Strong, warm hands rest lightly on my shoulders a moment before Soran slips his arms around me, pulling me back into the solid warmth of his chest. He points to the upper corner of the planet. "Just there are the Liral mountains." He places a gentle kiss atop my head, and I turn just enough to reach my hand to cup the back of his neck and bring his lips down to mine.

His silver reflective eyes stare down at me with so much love, it breaks my heart. "I'm so sorry, my love. You're giving up so much for me."

"No." He presses his lips again to mine. "I am blessed beyond measure. That you chose me, makes me happier than I have ever been, Liana."

I reach up to touch his face. "I am too. I'm so happy, I feel guilty sometimes. I hate knowing that others are still suffering as I was before you found me. And I...keep thinking about my crew." My voice breaks on the last sentence as I struggle to contain my emotions.

"After knowing what you and Tr'lani went through, Al'aneo seems as interested in ending the slave trade as we are. Perhaps before we leave Mosaura, I can persuade my mother to speak with him about shared patrols of the neutral zone between our two Empires." He rubs his hands up and down my arms reassuringly. "Al'aneo said the Aerilon Council has committed to finding your people. They already have agents searching for 'small V'loryns.'"

This gives me hope. I already know what happened to Amanda, but it kills me not knowing about the rest of my crew. Abby has people out there too. I pray that the Aerilon find them.

As my gaze turns back to the planet, nervous anticipation fills me. I look up at Soran. "Are there any cultural customs I need to be aware of?"

He glances up at the ceiling thoughtfully a moment before he lowers his gaze to mine. "Try not to smile."

This shocks me. He and Rowan smile all the time. Smiling is a bad thing? "Why?"

"We don't want to draw attention to your pitifully tiny fangs."

My jaw drops.

A slow grin spreads across his devastatingly handsome face and I realize he's teasing me.

I roll my eyes and laugh as I hit at his shoulder. "You maltak! I thought you were serious."

Rowan moves up beside us. He arches a brow and gives me a sly smirk as he gestures to his brother. "Is this male bothering you?"

I grin. "Always."

He laughs, and Soran punches at his arm.

Sadness fills me as I watch them tease each other back and forth, knowing this will probably be one of the last times they will ever be together.

The low rumble along the hull followed by an echoing thud means we've docked at the orbital station around Mosaura.

Soran's expression becomes somber. "I am glad you will meet my sister and mother before we must leave." He gives me a small smile. "We should ready ourselves. We will be on Mosaura within the hour. And I have sent word ahead to my mother, informing her that we will make use of the Ancient Archives during our short stay."

"Archives?"

"I've told you of how my people used to be explorers. They mapped thousands of star systems over the past three thousand cycles. All of their charts are kept in the Archives. If we are going to find your home world, that is a good place to start."

"Can we transfer the data? Take it with us to Aerilon?"

"I am uncertain, but that is my hope."

**Soran**

Liana is nothing short of stunning in the traditional Mosauran robes—a deep forest green to represent the colors of our House. Tr'lani had them specially made as a bonding gift. Even though I am Outcast among my people, we can still honor their ways. Presenting her in House Mosaura's colors will show everyone that she is my mate, and I am proud to be hers. Bittersweet happiness fills me at the thought of seeing my mother and sister.

She hugs Abby and Grex before we depart. They've chosen to remain on the Aerilon vessel, and I do not blame them. My people are not exactly welcoming to other races.

As we stand at the airlock, Rowan moves to the other side of Liana in a silent show of support for my choice of mate as we wait for the outer doors to open.

When they finally do, I take Liana's hand in mine before the three of us step off the ship and onto Doprava—the Mosauran orbital station. My mother and sister said they would formally greet us here before we board the Imperial transport for the surface.

I'm surprised to note that it is only my sister's guards that line the path on either side as we exit. They stare in rapt fascination at my mate. She is beautiful. I struggle to suppress the low growl rumbling in my chest at their open and curious stares.

Caryn stands in the center of her guard, waiting for us, a regal but neutral expression on her face as her sharp gaze scans Liana from head to toe. No doubt she is probably concerned by her small stature compared to a Mosauran female, and by the striking similarity of her appearance to V'loryns. A smile tugs at my lips. She and the rest of our people will quickly learn that my Ashaya may be small, but she is as fierce as any warrior of Mosaura.

Tr'lani and her brother walk a few steps behind us. They insisted on accompanying us in a show of support and acknowledgment that we are now part of their clan. Tr'lani is especially protective of her. No doubt they both question my people's unwillingness to accept someone just because of their race.

As soon as we reach Caryn, the three of us bow deeply in respect before I lift my gaze to hers.

"Future Empress Caryn of Mosaura," I begin solemnly. "I present to you, Liana Garza of Terra. My mate and my Ashaya."

Shocked gasps come from some of the guards. Caryn's expression is unreadable, but her eyes betray her sadness as she greets us with a formal nod. She steps forward and embraces me warmly before turning to Liana. A pained smile tugs at her lips. "I am glad to meet the female that holds my brother's heart."

Dressed in long flowing robes with the colors and insignia of Clan Al'ani—one of seven ruling clans of Aerilon—Tr'lani and Al'aneo step forward. The each place a hand on Liana's shoulders and begin the low trilling hum that tells everyone she is their family and part of their clan. My sister's eyes widen briefly in shock. An expression I'm almost certain is reflected on every Mosauran witnessing this event. Their acceptance of Liana is the highest honor an Aerilon can ever give to an outsider. That Tr'lani and her brother are from one of the ruling families on Aerilon means that much more.

Tr'lani moves closer to Caryn. "As the mate of our sister, we find Soran of House Mosaura worthy of acceptance into our clan. May the House of Mosaura and the House of Al'ani be joined in friendship from this day forward."

Now my sister's face is openly shocked. The Aerilon and the Mosaurans have never had anything more than a tenuous relationship between them. Our two races have a long history of mistrust.

Caryn dips her head in acknowledgment. "Thank you for returning my family to me."

I notice she says "family," instead of "brothers," and I wonder if she's intentionally done this to include Liana in her statement.

She turns her attention to me. "The Empress wishes to speak with you privately when we reach the palace."

Liana's eyes dart briefly to mine, but I force my gaze to remain neutral. I don't want her to see the disappointment on my face that my mother was not here to greet us. I will be Outcast soon enough. I had only hoped to spend at least a few hours with my family before we leave for Aerilon--never to see them again.

Caryn looks to Al'aneo and Tr'lani. "It would please the Empress if you would stay as our honored guests tonight before leaving for Aerilon."

My ears perk up. Perhaps Mother is not as angered by my taking Liana as my mate as I thought if she's inviting Tr'lani and Al'aneo to stay the night, and by extension, Liana and myself as well.

## Liana

Caryn's eyes rake over me once more with a hint of intense curiosity behind their gaze. Strange. From everything Soran and Rowan have told me about how much their people dislike the V'loryn's, I'd half expected her to look at me with disgust.

When she informs us that their mother wants to meet with us privately at the palace, my heart quickens its pace. I'm nervous not because she's the Empress of one of the largest Empires in the quadrant, but because she is Soran's mother. I don't expect her to like me, but I pray that their reunion will go well for his sake. This may be the last time they ever see one another.

Doprava Station is a hive of activity. Except, unlike Telvo Station, most of the people here are Mosauran instead of a mixture of different species. Much larger than Telvo, Soran explained that this place was designed so that each level could easily accommodate Mosaurans in draken form.

To my great disappointment, I'm not afforded much of a view. Caryn's guards surround us on all sides as we make our way to the transport. Much taller than me, they make it difficult for me to see anything. The few glimpses I get between the gaps of the warriors is mainly the curious stares of several onlookers that study us in rapt fascination as we pass.

I lock eyes with one, and he gasps. "V'loryn." The word escapes from his mouth and is soon uttered throughout the crowd as we continue on our path.

Soran's hand is in mine, and he gives it a gentle squeeze of reassurance. "They are merely curious," he whispers. "They do not know what you are and believe that I have taken a V'loryn as my mate."

Regardless of their intentions, I find their stares unnerving, and I'm glad when we finally board the Imperial transport.

From the viewscreen, I'm able to study the surface in greater detail. My jaw drops at the beauty of a lavender sky full of fluffy gray and white clouds, punctuated by the light of a soft orange sun. This entire region is nothing but mountainous terrain. A place that, on Terra, would not normally lend itself to a city due to the sheer drops of many of the towering rock formations. It seems Mosaurans have carved out their homes and buildings into the obsidian stone walls. Their structures are surrounded by a sea of deep green trees, similar to pine but taller than any that are found on my world. The dense vegetation is interrupted every so often by gorgeous cascading waterfalls that spill down from the tops of the mountains.

Winged Mosaurans in both draken and humanoid form fill the sky, and I stare in wonder as I take it all in. As we draw closer, the palace comes into view. Carved into a sheer cliff wall, the obsidian rock fortress gleams in the light. Closely resembling the ancient castles of Terra, with several formidable towers capped by silver domed roofs and built out terraces, it appears to have been constructed as much for defense as it was for aesthetics.

A waterfall drops from the mountain above, straight into a large overhang at the top of the palace. It cascades into a series of waterfalls down the front of the structure before flowing into a pool at the base, feeding into a river that runs straight through the valley below.

We land next to the gardens. As we exit the transport, I marvel at how wild everything appears. As if standing in a natural forest instead of carefully manicured castle grounds. Large trees that resemble the great pines of Terra line winding paths carved from the same obsidian stone as the palace, punctuated every so often by various sea-green pools of water.

Tr'lani and Al'aneo give us a quick smile before leaving with two of the guards to find their accommodations. It doesn't escape my notice how Rowan's eyes follow my friend longingly as she walks away, before he turns back to us.

When we finally reach the entrance, two Mosauran guards stand on either side of a large, open entryway. As we pass beneath it, a small pulse-like energy ripples through me and I stop in my tracks. I look up at Soran. "What was that?"

"A forcefield barrier. Only those permitted may pass through it."

"How does it recognize who is allowed?"

A smile tugs at his lips. "Such a primitive place, your Terra," he teases under his breath.

I roll my eyes in mock frustration before an answering grin quirks my mouth.

He explains. "Members of the Royal House are automatically granted access to every part of the palace." He lifts our joined hands. "It is coded to recognize the genetic structure of those belonging to the Royal House and our guards. Because I am touching you, it allows you to pass as well."

"What would happen if we weren't holding hands?"

"The energy barrier would be as a solid wall to you."

There are a million things I want to ask, but when Caryn stops to look over her shoulder with a slightly raised brow, I close my mouth, and we continue to follow. I'll save all my questions for later.

Our footsteps echo loudly as we move farther into the palace. Knowing that they are predominantly a warrior race, I had expected a mostly utilitarian space, and I'm surprised by the lovely interior. It has just enough soft touches to make it feel like an actual home instead of a fortified castle. The rooms are great, cavernous spaces, but remembering how big Soran's draken form is, I suppose that's the reason they're built this way—to accommodate a Mosauran in either form if necessary.

When we reach the end of a long hallway, the large door seems to disappear into the wall beside it. The farther we walk, the more comfortable and plush the furnishings become, as if this part of the palace is actually lived in and the outer rooms near the entrance are more for visitors and formal gatherings.

When we finally reach the Empress's atrium, my mouth drifts open in wonder. Mosaic tiles line the floor and walls in a beautiful pattern depicting forest scenes and Mosaurans in draken form. Light filters in from a glass ceiling above, lending an almost ethereal effect to the space as it reflects off a large sea-green pool of water that sits in the center of the room.

A woman dressed in traditional dark-green Mosauran robes stands at the edge of the water, hands clasped together in front of her. With a regal air and a slight tilt of her chin, her expression is at once stoic and yet almost predatory as she watches us approach.

Her sharp gaze scans me from head to toe, and I force myself to keep my eyes trained on hers. I am the bondmate of a Mosauran warrior. I will not show any weakness or fear in front of Soran's mother, the Empress.

She studies me a moment more before turning her attention to Soran. "She is small," she says impassively.

He bristles beside me. "She may be small, but she is as fierce as any Mosauran female."

Her nostrils flare, and her eyes widen briefly in shock as she stares down at me. "It is done then." Her gaze turns to Soran with a look I can't quite decipher, but if I had to guess, it's something between disappointment and sadness. "You have already mated her."

My cheeks burn red hot in embarrassment. *She can scent that we've mated?*

"Why would you take this female that looks so much like a V'loryn as your mate?" she asks, and this is the first time anger bleeds into her imperious tone. "What could you possibly have been thinking?"

Soran opens his mouth to answer, but I step in front of him, tilting my chin up defiantly. "I do not appreciate being talked over as if I'm not standing right here. Soran is my mate, and I am his. We *chose* each other. We do not come here for your judgment or approval. We came here so that your son can spend some time with his family before he is banished by your archaic laws."

Something akin to respect and admiration flashes behind her eyes, and now I'm thoroughly confused. She arches a brow. "So, not like a V'loryn then," she says in a low voice more to herself than to us.

She levels a hard gaze at me. "You call our law archaic, but it exists for a reason." She turns to face the far wall.

As I look closer, I notice the small tiles depict an image--a draken falling from the sky.

She continues. "Our people mate for life. Our very hearts even beat in synchronization at the moment the bond is forged, creating a link between our souls." She turns and meets my eyes evenly. "Our mates are our greatest strengths but also our greatest weakness."

She is silent a moment, allowing the magnitude of her words to hang in the space between us before she continues. "That is the reason for the mating battle. To ensure that the mate we choose is at least our equal or our better. They must be strong, because if they are not and they are killed, the other usually follows shortly after."

"You survived the death of your mate," I counter.

She levels a dark gaze at me. "But at great cost. I *do not* want that for my son." With a slight clench of her jaw, her eyes travel up and down my form. "You are a weakness now in the Imperial line. Not only because of your size but also because of what you represent."

Angered by her words, it takes everything I have to keep my voice even when I ask, "And what exactly do I represent?"

Her nostrils flare. "In his bonding with you, I can easily imagine the death of my son—his soul tethered to a species weaker than our own." She leans forward. "You are also an affront to the traditions of our people—a straying from the old ways. If I ignore the laws, I set a precedent for my reign—discarding the rules that have served our people for thousands of cycles. We have only just recovered from the last Civil War, and this could lead us into another."

I tilt my chin to meet her gaze defiantly. "I was taken from my people and forced into slavery. I've experienced things that you could scarcely imagine even in your darkest nightmares. There were times it would have been so much easier to die than to fight for life."

I continue. "When I chose your son, I gave him the warrior's vow. I will carry him. To victory or to death, but I will never leave him behind. I survived because my will is stronger than the ones who tried to break me." I meet her eyes evenly. "And I vow that I will fight fiercely at his side against any enemies that would see him fall, because I protect and defend what is mine."

With Soran's hand in my own, I wait for her to speak, but she says nothing. Her mouth drifts open, but she quickly snaps it shut.

Breaking the silence, I step forward. "Since when does a Mosauran back down from a challenge? You are an Empress—the leader of your people. On Terra, we've had two kinds of leaders throughout our history: the ones who cling to the old ways, afraid to embrace change because it could threaten their rule. Or those that are visionaries who usher in progress, adapting to create a better future for their subjects." I keep my gaze locked on hers as I stand tall. "Which one are you?"

Anger is no longer visible on her face. She stares at me with an expression that borders on disbelief, probably stunned that someone would dare speak to her this way.

I don't wait for her to answer, nor do I expect her to. Instead, I squeeze Soran's hand before I address her again. "My only desire in coming here was for my mate to spend time with his family before he's Outcast. Having been taken against my will from my home world and my family, I know the pain of being parted from those you love. It is not something I would wish even on my worst enemy. Whatever offenses you have laid against me, I do not hold you responsible. Your ignorance is to blame, and I will not waste any more time holding you accountable for it. I will leave you to spend time with your son."

Ignoring the shocked stares of the Empress, Caryn, and Rowan, I turn to Soran and stretch up on my toes to press a gentle kiss to his lips.

His eyes flash with love and admiration as a smile tugs at his mouth.

Releasing his hand, I look back at his mother. "I assume you wish us to spend the night here in the palace since you invited Tr'lani and Al'aneo to stay?"

She blinks several times before she answers. "Yes."

I give her a curt nod and then turn to one of the guards. "If you would be so kind as to show me to the Archives."

The guard's cheeks flush dark purple, nearly blending in with the charcoal scales that cover the rest of his body as his eyes dart to the Empress.

She gives me a questioning look.

Soran steps forward. "My mate was captured by the Zovians while aboard her ship in suspended sleep. She is searching for her home world. Perhaps the ancient star charts may provide some answers." He turns his gaze to me. "I will help you."

I place a hand on his chest to stop him, softly shaking my head. "No, my love. I want you to spend whatever time you can with your family before we leave. I will be fine on my own."

His silver eyes search mine a moment before he finally nods.

I flash him a warm smile before turning to leave with the guard.

When we reach the first energy field, the guard stops and nervously looks back at me. He clears his throat, and his cheeks flush dark purple again as he offers his arm. "My name is Tharin. You must hold onto me, Princess, to help you pass through the barrier. It has not been coded to recognize you yet."

"Oh." I rest my hand over his offered forearm and have to suppress a laugh at how nervous he appears. He's sweet the way he said "to recognize me yet." As if it will ever be coded to recognize me. Soran and I will never be able to come here again. He's Outcast. Because of me. Pushing down the lump forming in my throat, I address the guard. "You may call me Liana."

His jaw drops. "That—that would not be proper. You are a princess."

"Not according to your people," I counter. "My mate and I are Outcast because I am not Mosauran."

Regaining his composure, he softly shakes his head. "It is an outdated law."

His answer surprises me. "You don't agree with it?"

"No," he states firmly. "But, unfortunately, there are many that still do."

It's comforting to know that not all Mosaurans feel the way Soran's mother does.

Turning down another long hallway, we soon reach the archives.

This place is incredible. Long columns of books and scrolls line the walls from floor to ceiling, extending in every direction across the cavernous space, at least six stories high.

A Mosauran dressed in long silver robes greets me at the entrance. His dark hair is peppered gray near his temples, suggesting he may be older than he otherwise appears. "You must be Liana Garza, the mate of Prince Soran. I am Rolan, Keeper of the Archives."

"You know who I am?" I ask, shocked that word has already spread this quickly. We arrived less than an hour ago.

He dips his chin in a subtle nod. "Soran is well-liked among our people. It is...distressing that he will now be Outcast."

I don't know which way Rolan falls on the issue of interspecies bonding, but I don't have time to argue if it's on the opposite side of my own opinion. It's already midday, and I have a lot of information to comb through. "I'd like to study your ancient star charts."

He bows slightly. "Would you like to view them in the Immerser?"

"That's possible?"

"Of course."

Tapping the clear crystal globe on the stand beside us, he then types something into the control panel beneath it. The entire space darkens, and we're suddenly surrounded by a galaxy of stars and planets. It's so beautiful it takes my breath away.

"If you raise your arms," he instructs, "you may manipulate the charts as you see fit."

He demonstrates by waving his hands and scrolling through the chart so that the star system just barely visible on the outer edge of the display shifts closer to view, dragging along other stars and planets in range with it.

"This is amazing," I whisper more to myself than to Rolan.

He frowns. "Your species does not have this technology?"

I purse my lips. "No. But we have other technologies," I add for good measure, so he doesn't suspect we're as primitive as Soran and Rowan seem to believe. "I think I can handle this."

He steps to the side and bows again. "I will leave you then, but I will be nearby if you have questions."

The amazing thing about these charts is that each star system and planet are labeled. I recognize enough of their alphabet to know where Vylax Station is. It's the starting point of my search because that's where Soran found me.

My first master took me to several seedy stations, trying to find a buyer for his slaves. From what limited views I had while collared or caged, I've been unable to figure out the names or locations of those places to help in my search.

As I scroll through the charts, I recognize the ice planet we crashed on. Its name is Talv—the Mosauran word for winter. A small hieroglyph beside it designates it as habitable, but I think whoever labeled it as that, has probably never been there.

After a few hours, I struggle to keep my eyes open. Working on the idea that V'loryns must look similar to my people for a reason, I've been checking every system in their known Empire from a thousand cycles ago. It's exhausting, but I can't give up. I won't have access to these charts once we leave. According to Rolan, the files are too large to be loaded into a ship's immerser, so any hope I had that we could take this information with us is gone.

# CHAPTER 39

SORAN

My gaze tracks Liana as she leaves the room. When I turn back to my mother, I notice a look of deep contemplation on her face as she stares at the mural of the fallen draken warrior. "Losing your father and then believing you were dead as well...it nearly killed me." Her voice is thick with emotion. "When you returned, I swore I would do everything in my power to keep my family together...to keep you all safe."

She turns to face me with a thunderous look. "And now you have jeopardized everything. You took a mate outside of our race. A weak one that looks almost exactly like a V'loryn. You should be Outcast according to our laws. Our people will believe I am granting you leniency because you are my son. And they would be right."

My nostrils flare. "Liana may be similar in appearance to a V'loryn, but I can assure you, she is anything but weak. When our pod crashed on that frozen rock of a planet, she dragged my unconscious body several clicks across ice and snow, defending me from dangerous predators and keeping me safe when it would have been easier for her to leave me behind. You have no idea how strong she is, and you insult her each time you suggest otherwise."

Rowan steps forward. "He speaks truth. We would be dead right now if not for her bravery. Even after the A'kai violated her mind, she still risked her life to save us, knowing that she would face his wrath and her own death if she failed."

Mother's expression changes; sadness reflects in her eyes. "My sister was the strongest female I have ever known. During a border skirmish, the A'kai captured her transport. They violated her mind."

Caryn's eyes widen in shock. Mother never talks of the sister she lost when they were young.

Tears brighten her eyes as she stares at the opposite wall, a far-away look on her face as if reliving the terrible memory. "And my sister—the strongest female I ever knew...it broke her. She went mad and took her own life." Her gaze drifts to mine. "That your Ashaya survived it, tells me that she is undoubtedly strong. But it does not change what she is; what she represents."

Caryn steps forward. "Only a strong female would stand before the Empress of the Mosauran Empire and speak her mind where others would have cowered in fear. You, Mother, were the one who taught me that in the days of the Old Empire, women were considered unfit to rule until the law was changed." She darts a quick glance at me. "Perhaps it is time for the laws to change again."

Mother gives her a stern look. "There is already threat of another Civil War between the Great Houses. This could be the catalyst that stokes new flames of discord among our people. There will be many who will not wish to accept an Outsider among our people, especially in the Royal family."

She turns, pacing along the edge of the reflective pool in the way she always does when she's worried; mulling over a decision. "We could lose much of our support on the Council. That would leave us vulnerable to attack from another Great House like before, when your father was killed, and I thought I had lost you too." She stops speaking, clenching her jaw as if the words are too painful to even speak. "I'll admit, you have chosen a worthy mate. If she were Mosauran, I would have no objections to your bonding. *No one* would. But do you not see how this could place us in danger? Compromise my rule? And your sister's reign after mine?"

Caryn's eyes flash with anger. "We did nothing to provoke the attack that led to Father's death and the Civil War. And yet, it still happened." She holds mother's gaze evenly, allowing the heavy weight of her words to settle in the space between them before she continues. "Sending your son and his mate into exile would only weaken our family, lessen the circle of people we can truly trust. We will always have to be vigilant against those who would seek to take the throne for themselves. Don't you understand? We are much stronger if our family is united."

"Besides." Rowan speaks. "The laws will have to change eventually. After the last plague that swept through the Empire, we lost so many females we are almost in as dire straits as the V'loryns. Interspecies bonding is the answer to replenish our numbers." He gives her a pointed look. "And with it could come new allies for the Empire. Allies that are loyal to our House."

"He's right," Caryn adds. "Clan Al'ani accepted Liana into their family. They are one of the seven ruling clans of Aerilon, and they have pledged their friendship to our House because of Soran's bond to her."

Mother moves toward me, placing her hands on my shoulders. Her eyes are bright with tears as they meet mine. "I cannot lose you again. It would break me. I will inform the Council of my decision and deal with the fallout as it comes. Please bring your Ashaya before me. I must formally welcome her into our family as I should have done when she first arrived."

# CHAPTER 40

LIANA

**W**arm hands come to rest on my shoulders, and I immediately recognize Soran's touch. Leaning back against his broad, muscular chest, I let out a breath of exhaustion as he nuzzles my hair before placing a gentle kiss to the top of my head. "You are tired," he whispers in my ear. "Come to bed, my love."

Sleepily, I barely manage to nod.

Without warning, he scoops me up into his strong arms. A surprised gasp escapes my lips before I laugh. "What are you doing? Put me down," I half-heartedly protest, pushing against his chest. "I can walk."

He grins and tightens his grip. "My Ashaya is tired, and I wish to carry her."

Melting against him, I arch a brow. "Well, in that case, your Ashaya is starving too. Is there anything to eat?"

"I have already asked for food to be sent to our rooms." His expression turns serious. "Though, you may not like sharing a bed with me tonight."

"Why?

He gives me a teasing grin as he presses a quick kiss to my nose. "Because I doubt I will be able to keep my hands off you long enough to allow you to sleep."

His silver eyes stare into mine with a smoldering gaze, and as his arms tighten around my form, heat pools deep in my core, and all traces and thoughts of fatigue have fled my system.

Running my fingers through the hairs at the nape of his neck, I kiss his soft, perfect lips. When he pulls back, his nostrils flare slightly before a slow and devastating smile curves his mouth as he picks up his pace.

As soon as the door shuts to our room, I blink several times when I realize the sheer size of our accommodations.

A large, four poster bed floats in the center, surrounded on all sides by beautiful green sheer fabric panels. A deep green comforter on top of the bed appears so plush and inviting. Massive by any standards, I imagine a Mosauran in draken form could probably use this space just as easily as they can in humanoid form. Something, a low rumbling sound in the background echoes throughout the room. I motion for Soran to put me down.

Gently, he sets me on my feet, and I take his hand as I move toward the strange noise. I gasp in surprise when I step through an invisible barrier and suddenly find myself standing on a balcony outside.

It's a large terrace that overlooks the gardens and the city. Water cascades from the level above, collecting in a small pool near the edge before it flows over the side and down to the next level. This is beautiful. As I turn back, I notice that I cannot see the entrance to the room. It appears as though a solid part of the structure.

I gesture back in the direction we came. "Where did—"

Soran explains. "After the attack on our family, Mother added extra security to the palace, including cloaking and concealment of the family rooms."

My mouth drifts open slightly. He and Rowan are right. My people *are* primitive compared to theirs, but I'm certainly not going to admit it to them.

Soran continues. "These were my rooms, but now they are ours."

I stare up at him in confusion. "Ours?"

He nods, a dazzling smile lighting his face. "I've spoken to my mother. We will not be Outcast."

Shocked by his statement, it takes me a moment to gather my thoughts. After our conversation, I believed she hated me. "What made her change her mind?"

Instead of answering my question, he crushes his lips to mine as he rushes us back into the room and the large floating bed.

Gently, he lowers me onto the soft, green comforter. As he lays down beside me, the shimmering bolts of light-green sheer fabric lowers into a canopy encircling the bed.

Soran's warm hand moves up my thigh, beneath my robe, and I gasp as he dips his fingers into my already slick folds.

"My beautiful Ashaya." He softly skims the tip of his nose from my jaw down to the curve of my neck and shoulder. Extending his claws, he carefully slices a line down my robe. That fabric falls away, leaving me bare beneath him. He stares down at me with a heated look. "Your scent calls to me, and I can feel the effects of my mating heat. I will try my best to not keep you awake all night. I don't want you to be tired for your welcoming ceremony tomorrow, but I cannot promise anything."

I start to ask what a welcoming ceremony is, but he captures my mouth in a kiss, swallowing my gasp as he pushes a finger just inside my core as his thumb makes slow circles around the small bundle of nerves at the top of my folds.

"You are perfect," his breath whispers across my skin as he trails kisses along my neck and down the valley of my breasts. He closes his mouth over one soft globe, and I moan as his tongue moves across the already sensitive peak.

Running my fingers through his hair, I trace the hard, cranial ridges along his skull and feel an answering ripple move through him.

He turns his attention to my other breast with more fervor and I wrap my arms tightly around him.

～

**Soran**

Liana caresses my sensitive cranial ridges and I groan at the sensation. The soft give of her body and her intoxicating scent are more than I can bear. The need to bury my stav deep in her core is all consuming.

I want her to become as addicted to my touch as I am to hers, so I continue kissing a trail down her abdomen until I reach her soft folds.

As soon as I press my tongue to the sensitive bundle of nerves at the top, she gasps and arches up against me. Circling the small nub with my tongue, I press one finger into the entrance to her core.

The small muscles tighten and flex around my finger as I stroke in and out. She raises her hips off the bed as she cries out my name. Each time I touch her, I'm fascinated by all the difference between us. Mosauran females do not have any muscle here, and the first time we mated, it was difficult not to spill my seed the moment I entered her channel and she clenched tight around my length.

I love the small sounds of pleasure she makes as I continue to tease the sensitive flesh with my tongue. She writhes beneath my attentions and I band my other arm across her hips, holding her in place as her breath quickens and she digs her heels into my back.

The taste of her on my tongue is exquisite, and I cannot get enough as I continue to explore her. The muscles of her core begin to quiver in response as she approaches her release.

"Soran, I want you," she pants. "I want you inside me." I look up into her sea green eyes. Her face is flushed, and her gaze is heavy with desire as she pulls at my shoulders.

Slowly moving back up her body, I lean down and capture her mouth. She moans low in her throat as she opens her hips to receive me. She takes my stav and positions me at her entrance. The breath rushes from my lungs as I enter, and her tight, wet heat envelopes me completely.

The tight clasp of her channel is exquisite. Her muscles flex and quiver around my stav as her body adjusts to the invasion of mine. I stroke deep inside her and she arches her hips to meet each thrust, intensifying the friction between us.

I'm breathless as I stare down at my beautiful Ashaya. I know she is close as she calls out my name. Shifting my hips, I adjust my angle and sink even deeper into her warm, wet heat.

A breathless moan escapes her as our bodies move as one. I love the way my name spills from her lips as I stroke deep inside her. I reach down and cup my hand to her face.

Her eyes stare into mine, and her soft lips part as she cries out her pleasure. Unable to hold back any longer, my stav pulses deep inside her as my release erupts from my body, filling her with my seed. The small muscles of her channel clench tightly around my length as her body pulls every last drop of my essence deep into her open womb.

Gently rolling our bodies to the side, I wrap my arms and wings tightly around her, pulling her to my chest, my stav still buried inside her. I don't make any move to leave her warm channel. She loves to stay connected in this way as much as I do. I revel in the tight clasp of her body around mine and can remain this way as long as she desires.

Her cheeks are flushed as she gives me a beautiful smile. Running her fingers through my hair, she presses her soft lips to mine before resting her head on my bicep. She shifts slightly, and the movement stirs my desire anew, but her eyes remain closed. The even and steady rhythm of her breathing tells me she's starting to drift off to sleep.

Running my fingers through her silken, auburn locks, I stare down at her beautiful face. She is everything to me and I will do whatever it takes to help her find her people and her world. My hand trails lightly down her back, over the thick and irregular pattern of scars that mar her delicate skin, and my thoughts turn toward Talel.

After his comments about having allies on Mosaura, Al'aneo ordered that he be left under guard on their ship. We will go there tomorrow, and I will bring one of our Healers. They have ways of making people talk.

# CHAPTER 41

SORAN

When I wake in the morning, Liana is still asleep in my arms. Wrapping my wings tightly around her, I gently nuzzle her hair and breathe deeply of our combined scent.

"Mmmm," she mumbles softly, stretching against me before opening her eyes to give me a sleepy smile.

"Good morning, Princess."

She grins and nestles against me.

I love when she does this, as if she cannot get close enough to me. So, I'm reluctant to ask her if she wants to leave the bed, but I know how important bathing is to her. "Shall I carry you to the cleansing room where we may shower together?"

Her eyes sparkle with amusement. "Is that code for 'let's make love in the shower' this morning?"

"If we had time, I would make love to you all morning...starting in the shower." I tuck my wings tighter around her. "But we have to get ready. Ceremonial robes are being brought here as we speak so that my mother may formally accept you into our family."

"What made her change her mind?"

I press my lips to hers. "You did, my Ashaya, when you stood up to her during your first meeting. Rowan and I told her all about you and how you saved us...how you saved *me*. You have the heart and strength of a Mosauran warrior, and you chose me to be yours. What better or more worthy mate could I have asked for?"

A soft knock at the door is one of the staff with her new robes. Although they were hastily made, they are not too large as I'd feared they might be. The long, shimmering green fabric hugs her small form perfectly, accentuating the sensuous curve of her breasts and the taper of her waist before reaching the gentle flare of her hips.

She is so beautiful and perfect, I want to tear the robes from her body and make love to her all over again. The only thing that stops me is Rowan arriving unannounced to walk with us to Mother's chambers.

When we reach them, Tr'lani and Al'aneo are already there. At least my mother remembered Liana is now part of their clan, and it is only proper for them to be here when she is accepted into our family. In effect, this will form a blood alliance between Aerilon and Mosaura. Something that has only ever been done among the Great Houses but never outside of our race.

Rokar, my mother's advisor, rushes to her side, whispering in her ear.

She clenches her jaw and then turns her gaze to us. "An A'kai cruiser has been detected entering our system."

Liana squeezes my hand, but her expression betrays nothing as she trains it into a stoic mask. In this, she is much like the V'loyrns—able to hide her emotions well.

Rokar taps the console nearby, and the image of an A'kai fills the viewscreen. "Why have you entered the sovereign space of Mosaura?" My mother's voice is deep and cold as she glares into the display.

The A'kai captain makes no effort to hide his anger. "The First Prime of A'kaina is demanding the release of his brother, Talel."

Al'aneo glares at him, baring his fangs. "Inform the First Prime

311

that, according to our laws, his brother's life was forfeit the moment he took my sisters as his slaves."

The captain's glowing green eyes narrow. "We are willing to offer an exchange." He presses a button, splitting the viewscreen so that two females are visible. Two Terran females.

Liana gasps and moves toward the display.

The females appear similar in age to my Ashaya, but one has long brown hair with golden-brown eyes, and the other has short blonde hair with gray-blue eyes. Both of them have the same haunted look my Ashaya had after her mind was violated by Talel. Anger floods my veins, and I curl my hands into fists at my side as I struggle to contain my rage.

Caryn gives me a surprised look, but when I whisper the word "R'ugol," she understands exactly what has been done to these females. Her lips curl back in a snarl as she turns to face the screen.

"Release the females at once!" my mother says in a loud and booming voice, startling Rokar beside her.

Liana reaches up as if to touch them through the display. "Gwen? Aria?"

Both female's eyes snap up at the sound of their names. The one with dark hair lifts a trembling hand to the screen. "Liana? Is it really you?"

A single tear slips down my Ashaya's face as she struggles to keep her voice even. "Yes, it's me. Don't worry. We're going to get you back."

The A'kai captain sneers. "Only if you release Lord Talel."

My mother lifts a dark gaze to the A'kai captain. "Done," she grits through her teeth. "But then you must leave this system immediately."

The captain's mouth curves into an evil grin. "I will send a transport to the orbiting station, and I expect Lord Talel to be ready when we arrive."

With a quick jerk of her head, the Empress waves at the screen and it cuts off.

Disbelief ripples through me. "He's a monster. You cannot let him go free."

My mother raises a hand in a silent bid to allow her to speak. With a raised brow, she smirks. "The A'kai are in Mosauran space. The possession of slaves is a mandatory death sentence according to our laws." Her gaze sweeps to Al'aneo. "I believe that is the case for your people as well, is it not?"

He dips his head in a subtle nod. "You are correct."

"Good," she replies. "Then, the moment we have the females, we will fire on their ship."

Rokar, my mother's advisor, interjects. "Empress, if we do this, we risk starting a war with the A'kai."

She turns a hardened gaze to him. "No! It is *they* who risk starting a war with us. They know the laws, and yet they dare to violate them. Mercy, in this case, would be viewed by the A'kai as weakness. *We* are Mosaurans. We fear no other race."

# CHAPTER 42

SORAN

Despite my mother's insistence that Liana and I remain on the planet, I could not persuade my Ashaya to listen. Her concern for her friends is admirable, but I do not want her anywhere near the A'kai.

As soon as we reach the station, I turn to her, staring deep into her sea-green eyes. "Please, stay close to me."

"I will."

Reaching for the small knife tucked into my belt, I place it in her palm. "Keep this close."

Instead of questioning me like I'd expected, she nods and tucks it under her sleeve.

Tensions are high as we wait for the A'kai transport to dock. Two A'kai Centurions disembark, dragging the Terran females behind them with slave collars around their necks. Low rumbling growls fill the silence as every Mosauran, including myself, glare at the A'kai. To treat others this way, especially life-givers, is abhorrent.

Liana bristles beside me.

Baring his teeth in a show of displeasure, Talel is dragged from Al'aneo's ship by Aerilon soldiers. His eyes burn with anger as they meet my Ashaya's. "I will have you. You think you are safe, but there is nowhere you can go that I will not find you." His gaze sweeps to mine. "You think she is safe with you here, but you are mistaken. We have allies within your Empire that want to see your mother's reign end as much as we do."

It takes everything I have to not kill him right now. But knowing he and his people will be dead as soon as they return to their ship is enough to help me maintain my control.

When the A'kai release the women, the Aerilon reluctantly free Talel. Several guards track his movements carefully, their blasters pointed and ready to fire if he tries to attack as he stalks past them.

The females look to Liana, tears in their otherwise broken expressions. As soon as they are handed over to the Mosauran soldiers, Liana releases my hand and goes to her friends. Fierce protectiveness rushes through me, but I force myself to stand back, not wanting to crowd them. My mate will signal me when she wishes me to come to her.

As she embraces them, the females break down. The one with light hair releases a pitiful and agonizing wail as tears flow like rivers down her face.

One of their Mosauran escorts, Tharin, appears as anguished as they are as he watches their reunion. As my gaze scans over the rest of our warriors and the Aerilon that surround us, it is easy to see that they are as equally affected by the females' agony.

Despite the trauma they have no doubt endured, the dark-haired female turns to thank the Mosauran warriors that retrieved them. How terrible must the A'kai have treated them that they would not look upon my people with fear?

We watch as Talel and the two A'kai Centurions board their transport, sealing the door behind them.

All eyes then turn to Al'aneo. His gaze shifts to his soldiers as he speaks into his communicator. "Now."

The station tremors beneath our feet as the Aerilon ship's cannons fire.

A deafening boom splits the air as the fiery impact engulfs the A'kai ship, breaking it apart into a floating mass of destruction.

Bracing myself for the secondary assault on Talel's transport, I look to Al'aneo in confusion when I don't feel another explosion.

His eyes go wide as he looks toward the docking ring, crying out to his men as the doors slide open. Like a nightmare, everything shifts into slow motion as Talel and the two A'kai emerge from their vessel. Fire burns in their eyes as they charge our soldiers.

Able to move with lightning speed, I watch in horror as Talel splits from the others, charging straight for the Terrans.

Fangs bared, he rushes past two Mosauran warriors. One of them manages to cut his arm with their sword, but it does little to slow his advance.

My pulse pounds in my ears as I race toward Liana.

She pulls the two females behind her to shield them.

I cry out for her to run, but it's already too late.

Talel reaches Liana, and she cries out as he slams into her smaller form.

I howl with rage as he locks his arms around her in a deadly embrace.

Out of the corner of my vision, I see the other two A'kai have already fallen—taken down by blaster fire.

"Stop!" Talel yells as every weapon turns on him.

Everyone stills and falls silent. Positioned behind Liana, his hand is wrapped around her throat in a dangerous hold.

Rage burns through me like fire as a low growl rumbles deep in my chest. "Let. Her. Go."

He glares at me. "Never."

Her eyes find mine, and instead of fear behind them, I see anger tempered with steeled determination.

Forcing myself to focus beyond my blinding panic, I realize she knows this hold. We've practiced it many times during our sparring sessions.

Light catches my eye as it reflects off the knife, just barely peeking out from under her sleeve. Her knuckles turn white as she grips it firmly in her palm.

Talel is already dead, and he does not know it.

Clenching her jaw, her nostrils flare as she draws in a steadying breath. With perfect form and fluid grace, she twists free of his hold. Grasping his hair, she takes advantage of his shock and jerks his head back, exposing his neck. In one swift movement, she pulls the knife across his throat, cutting deep and true.

Obsidian blood bursts forth in an explosive spray, gushing down the front of his chest. His eyes are wide in disbelief as he grips his open throat. Liana grits through her teeth as he meets her gaze. "You will *never* hurt anyone again."

He drops to his knees before collapsing to the ground in a pool of dark blood. My Ashaya, looking every bit as fierce as a Mosauran warrior, steps over his body to return to me. I pull her into my arms, releasing the breath I hadn't realized I was holding until now. My mate is safe, and I send a silent prayer of thanks and gratitude to the Creator for sparing her this day.

All eyes are on my Ashaya with looks of awestruck admiration and wonder. Although they'd heard rumors of her strength and her bravery, this is the first time my people have witnessed it with their own eyes.

This brave, fierce female chose *me*, and I am full of immense pride as she takes my hand, displaying for all to see that I am hers, as she leads me to the two Terran females.

The trauma they have faced is unimaginable, and I'm certain it will be a long time for them to recover. Aerilon and Mosauran Healers greet them, and I listen with pride as Liana explains that my people and the Aerilon are honorable and that they are safe in the care of our Healers.

When she lifts her gaze to me and explains that I am her "husband,"—the Terran word for "mate"—the females' eyes widen in shock before one of them extends her hand in the greeting that is customary of their people. She gives me a watery smile. "It is nice to meet you,

Soran," she says, and I'm astounded once more by the strength of Liana's people. They may appear similar to V'loryns, but their hearts and minds are as resilient and fierce as any I have ever met.

# CHAPTER 43

LIANA

Although it has only been a week since I killed Talel and the A'kai cruiser was destroyed, it feels much longer than that.

Tr'lani wraps her arms around me, and I return the embrace as tears well up in my eyes. She gently runs her fingers through my hair. "I will miss you, my dear sister. You must promise to come visit me."

"I promise."

Al'aneo steps forward. "Our people have already begun looking for yours. Hopefully, we will find both your crew and Abby's."

"Thank you," I hug him. "You have no idea how much that means to me."

"It is the least we can do until the formal alliance is signed." He levels a frosty gaze in the direction of the Empress before turning his attention back to me. He still has not completely forgiven her for the less than welcome reception we had when we first arrived. "If you are ever made to feel unwelcome in your new home, all you need do is send a message to us on Aerilon, and we will come get you as quickly as possible. You are part of our clan, and you will always have a place among our people." He looks to Soran. "Both you and your mate."

Tr'lani gives me a sad look. "It is hard to leave you, Liana. I wish you and Soran were coming with us, but I know you are eager to find your world. The star charts here are much more extensive than the ones we have on Aerilon."

Al'aneo claps Rowan on the shoulder. "I have already arranged for the High Clans to meet with us as soon as we land. I'm certain you will represent your people well. Hopefully it will not take long to reach a formal agreement between our two races. Especially now with the threat of war from the First Prime of A'kaina in response to his brother's death."

Soran looks to Al'aneo. "The sooner, the better. Together, we can search for the missing Terrans and for their home world. Their people must be warned about the dangers that they face."

I shake my head. "I suppose it's a mixed blessing of sorts that we do not know where Terra is. When the A'kai searched Gwen and Aria's minds, they found out the name of our planet, but not its location because we don't even know it ourselves."

Tr'lani nods. "At least with Talel's death, perhaps it will take the A'kai longer to make the connection that his beloved knew of your world."

I swallow against the knot of worry in the pit of my stomach. I hope she is right.

Soran and Caryn embrace Rowan warmly, and I do the same. Before he pulls away, I whisper in his ear. "Promise me you will tell Tr'lani how you feel about her before you return to Mosaura."

Despite his usual carefree demeanor, his uncertainty shows in his eyes. "You are certain it is something she would wish to hear?"

I give him a warm smile. "Yes, I believe so."

He nods and I notice her eyes follow him as he goes to speak with her brother.

Turning, I find Abby and Grex standing off to the side.

I give Abby a warm hug. "Are you sure I can't talk you into staying here?"

She gives me a hesitant look as she places her hand over her belly. "I'm sorry, Liana. I wish we could, but Grex and I want to raise our baby somewhere that she won't be judged so harshly for being different." Her eyes drift to Soran and his mother. "I know not all Mosaurans are speciest, but so many of them still are."

Although I wish I could convince her otherwise, I know she is right. "We'll try to visit as soon as we can. I'll miss you, Abby."

"I'll miss you too." Tears fill her eyes as she looks between Soran and me. "I'll never be able to repay you for saving us." Grex wraps a protective arm around her waist. Her hand settles over her pregnant belly, and his tail curls around it as if cradling their unborn daughter. "All of us."

With a final embrace, she and Grex step onto the transport with Al'aneo, Tr'lani, and Rowan. With a heavy heart, we watch them leave.

# CHAPTER 44

LIANA

For the past three weeks, Gwen, Aria, and I have taken turns searching the archived star charts for our system. They usually stay up late, studying the ancient maps because they still have nightmares. We all do. But the difference between them and me is that I have Soran.

He whispers soothing words of comfort into my ear as he wraps his solid arms around me, always reminding me of where I am and that I'm safe when I wake from a bad dream.

So, when I wake up this morning with his arms wrapped tightly around me as he stares at me with a worried look on his face, I reach across to gently run my fingers through the hair at the nape of his neck. "What's wrong?" I whisper.

His eyes search mine. "Are you well?"

"I feel all right. Why?"

He shakes his head softly before gently pressing his forehead to mine. "I have a strange impulse to shift into draken form, as if I need to protect you from something, but I...I do not know what." He runs his hand roughly through his hair as he huffs out a frustrated breath.

"I don't understand why I feel this way. I always experience this urge when you wake from a nightmare. It's instinctual. But this...this is different. It's stronger somehow."

I snuggle into his chest. "Well, I feel fine, Soran. You don't have to worry about me."

He doesn't answer. Instead, he skims the tip of his nose from my temple and down my cheek before nuzzling my neck. Pressing a line of tender kisses down my body, I moan lightly as his strong hands gently caress my skin. Placing his hand on my inner thigh, he gently parts my legs and moves his delicious ridged tongue between my folds. "Your scent...your taste," he whispers between strokes of his tongue. "It's intoxicating. So much stronger than it normally is."

He goes still.

Confused, I look down as he brings his face up even with my lower abdomen. His nostrils flare as he scents me, and I laugh softly as a short puff of air tickles my sensitive skin.

Sitting up on my elbows, I smile and stare down at him. "What are you doing?"

His brows crease into a deep frown as he presses the side of his face against my stomach. I wriggle just enough to get his attention. "Soran?"

When he lifts his gaze to mine, his eyes are bright with tears. "You are with child," he whispers in amazement.

Shocked, I stare at him in disbelief. "Are you sure?"

He nods and quickly moves up my body. Pressing his lips to mine, he wraps one arm tightly around me, placing his other palm over my lower abdomen. "We are going to have a fledgling. That's why I feel so protective of you. Usually, this instinct is strong when we are nesting —guarding our egg. But you are Terran, and our child grows inside you."

His expression changes as he gives me a solemn vow. "I will not leave your side for even a moment while you are gravid."

My head jerks back in surprise. "What? Why?"

"In my species, the males are the ones that guard the eggs."

"But..." I give him an incredulous look, motioning to the area around us. "We don't have an egg."

"Exactly," he grins. "Our child grows inside you. So, you"—he possessively pulls me closer against him—"will not leave my sight while you carry our fledgling."

My mouth drops at his statement. *If* I really am pregnant. It could be months before our baby is born. He can't be serious about me not leaving his sight. Can he? Drawing in a deep breath, I can almost hear my father's voice in my mind. *"One step at a time, Liana."*

I press a quick kiss to Soran's lips. "Let's go see the Healer so we can be sure we're actually pregnant, all right?"

He nods. "All right. We need them to check that the child is healthy."

I open my mouth to argue that we're not completely sure that there even *is* a baby, but he seems so certain of himself that I'll just wait until we speak to the Healer.

As the Healer runs the scanner over my abdomen, tears fill my eyes when I see the baby's tiny little wings. I place my hand over my mouth, attempting to hold back the sob rising in my throat. "She's going to look just like her father." My voice quavers as I pull Soran to me, hugging him tightly.

The Healer gasps, and my heart stops.

"What's wrong?" Soran's face is full of panic.

Healer Krinan cocks his head slightly to the side in a questioning look. "Do Terrans possess the gift of foresight?" His piercing gaze meets mine. "How did you know your child was a female?"

Now, the tears are freely flowing down my cheeks. Emotions lodge in my throat, and I'm unable to even answer him. My mother was the one with the gift, and she always told me I'd have a little girl first. As I picture her face, my heart breaks at the thought that she may never see her grandchild.

The look of pure joy on Soran's face quickly chases away my

sadness. He presses his mouth to mine, and I smile against his lips. "We're going to have a daughter," I whisper as he places his hand over mine, low on my abdomen.

Healer Krinan clears his throat. "The scanner estimates that gestation will be eleven months."

My head jerks up, and I blink several times in shock. "Eleven months?"

His brow furrows. "How long is normal gestation for a Terran?"

"Nine months."

"Ah, I see," he says before turning his full attention to Soran with an intense look on his face. "Because there will be no egg, you must remain by your mate's side at all times, just as you would if you were guarding your nest."

My mouth drifts open. "Wait, I don't think he needs to do that."

Ignoring me, he places a firm hand on Soran's shoulder and looks him straight in the eye. "Your task will be difficult because you must guard not just an egg, but your mate as well because in your case...they are one and the same."

As he listens closely to what the Healer is saying about not letting me out of his sight, Soran's face is a mask of fierce determination. These people are insane. I'll go crazy if Soran is constantly hovering over me for the next eleven months.

We're supposed to go to Aerilon soon. I'm looking forward to spending time with Tr'lani. *Alone.* If Soran keeps listening to what this Healer is telling him, that's definitely not going to happen.

"Excuse me." I look to the Healer. "I'd like to speak with my mate alone for a moment."

He bows his head. "Of course, Princess."

Soran gives me a worried look. "What's wrong?"

I take both of Soran's hands in mine and meet his eyes evenly. "Okay, look. We're going to have to talk about this 'me not leaving your sight' situation."

His expression turns serious. "Do not worry, my Ashaya, I will remain at your side at all times. I will be an ever-constant shadow hovering over you and attending to your every need; I will not fail you."

His vow melts my heart. With a heavy sigh, I decide I'll let him hover for today since it means so much to him. We'll talk about it tomorrow.

# CHAPTER 45

LIANA

We leave tomorrow for Aerilon, and we'll be gone for two weeks. As I enter the archives, I find Gwen studying the star charts. "Are you sure you two don't want to come to Aerilon?" I ask.

She gives me a pained smile. "I...it's safe here. After everything we went through, I'm not ready to go back out there." Her voice grows thick with emotion "The Mosaurans have been so good to us. I'm...I'm just afraid to leave. The A'kai are still out there."

A broken sob escapes her throat, and I rush forward to embrace her as she breaks down in my arms. I know what she's afraid of, and I'd be lying to myself if I didn't admit that I was afraid too. But I realize that I can't live in fear for the rest of my life. I know that Gwen and Aria know this as well, but they're not ready, and I can't push them.

Their traumatic experiences are still very fresh in their minds. They haven't been free as long as I have. They were held by the A'kai much longer than I was, and I can only imagine how awful it must have been.

They haven't told me everything yet about what they went through, and I understand, from experience, that it will take time before they are able to. The only other member of our crew that I know for certain is safe is Amanda. She is still on Garkolna.

I sent word to her and heard back that she is well. But she is like Gwen and Aria. Afraid to leave the safety that she's found. Soran has promised we will travel there soon, but we have to get permission from the Garkol Council. They have a deep mistrust of the Mosaurans, and it may be a while before they allow us to visit their planet.

Tharin, one of Soran's guards, walks in. He bows low as he greets me before turning to Gwen. "It has been several hours since you had anything to eat," he tells her softly. "I have prepared a meal for you. We can eat in your favorite part of the garden."

She gives him a warm smile. "That sounds wonderful. Thank you, Tharin."

I've noticed he's very protective of her. Ever since the day he escorted her and Aria from the A'kai, he's been an almost constant presence at her side. He looks at her as if she were the most precious thing in the world. I recognize that look because that's how Soran looks at me. But I wonder if Gwen realizes this.

She turns to me. "I'll see you before you go?"

"Yes. I'll be sure to come say goodbye."

After she leaves with Tharin, I turn my attention to the star charts. Scrolling through them, I focus closely on the ancient V'loryn Empire. Vast and encompassing many systems and planets, it's proving exhausting trying to wade through it all. But, like Soran believes, I don't think it's just coincidence that my people look so similar to them, nor that their elf-like appearance is so heavily embedded in our ancient Terran mythology. Even their language is remarkably similar to the one spoken by the Ancient Celtic people. Surely, their race interacted with mine over many years for them to have heavily contaminated our culture to such a degree.

Warm hands come to rest on my shoulders, and I instantly recognize them as Soran's. Leaning back against his chest, I practically melt in his arms as he begins to knead the muscles in my neck and shoulders. "I have something I must tell you."

The tone of his voice gives me pause, and I tense as I turn to face him. "What is it?"

"There are rumors of Terrans being held on one of the stations in the neutral zone between here and Aerilon. Al'aneo has offered to send two cruisers to meet us there."

I shudder inwardly at the thought of my crewmates as slaves. As if sensing my distress Soran wraps his wings tightly around me in a comforting embrace. "We have to go, my love. If there's a chance my people are there, we have to find them."

"We will." He turns me to face him and stares deep into my eyes. "But you must agree to stay on the ship while we take care of the slavers."

By "take care," he means "execute." It's a death sentence to traffic slaves according to the laws of the Mosauran, Aerilon, and V'loryn Empires. After what I saw and everything I went through during my time as a slave, I'm not going to disagree with how they handle things.

"But tonight, you must rest. We leave early in the morning for Aerilon."

# CHAPTER 46

LIANA

As we stare out the transport viewscreen to Mosaura, the curve of the planet glows brightly as we ascend from the surface. Soran slips his arms around me, and I lean back against his solid chest. A wistful smile curves my lips as my thoughts turn to my father, imagining what he would think if he were here with me now.

I don't know what the future holds or if I'll ever see my family again. Zuran told me I would find them, and I choose to hold on to that hope.

~

**Soran**

After three long days traveling at full speed in the Mosauran cruiser, we've finally arrived. Liana is hopeful we will find some of her crewmates here, and I wish the same. I can only imagine the fear of the people manning the bridge of this wretched station as they see two Aerilon and Mosauran cruisers approach.

Sweeping my gaze over her form, I double-check that her blaster is firmly attached to her hip. Although she will not step foot on the station until we've taken care of the slavers, I want to make sure my mate is well prepared.

Warriors line up in formation, battle-ready and eager to enforce the anti-slavery laws once we disembark.

As Liana docks our lead Mosauran ship, a Zovian face appears in the viewscreen.

With a harsh and frantic clicking of his mandibles, he demands she explain why we're here.

She turns to the captain. "Broadcast on all feeds so the entire station can hear us."

He dips his chin in a subtle nod as his hands fly across the control panel. After a moment, he turns back to her with a hint of a smile on his otherwise stoic face. We have to keep up appearances after all. Mosaurans are one of the most feared races in the quadrant, and it works in our favor if we encourage this belief.

Dressed from head to toe in Mosauran battle armor, she looks every bit the warrior that she is as she stares into the viewscreen. My chest fills with pride. She will be an excellent mother to our fledgling.

"I am Liana Garza of Terra and the Aerilon Clan Al'ani, Princess and Bondmate of Soran of House Mosaura. To the slaves that are held on this station, locked away in cages and kept in dark cargo bays...I was once as you are now. I survived because my will is stronger than the ones that tried to break me. A single light can defy the darkness of despair. This message is for you. There is hope in the darkness. Hold fast to the light. We are coming to free you."

# ABOUT JESSICA GRAYSON

Thank you so much for reading this. If you enjoyed this book, please leave a review on Amazon and/or Goodreads. If you enjoy my writing, I also write under the pen name *Aria Winter.*

If you'd like to read Tr'lani and Rowan's story, it's available. **(Shape of the Wind).**

If you want more Mosaurans, I have an Ice World Series featuring Commander Markus (the Mosauran warrior that was enslaved with Soran) available here: **Claimed: Dragon Shifter Romance**

*Mosauran Series (Dragon Shifter Alien Romance)*
    The Edge of it All
    Shape of the Wind

*Ice World Warrior Series*

**Claimed: Dragon Shifter Romance**
**Bound: Vampire Alien Romance**
**Rescued: Fae Alien Romance**
**Stolen: Werewolf Romance**
**Taken: Vampire Alien Romance**

**Want more Dragon Shifters?** Check out my Dragon Shifter Beauty and the Beast below
    *Fairy Tale Retellings (Once Upon a Fairy Tale Romance Series)*
    **Taken by the Dragon: A Beauty and the Beast Retelling**
    **Captivated by the Fae: A Cinderella Retelling**

**Rescued By The Merman: A Little Mermaid Retelling**
**Bound To The Elf Prince: A Snow White Retelling**

Do you like Elves and Vampires? I have a Vampire Alien Romance series you might enjoy.

*V'loryn Series (Vampire Alien Romance)*
**Lost in the Deep End**
**Beneath a Different Sky**
**Under a Silver Moon**
**V'loryn Holiday Series** (A Marek and Elizabeth Holiday novella takes place prior to their bonding)
**The Thing We Choose**

*V'loryn Fated Ones (Vampire Alien Romance)*
**Where the Light Begins** (Vanek's Story)

*Aerilon Fae Series (Fae Alien Romance)*
**Trace The Sky**
For information about upcoming releases Like me on

Facebook at Jessica Grayson
http://facebook.com/JessicaGraysonBooks.

OR

sign up for upcoming release alerts at my website:
Jessicagraysonauthor.com